D1592076

Creative Drama and Imagination

Transforming Ideas into Action

Foreword

Jerome L. Singer
Professor of Psychology
Director of Graduate Program
in Clinical Psychology
YALE UNIVERSITY

What a pleasure it is for someone who has labored long in the vineyards of research and clinical work in the area of the psychology of imagination to see a book that takes the fruits of these efforts and applies them so effectively to the educational process. In *Creative Drama and Imagination* Dr. Helane Rosenberg has gone well beyond the intuitive efforts of the fine writers about the acting profession beginning with Stanislavski and moved to the realm of solid clinical and scientific research. But she has done so with a personal style, a liveliness, and a didactic clarity that, in my judgment, surpasses the previous efforts I have seen of this type.

Let me try for a moment to cast this book into a broader perspective from the standpoint of the current status of psychology research and theory. After a period of almost fifty years, from 1910 to 1960, when psychologists were preoccupied with understanding overt behavior (usually by studying rats in mazes), we have witnessed what might be termed a paradigm shift in thinking in the behavioral sciences. We now recognize the considerable importance for human emotion and action of the ongoing thought processes of individuals and the nature of the special human capacity for producing images in the various sensory modalities. Through our capacities for imagery we can in effect create at least briefly alternative contexts and, indeed, even alternative personalities which we can, as Freud long ago suggested, try out for size as a form of "experimental action." Research with which I, among others, have been involved in the past two or three decades has increasingly supported the view that human beings who can rely freely upon their capacity for positive constructive daydreaming or imagery seem to have "the best of both worlds." They need not by any means be ineffective in direct interactions with the people and settings around them. On the other hand, they can also by the use of their imagery and fantasy rehearse alternative courses of action, use the advantages of playful fantasy as an escape from boring or momentarily frustrating situations, and gradually develop whole new sets of plans and intentions. The research also supports a close link between imagination and both the expression and control of emotion.

Some of this work has been extended to careful studies of the development of young children. We find again and again that those children who because of parental support through story-telling and encouragement of imaginative play show more indications of pretending and fantasy in their spontaneous activities do benefit considerably from this tendency. Thus, preschoolers or early-school-aged children who engage in a good deal of make-believe play turn out to show more self-control in other situations, to be able to persist longer at tasks, to sit quietly in a situation that calls for necessary waiting, to show leadership with other children in preschool or kindergarten situations, and to develop certain cognitive skills even more rapidly. Given these indications of the power of the human imagination, Dr. Rosenberg's work develops and elaborates much further the tremendous educational potential of carefully graduated exercises in creative drama and imagination. What an enrichment one can hope for if parents initially, through careful games and exercises that are as enjoyable for them as for the children, begin early to help children develop their own internal capacities for fantasy and play. But what of those children who have not had the advantages of such parental interaction early on? And what of those children whose parents because of pressures of work and their own limited skills or capacities in this respect cannot continue what they may have begun in earlier childhood? The role of the school may well be critical here. Dr. Rosenberg's proposals not only can help those children who seek to become good actors or who are interested in theatre for itself but also can be of tremendous advantage to children whose ultimate goals are quite different. The joy of imagination is open to all through the kinds of training offered in this delightful book.

Preface

Creative Drama and Imagination is about conducting drama activities with young people, ages K–12. It is a comprehensive textbook for university students in schools and departments of theatre and of education who are seeking an introduction to creative drama. It is also intended for the generalist and arts specialist teachers already in the classroom, directors of after-school drama programs, recreation leaders, camp arts coordinators, and all others interested in encouraging imaginative drama abilities in young people.

The book is divided into two parts: The first part focuses on theory, bringing together the fields of psychology, education, theatre, and mental imagery as a way of clarifying the complex nature of the creative drama experience. This first part also presents a historical overview of creative drama and contemporary analysis of the field. The second part of the book focuses on practice, detailing a creative drama approach that is strongly connected to the theories presented. This approach is divided into three levels, each of increasing difficulty. Included in the creative drama approach are exercises, activities, case studies, explanatory material, and evaluation/assessment guides.

Chapter 1 introduces readers to the phenomenon of creative drama and establishes its connections to play and theatre. Chapter 2 provides an overview of the history of creative drama and analyzes five significant contemporary approaches. Mental imagery is the topic of Chapter 3; it is in this chapter that readers begin to explore their own imaginative abilities. Chapter 4 presents the theatre information that is a vital part of creative drama; differences and similarities between theatre and creative drama are also explored in this chapter. Chapter 5 covers the theory of imagination in action, which is the foundation of creative drama practice. Chapter 6 presents an overview of the Rutgers Imagination Method (RIM) and concludes the first half of the book. At this point, readers are armed with sufficient information to begin conducting creative drama activities.

Chapters 7 and 8 are filled with Starter exercises. Within these two chapters are the exercises themselves, explanatory material, and practical pointers. Chapters 9 and 10 are similarily organized, but focus on the second level of activities, termed Transformations. Chapter 11 presents case studies which chronicle Mastery, the third level. Because each group is unique, case studies, not a series of exercises or activities, are models for advanced creative drama work. Finally, Chapter 12 focuses on issues of assessment and evaluation and concludes with a discussion of the future of creative drama.

Preparing readers to be confident, knowledgeable, and imaginative leaders of creative drama is of primary importance. To assist readers in accomplishing this objective, various thematic threads strengthen and give consistency to *Creative Drama and Imagination:*

- **Throughout the book, creative drama and its parent art, the theatre, are tightly linked.** The art form of theatre has contributed many principles, conventions, and artistic models to the art of creative drama. Early practitioners instinctively understood this strong tie. More recently, in trying to respond to "back to basic" educators, practitioners often dismissed creative drama's artistic core; this sad error reduced creative drama to a mere methodology. As it reestablishes essential links with theatre, creative drama can be seen as an art form distinctively valuable in its own right. A firm understanding of what theatre and creative drama have in common helps new leaders understand the potential shape of the planning process, the potential form and structure of the enactment, and the potential artistic roles to be emulated by drama participants.
- **Imagination plays a similarly essential role.** The field of mental imagery has clarified the way people retrieve, manipulate, and utilize their personal memory images in everyday life. Based on this information, the imagery-based theory presented throughout the book can help readers understand and encourage the imagination of participants. (An added bonus is, of course, that readers have the opportunity to practice their own imagery skills.) Although leaders help participants develop a large repertoire of skills and behaviors — including verbal, physical, problem-solving, social, and expressive — at the core of all of these is the pivotal ability to imagine.
- **The focus is on how to assist the connection of ideas and action.** Young people are often drawn to creative drama because of the opportunity it provides them to explore, mold, and communicate their own personal views of the world. Participating in drama can become frustrating when these intentions become difficult to realize and participants are unable to connect ideas to behavior. In order to provide readers with models, we discuss how various artists and drama participants have developed unique connections.
- **Both sections of the book — theory and practice — are strongly interrelated.** The first part of the book, the theoretical framework, sets the stage for the practical information that follows. In these exercises, activities, and practical pointers, this essential material remains a consistent focus. The objectives in each exercise, for example, as well as the warm-up material, include many imagery-based elements. Potential leaders are encouraged to utilize theatre terminology in discussing enactments, as well as principles of dramatic structure in evaluating the drama product. No creative drama book can be complete without a carefully wrought connection between the theoretical and the practical.
- **The creative drama approach detailed in this book is not a personal style approach.** Many early approaches quite logically reflected the particular training and perspective of leaders who developed them. Be-

cause their approaches were natural and instinctual, they were usually difficult for others to master. Without direct knowledge of what had gone into the method, many novice drama leaders became only shadows. The Rutgers Imagination Method, with its three-part focus — imagination, dramatic behavior, and their connection — is universally effective. Knowing the "why" makes leading the "what" much more dynamic.

As you page through *Creative Drama and Imagination,* you will notice immediately that it has many components. This format and style were developed to obtain maximum benefits for its readers. A book that details a method built on the aesthetic must be aesthetically pleasing. A book about imagination must stimulate the imagination of its readers. Consequently, we have included:

- **Reproductions of art works of the masters,** primarily contemporary, to illustrate the concepts presented in the text. Readers of the book can view these art works as end products of imaginative art-making, as well as works which can in turn be used to stimulate creative drama activity.
- **Quotes from famous people** to reaffirm the concepts presented. The words of Einstein, Picasso, Aristotle, and even Lily Tomlin help the reader develop a sense of the importance of imagination in the world at large, as well as in the drama arena.
- **Photos of people, places, animals, and objects** to stimulate the imagination of readers and at the same time to serve as models for the kinds of photos to be used in creative drama activity. Michael Rocco Pinciotti, Peter Byron, and Rutgers University students in classes in arts and imagination provided us with variety and beauty to share with our readers.
- **Photos of young people in the creative drama setting.** These are not intended as models, but more as examples of young people having a wonderful time, while they explore the drama activity. These photos capture the essence of imagination and action.
- **"You Are There" descriptions of drama activities.** Since many readers may not have observed creative drama, the guided fantasy, a technique presented for use in creative drama settings, similarly helps readers expand their observation experiences. Readers are asked to travel to many creative drama settings, theatre rehearsals, and natural play settings — in the past, present, and future — and picture the actual situations in their minds' eye.

Creative Drama and Imagination represents the work of a two-stage five-year project, in which faculty, students, and former students (all affiliated at some time with Rutgers University in New Brunswick, New Jersey) have participated. A Junior Faculty Fellowship funded my work as a new assistant professor and enabled me to devote full time to this project. A team, made up of me and three doctoral students (Patricia Pinciotti, Rose Castellano, and Geri Chrein) developed the imagery-focused Framework detailed in this book. This aspect of the project received the Children's Theatre Association Research Award in 1982 for Best Research in the field of Child Drama.

The second stage of the project involved the crafting and testing of a creative drama approach based strongly on the theories that had been formulated. As mentioned throughout the book, a theory is not a method. After careful development, much field testing, and outside evaluation from researchers and practitioners in theatre, psychology, and creative drama, the

Rutgers Imagination Method in its current state emerged. This approach to creative drama represents the "state of the art." I have used the book (in manuscript form) with great success to teach courses in creative drama on both the undergraduate and graduate levels. Both Patricia Pinciotti (now herself a university professor) and I, as well as many numbers of our students, have conducted the activities with many populations representing many ages, socioeconomic levels, and regional backgrounds. We feel confident that the method teaches well to potential leaders and works well with young people. The framework can also be invaluable for the leader already working in a creative drama situation.

I wish to thank the following people. First, to Dr. Patricia A. Pinciotti, who worked long and hard on both phases of the book: the evolution of the theory and the refinement of the method. Pat's practical suggestions, knowledge of children's artistic process, boundless enthusiasm, and personal integrity helped shape the book. Second, to the Rutgers University Research Council for its initial financial support and, also, to Rutgers University Graduate School of Education faculty, staff, and students for continued support. Many of my students share an interest in mental imagery and likewise believe in the role imagination plays in validating the arts-making process of young people. It is impossible to thank each and every student, but I would like to mention those people who researched mental imagery, tested the method, and contributed photos to the book: Kathy Brailove, Mary Carter, Soon Choi, Janet Clausi, Pat Crompton, Marc Finkelstein, Joanne Friel, Alison Gallagher, Merald Goldman, Caryl Harris, Phyllis Heim, Therese Hembruch, Dale Hirsch, Cindy Levy, Susan Niedt, Joanmarie Penney, Pam Rich, Elizabeth Eron Roth, Susanne Sachs, Renee Schnitzer, Ann Smalser, Angie Sturgis, Bob Thomas, Bill Trusheim, Evelyn Van Nuys, and Gail and Jim Williams. These RIM students have captured the imaginations of countless artists, scholars, and schoolchildren, including my own!

I would also like to thank the organizations whose classes served as models for the Mastery case studies, particularly Creative Theatre Unlimited in Princeton, New Jersey, my Teacher as Performer class at Rutgers, and Brick Township Memorial Middle School, New Jersey. Finally, I would also like to thank the faculty and staff at East Stroudsburg who were of enormous help to Pat and me, specifically Dr. Arthur Mark for his savvy encouragement, Dr. Robert Walker who carefully edited the manuscript, and graduate assistant Donna Miller who organized the graphics program.

Throughout this project, both Pat and I have had the support of wonderful associates, friends, and family. Thank you to Elva C. Shapiro, Ruth Bonvillain, Andrea Zakin, Zaro Weil, Susan Golbeck, Joel Vig, Marlene Birkman, Jeffrey K. Smith, Suzanne Bennett, Virginia Koste, Geraldine Siks, Judith Kase, Nancy Smith, Scott Laughead, Jerome Singer, Zak Adams, Howie Rappaport, Dino and Lisanne Pinciotti, Mary Lisa Vertuca, Suzanne Gagnet, Rosemary Pinciotti, Michelle Rockoff, Esther Glat, Rita Pinciotti, and Don Pinciotti.

I'd also like to thank those steadfast, yet imaginative, editors at Holt—Karen Dubno and Herman Makler—who remained reality-bound (but daring) through it all. And, finally, thanks to the following people who added their perspective and encouraged imagination to give shape to this drama: Robert W. Colby, Emerson College; Charles E. Combs, Plymouth State College; Patricia M. Harter, University of California, Los Angeles; Robert R. Pevitts, University of Nevada—Las Vegas; and Julie Thompson, Specialist in Theatre Arts as Education.

H. S. R.

Contents

CHAPTER 11 MASTERY 281

CHAPTER 12 EXPANDING CREATIVE DRAMA 308

List of Starters and Transformations

Starters

Transformations

Events/Stories into Plots

Place Becomes Setting

Adding Conflict

Creating Spectacle

ALL ABOUT CREATIVE DRAMA

CASE STUDY

A MAGIC MOMENT As Mr. Winters the principal walks down the hall, his attention is diverted by the students in Ms. Chumley's sixth-grade class. More than half the class is riveted to something happening in the front of the room. Quietly, Mr. Winters slips into the back of the room; no one even notices him. Very quickly he realizes that the eight sixth-graders in the front of the room seem to be in another time and place. He's reminded of an Old West saloon. Five cowboys sit playing a pretty serious game of poker: an old codger, a big cowpoke, another with a grey moustache, a dapper gent who smokes expensive cigars, and a fancy dude with a black hat who's obviously the big winner. A bartender, a piano player, and a silent, lone patron watching from the bar complete the scene. The tension builds along with the size of the pot until the big cowpoke jumps to his feet shouting, "Cheater! Cheater!" The table is overturned; cards fly and shots are heard; the silent lone patron emerges as the New Law of the Town. The principal, captured by the moment, shouts, "Bravo!"

CASE STUDY

A SECOND MAGIC MOMENT James T. Peabody School is an elementary school in a sprawling urban city. Many of the children come to Peabody knowing only their native language. Much of the curriculum in the early grades emphasizes language development and social skills. Mrs. Temple utilizes creative drama activities with her first-graders because the relaxed, playful atmosphere allows the students to build trust and language skills more quickly. Creative drama activities also provide an opportunity to share the rich cultural heritage of the students. She recounts a particular example of creative drama's impact:

> We were working on pantomime exercises to show basic daily activities, such as brushing teeth or eating breakfast. These pantomime sessions include a great deal of discussion before and after, so that the activities don't turn into charades. During one particular lesson, Dru Pan, a Vietnamese child who had been with us for

almost a month, enacted an entire morning ritual that she recalled from her life in Vietnam. Dru Pan was very withdrawn and had never spoken in class, yet her actions were so expressive! When she finished, her classmates applauded enthusiastically. Creative drama activities provided the medium that motivated her to draw from her past experiences and share them with people who could not speak her language. This was a breakthrough for Dru Pan; her smile confirmed it.

THE PERPLEXING PHENOMENON

These two scenarios describe the phenomenon of creative drama. Many people who are familiar with creative drama find these moments magical and believe that every person, young or old, can experience the wonder and excitement of creative drama. Unfortunately, many administrators, parents, teachers, and diehard cynics, all outside the field of arts education, would not describe these experiences as magical or essential for growth and development. This negative point of view is evidenced by their comments that creative drama is little more than glorified recess or an inefficient rehearsal of a second-rate play.

Creative drama seems to share characteristics of many other methods and art forms found both in and out of schools. Using personal images and experiences to enhance learning, growth, and behaviors is not a new idea. Teachers in many disciplines find that connecting imagination to action is a motivating and powerful force. The creative arts are especially suited to engaging the whole child in this type of learning activity. Even so, creative drama's similarity to other activities makes it as elusive as it is familiar.

Isn't It Just Like . . . ?

The people most often confused about creative drama are those theatre artists, educators, or counselors/therapists who use procedures that, on the surface, seem similar to creative drama. No one has clarified for them how creative drama is similar to and yet different from what they do. These comments come from our own series of interviews conducted to discover prevailing attitudes concerning creative drama:

> I use lively activities like this to enhance learning in my classroom all the time. Isn't creative drama merely creative teaching?
>
> *Second-grade teacher*

> Dealing with feelings and life situations falls into the realm of therapy or counseling. Role-playing is one of my most effective strategies. Isn't this just like creative drama?
>
> *School counselor*

> I'm tired of watching my child make up dramas. Aren't plays from books better? When I go to a play, I want something familiar.
>
> *Parent of nine-year-old*

When I walk into the drama room, it looks like the students are merely playing. How is creative drama different from the play my preschoolers do in the housekeeping area?

Elementary principal

Drama Shares Characteristics

Creative drama and creative teaching may consist of similar activities, but these exercises are used for very different purposes. Both procedures have learning as their primary objective. Creative drama and creative teaching, however, differ in terms of what is to be learned. In creative drama, the goal is mastery of the various aspects and skills that make up creative drama. In creative teaching, the learning objectives are suggested and structured by a subject that is nonarts related.

For example, teachers who ask students to write a paragraph about how it might have felt to be Columbus or to act out the Civil War are using arts activities to stimulate learning in social studies. These activities are used to motivate learning, to enhance the students' knowledge of the subject matter, and to provide a varied learning experience. At the conclusion, the teacher will test and assess the students' social studies knowledge, not the artistic product. Even though a creative drama enactment and a creative teaching activity may seem to be similar, their goals for learning are very different.

Creative drama has educational, not therapeutic, goals; role-playing constitutes only one aspect of the creative drama experience. Role-playing activities, often utilized in therapeutic situations, focus on the feelings the participants have for a particular role or situation. In these role-playing experiences, the role playing has particular value for the participants alone and communicates social, not artistic, messages. Creative drama does help participants change their behavior and their thinking—but by allowing them to put their own ideas into action, not by directly modifying or reshaping "inappropriate" behavior.

Creative drama is different from, yet draws many of its principles from, the art form of theatre. The unique aspects of creative drama and those it shares with theatre are difficult to distinguish from each other and even more difficult to explain. Theatre is the parent art of creative drama; creative drama has been around for a mere sixty years as compared to theatre's history of 5,000 years. Yet creative drama and theatre share many writing and production conventions.

Creative drama is not merely an extension of the play of young children; it shares many characteristics with dramatic play, but it also possesses unique characteristics. Participants involved in creative drama utilize many of the same imaging strategies as do young children in dramatic play. Creative drama, however, is a more complex and structured type of learning activity. If Mr. Winters had watched the sixth-grade class for a longer time, he probably would have concluded that play and creative drama have similarities, as well as important distinctions. Both dramatic play and creative drama involve the transformation of images and ideas into dramatic action. Both are forms of communication about an imagined object, event, or character. In both, the individual communicates an imagined reality by means of movement, gesture, and/or dialogue.

The most obvious difference, however, is the presence of a leader in the creative drama experience. This leader sets the learning goals, introduces the lessons, weaves the continuity from one lesson to the next, and assesses the learning of the participants. Most creative drama sessions are artificially stimulated by the leader, unlike the play situations, which almost always reflect the natural choices of the young children involved and may or may not have an adult present. Also, reflection and rehearsal are rarely a part of young children's dramatic play. Participants in creative drama, on the other hand, are often involved in the planning and evaluation of their dramas — an important factor that helps them improve their creative drama skills.

THE UNIQUE NATURE OF CREATIVE DRAMA

Creative drama is valuable for precisely the same reasons that it is misunderstood: it involves diverse procedures; it is related to theatre and to play; and its benefits are far-reaching. In fact, creative drama is a unique art form and affords participants learning experiences not available in any other activity currently found in the school curriculum.

A good way to begin to understand creative drama is to look at the definition developed in 1977 by the Children's Theatre Association of America (CTAA): "Creative drama is an improvisational, non-exhibitional, process-oriented form of drama, where participants are guided by a leader to imagine, enact, and reflect upon human experiences, real or imagined."

An elaboration of the definition can help clarify its meaning: The word *improvisational,* derived from theatre terminology, means "without a script." Unlike formal productions, enactments done within the confines of a creative drama session rarely begin or end with a script. *Nonexhibitional* means that the primary objective of the enactment is *not* the pleasure of the audience, but the development of the participants, as designated by the term *process-oriented.* Notice that the people who work within the creative drama arena are called *participants,* not *actors* or *performers.* Notice, also, that the person in charge of the creative drama session is called a *leader,* not a *teacher* or a *director.* The creative drama leader's job encompasses aspects of these and other roles, including *guide,* as indicated by the use of the verb *guided* within the definition. To go on, the three-stage process of creative drama — *imagine, enact,* and *reflect* — must occur if change is to take place. Similar terms — *plan, play,* and *evaluate* — may help you understand more about what happens during each stage. Finally, *human experiences,* those of each participant as well as those presented by the leader, are the source of all drama work. Initially, the source of material for drama is memory of past experience, but subsequently, participants develop richer and more elaborative imaginative material for drama.

The participants in creative drama range in age from preschoolers to senior citizens. Our recent survey suggests, however, that the majority of creative drama sessions are conducted with young people from five to fourteen. Before the age of five, young children are typically engaged in their own unique form of imaginative play, which is not adult directed. After fifteen, much of the drama curriculum begins to focus on the theatrical enactment, such as the school, class, or drama-club play. Our survey also suggests that more and more drama teachers are using creative drama with young people as old as seventeen. Creative drama is most often found in school settings; creative drama is also popular in after-school/recreational programs, in religious schools, and in summer camps.

LEARNING AND CREATIVE DRAMA

Teachers, parents, administrators, and even the participants themselves want to know what they learn by doing creative drama. Learning in creative drama involves the whole child. **One of creative drama's strongest assets as a learning medium is that it integrates cognitive, affective, social, and psychomotor abilities.** Many skills, found in each learning modality, are acquired through participation in creative drama. In creative drama activities, participants think, feel, and move together with others in order to enact a drama.

Learning in creative drama is, as is learning in any other discipline, dependent on the teacher, the method, and the learner. Much of this book deals directly with the leader's role and with a particular drama method. The learner's developmental level and capacity for learning are equally important components. That is why it is important for you, in your role as drama leader, to understand the similarities and differences among children. A group of five-year-olds is not only less experienced and less skilled than a group of ten-year-olds but also views the world very differently. An understanding of how children develop and how they learn is critical.

In the last thirty years, many researchers have provided unique insights into how children grow and develop physically, mentally, socially, and emotionally. The field of child development continues to explore new and important aspects of the essential question of how children learn and change. The following introduction to child development can provide you with only a cursory knowledge of children. We encourage you to investigate the learning and developmental potential of any group with whom you conduct creative drama.

The foundation of civilization rests not in the mind, but in the senses.

Sir Herbert Read

Development and Learning

Children grow and change; sometimes these changes seem to occur right before your eyes. Sometimes they are gradual, taking months or even years. These changes occur in three ways. Some skills are acquired merely because children get older. Speaking and walking are skills of this type. These abilities are part of being human and will occur even with minimal adult intervention; these skills are the result of *maturation*. As they get older, children also acquire unique skills and increase their storehouse of information about the world in a particular way. Using precise terminology for stamp collecting, playing the flute, or jumping rope are learned skills and abilities. These abilities are acquired by watching or listening to others and imitating these behaviors, or by being taught in formal or informal situations. Experiences of this type are categorized as *learning experiences*.

As they get older, children also change the way in which they experience, interpret, interact, and communicate. When a two-year-old points and says, "dog," he or she could be referring to a dog or a cat or squirrel or any other animal with four legs. When an eight-year-old refers to "dog," he or she may be talking about his or her own dog—"My Irish setter who hunts pheas-

Children learn about the world through their senses. The children in the photos on this page and the next are intently observing and jubilantly experimenting with objects in their environment. (Photos courtesy of Patricia Pinciotti)

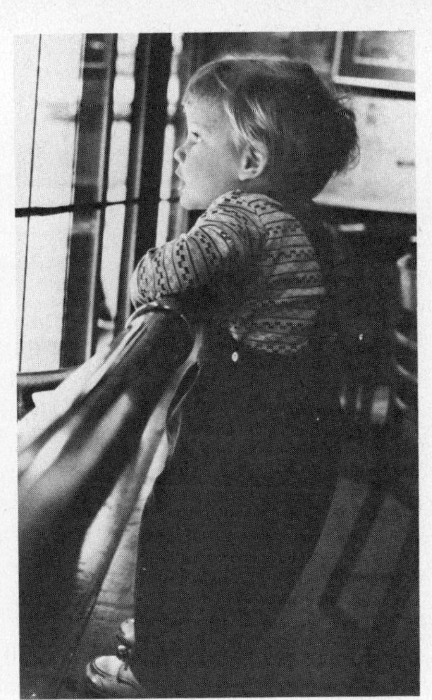

ants"—or describing any number of specific experiences with dogs. This young person not only has more information about "dogs" but also organizes it in a way different from the toddler. These differences are reflected in thinking, behavior, and language. Changes of this sort are the result of *development*.

General Notions Concerning Development

Developmental psychologists are constantly investigating the world of the child. They have provided the field of creative drama with a myriad of potentially valuable theories. One development theory, taken alone, cannot provide a total picture of the growing child. Each theory focuses on a particular aspect of growth or development (physical, socioemotional, or cognitive, for example) and is based on the focus and training of the researcher to whom the theory is credited. Perhaps the best known and most comprehensive of these developmental theories is Jean Piaget's *theory of cognitive development*.

Swiss psychologist Piaget spent the major portion of his adult life observing children in order to solve the mystery of how knowledge is acquired. Piaget's theory on how children develop focuses on children's experiences with their environment, specifically, how they assimilate new information and how they accommodate their behaviors in light of this knowledge. Piaget theorized that as children develop, they move through a series of stages. Each stage marks a reorganization of thinking and is therefore more complex than the previous one. Piaget suggested that development occurs at its own pace and cannot be pushed ahead; all children reach each stage in the same consecutive order. By observing children of different ages involved in various cognitive tasks, Piaget was able to describe and outline the discrete and definable abilities of children in each stage.

As a drama leader, it's important to remember that Piaget's work describes a particular kind of development—the development of scientific or logical thinking. Unfortunately, other types of thinking and reasoning are not accounted for in his theory. As arts psychologist Howard Gardner explains, "We learn much from his writings about children's conceptions of water, but little about their fear of floods, their love of splashing, or their desire to be minnows, mermaids or mariners." Nevertheless, Piaget's framework is one of the best models of child development to date and can provide you with the essential understanding of how children change as they grow older.

Development involves a continuous accumulation of skills. Children do not move from one developmental stage to another as if climbing steps or moving up the rungs of a ladder. It may be more helpful to think of the entire process as a series of *developmental levels* rather than absolute stages. Each individual experiences a gradual transition from one level to the next, although the movement to a new stage is often marked by a "quick spurt" or "learning explosion."

Movement from one developmental level to another is indicated by a major behavioral reorganization. This developmental shift permits children to be able to think about their world and to behave differently. Once each new level is reached, children take time to internalize and broaden these new skills. The developmental spurts that you may have observed in children create a new potential for more complex sets of behaviors and reasoning and signal *developmental milestones*. Thus, development is characterized by spurts and plateaus.

Learning occurs within developmental stages. Although you cannot hurry development from one stage to another, you can encourage and stimulate learning within each developmental level. Learning always leads development and is therefore the critical factor in the "spurt" from one stage to another. Russian psychologist L. S. Vygotsky provides a term—the *zone of proximal development*—that describes the relationship between learning and development.* The zone of proximal development is the distance between the actual developmental level, as determined by independent problem-solving, and the level of potential development, as determined through problem-solving under adult guidance or in collaboration with more capable peers. Most precisely, it is in this zone that learning occurs.

Interactions with other children and adults provide the growing child with models to imitate and with stimulating experiences. Good learning leads the child. This learning is in advance of development just enough to provide both the model and the motivation to learn. Through practice and repetition, the new learning behaviors and/or skills become integrated and internalized. A positive social relationship with more capable peers and interested adults allows children to demonstrate abilities beyond their current development level. A playful attitude on their part helps encourage these children to "work ahead of themselves" in a nonthreatening environment. This social interaction plays a key role in the development of higher social, physical, and cognitive functioning.

The Importance of Play in Development

Play is a central factor in the development of young children. The onset of play behaviors in a young child signals an important developmental change. All children play; this capacity allows them to experiment with thinking about and acting upon their world in new ways. If you observe children at play, you can see how easily they transform objects, places, self, and others. A block of wood can become a truck, "Brrrrummm. Brummmm." Three chairs become a train. An empty bowl allows children to act *as if* they were eating ice cream. With a necklace of beads, a child can become medieval royalty, an Indian leader, or a being with superhuman powers. This play is serious work. **Play provides opportunities for children to master new skills, interact with others, and transform their world of reality into a world of the imagination.**

Dramatic play is one of the specific interactive learning activities that leads development and allows children to work in advance of themselves. Dramatic play in children begins with imaginary situations that closely resemble real ones. Play behaviors at this stage may appear more imitative than imaginary. As the ability to play dramatically develops and personal knowledge of the world increases, children become more aware of play's purpose and its power. Children become more able to entertain endless possibilities as they readily transform self, objects, place, and others. It is during imaginative play that children's greatest self-control occurs because they must abide by new sets of rules that they have created for themselves; all behaviors and dialogue must fit. Play then allows children to experiment with, rehearse, and recreate actions and words. Play leads thinking and doing forward.

* *The writings of Vygotsky, a noted Russian psychologist of the early twentieth century, have only recently been rediscovered in America. His book* Mind in Society *helps to clarify many developmental issues.*

Helping children develop and expand their ability to make believe may keep the sense of magic alive for them throughout their lives.

Dorothy and Jerome Singer

Creative Drama, Development, and Learning

Children at various developmental levels are able to learn the skills and processes that make up creative drama. Of course, the ultimate mastery of dramatic learning presupposes a sophisticated developmental level, as well as a body of totally realized and integrated creative drama behavior. Each child, however, can be master of dramatic learning in a manner appropriate to his or her developmental level. Creative drama skills are learned within the individual's current level while at the same time facilitating the participant's ability to move from one level to the next.

What is learned remains the same. It is the manner in which these creative drama components are able to be learned and integrated that changes as children move from one developmental level to the next. The creative drama activities included in the second half of the book have not been geared for any particular age group. They can be used with children on a variety of levels. It is up to the leader, however, to establish the behavioral expectations based on the children's developmental level.

Vygotsky's notion of the proximal zone of development also has particular implications for the conduct of creative drama. The existing elements of creative drama — collaboration with capable peers, problem-solving under adult guidance, and independent problem-solving — seem to match up with those experiences that lie in the zone of proximal development. Creative drama is an ideal experience to stimulate learning and meet potential developmental growth.

Dramatic Learning: Imagination in Action

Individuals who master dramatic learning are able to connect imagination and action and to communicate this connection. Dramatic learning is shown by two preschoolers in the bathtub as they act out their nightly "mermaid and fish" piece in which they imagine swimming in the ocean. Likewise, appropriate dramatic learning is demonstrated when a group of fourth-graders plans and implements a drama about a whaling expedition. One example of ultimate mastery of dramatic learning is a cast of well-trained professional theatre artists who rehearse and perform a wonderful production of *South Pacific*.

Dramatic learning for each group or pair involves imagination and dramatic action. Each situation requires that the individuals involved recall past images, manipulate these images, and create new material mixed with these personal experiences. Each group also physically explores the situation and learns to demonstrate and communicate through behaviors that are inherently dramatic. In each situation, to the best of their abilities, the "performers" select actions, dialogue, gestures, and objects that fit the imagined event or situation — the new imaginative reality.

The connection between imagination and dramatic action is the central factor that propels the drama forward, creates continuity, and allows the

Philip Guston's *Martial Memory* pictures children playing dress-up with everyday objects easily found in their everyday world. (St. Louis Art Museum, Eliza McMillan Trust Fund)

participants to improve. This improvement is evident in every dramatic learning experience. Preschoolers learn to "play" longer and more elaborately. Creative drama participants integrate a plan/play/evaluate format into their procedure. The production team uses rehearsals to refine its performance.

The group also develops a particular way to connect imagination and action. Although each individual functions independently, the group must also function as a unit. In all three situations, the individuals work with others to communicate the imagined reality and to develop consistent dramatic action.

CREATIVE DRAMA'S POTENTIAL

Creative drama is the specific activity that helps children extend their abilities discovered through imaginative play. Through creative drama, participants explore the potential of their imagination. In one sense, they are able to rummage through their storehouses of images to select the best one for drama. Their dramatic behaviors are also extended as they learn to connect imagination and action by being actor, playwright, designer, or director. Since creative drama is a group art, it provides ample opportunity for participants to share ideas, plan and negotiate their actions, and reflect upon their work. Through the dramatic learning process, participants come to know their abilities both mentally in their mind's eyes and physically through action.

Images and Imagination

The source material for dramatic learning is of two basic types: facts and experiences. People acquire facts, usually secondhand, by being told or reading information about something. Facts of this sort make up a large part of what is known by people, but often are not the ideal source for drama-making. The other way of knowing about the world (and the one that can provide the best material for drama) is developed through personal experience. These experiences, filled with sensory impressions and personal feelings, provide information unique to each individual. Most people have access to both types of information as they develop ideas.

As a way to clarify the differences between fact and experience, we ask you now to think about a roller coaster. First, recall all the facts that you know about roller coasters: how they are built, who invented them, and where the largest one is located. Jot down all the information you can. Now, recall an actual roller coaster ride. Remember the slow ascent, the sudden plunge, the speeding up, and the final stop. Try to recall the whole experience.

Which kind of information provided you with the more intense experience? Which kind of information seemed to encompass more than one sense? Most of the people who answered these questions selected their personal experiences as the more powerful, intense, and stimulating source for ideas, even if their recall of the roller coaster was more negative than positive. **Experiential knowledge focuses on images that are unique to each individual,** as opposed to factual information that is available to everyone. The vast differences among individual experiences helps explain why one person's enactment may be very different from another's. Drama's personal nature is highlighted by the ability of each individual to use his or her own experience as the impetus for action.

Second, **experiential knowledge involves multisensory information, vivid images, and resulting feelings.** The recalled sensation in your stomach as the roller coaster rises and the rush of air as you descend can provide material for countless dramas, even ones that deal less with roller coasters than with fear or excitement. Creative drama, as do all the arts, relies heavily on the experiential knowledge of its creators. The wealth of images and experiential knowing that each participant brings to the drama class influences the action that occurs.

If actual imagination and actual sensation were the same, imagination would be found in all the brutes; this is not the case, it is not found in ants or bees or grubs. Visions appear to us even when our eyes are shut.

Aristotle

All participants do not enter the drama arena with the same or even similar sets of rich and vivid images. In fact, you and even some of your future drama participants may never even have ridden a roller coaster. Or, the experience may have happened so long ago that you and they have forgotten it. Don't worry. In the early stages of creative drama, the leader provides many opportunities to increase or enhance both the quantity or quality of the participants' images. In fact, if you work through many of the suggested activities, you too can develop your own ability to remember and use past experiences. Many of the creative drama exercises emphasize sensory awareness and utilize here-and-now objects to help participants retrieve and cultivate a vast storehouse of images. Participants come to know that their own storehouse is the richest resource available to them.

Dramatic Action

Within each creative drama exercise and activity, participants are encouraged to transform these mental pictures into dramatic action. Behaviors modified from those used by the actor give much of the early creative drama activity its form. Exercises that deal with pantomime, movement, and dialogue develop participants' abilities to transform themselves into a character. As their dramatic abilities develop, creative drama participants also model the behaviors of other theatre artists, such as director, playwright, designer, and critic. Ultimately, dramatic action expands to include the full range of dramatic behaviors and theatre skills provided by the model art form of theatre.

Working with the Group

Just as theatre is an ensemble art, so creative drama focuses on the development of a group-conceived product and a cooperative group process. The necessary negotiation skills build from work in pairs to small-group to whole-group enactments. The development of group skills is an important aspect of dramatic action and a purpose integral to creative drama and dramatic learning.

Group skills build gradually. Participants first must develop an awareness of self alone before they can consider self within group. Gradually, through discussing, sharing, and working together, a sense of group begins to emerge. As the group grows closer, individuals begin to share ideas and images and to listen to one another. These basic negotiation skills are enhanced by having to work together on a single improvisation. Individuals must make decisions about selecting and rejecting ideas. A sense of collaboration becomes paramount.

Since groups are made up of individuals, one group is never exactly like another. There are similarities among groups of the same age or among groups who, for example, live in the same community. Each group, of course, has its own personality and set of idiosyncratic work habits.

The uniqueness of group is both fascinating and frustrating. Some groups work quickly, enjoy each other, and rapidly reach mastery. Others are filled with individuals who hold on too tightly to their individuality and are unwilling to cooperate. Most groups fall somewhere in between. Remember that, as you arbitrate early disagreements and soothe hurt feelings, a truly collaborative drama creates a level of joy and success not unlike a great theatrical production. Once the group has gelled, all your careful coaching will be worthwhile.

Metacognitive Abilities

Metacognitive abilities involve a special type of awareness. This awareness extends beyond just having knowledge and using it to create or solve problems. **Metacognition involves knowing that you know and often how you know that you know.** People with high metacognitive abilities are able to know whether they can accomplish a task before they have begun; people with strong metamemory abilities are able to know how they know — they can describe how they went about solving a problem. This awareness or *self-monitoring* can occur in terms of self-knowledge, knowledge of others, or in reference to tasks or strategies. Metacognitive abilities in creative drama permit participants to create and enact a character consistently and to behave within the confines of the imagined reality.

Creative drama stimulates a certain physical and mental facility to "think on one's feet." **The cognitive and metacognitive skills mastered through creative drama emphasize the connection between thought and action.** Participants learn to trust themselves and their ideas. Participants become proficient in selecting some of their ideas and rejecting others. (If you have ever had to choose your own best poem or painting from among many, you know this is no small task.) Participants learn to compress time and space and to rehearse behaviors in their mind before action.

Participants also learn to view themselves from the standpoint of others. This ability helps them create a self-monitoring system that can enhance their view of themselves as solvers of everyday problems that come their way. As you can see, learning these cognitive abilities makes creative drama an excellent "rehearsal for life"— one of creative drama's known strengths since its inception.

Just as with imagination, dramatic behaviors, and group skills, metacognitive abilities build gradually as drama participants plan, play, and evaluate their drama work. Creative drama is well suited to developing these abilities, because it requires that participants search within to find images and experiences to connect to dramatic action. Drama participants must monitor the connection between imagination and dramatic behavior both individually and as members of groups in order to clearly communicate the imagined reality.

The Impact of Creative Drama

Creative drama's primary focus is the connection of imagination and action. This connection occurs individually and with the group. One of creative drama's strengths within educational settings is the opportunity it provides children to cooperate and collaborate with others to create a realized whole. As in all other arts, imagination is essential to the growth and development of skills. Unlike the other arts, self and group are the sole medium. Participants must develop a great deal of physical and mental control to work individually and collaboratively at drama.

Since creative drama has at its core the connection between the internal workings of the imagination and the external manifestations as evidenced by action, it provides practice in this essential life skill. In fact, it may be this very skill that permits creative drama to have an impact on learning in a variety of other subject areas. It may also be this skill that is at the real core of the testimonials that focus on creative drama's nature as a "rehearsal for life."

THE LEADER OF CREATIVE DRAMA

In creative drama, the leader plays a pivotal role. With no script, no musical instrument, no set of time steps to teach, the leader must truly have a grasp of drama and of expected behaviors to be mastered by the participants. Initially, the leader must assess the participants' current dramatic abilities and future potential. The leader must structure a set of activities that meets these needs. In order to assist dramatic learning, the leader must create a safe, supporting, and stimulating environment. The leader must be concerned with the whole of dramatic learning—what is occurring within the participant and for the group as a whole, as well as with the enactment itself. The list of "musts" could go on and on. If the "musts" have made you feel somewhat uneasy, remember that this entire book is devoted to helping you develop the required knowledge and ability.

At this point you have an introductory understanding of the complex and interesting phenomenon called creative drama. You may already be picturing yourself leading wonderful drama sessions. You probably are also feeling somewhat overwhelmed. Be patient. Leader's skills develop slowly, just as participants' skills do.

Keep in mind that good creative drama leaders are not all alike — there's no cookie-cutter mold that turns out good leaders. Many types of individuals, with vastly different training and experiences, have the potential to become skilled leaders. Certain common characteristics, however, do exist among excellent leaders; these good leaders have usually immersed themselves, through formal instruction or independently, in knowledge-gathering and personal introspection.

Your first goal should be to arm yourself with as much information as possible in such areas as theatre, child development, imagery and imagination, and creative drama itself. This work requires that you read what others have written, particularly in the areas of cognition and creativity. (We include a helpful bibliography at the end of the book.) But not all information is found in books. In fact, much of your early information-gathering can be focused on direct observation and active participation. The following activities are good ways to start your investigations:

- Observe young children between the ages of two and eight at play. Note how they interact with each other, how they develop imaginary situations, and how they use "as if" behavior.
- Talk to children about what they know, what they remember, and how they know those things. Listen for descriptions of past sensory experiences and metacognitive experiences.

- Attend as many plays as possible. Note similarities of each play to the other; consider how they differ.
- Attend a rehearsal for a play. Watch the various theatre artists at work. Notice how they work both separately and in conjunction with one another. Consider how rehearsal and performance are similar and different.
- Listen to the director coach the actors. Talk to actors and directors about their crafts.
- Read interviews with theatre artists. Pay particular attention to how they talk about the sources for their ideas, how they cultivate their imagination, and how they choose to communicate their images.

Second, you must also turn the search inward. Just as you intently observed the work of others, so must you become aware, just as systematically, of your own dramatic abilities. Think for a moment about what makes up dramatic learning. Which skills do you possess? Which skills need sharpening? Even though you will not be expected to be Joseph Papp, Brooke Shields, or Bruce Springsteen, you still must work to build necessary skills. Only a first-hand knowledge of how to put imagination into action can provide the necessary foundation for your work as a leader. Here are a few suggestions about how to proceed:

- If you have not already done so, take a movement, drama, or acting class.
- Work to increase your awareness of and artistic sensitivity to the world around you.
- Read.
- Travel.
- Daydream.
- Observe other creative drama leaders at work.
- Experiment with another art form—poetry, drawing, music.
- Visit art museums, attend dance and music concerts, involve yourself with the arts.

Finally, you must cultivate the "mind set for success as a leader." All good leaders seem to have kept alive or rekindled the spark of childlike wonder, which everyone initially possesses but many eventually lose. Good leaders share a certain openness toward life, an enthusiasm for ideas, and an interest in others. Good leaders are flexible and adaptable to moment-to-moment changes as dramas metamorphose right before their eyes. So, as you begin your study as a creative drama leader, find and hold your sense of adventure. And don't forget to be open enough always to entertain the possible!

How This Book Is Organized

The following eleven chapters are organized to facilitate your development as a creative drama leader *extraordinaire*. *Creative Drama and Imagination* provides a step-by-step approach to help you think about and do creative drama. The first half of the text provides the information and strong theoretical base for your practice, which is detailed in the second half of the book. Both sections are essential for obtaining a complete understanding of the complex phenomenon of creative drama.

Chapter 2 overviews the history of creative drama and analyzes some of the significant approaches. Mental imagery is the topic of Chapter 3; theatre of Chapter 4. Chapter 5 covers the theory of imagination in action, which is the

The power of the drum major to lead children in a joyous parade, photographed by Alfred Eisenstaedt, can be likened to the power of the drama leader to guide young people into the world of the imagination. (Time-Life Picture Agency, © Time, Inc.)

foundation for drama practice. Chapter 6 deals exclusively with the Rutgers Imagination Method (RIM) and ends the first half of the book. Chapter 7 and Chapter 8 are filled with Starters, the first set of drama exercises, and helpful leader tips. Chapter 9 and Chapter 10 contain the second-level activities, called Transformations. Chapter 11 presents case studies to chronicle the final Mastery level. Finally, Chapter 12 focuses on issues of assessment and evaluation.

THE HISTORY OF CREATIVE DRAMA

You are entering the field of creative drama at a very exciting time. Creative drama is now recognized as a subject and is included in the curriculum of most schools. No longer confined to the field of education, creative drama is also widely used in recreation, therapy, and even in actor training. The future of the field will depend on you and on your experiences and accomplishments as a leader. You can only begin to assume your role as a confident leader, however, after you have an acquaintance with the history of creative drama.

This chapter is divided into two sections. The first section overviews, decade by decade, the chronological events important to creative drama's growth as a field. The second section analyzes the approaches of five representative creative drama leaders: Winifred Ward, Brian Way, Viola Spolin, Dorothy Heathcote, and Geraldine Siks. Within each analysis we will discuss representative exercises, overall goals, the role of the leader, and the manner in which dramatic learning takes place.

CREATIVE DRAMA DECADE BY DECADE

Historians of creative drama correctly date the beginning of the field to the 1920s, but the history of drama in education dates back to Plato and Aristotle. Teachers with creative inclinations have always conducted drama activities to enhance learning. Countless generations of children have acted out holiday plays and dramatized historical events. What is new in the last sixty years is the systematic conduct of these activities, as well as the training of people to lead them. We will begin our history in the 1920s and proceed decade by decade, discussing how the field was shaped by external events in society and education, as well as by the internal experiences and insights of creative drama leaders.

The 1920s: Setting the Stage for Creative Drama

The United States was ready in the 1920s for the development of the field of creative drama. Americans became more receptive to the idea of arts instruction with the social changes brought by the twentieth century. Look at what was happening. As the agricultural society of the nineteenth century gave way to the Machine Age, people increasingly left the farm to work in factories and live in developing urban centers. No longer needed for farm chores, young people could stay in school for more years. The curriculum expanded to include more than the three "R's," and more teachers' colleges developed to meet the increasing demand for qualified instructors. New immigrants came from European societies to escape an unstable European economy. Having been exposed to a tradition of art and drama from the time of the Renaissance, these immigrants valued the arts more than our Puritan forefathers. Settlement houses originated to bring cultural enrichment and after-school activities to the children of immigrants and urban factory workers. To a large extent these programs focused on the arts and arts instruction. Finally, as the new film industry grew and reached all Americans, an interest in drama and acting reflected society's enchantment with the celluloid art.

As these changes paved the way for new forms of art instruction, so changes in educational theory contributed to the development of creative drama. Progressive Education, the name given to the new educational movement, focused on how to educate children in the twentieth century. Such progressive educators as John Dewey, Francis Parker, William Kirkpatrick, and Hughes Mearns emphasized the education of the whole child. Educating the whole child meant that the education of children's spirits and emotions was as important as the education of their minds. Experience rather than rote memorization was the key to learning. These progressive educators valued all the arts as natural media for experiential learning and self-expression, but they felt drama was particularly important for its ability to create experiences in the classroom not easily accessible in any other place.

As progressive educators documented their successful programs, more schools across the country began to include their ideas in the curriculum. The superintendent of the Evanston Illinois Public Schools invited Winifred Ward to define a program of dramatics. Remember, until that time, "drama" had been part of the curriculum, but drama was thought of as memorizing and then reciting plays and poetry to commemorate holidays and events. But Ward, like her progressive education colleagues, believed that the process of working was more valuable than the actual performance. As she and her students experimented with exercises, Ward, carefully observing and documenting the successful activities, developed the systematic approach to dramatic activity and dramatic learning; this she later termed *creative dramatics*.*

The 1930s: Beginnings

Although Winifred Ward had begun experimenting with creative drama in the 1920s, the publication of her text *Creative Dramatics* in 1930 marks the official beginning of the field. Nellie McCaslin, noted leader in the field of creative drama, has called the 1930s — the Depression era — a decade of "expansion in depression" for creative drama. The 1930s was the decade of developing social consciousness as people began to question American institutions, particularly cultural and educational ones. Government supported the arts through such programs as the Federal Theatre Project, and the arts prospered.

Creative drama prospered, too, in this environment. The experiments conducted by Ward are documented in her book. Her training program at the School of Speech of Northwestern University in Evanston, Illinois, was respon-

* Creative drama *is now the accepted term, having replaced the term* creative dramatics.

Winslow Homer's *The Country School* shows the potential sharing of ideas and experiences among children of all ages that could occur in the American one-room school. (City Art Museum of Chicago)

sible for training the majority of drama leaders until the 1950s and still enjoys a healthy enrollment.

Ward's approach to drama became the model for the next two decades. Ward hoped her book would serve as a starting point for other teachers. In fact, young people in creative drama classes across the country were taught by Ward-trained teachers and participated in classes very similar to each other's. In a decade of terrible economic hardship, creative drama flourished. Due largely to the monumental efforts of Winifred Ward, the 1930s was an active period for this plucky endeavor. By the end of the 1930s, Ward had a large and popular program that trained teachers and presented classes to scores of young people and had established creative drama procedures that were to be virtually unchallenged in America until the 1960s.

The 1940s: World War II

America was again troubled by problems, this time of a different life-threatening nature. The 1940s saw America pull itself out of economic difficulties and become involved in an overwhelming global war. Many arts and education programs were put on hold while the United States focused on World War II.

Perhaps the most significant development for the field of creative drama in the 1940s was the founding of the Children's Theatre Committee in 1944, an affiliate of the American Educational Theatre Association. Founded to promote more and better theatre and drama for young people, the Children's Theatre Committee (which was known for many years as the Children's Theatre Association of America, and now is reconstituted as the American Association of Theatre for Youth) [AATY] has been the organization most influential in child drama. At the invitation of Winifred Ward, the participants attended the first of a series of annual conferences on the campus of Northwestern University in the summer of 1944. Objectives printed in the first program included "new materials and ideas, a rethinking of recreational standards to fit wartime and post-wartime needs, and a renewed confidence in the field of children's drama."

The 1950s: Expansion

The 1950s was the creative drama movement's most expansive era. Its is a credit to the professionals in this field that such tremendous growth could occur in an era marked by the Cold War and a nationwide effort to focus education on the training of scientists. The most significant changes in the field included the burgeoning number of textbooks and the development of many new university programs offering programs in child drama.

In 1950, interest in the field was sparked by the White House Conference on the Arts, whose theme was the "significance of aesthetic experience and artistic expression for healthy personality development." This conference not only recognized drama but secured a place for drama as an important component of a total education package.

Many new books were written by leaders, who by now had developed and tested creative drama methods with a variety of different students. Some of these authors, most notably Geraldine Siks, went on to make even more significant contributions to the field. Their output suggests that creative drama had become a scholarly pursuit, one meriting research and evaluation. Articles about creative drama began to appear in the 1950s in such journals and magazines as *Theatre Arts, Players,* and *Educational Theatre Journal.*

Throughout the 1950s, university programs in child drama continued to produce fine scholars. Many of these programs had begun in the 1940s, but came into their own during the early part of the fifties as returning veterans enabled their families to attend school or attended school themselves. Most notable of these programs were those at the University of Minnesota, Hunter College in New York, San Francisco State University, The University of Delaware, and Brigham Young University. As the decade closed, master's and doctoral students conducting research on creative drama began to make a contribution to the literature in the field.

The 1960s: A Time of Possibilities

The authors of this text came into their prime during the 1960s. We remember this period with great fondness because it triggered our own interest in creative drama. Many advances for the arts occurred during the sixties as Americans pulled back from science/math pursuits, recovered their balance, and looked again to the arts for a way of expressing and understanding life. The decade began with President John F. Kennedy publicly supporting the arts and ended with the Artist-in-the-Schools program of the National Endowment of the Arts.

The most significant societal impact of the decade was the amount and scope of federal and state funding of the arts and education. This easy money gave practitioners an open ticket in the sixties. Within creative drama, this funding permitted wide experimentation and led to a variety of procedures — many good and some bad. The sixties marked the beginning of drama with special populations, as a personality enhancer, and as part of an integrated arts curriculum.

As practitioners in U.S. schools began to feel comfortable, they began to look to other countries — particularly England — and to other disciplines — notably mainstream theatre — for possible new methods. Ward's story drama approach was challenged by such works as *Development through Drama,* written by Brian Way and published in 1966, and Viola Spolin's *Improvisation for the Theatre,* published in 1963.

Enrollment in universities surged in the 1960s as "baby boom" students made decisions to study humanistic fields. Both men and women began to major in arts as undergraduates; many of them also pursued advanced degrees. Grants were available for all types of arts investigations. Northwestern University, the Universities of Minnesota, Washington, California at Los Angeles, Colorado, and Utah continued to lead in size of program and scope of offerings.

It seemed in the late sixties in America that all people regardless of race, color, or creed could be unified through arts activities. The kind of optimism that hoped peace marches would stop the Vietnam War waned as this socially active, arts-oriented decade drew to a close and has yet to return to the field of creative drama.

All societies have battled with that incorrigible disturber of the peace — the artist. How do artists disturb the peace? With anti-government slogans? With creations that offend society's moral? With lawbreaking ideas? Sometimes. But the most peace-disturbing feature of artistic creations is their imaginativeness.

James Baldwin

The 1970s: An Up-and-Down Decade

No decade in the history of creative drama has been so full of turmoil as the roller coaster 1970s. The rapid economic decline that followed the end of the Vietnam War and deteriorated with the oil crisis greatly affected the field. This economic recession, the severest since the Great Depression, caused universities, school boards, and arts agencies to re-evaluate their priorities. Money did not completely dry up — fortunately — but many projects slowly began to lose funds after long-term commitments had been met. Within education, the focus was a back-to-basics, no-frills one. The arts faced a renewed challenge — to prove that their subjects also qualified as basic to learning.

The challenges creative drama faced from external sources brought unity, a characteristic of the movement in the seventies. The Children's Theatre Association of America (CTAA), the primary educational association, began to work for more regional meetings and better attendance at the national convention. This united front peaked with the Wingspread Conference, held in August 1977, in Racine, Wisconsin. The group of thirty-five participants considered such issues as using the arts to enhance education, preparing the specialist and generalist to meet the needs of education through drama in the schools, and isolating the unique properties of theatre and dramas. A carefully researched document was the result of their deliberations. A growing creative drama network helped spread the word of drama's potential to the cities and universities where the participants resided.

Integrated arts activities also characterized this decade as leaders in all arts disciplines began to pool their resources. On the local scene, many successful projects that focused on the integration of the arts occurred in the seventies. On the regional scene, such large centers as Central Midwest Regional Education Laboratory (CEMREL) expanded their teacher training in the integrated arts. On the national level, the Alliance for Arts Education, formed in 1973, worked to bring the arts to the attention of school administrators, community leaders, university professors, and the general population. Also, documentation of the integrated arts movement by the John D. Rockefeller III Foundation resulted in the 1977 publication of *Coming to Our Senses*.

During the 1970s, creative drama activities were expanded to include work with diverse populations. Although it began earlier, with the publication of Sue Jennings' *Remedial Drama,* the trend to use creative drama with special-needs populations experienced tremendous growth in the decade of the seventies. Encouraged by federal funding to the handicapped, CTAA and ATA designated a special committee to explore the potential of drama with handicapped individuals. ATA also published the excellent *Drama/Theatre by, for, and with the Handicapped,* edited by Ann Shaw and C. J. Stevens. Older Americans, increasing in numbers, began to make up an important segment of the population, demanding leisure-time activities. Drama leaders began to expand creative drama's repertoire to include drama for senior adults. (An important text for this population is Isabel Burger's *Drama with Senior Adults*.)

The 1980s: Research Is the Key

In the mid-1980s arts and education began to make up for the losses incurred earlier. Cuts in federal support to the National Endowment for the Arts (NEA) and the Humanities (NEH), as well as the abolishment of the Office of Education in the early 1980s, struck a tremendous blow to all the arts. Recent reinstatement of funding to NEA and NEH plus better economic conditions generally have turned the tide. As the United States approaches the end of the decade, arts and education seem to be making slow and steady advances.

Research is the important work of the 1980s. This trend started in the 1970s—as CTAA created the office of vice-president for policy and research—but research began in full-force in the 1980s. More graduate programs have begun to offer advanced degrees, and these students are completing their university programs with interesting and valuable dissertations and theses. Older programs also are producing valuable research contributing to the knowledge in the field. In the eighties, scholars who in the previous decade had been working merely to keep creative drama from being cut out of their programs are attending seminars and institutes and conducting long-term research projects. CTAA has established a Research Award to encourage these activities and has sponsored a special Research Issue of the *Children's Theatre Review* to publish these works. AATY continues this trend by its support of scholarly meetings and practical training-oriented seminars.

At the core of all this investigative activity was the field's realization of the importance of connections—not only connections among the arts but also between the arts and other disciplines such as psychology, sciences, and philosophy. What leaders had felt instinctively concerning the importance and value of drama could now be described systematically and tested empirically. The road to research, of course, remains relatively uncharted. Various opinions, for and against the emphasis on empirical research, have developed, but argument is healthy; and disagreement helps stimulate critical thinking.

The only clear focus in the field is on the importance of research for drama's future growth.

You are entering the creative drama movement in the 1980s. You may feel it was easier to be a pioneer back in the early days of creative drama, but remember that each decade brought its own set of needs and challenges. The field is still young and receptive to new ideas. Your contributions are eagerly awaited.

A POTPOURRI OF APPROACHES

A creative drama approach is a specific method used to help leaders teach creative drama in a particular manner so that they can assist participants in their dramatic learning. In the first section of this chapter, you followed creative drama's growth as a field. Many leaders learned and practiced their art in various settings and with specific types of groups in order to reach a variety of goals. In the United States, the Ward approach formed the early and most popular model for creative drama. Geraldine Siks and Nellie McCaslin, both trained by Ward at Northwestern University, began their own programs in Washington and New York, respectively. Both wrote books based on their experiences with the Ward approach. Leaders from England—Brian Way and Dorothy Heathcote—reached the American scene during the 1960s and 1970s with unique approaches that greatly varied from Ward's, while Viola Spolin, an American, modified actor-training techniques for use in creative drama situations. Late in the decade, Siks introduced the process-concept method as a more theoretically based approach to teach and evaluate dramatic learning.

Essentially, all of these approaches, although different from one another, are creative drama. If Leader A employs Way and Leader B employs Ward, both are teaching creative drama, because all approaches share several characteristics. First, each creative drama approach consists of a leader, participants, and the dramatic improvisation. For the participant, there is some kind of exhibited external behavior, as well as internal stimulus for this behavior. The overall process of drama must also have, at one time or another, *an imagine, an enact, and a reflect phase.*

At this point, however, the approaches begin to follow different routes. Each mirrors the personal teaching style, life experiences, and knowledge base of the person who developed it. The stimulus for drama, the role of the leader, the environment, and the amount of time necessary for optimum dramatic learning vary among approaches. Later in this book, we present the Rutgers Imagination Method, an imagery-based approach to drama, and we wrestle with these inconsistencies among methods. For now, we offer an overview of the contemporary field of creative drama as a way of acquainting you with creative drama as a whole. Remember, each of these approaches has a certain magic and has worked for countless leaders. In fact, many of these techniques and theories can be incorporated into your evolving knowledge and practice of the art of creative drama.

Since much of this book focuses on imagination, we would like you now to journey with us to an imaginary school where creative drama approaches are being conducted in five classrooms by the very practitioners who originated each. Because you can compress time and space in your mind's eye, a brief lesson may actually be the symbolic representation of a whole series of lessons. In an attempt to capture the essence of each approach, we first describe a lesson. We then present a brief historical background, the major theories, and the key practices most important for your understanding of each approach.

WINIFRED WARD: MOTHER OF CREATIVE DRAMA

Young people cluster around Winifred Ward, seated center. The clothing suggests that the photo was taken approximately fifty years ago, but the power of Ward's ideas will never dim. (Winifred Ward Archives, Northwestern University)

CASE STUDY

GOLDILOCKS We enter a classroom of fifteen seven-year-olds just as the leader is telling a story. The leader, a white-haired lady, is kind and enthusiastic. Only when she is giving directions, introducing the lesson, or leading evaluation does she speak. The class has obviously heard the story of "Goldilocks and the Three Bears" before. As we begin to observe, the children are counting the number of characters and the number of incidents in preparation for the story drama that will conclude this lesson unit. The class is eager to act out the entire fairy tale, but the leader explains, "First we must prepare. Remember when we went for a walk in the woods? What was the forest like? What did you do in the forest?" After a bombardment of answers from the children, the leader asks each of them to pantomime an activity that might be done in the forest. Each, in turn, demonstrates for his or her fellow classmates.

After one particularly fine pantomime, the leader asks, "What did Andrew do to help you know he was picking flowers?" When all the children have shown their pantomimes, the leader explains that they now will pretend to be bears in the forest. "How does a bear move?" The class suggests "slowly" or "on four legs" or "with big movements." The class acts out the forest activity, this time as bears. Then the leader reviews with the class the breakfast scene from "Goldilocks" in which Papa Bear, Mama Bear, and Baby Bear eat their porridge. She divides the class of fifteen into five groups of three bears and assigns each child a role. She also reminds the class how different characters use different voices, and she urges each student to speak like his or her assigned character. Each group rehearses a short breakfast scene with dialogue. After a brief planning period of several minutes during which the leader remains seated, each threesome shows its scene to the others. The leader is quiet until the completion of the performances and ends the activity with a brief evaluation. We leave as the leader explains that, "Tomorrow we will work on some other scenes and other characters. Soon we will be ready to act out the while story of 'Goldilocks'."

Background

What you've just witnessed is the approach developed by Winifred Ward, who is affectionately referred to as the "mother of creative drama" in America. Ward was the first to establish creative drama as a field apart from formal theatricals with children. Ward's landmark books, *Creative Dramatics* published in 1930 and *Playmaking with Children* published first in 1947 and then revised in 1957, established theories and activities still in use in contemporary classrooms.

This pragmatic spokesperson had a great gift for understanding the dramatic behavior of young people. Through observation of these young people, Ward and her students began to develop a systematic approach to dramatic activity and a justification that would speak to people less "pro-arts" than herself. In retrospect Ward explained, "For it was the children who taught us this free, informal drama. All we had to do was work out the way to use it and convince the administration that it belonged."

Winifred Ward's campaign for a more open-minded attitude toward children may not have been unique to her. What was special about Ward was her ability to establish practical programs of creative drama training, to act as spokesperson extraordinaire for the rapidly developing field, and to write the first works in the field. The program Ward established at Northwestern University is still responsible for training many of the leading experts of today. Ward's second book, *Playmaking with Children,* is still a respected work in the literature. Ward remained active and innovative until her death in 1972. To honor her memory, the Children's Theatre Association of America developed the coveted Winifred Ward Scholarship awarded yearly to an outstanding student-scholar in the field.

View of Dramatic Learning

Earlier in this chapter, it was noted that Ward's theory of creative drama was derived from and nurtured by the progressive education movement, whose main goal was to educate the whole child, with the idea that the child could achieve an understanding of self and society. Ward believed that drama was a perfect subject to meet these goals because drama integrates all the arts, thus offering participants the most complete opportunity for personal development through the expression of imagination. As participants assume characters in the cooperative environment of creating a drama, they learn to understand themselves and to work with others.

The Ward approach focuses on drama as an art, with the balance of process and product. In her approach, participants acquire a series of *internal skills* — concentration and sensitivity, for example — and *external behaviors* — pantomime, dialogue, and characterization — that almost always culminate in the dramatization of a story. Although personal experiences are part of the early work in the Ward approach, individuals turn aside their personal desires as they become part of the group enactment of a story, legend, or fable. While the Ward approach teaches specific drama skills, the overall thrust of the method is the affective and social growth of the participants.

Distinguishing Characteristics

The Ward approach offers some specific guidelines in terms of types and sequences of activities, lesson structure, ultimate goals, and role of the leader. Perhaps because it is so focused on the development of skills necessary to enact a group story, the method is easy to learn. Although sometimes tedious, Ward's approach offers a series of foolproof activities.

1. A Building-Block Sequence of Activities

Ward's method is based on a building-block development of skills acquisition. By building block we mean that one skill must be worked on and mastered to a certain extent before participants may proceed to the next. Several possible frameworks are presented in Ward. The most typical is exemplified in *Give Them Roots and Wings: A Handbook for the Elementary School Teacher*. Developed by many leaders who at the time embraced the Ward method, the objectives are ordered like this: Movement/Pantomime, Sensitivity, Characterization, Dialogue, and Dramatic Form, also called Story Drama. **The leader presents these various drama elements in an inductive progression starting with the nonverbal skills of movement/pantomime to the more complex skills of characterization and dialogue, culminating in improvisational playmaking.** This step-by-step development could take place over an entire fifteen-week term and/or be utilized as the organization for each daily lesson, as portrayed in the scenario.

In each of the areas the leader presents various activities that are designed to develop a specific external behavior. Leaders can select from the activities presented in each of the areas in such sources as Ward, McCaslin, or

Roots and Wings, or can develop original ones. The given activities can be used as separate exercises or as part of a unit having as its culmination the playing of a story.

2. Literature as Stimulus/Story Drama the Outcome

One of the major aspects of the Ward approach is the importance of literature as the stimulus for drama. The acting out of fairy tales, poems, fables, classics, or contemporary stories is the primary goal of the Ward approach. Ward believed that literature is the perfect fabric of creative drama because it is closest to drama and to life itself. Ward emphasized stories, but valued the dramatizing of them even more. Much of Ward's 1957 book attests to the importance of stories: 75 percent of the book is devoted to choosing stories, developing scenes, working on characters, improvising speech through stories, and presenting plays based on stories.

3. Character at the Core

Character analysis becomes one essential key to meeting the social and affective goals of creative drama. In her 1930 book, Ward explained that analysis of character is the most valuable aspect of creative drama. Participants in drama must understand people before they can portray them. This experience in comprehending points of view different from their own gives children a true perspective on life, helping them to formulate their own values and to understand others. Trying on people is an idea compelling to young people. The Ward approach considers this rehearsal of behaviors integral to the personal development of the participant, both theatrically and cognitively.

4. Leader as Guide

All of this story drama must, of course, be planned and implemented by a leader well trained in all aspects of theatre, child development, and language arts. The particular role to be assumed by the leader in Ward's approach is a pleasant one — that of guide. Certainly not a passive role, nevertheless the role of guide implies that at least some of the responsibility for the development of the drama is in the hands of the participants. The leader must choose the story, tell the story, and assist the participants in developing appropriate skills. And the leader must also assist the participants, through careful questioning, to think of more possibilities and to draw connections between the dramatic situation and their own lives. Yet, in the Ward approach, the group is often left to develop on its own. At times, the leader may even bow out, silently observe the enactment, and pose questions at the conclusion, as described in the scenario.

5. Enact Is the Vital Phase

Of the three phases of creative drama — imagine, enact, and reflect — the enact phase is most essential to the Ward approach. Most day's activities culminate with the performance of the story by one part of the group for the rest of the group. Ward also encouraged the performance of these dramas, usually in the form of demonstrations, for invited guest classes or for adults. The second most important phase is the imagine phase (more appropriately termed the planning phase in the Ward method). During this phase, participants organize and rehearse their improvisation, readying it for performance. The reflection phase includes leader evaluation, focusing on the replaying of the scene, or on the skills/behaviors to be mastered for subsequent performances of other story dramas.

WARD AT A GLANCE

- Major texts: *Creative Dramatics* (1930), *Playmaking with Children* (1947, 1957)
- Books derived from Ward approach: Siks' *Drama: An Art for Children* (1958); McCaslin's *Creative Dramatics for the Classroom* (1968, 1984); Schwartz and Aldrich's (editors) *Give Them Roots and Wings* (1972)
- Major goals are the individual and social development of the participants.
- The five major objectives and categories of activities are movement/pantomime, sensitivity, characterization, dialogue, and story drama. The activities move from simple to more complex skill acquisition.
- Characterization is a main key to drama's value for children.
- Literature is the main stimulus for drama; the acting out of stories is the culmination of dramatic learning.
- Performance is a vital aspect of the approach.
- The leader is a guide.

BRIAN WAY: THE EVOLVING VIEW OF DRAMA

CASE STUDY

A ROBBERY We enter the next room to find a tall, British-sounding man with gray hair and a beard. He is putting away a large card with a rotating arrow on it. (This arrow moves from nine o'clock on the circle, which indicates "soft," to three o'clock, which indicates "loud." This control device allows the class to become noisy, but only at certain times.) "Okay, class," he says in a booming voice, "we are going to work on movement." This class of twenty-five nine-year-olds has just begun to participate in drama work.

"I am going to put on some music for you to do a short activity with only movement, no words. When I put on the record, please move the desk which is closest to you so we can clear a space for drama. As you move the desks, imagine that you are really doing some other activity like cleaning the attic or preparing the booths for a bazaar. Please begin when the music starts and end when it stops." He turns on the record; the music is soft, slow, and steady. "Now I'm going to go around the room and each

This photograph records Brian Way's intense and concentrated style of drama leading. (Photograph courtesy of Baker's Plays, Inc., Boston, Massachusetts)

of you can whisper to me what you were doing." The leader does this so as not to put any one person on the spot. He listens earnestly to each one's *private whisper.*

"Okay, now we are going to do a small story, this time also with just movement, no words. Please get into the small groups you were in yesterday." The class breaks into groups of three or four. Typically, the boys are grouped with other boys and the girls with girls. "I'd like you to think of the silliest character you can. In this situation you have just robbed a bank. The improvisation will start just as you leave the bank. The action will begin when the music starts and finish when the music ends. Take a few seconds to talk over the situation with members of your group." The class talks quickly and just as quickly is finished planning. "Each group now make a still photograph of the robbers leaving the bank." Each group gets into position. "As soon as the music starts, bring the photo to life. When the music stops, freeze the action." The music is peppy and gradually gets louder. Each group works simultaneously and each acts out the episode. After the enactment, the leader conducts a short discussion with all groups at once. He questions primarily about what went well; he does not talk about how to improve the improvisation. We depart just as the class is about to begin the next exercise.

Background

The method just described belongs to Brian Way, author of *Development through Drama,* written in 1967. Brian Way was strongly influenced by Peter Slade, author of the 1954 pioneer text *Child Drama*. Way modified and incorporated much of Slade's work, but gave his own book both a theoretical and practical slant. *Development through Drama* made a strong impact on the British educational drama field as well as on the American creative drama scene. In a 1974 survey of the field, Brian Way's book was the drama text most utilized in American universities, surpassing the previous first-place holder, Ward's *Playmaking with Children*.

Brian Way began his career as an actor, then became a director and a playwright. Author of many participation plays for young people, among them *Pinocchio* and *The Mirrorman,* Way remains active in the theatre field as well as in drama education. Way is much in demand as a lecturer in America and has participated in university summer drama programs throughout the United States.

View of Dramatic Learning

The kind of dramatic learning cultivated by the Brian Way method relates specifically to Way's interest in humanistic education, training in theatre, and the influence of Peter Slade, his mentor. Both Peter Slade and Brian Way were intrigued by the humane educational theories of the early twentieth century. Caldwell Cook, who inspired both Slade and Way, focused on play as a natural learning environment for children. In *Child Drama,* Peter Slade summarized his twenty years of improvisational drama by concluding that drama is an extension of children's play.

Consequently, Way's main focus — the process of drama — constantly outweighs the importance of product. In fact, participants play activities in pairs or simultaneously, making leader evaluation unnecessary and often impossible. As you will see, the thrust of these activities is the personal experience, not the overt behavior. It often seems that Way never gets to the drama at all, in contrast to Ward, who always ends with a drama.

Way believes that the process of drama is in sharp opposition to the theatre product and that young children should not be encouraged to view formal theatre because such theatre attendance can only undermine creativity. This contrast between theatre and drama distinguishes Way from many other approaches analyzed in this chapter.

Way believes that dramatic learning occurs in seven areas: concentration, the senses, imagination, physical self, speech, emotion, and intellect. Instead of a step-by-step acquisition of skills, as prescribed by Ward, Way believes that a more appropriate model is the circle. This circle expands symbolically as the participant develops from discovery of personal resources to the more complex interaction of self and environment. Way explains that the leader should start at any point in the circle, based on his or her own needs and interests, and those of the participants. The main issue is that the activities help develop a human being.

Distinguishing Characteristics

Development through Drama is a compelling book that intersperses personal philosophy and theory with more concrete examples and specific descriptions of behaviors. The diversity of the discussion makes it speak to a variety of readers. Written almost twenty years ago, Way's book is a significant contribution to creative drama in America. Brian Way's approach is based on several features that are almost in direct contrast to Ward's.

1. The Circular View of Development

No single linear progression of drama activities can be the norm because of the variety and complexity of human beings. Way advises leaders to "begin where you are" and to choose activities from one resource area to another to a third and back to the first. If you as leader believe that the group has mastered one area or is bored, you should move to another area for the remainder of the day or for the next week. In fact, because there is no prescribed final product and each area is self-contained, drama lessons can last for as long as necessary or be as short as five minutes.

2. Past Experiences as Stimulus/Material for Drama

Way views music, history, and everyday life as potential stimuli for drama activity. The pragmatic Way truly believes that not simply stories but television, current events, and personal experience may be used to pique the interest of the student. Unlike Ward, who focuses largely on stories, Way remains consistent in his belief that leaders must begin drama where the students are and that drama is an integral part of living. Way stresses the use of past experiences as stimuli for exercises — in contrast to other theorists who believe in the importance of the actual stimulus at hand.

3. Leader as Learner

The Way approach is based on the notion that the novice leader need have little if any exposure to theatre or to drama procedures. Because the circle approach suggests that many beginnings are possible, new leaders may begin where they feel comfortable. In no other approach are leaders encouraged, for example, to sneak drama into the classroom for five minutes. A supportive learning environment is an important element of this approach. The leader must therefore strive never to make drama threatening to the participants. Way also believes that the leader must never demonstrate to the students how to perform an activity because he believes theatre skills are unnecessary. Consequently, nonelitist Way has a great appeal to departments of education and to leaders not well versed in theatre. Leaders may learn about drama along with their students.

The novice leader is taught to handle discipline problems through what Way calls "crowd control." For Way, crowd control must be part of the exercise. Various techniques, such as slowing down the action, using an arrow (as mentioned in the scenario), and establishing that people in this scene are too tired to speak to one another, are built into the activity. A clever leader who learns to structure such control has fewer discipline problems. According to Way, the leader must never entirely "give up the arrow."

4. Nonperformance Orientation

Way's approach does not stress performance. Way makes a clear and sharp distinction between drama and theatre. Theatre is concerned with communication between actors and audience; drama is concerned with the experience of the participants, irrespective of the audience.

Way recommends working in pairs or simultaneous individual work within the group context—both of which make working with larger classes easier, especially in the earlier stages of the drama. Way believes that each activity may exist as a separate entity, unconnected to all other activities. In fact, Way feels that leaders do not have to offer explanations to their participants about the total scope of the drama curriculum.

5. The Importance of the Imagine and the Reflection Phases

Of all the phases of the creative drama process, Way seems to be most concerned with the imagine phase. Because scene work is his focus, Way's imagine phase involves much personal remembering of past experiences and thinking about possible solutions to the exercise, rather than the group planning the scene to be played. Reflection in Way is equally personally oriented. Participants don't really reflect on the enactment itself, but on what has been learned and its application to daily life. A Way reflective question is "What would you do if you were called upon to cope with a disaster such as the one we worked with today?" instead of "What kind of character did Shellie play?"

WAY AT A GLANCE

- Major text: *Development through Drama* (1967)
- Major goal: The development of the human being
- Structure: The circle model of human development, from self-discovery to interaction of self with environment
- Activities stress drama process, not theatre product.
- The environment is noncompetitive; it has an atmosphere of trust and cooperation. There is simultaneous individual and pair work, with few performances and little leader evaluation.
- Leader is also a learner.
- Life events are the stimuli for drama.
- Five-minute segments of drama performed consistently are preferable to longer chunks of drama performed on an irregular basis.

DOROTHY HEATHCOTE: DRAMA WITH LEARNING AS THE FOCUS

CASE STUDY

ACTION SHIP As we enter the classroom, we see a rather large woman who speaks with a British accent. She is dressed in modern dress,

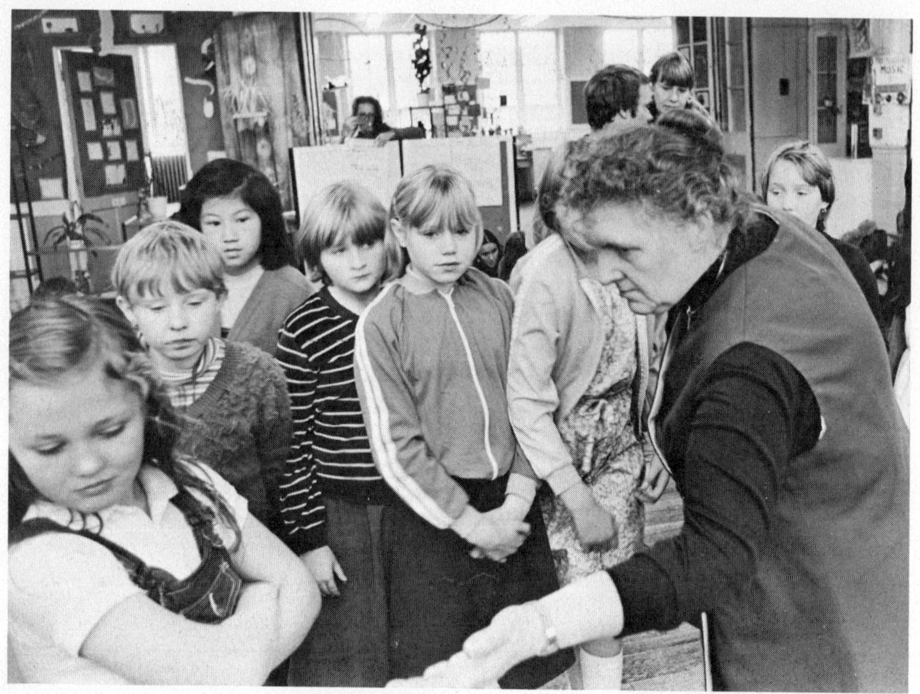

The power of Dorothy Heathcote, pictured here in a drama in progress, is apparent as she gathers her group by means of a stoic stance and a simple gesture of her hand. (Photo courtesy of Dorothy Heathcote)

but she wears a military hat, carries a clipboard, and strides around the classroom. "Take me to the captain of this ship," she bellows. The thirty twelve-year-olds, who have never had a drama class, are silent; they don't know what to make of this very serious woman who stares at them until one boy responds, "We have no captain since the last battle." Still in role, the leader says, "That is obvious. Look at the condition of this ship. How can you expect to win the next battle if this ship is in such terrible shape? What can we do to prepare?"

The class responds, giving many suggestions, some silly, some serious. The leader, still in role, responds to the sillier ideas ("Wear clean underwear") with statements like, "Well, mates, what do we do with traitors?" One boy comes up with an answer, "We must reorganize our arsenal and our supplies." To which the leader responds, "Good, now show me what supplies are left. I can assist you." The leader now has an ally in this boy, whom she perceives as a popular member of the class. The class has taken various props, such as maps and math supplies, from around the classroom and is stacking them near the leader. Some class members scurry around the room, collecting more and more; others are sorting the materials. It's obvious to us that the class has begun to work together and to participate in drama, without ever having a preparatory introductory drama lesson. As the class gets more rambunctious, the leader realizes that she is about to lose control of the children and announces, "Wait. This is important. I would like each of you to present each piece of equipment to me and say something about how it served you in previous battles." Immediately, we notice a change: many of the members of the class move slowly and in a dignified manner, using archaic language. They make statements like, "Once this vestment covered my chest as a bullet tried to pierce m' very heart."

As the ritual draws to a close, we notice that the leader's role is evolving. She seems more like a teacher now as she says in a quiet voice, "What do you do on this ship? Write your job on the board next to your name." Each class member does so. One writes "pilot"; another writes "first mate"; a third writes "cook and look-out." Once they have finished, the leader assumes a more shadowy role by saying, "I'm weary of being in charge." The class at first does not know how to respond. Finally, a girl offers the leader a chair and says, "Tell us how we can be on our own. What must we do?" Knowing that the drama is in very capable hands, we depart as the leader answers the question with another question.

Background

The scenario you have just viewed is based on the Dorothy Heathcote method as recorded in *Dorothy Heathcote: Drama as a Learning Medium,* written in 1976 by Betty Jane Wagner. Unlike most drama books written by the person whose approach is portrayed, the Heathcote book was written by an observer, one who remained objective enough to record accurately, yet who is full of praise and wonder for her subject.

Drama as a Learning Medium is an appropriate title for this book because of the dual meaning of the word *medium.* In one sense, the Heathcote approach focuses on drama as a way or medium to learn. The skills each participant acquires as a result of the drama experience are important life skills. In another sense of the word, the book inspires the leader to become a medium and "bring into the present the distant time or space, making it come alive in participants' consciousness through imagined group experience."

Art is the only way to run away without leaving home.

Twyla Tharp

Heathcote developed an approach that sums up her various strengths and mirrors her personal view of the world. A physically large woman who uses her great presence to her advantage, Heathcote thrusts herself into situations just as she thrusts her students into drama. Heathcote's training in theatre is apparent in her method, as are her strong trade union family experiences. Poverty and a family who worked at the looms in the weaving industry most likely make Heathcote aware of various sociological conditions in ways no indirect exposure could. The strength that Heathcote acquired in her difficult situation perhaps accounts for her own strength as a teacher and the powerful position she allows the drama leader—one of real control of focus in the drama situation. This eclectic approach also utilizes philosophies and theories from sociology, anthropology, and religion as a way to help participants view the human condition.

Heathcote was discovered by U.S. leaders in the early 1970s. Quickly her ideas were embraced by educators who realized their tremendous potential. Many of these leaders in the field traveled to England to study with her. Into the 1980s Heathcote remains a popular lecturer in America. She is often invited to lead courses in American universities with large drama programs. She also holds a full-time position as a lecturer in the University of Newcastle in England, where she often allows guests to observe her demonstrations.

View of Dramatic Learning

The main theoretical bases for the Heathcote method are tightly bound to two strongly felt principles: **drama itself is learning; and the leader is the essential catalyst of the drama.** The goal of drama in education is to provide the forum for reflecting and analyzing life's experience and a place to test it in action. For Heathcote, improvisation is perfectly designed to meet this goal. The leader, using a variety of methods, challenges and directs the group to retrieve, combine, and elaborate upon their experiences and then test them in acting through the developing drama. For Heathcote, drama is the perfect medium for learning about self and society because drama is both individual expression and social interaction.

Many of the activities thrust participants into the center of the improvisation without giving them prior opportunities to experiment with internal strategies or develop theatre/drama behaviors. Heathcote assumes that the immediacy of the situation will force participants into action. She believes that if the problem-solving potential of each participant is appropriately challenged, the behavior will exhibit itself and can be immediately modified by the leader.

The method is also based on the assumption that a leader can draw on his or her own vast repertoire of theatre and problem-solving experiences to cope with the situation at hand. A leader with a more limited background in theatre, anthropology, and psychology may be less able to confront the developing situation. Heathcote's vast and varied background allows her to shape the dramatic learning of a wide age range, even the adolescent — an often forgotten group.

Distinguishing Characteristics

In order for you to understand the Heathcote method, we've tried to compartmentalize a method that is not so easily broken down as were the previous two. Within the method, the leader has great responsibility for directing the drama. Because of this great responsibility, the leader-in-training must master a complex series of procedures for drama implementation, including *teaching in role or in register, questioning,* and *dropping to the universal.* Material for the drama comes from a variety of situations but always highlights the individual interacting with society. Because drama has a larger scope when more than stories are used as stimuli, drama can be viewed as having applicability in more curricular areas.

1. Leader Directs Drama

The leader in this method has absolute control. Unlike the story-centered Ward method or the child-centered Way method, the Heathcote approach, as written by Wagner, focuses on the practical techniques to be acquired by the leader. These techniques account for almost 75 percent of the book. Although Heathcote believes that the leader must thrust young people into sink-or-swim drama, she does not thrust untrained leaders into drama situations. The leader-in-training must undergo a long and arduous apprenticeship in order to be appropriately equipped to deal with all situations. Heathcote advises the leader to develop group involvement and focus within the context of the improvisation through some very clearly defined techniques.

Teaching in Role or in Register Heathcote believes that leaders need not always be themselves, but must assume attitudes or even full-fledged characters to direct the flow of the drama. Leaders must adopt an attitude that may be very different from what they truly feel to push or prod the participants into action. Instead of being leader as smiling guide (a role often assumed by the novice), Heathcote describes such registers as one who has no idea, a suggester of implications, interested listener, or devil's advocate. Often leaders withhold expertise so that the participants must find out themselves or think they know more than the leader.

Going a step further, Heathcote encourages leaders to start drama by assuming a character entirely different from themselves. This character can react in ways the leader might not. Leaders can, for example, be the principal of the school, the bill collector, the captain of the ship—any role that may press the students into participating. Assuming a character different from yourself may appeal to you if you have a flair for the dramatic or find it convenient to hide for a time behind another identity.

Questioning Another aspect of structuring the drama involves interrupting it to ask questions, seek information, supply information, call for decision, or control the process. Heathcote often charts the answers she receives on the chalkboard. Heathcote's questions are not the types that require pat answers but rather encourage reflection. It is through reflection, she believes, that drama changes people.

Dropping to the Universal Heathcote also recommends several other ploys classified under the umbrella-term *dropping to the universal*. Heathcote uses what is happening in the drama as a means to remind the group that there is an underlying significance in it that can be recognized by examining its implications. Stopping the drama to reflect or to ask "how do you feel now?" is a distancing technique that she believes encourages the reflection necessary for assimilating knowledge.

2. Material for Drama

Material for Heathcote's dramas comes from a system called the *Brotherhood Code.* Instead of wasting energy searching for material, Heathcote encourages leaders to "jump sideways through time and across social strata, hanging on all the while onto one constant or element in the situation." Any situation then becomes a potential dramatic improvisation. Cinderella is seen in the sisterhood of all those who have suffered at the hands of their siblings. Having a connection like this makes all situations possible dramatic ones and assists leaders in getting out of the trap of "acting out" stories and into the practice of dealing with human experience. The individual's own personal images become, in a sense, stimuli for larger, more symbolic imagery.

3. Enact/Reflect in Balance

The ultimate goal of a Heathcote drama is the discovery of the universal human experience. The participants develop this knowledge by enacting meaningful dramas and by reflecting on the essence embedded in them. Heathcote encourages participants' development by involving them as questioners as well as participants. She tries to encourage a balance of time spent in the enact and reflect phases of drama.

HEATH-COTE AT A GLANCE

- Major text: *Drama as a Learning Medium* by Betty Jane Wagner (1976)
- Major goal: to provide the focus for reflecting on and analyzing life's experiences and also the place to test them in action
- Structure: Not developmental or circular, but thrusting participants into sink-or-swim drama
- The leader is a participant in and has great responsibility for the drama. Leader-in-training must master a variety of specific techniques including Adopting Registers and Assuming Roles.
- The material for drama focuses on the human condition and evolves through a Brotherhood Code.
- The style of the approach is flamboyant—possibly because it mirrors the personal teaching style of Dorothy Heathcote herself.
- Drama is valued for its own cognitive and affective components.
- Appropriately chosen and structured activities achieve almost immediate results.

VIOLA SPOLIN: A GAMELIKE APPROACH

CASE STUDY

JOINING IN We enter the room to see twenty-five fourteen-year-olds, an age group usually very difficult to involve, about to begin an exercise. The leader, an energetic older woman, announces that the game to be played as a warm-up is called Part of a Whole #1. The class is attentive and eager to begin. The leader says, "I would like a volunteer to enter the playing area and become part of a large object or organism. As soon as the object becomes clear to the others, I would like each of you to join in, one at a time, and become part of that object. Begin."

One very agile girl jumps into the center and holds her arms up in the air and points her fingers to the ceiling. She makes a rhythmic clicking sound. The leader responds, "Good, use your whole body to become that object." The girl responds by moving one arm in a circle. No one moves to the center for a few seconds. The leader calls out, "Take a risk. Become another part of the object." Almost immediately, each class member, one at a time, becomes part of the "alarm clock." The leader talks for almost the entire exercise, giving verbal encouragement as each player becomes "Part of a Whole." During evaluation, the leader asks questions such as "What was the whole object? What did you think the object was before you joined?"

She explains that the class is going to move on to a more difficult exercise, titled Part of a Whole #4. The leader explains, "Please count off

This exuberant photo of Viola Spolin captures her lively personality. The drama method she developed is equally theatrical. (Photo courtesy of Virginia Glasgow Koste, Eastern Michigan University Theatre Department, Ypsilanti, Michigan)

by five's so we can make five teams. Each team, one at a time, will play the scene. Let's begin with Team 1." She turns to Team 1, "Okay, Team, the focus of this exercise is on communicating your relationship to other players through your activity. One player — you Jessica — begin a simple activity like hanging a picture. The second player — maybe you Zachary — choose a character relationship to the first player and join the activity. First player — you must accept the second player as his character and relate to him. Other players — you come into the activity until all five players are in the scene. Okay, ready. Remember, show, don't tell your relationship."

The scene begins. Jessica starts to hang up the picture. Zachary comes in and says, "Now dear, you know how I hate having pictures in the middle of our room." He is playing her husband. The leader coaches, "When you know who you are, show us." The scene continues. Various team members assume roles as child, neighbor, and interior decorator. The energy has been awe-inspiring. What the class lacked in believability, they made up for with enthusiasm.

As Team 1 sits down, the leader begins the evaluation, referring to the twenty children who didn't play as the "audience." "Audience, who were the players?" The audience describes the scene. The leader continues, "What were the relationships? Did the players show through activity?" The answers are thoughtful and show us that the audience has been watching, not simply worrying about their own enactments. As we leave, Team 2 is about to begin.

Background

In 1963 Viola Spolin wrote *Improvisation for the Theatre,* a book intended to be used by workshop leaders to help train actors in improvisational techniques. Because of the similarity between the goals and structure of an acting workshop and a creative drama classroom, the book was quickly discovered by creative drama leaders. In 1975 Viola Spolin modified *Improvisation,* using a recipe-file format, and it was published by CEMREL as the *Theatre Game File.* Spolin also added a handbook that assisted leaders by resequencing activities for specific age groups and classifying activities by theme. The intended user is the classroom teacher, with or without theatre training.

Viola Spolin attributes her interest in theatre to playing charades and to playing dress-up as a young person. This childhood of pleasant "gaming" became the basis for the method that we are describing. Spolin believed so strongly that games should be the focus of theatre training that even her earliest articles described the beginnings of this improvisational approach.

Spolin experimented with this method as she directed improvisational theatre troupes in the 1930s in settlement houses and in the Chicago WPA Recreational Project. In the 1940s she established the Young Actor's Company in Hollywood where the method was further refined. Spolin added the notions of *point of concentration* and *physicalization with feeling* to her approach. To encourage a more gamelike atmosphere, she also began to call participants *players* instead of actors. The final modifications for the book developed as she observed professional improvisational theatre and assisted in the training of actors, both at the Chicago Experimental Theatre and at Second City. It is perhaps in conjunction with her son Paul Sills' work at Second City that Spolin first came to national attention.

View of Dramatic Learning

The Spolin approach is based on the assumption that players will make educational, psychological, and social gains as they participate in theatre games. The major premise is that dramatic learning can happen only when the individual drops self-conscious inhibitions and spontaneously reacts to the here-and-now situation. The game structure is vital because it provides an environment defined by rules and draws attention away from the performance of the individual player and onto the team goal. Spolin believes players will become freer to lose inhibitions, open selves, and gain intuitive knowledge as they are thrust into confrontation with self, others, and the game environment.

Participants are required to personalize situations described on each notecard, but rarely to use their own life experiences as sources for the drama. Many of the activities demand that the players have more than basic knowledge of voice and body work. Yet rarely are these behaviors introduced; they are merely evaluated. Actors, the original Spolin population, used these activities in conjunction with other theatre training. Less experienced participants can have trouble both with the skills necessary to externalize the ideas and with the development of believable characters. For those who work well in highly competitive group situations and for those who have had other drama experiences, the Spolin method can stimulate dramatic learning.

Distinguishing Characteristics

Each activity, or game, in the *Theatre Game File* is presented on a notecard. The notecard is titled, numbered, and color coded and includes seven categories of information. Two unique features of the notecards are the way in which the activities have been divided and the specific guidelines, directed to the leader.

1. Organization

Over two hundred games and a guidebook are included in the *Theatre Game File*. The games are sequenced in three sections of increasing difficulty. Section A contains material that can be pulled out of sequence and presented at any time during a *workshop* session. (Spolin calls each drama lesson a workshop.) Spolin suggests that these games can be repeated. Section B deals with the development of actions, activities, settings, characters, relationships, and situations. Section C presents more advanced activities to develop further the skills of Section B.

2. Leader as Coach

The main objective of the leader is to provide an environment and a series of rules that draw each player away from self and permit a here-and-now spontaneous reaction to the rules or situation. Once this real-life reaction is achieved, the leader coaches each participant to be able to reachieve this reaction, as well as to work in groups. **Spolin believes that the leader should ask participants to see and do, not to imagine or feel.** The here-and-now is more objective, more tangible, and therefore more accessible. Side coaching, focus, and evaluation are methods used by the leader to reach the objective.

Side Coaching Side coaching is the calling out of statements by the leader during the enactment. Spolin made it clear that the leader may talk to participants during enactment and that such vocal assistance is extremely desirable. In the described scenario, young people were acting out improvisations, while the leader called out such directions as "Listen to my voice, but don't look at me," "Show, don't tell," and "Explore the object." (These directions do not at all divert the attention of young people accustomed to television and stereo noise while, say, doing homework or reading.) During a Ward lesson, on the other hand, the leader gives directions during the planning phase and conducts evaluation during the reflection phase, but rarely speaks during the enact phase. Often, the enactment takes place in total silence.

In order to be a good side coach, it is necessary to feel like a participant in the game. Spolin believes that anyone can be good at side coaching. She urges the side coach to use active verbs like *see* and *use,* not words that suggest imaginary situations. She suggests that the leader not direct the participants with such words as *imagine* or *pretend* or with references to the past. Spolin aims for the here-and-now. She does not focus on playing with images in the mind's eye but rather on immediately activating images. Participants who need time to manipulate their images may fall back on stereotypic behavior that can often characterize the Spolin approach.

Focus The goal of side coaching is to focus the participant on the current objective. Termed *point of concentration* (poc) in Spolin's earlier work, focus should be viewed as the physical and psychological anchor for the whole exercise. Used as a tool, focus helps participants stay on task and not worry about outcome. As developed by Spolin, focus also helps pairs or groups mutually work on the same task. The focus in the game of baseball, for example, is on the ball: on pitching it or hitting it or catching it. The objective, of course, is to win, but winning is achieved only by focusing on the ball, moment by moment.

Evaluation Spolin's other contribution is in terms of the evaluation phase of creative drama. What was communicated to or perceived by the audience is the subject of the evaluation discussion. Consequently, those who participated and those who observed become involved in the discussion by presenting their own special view.

As leader you are cautioned to make sure not to slant evaluation questions toward your own point of view. Making sure that evaluation is based on whether the problem was solved helps do away with criticism and value judgments. Statements like "He was good" and "I like it" are not acceptable. An evaluative statement like "The hitting of the baseball was clear to me" is more appropriate.

SPOLIN AT A GLANCE

- Major texts: first work is *Improvisation for the Theatre* (1963); evolved into more creative drama-oriented *Theatre Game File* (1975)
- Major goal: to enable participants to lose inhibitions, open selves, and gain intuitive knowledge
- Structure: Games are the key. Participants are called players and activities are called workshops. Games are presented in a notecard format with tightly structured and categorized activities.
- The leader as coach directs participants to respond to the here-and-now situation through side coaching, focus, and evaluation.
- Here-and-now images, not past experiences, provide the material for drama.
- The method has strong ties with the theatre; it was originally an actor-training method.
- Performance is a major objective — in pairs and groups.

GERALDINE SIKS: A METHOD BASED ON RESEARCH

CASE STUDY

STORY TIME As we enter the last classroom we see a small group of students clustered around the leader, who is holding a Dial-a-Story

Geraldine Siks, Professor Emeritus of the University of Washington, has traveled around the world to lecture about creative drama. Professor Siks is pictured here with a tambourine, as she demonstrates drama to college students in Japan. (Photograph courtesy of Geraldine Siks)

Wheel that looks like a large roulette wheel with numbers on it from 1 to 12. On the chalkboard behind the leader are four columns with one heading written on the top of each: place, character, situation, conflict. This group of nine is only part of a larger class. These students are participating in this drama lesson as part of their language arts curriculum; the rest of the class is in another room where a more traditional lesson is being taught. The drama leader is also an older woman who is in her sixties; her manner and dress, however, suggest a much younger woman.

She begins, "Today we are going to continue working on your role as player. What we are going to work on is how to begin a play. Does anyone know how a play begins?" This group is full of suggestions: "When the curtain rises," "When the orchestra stops playing," "When something bad happens," "When the hero has to rescue somebody." The leader smiles at all the suggestions and says, "Good ideas. All of you are right. Let's suppose, however, that we don't have a curtain or lights, but only ourselves. If we are to be players, we need to know at least four things: where the story takes place, who we are, what we are doing, and the nature of the opposing forces against us. I have here a Dial-a-Story Wheel that can help make the environment and the circumstances very specific so we know what we're doing in the beginning of the drama."

The leader then reviews the directions with the first group. Student A—in this case we discover that this boy is named Sam—will dial the wheel to discover who he is: he's a scientist. Susan dials and becomes a refugee. Amy becomes a spy. Then Sam dials to determine their situation: they are experimenting. These three then go into a corner of the room to discuss and improvise the action. Their main objective is to give reality to the environment and circumstances in the opening sequence of the play. The other two groups dial the wheel in a similar manner and each goes into a separate corner to prepare the improvisations.

After a few minutes planning time, the first group is ready to perform. The improvisation goes on. Each player walks and talks like the character he or she is portraying. The behavior is somewhat stereotyped; the class has only been working for about two months. After the improvisation is completed, the leader questions the audience: "Where were they?" "Who were they?" "What were their relationships?" The leader has been careful not to allow the members of the audience to call out during the improvisation; this enactment is not a game of charades. Now the audience answers, "They were trying to discover something." "They were hiding something." When the evaluation is completed, each of the next groups performs in turn and is evaluated. As we leave, the leader begins discussing how the next element of the wheel — conflict — will be incorporated into the improvisation.

Background

Geraldine Siks has been well known in the field of creative drama since her book *Creative Drama: An Art for Children* was published in 1958. Her next book, *Children's Theatre and Creative Drama*, followed quickly in 1961. Edited by Siks with her sister, Hazel Brain Dunnington, this collection provided the field with an overview of the state of drama and theatre for young people. Siks continued to write a series of articles and books that traced her developing theories. *Drama with Children*, published in 1977 and revised in 1983, represents thirty years of research in the field.

Siks had a wonderful arena in which to experiment. With her colleague, Agnes Haaga, she developed the child drama program at the University of Washington at Seattle. Housed in a School of Theatre, this program continued to be influential in the field of creative drama until its demise in the early 1980s.

Siks' early influence was the work of Ward. Throughout Siks' own work (more clearly in the early books), you can see the similarity between the two scholars, particularly in terms of the significance of literature. Also influential to Siks' work were the research projects she conducted in the 1960s and 1970s. Siks credits her new theories first to her participation in the First International Conference on Theatre Education held in Washington in 1967, and later to her membership on the research task force of the Central Atlantic Regional Laboratory; this group aimed to identify the basic processes and concepts of drama. Certainly Siks' years of working with students on the college level gave her the necessary forum for presentation of her new ideas.

View of Dramatic Learning

To understand Siks' approach, you must first understand the nature of drama. Drama, according to Siks, is a multifaceted subject that is both an art form firmly rooted in theatre and a language art basic to education. As such, Siks reasons, drama is uniquely suited to develop both the participant's creative and expressive abilities, which are the main goals of the approach. Siks offers the *Process-Concept Approach* (also known as the Conceptual Approach) as a unifying theory that helps leaders organize curriculum and participants view the connections between drama and theatre and drama and the language arts curriculum. The various components of this approach focus on drama as an art, drama as a language art, and the Process-Concept Approach.

1. Drama as an Art

Although this idea is not unique to Siks, Siks certainly makes a case for believing and understanding that drama is an art. Siks traces drama-making back to its roots and points out that the very stimulus of these ancient tribes to make drama exists in the dramas of young people today. Siks explains that drama as an art is a "created object that is formed according to universally established principles of theatre." The relationship between drama and theatre is so strong that no question exists in Siks' mind as to the certainty of drama as an art.

> ***When the artist is alive in any person, whatever his kind of work may be, he becomes an inventive, searching, daring, and self-expressive creature. He becomes interesting to other people. He disturbs, upsets, enlightens, and opens ways for a better understanding. Where those who are not artists are trying to close the book, he opens it and shows there are still more pages possible.***
>
> Robert Henri

2. Drama as a Language Art

Another aspect of the theory, again not unique to Siks, is drama's importance to the language arts curriculum. What Siks does, however, is clearly delineate why she feels that drama is so closely linked with language arts. The very same language skills of listening, speaking, reading, and writing are, she believes, at the core of the drama experience. As player, each young person must speak and listen. As playmaker, each must read and write. Each must also explore language and gain competence in oral composition, oral interpretation, and oral communication. Language development skills in the role of audience member center around making judgments and constructing evaluations.

3. The Process-Concept Approach

Certainly the most original aspect of Siks' approach is the process-concept theory. As a dynamic drama leader, Geraldine Siks has discovered that, as an art and a language art, drama is a powerful subject that deserves a place in the curriculum. As a realist, she recognized that, like the other arts, drama is often not given priority in the general education curriculum. She also observed that a better rationale and method were needed to help drama obtain its rightful place. Siks offers the process-concept theory as the structure for leaders to use to present the art of drama in such a way as to make it basic to education. She believes that leaders and participants must understand the nature of drama, so that both become conscious of the learning experience.

The process-concept theory helps leaders understand that participants are involved in the processes of doing drama while they explore drama concepts. Process describes "how" and concepts "what."

Distinguishing Characteristics

The teaching/learning processes are at the heart of Siks' approach. The focus of this approach is always the child, who, as player/playmaker and audience member, learns new concepts and explores various processes to meet increasingly more challenging goals. The leader is a skilled teacher who carefully observes students' progress and plans to meet their needs.

1. Child as Player, Playmaker, and Audience Member

Related to the concept that drama is an art are the participants' roles, which as delineated by Siks, are *player, playmaker,* and *audience member.*

Player Probably the most basic role is the one of player. The basic elements utilized by the player are those used by any participant in an improvisational situation. They include relaxation, imagination, movement, voice, sensory experience, and characterization.

Playmaker According to Siks, young people progress from the role of player to that of playmaker by consciously learning how to create a piece of drama. Participants, guided by their leaders, learn the principles of play construction and acquire a working vocabulary. Leaders delineate the nature of conflict, protagonist, antagonist, plot, action, climax, characterization, theme, and dialogue. During their experiences as players, participants may have already come into contact with these concepts. This set of playmaker activities, however, helps formalize the experience.

Audience Member Another role assumed by the participant is that of audience member. Siks explains that the audience component is essential to the art of drama, because a script is fully realized only when it is performed for an audience. During many drama activities, some young people must observe. Instead of just ignoring them, Siks explains that the leader must strive to get them involved so that each child in the audience learns to perceive, to evaluate, and to respond to the drama. Assuming the role of audience member helps participants perceive the relationship between drama process and theatre product, and develop potential interest in theatre-going.

2. The Workshop Procedure

Siks sets up working situations in which participants solve problems or reach goals. She classifies these workshops by major procedures: directed, problem-solving, exploratory, competency-based. A workshop can consist entirely of one type or be based on any combination of the four.

Directed In this type of workshop or part of a workshop, the leader gives the participant simple directions to follow, but does not qualify these directions or act as model. For example, "Walk on the outside of your feet" might be one of the tasks directed by the leader.

Exploratory In this procedure, the leader sets up an exploratory question: "See how many different ways you can make your body into the shape of a circle." These activities often deal with the physical and are accomplished individually or with only one other person. Exploratory work introduces participants to simple drama questions and prepares all participants for problem-solving questions.

Problem-Solving This is the core of most of drama's benefits. The leader introduces a concept and then presents a problem in terms of task to be accomplished. It is essential that the leader design experiences that are problem-solving in nature.

Competency-based This procedure encourages self-directed learning. Children work in groups without leader direction; the motivated children encourage the not-so-motivated ones. Leaders evaluate the finished product, not the work in progress.

3. The Leader as Teacher

The leader has the responsibility for selecting the roles, the activities, and the workshop procedures that will further the dramatic learning of the participants. Because the approach is developmental, proceeding from easier to more complex skills, the leader plans the drama program first through an initial evaluation of the participant's needs and then through an on-going evaluation of progress. Therefore, the leader must be not only well versed in the art of theatre, but also be a skilled teacher who knows child development and can make appropriate educational decisions. This dual training seems essential for those leaders embracing the Siks approach.

SIKS AT A GLANCE

- Major texts: *Creative Drama: An Art for Children* (1958); *Drama with Children* (1977, 1983). The process-concept approach is discussed only in the later works
- Major goal: to develop the participants' creative and expressive abilities
- Structure: developmental based on participants' needs and progress
- The method has strong ties to both theatre and the language arts curriculum. Drama is first and foremost an art, but it is also a language art.
- The process-concept approach ties drama to theatre and to the educational curriculum and is the underlying premise of all work.
- The participants assume three roles during drama: player, playmaker, and audience member.
- The leader must be knowledgeable in theatre/drama and also be capable of making educational decisions based on knowledge of child development.
- This method is the first popular approach to be based on more than personal teaching style and observations; the approach is developed from systematic observation and well-constructed theory.

IN CONCLUSION

The work of the past sixty years brings the field of creative drama to a new threshhold. The changes evidenced by educational reform, measured by scholarly research, and personified through master drama leaders can stimulate further study of creative drama. New leaders can proceed with their own individual mastery of creative drama based on the work of these theorists. Yet new leaders also embark on an even newer adventure: connecting theory and practice in the pursuit of excellence. The remaining decade of the twentieth century may witness the enhancement of dramatic learning through systematic conduct of drama exercises and activities. Creative drama can now be viewed as a pivotal learning and developmental experience, second to none. In education, creative drama can return to its rightful place in the curriculum—center stage!

MENTAL IMAGERY

Dramatic learning embraces both internal processes and external behaviors. Among the internal processes mastered in dramatic learning are the abilities to experience the world through the senses, to recall images of past experiences, and to select images to be the source of drama. The important external behaviors have to do with creating characters, stories, and places — in ways that closely resemble what actors, playwrights, and designers do.

This chapter and the next discuss the *basic skills of dramatic learning* and the theories of a field of psychology commonly termed *mental imagery*. Researchers in mental imagery study how individuals acquire, retrieve, and manipulate images in the mind's eye. This valuable information is directly applicable to an understanding of the creative drama experience. The vast body of literature about theatre has similarly provided information to help explain the dramatic actions seen in creative drama.

As you read Chapters 3 and 4, keep in mind that the information has been spread over two chapters only to help demystify this complex phenomenon. In real life, imagination and action occur swiftly, startlingly, and with exciting results. Naturally, as leader, your goal is to assist in and to stimulate this connection. If a participant is having difficulty, he or she may not have a clear picture in the mind's eye that can act as a strong sensory stimulus. The information that follows can help you understand and expand your own imagery abilities and help others do likewise.

Imagination is more important than knowledge.

Albert Einstein

GENERAL INFORMATION

The acquisition, cultivation, and manipulation of images, as well as the way in which these images evolve into active imagination, have long been sources of fascination for scientists, psychologists, and artists. Until recently, imagination had not been the focus of systematic investigation. In the last several decades, however, serious studies that focus on mental imagery are on the increase. These studies are astoundingly far-ranging: from how imagery affects learning and psychological state, to how various artists use childhood experiences as sources for art-making, to how fantasy shapes one's choice of friends. Researchers in the field of mental imagery agree that the study of imagination can help clarify many cognitive and creative processes.

Many people use the term *image* freely and less than scientifically. For example, people use the word "image" when they describe how a person views himself, as in, "He has a low self-image." Advertising executives often say they want to change the "image" of their product, when what they mean is they want to change the way the public views it. Art collectors may call a work of art the "image." These familiar expressions are popular phrases, but have little to do with the particular way in which the term *image* is used in this book.

Mental imagery is the ability to reproduce internally a variety of sensations when the object or experience that stimulated them is no longer physically present. Those working in the field of mental imagery use many words with the "imag" root. We define the most important here:

Image (noun): The sensory record of an object or experience that remains in the mind's eye in the absence of the here-and-now object or real-life experience.
Image (verb): To acquire or retrieve images.
Imaging: The ability to manipulate images in the mind's eye.
Imagination: The ability to develop original or novel images (based in part on a number of here-and-now objects or previous experiences) and to act upon them.
Imagery: A term encompassing all of the above phenomenon.

All people have stored images of past experiences. These images often pop up or are called forth at will as people go about their daily activities. Scientists, artists, and students use these images to solve problems, to create works of art, or to entertain themselves during boring lectures. Many people who say they do not have images, in fact, do, but because of early negative reinforcement or lack of information, they are unaware of their presence, particularly in nonvisual modalities.

HOW PEOPLE ACQUIRE IMAGES

Perceiving occurs in the real world; imaging in the mind's eye. How well you image something depends on how well you perceive it. Throughout life, human beings attend to and absorb the sights, sounds, and smells around them. These sensory experiences form the basis of their imagery storehouse. When asked to image some aspect of your childhood, for example, you may have a quick flash of many childhood memories, or you may have a single image that collectively represents your childhood. Particular images may be very clear, as if they are happening at this very instant. Others may be faded and seem distant. You may remember visual images exclusively, such as your room at home or the corner house that is no longer there. You may recall sound images, such as your mother's voice as she calls you. You may recall smell images more often and more intensely than you remember any other sensory ones: Can you close your eyes and recall cookies baking in the kitchen or the way the lilacs smelled blooming in your backyard? All of the images you recalled have as their source, for the most part, perceptions from your childhood.

Childhood memories of special events are part of everyone's imagic storehouse. Pictured here is the author (*right*) in one of her many dance recitals. Similar childhood photos from a family album can stimulate memories of people, places, and events long forgotten. (Photograph courtesy of Elva C. Shapiro)

People rarely remember the past exactly the way it existed or events in precisely the way they occurred. Consciously or unconsciously, they combine places and merge experiences, forget insignificant details, or repress unpleasant experiences. They remember images that they want to remember. The memory often plays tricks. People also take images from literature, theatre, and/or television and build an imaginary world based on them in which they see themselves as the heroes or heroines. Playing imagination games or fantasies of this type is called *daydreaming* and may be productive or unproductive.

Most people do not go through life consciously searching for objects or experiences to record, even though the unconscious mind does a lot more record-keeping than supposed. Artists, however, do consciously look for objects and experiences to remember and to catalogue. Artists are often credited with having special powers of perceiving, but, in fact, they may merely pay more rapt attention to the world around them. Early twentieth-century theatre director Max Reinhardt in his famous directing notebooks explains how important the world was in stimulating his imagination: "I am surrounded by images." This *artistic sensibility* can be cultivated by nonartists who consciously focus on what they are experiencing, just as people in love try to record every nuance of their true love's face, or as a college student about to leave home for the first time moves about the house trying to record every detail so that he or she won't forget it while away.

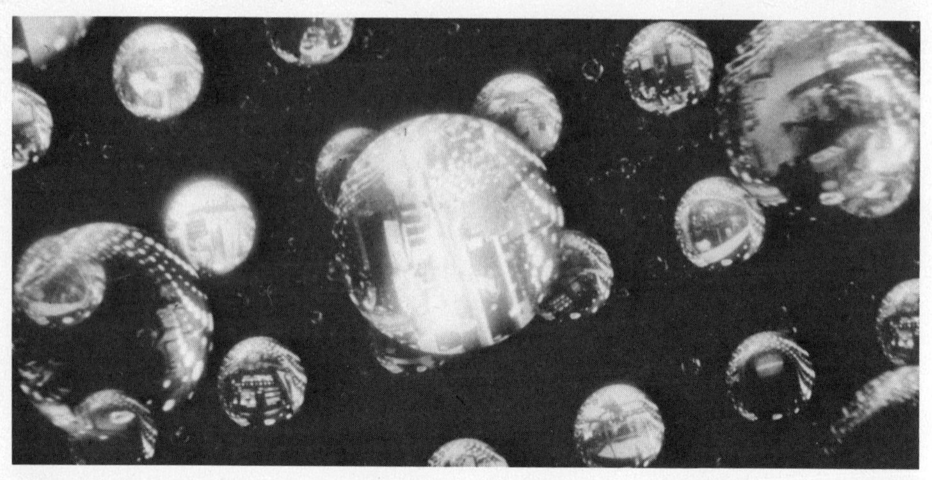

This still from the 1981 film *Brainstorm* shows the stored memories of the dying scientist. This film centers on a scientific discovery that enables people to have access to another's imagery storehouse — a fantasy for some and a nightmare for others. (MGM Films)

Not all the images people remember are consciously acquired; many are introduced by the unconscious mind. *Unconscious images* are those over which people have no control. They may surface during sleep, or while awake but in a state of altered consciousness achieved through meditation, drugs, or alcohol. Artists have been known deliberately to alter their consciousness to "capture" certain images, and the art they produce in these altered states is often surprising. Edgar Allan Poe for instance, imaged and wrote "The Raven" while under the influence of opium.

Many circumstances contribute to how well or how long individuals are able to experience an image. Obviously, the experience with the here-and-now real-life object, person, or episode affects the ability to recall the image. If someone has had many experiences with another person, he or she may have strong images of that person. Even if a person has had a brief, but very significant experience with someone else, the memory is very intense. In a recent television movie, an older man recalls a fleeting experience that occurred many, many years ago of seeing a woman in a white hat sitting in a train across the platform from him. Even though the man never spoke to the girl, something about her caused him to return over and over to his memory of her. In fact he says, "Hardly a day goes by when I don't remember that girl."

Another factor that influences the ability to recall images and to utilize them is how a person's parents or teachers felt about the time he or she spent playing. If these young people were allowed and/or encouraged to develop a rich fantasy world and to play make-believe, they have had much practice and, consequently, retrieve and manipulate images easily. Or, if they were encouraged not to play, but to deal with "reality," or were deprived of strong sensory stimulation as a child, they may be less prone to retrieve and play with their images. Research suggests that almost all "normal" people can naturally retrieve and manipulate images or can be taught to do so.

Another factor in the type of images recorded is which sense an individual naturally favors. Just as a blind person depends on touch and hearing to compensate for a lack of sight, so can a person who has the use of all his senses still gravitate toward one sense over the others. In assisting people in their acquisition of images, encourage them to experience and use all senses to their fullest capacity.

A Variety of Sensory Images

A mental image is the sensory picture that exists in the mind's eye in the absence of the here-and-now object. There are as many sensory types of images as there are types of experiences that they record:

A visual image — one recorded through seeing.
An olfactory image — one recorded through smelling.
An auditory image — one recorded through hearing.
A gustatory image — one recorded through tasting.
A tactile image — one recorded through touching.
A kinesthetic image — one recorded through moving.

Think about your own images and try to classify them by type. You may, for example, have a clear sight and smell of lilacs in your backyard. You may have a strong image of the sound of your cat meowing and of the touch of the cat's fur. You may have a clear image of the taste of your favorite ice cream. You may have a strong kinesthetic image of the movement of riding a bicycle or a roller coaster.

The types of images that are readily stored vary from person to person. Research suggests that olfactory images may be the most primitive. Research has also shown, however, that most people store visual images, possibly because they use their visual abilities more than any other sense. It stands to reason, then, if you work on developing your other senses, you will increase your ability to perceive and recall in all sensory areas and, thus, increase your storehouse of images.

It is important to distinguish the here-and-now source of an image from the type of sensory image stimulated by it. The here-and-now smell of an orange may cause you to recall a taste image of today's breakfast, or more possibly a sight image of your vacation in Florida. This is an example of a here-and-now smell stimulating nonsmell images of previous experiences and is an everyday type of imagery-related activity. But if asked to recall the smell of an orange, you may have difficulty doing so, for this is much less common and requires that you retrieve a sensory image on demand. Even if you are unable to do so now, with practice many people are able to retrieve all kinds of sensory experiences.

Rarely, if ever, will you experience an isolated mental image in only one sensory modality. Mental images in one sensory modality tend to change or develop in conjunction with images in other sensory modalities. When asked to image smelling a rose, for example, you may not merely smell the rose, but see the entire rose garden, or perhaps actually experience touching it.

Kinds of Images

Images usually come from two sources: the general knowledge of an object or the personal knowledge of a specific object. Thus, there are two kinds of images: *generic images* and *personal images*. Generic images are images for which there is no personal, real-life reference. When asked to image an old man crossing a street, you may have a generic image of a faceless man walking across any street. Personal images, because they are based on a real-life experience, have very specific qualities. The personal image you have of an old man crossing a street may be of your grandfather crossing the street where you lived as a child. You probably will have a strong affective reaction to this image.

In the course of the day, you probably experience both generic and personal images. It stands to reason that the better source of images to stimulate art or drama-making are personal ones. Dramas based on generic images are often vague and stereotypic. Young people often enact an "old person" as a bent over, limping, quavery-voiced grump. Granted, a few old people fit this stereotype, but many do not. Close observation of the wide variety of ways in which particular people age, however, can form clear personal images that, in turn, stimulate more personal and more realistic characters. These personal images are richer and more vivid because of the meaningful feelings associated with them.

Images can also be classified in another way, based on whether the image is of a real-life object or experience or is a mental construction. Images based on real-life situations are called *memory images* and are records of what was actually experienced. Although these images are often easy to retrieve, memory images are often more difficult to manipulate, simply because they are records of real life. Also, memory images can be vague and sometimes general. *Imagination images,* on the other hand, are images based on abstract associations of memory images or on projections of fantasy. Of course, they are based on real-life experiences, but imagination images are combined or recorded in ways that give them a life of their own. Consequently, imagination images can be more vivid than memory images.

In their mind's eye, people have travelled to fantastical other worlds. This etching *Things Seen by J. Wilkins on His Famous Voyage to the Moon,* made over two hundred years ago by Filippo Morghen, shows us just how timeless and universal are fantasy journeys. (The Metropolitan Museum of Art, Harris Brisbane Dick Fund, 1932)

Artists often speak of this phenomenon when writing or speaking about a particularly exciting creative process. They explain that images seem to take over and exist outside them. Twentieth-century theatre director and acting theorist Michael Chekhov wrote about the actor's need to acknowledge images outside self. In *To the Actor,* Chekhov elaborated upon techniques for utilizing the external image:

> You must ask questions of these images, as you would ask questions of a friend. Sometimes you must even give them strict orders. Changing and completing themselves under the influence of your questions and orders, they give you answers visible to your inner sight.

The early twentieth-century playwright Luigi Pirandello wrote an entire play about characters who come to life outside an unfinished play and search for an author to complete their lives. In the preface to this play, *Six Characters in Search of an Author,* Pirandello describes how in his own life these characters seemed also to have a life of their own:

> I can only say that, without having made any effort to seek them out, I found before me, alive—you could touch them and even hear them breathe—the six characters now seen on the stage. . . . [They] went on living on their own, choosing certain moments of the day to reappear before me in the solitude of my study and coming—now one, now the other, now two together—to tempt me, to propose that I present or describe this scene or that, to explain the effects that could be secured with them, the new interest which a certain unusual situation could provide, and so forth.

To all of you who have been visited by fantasy creatures or who have experienced your own ideas outside yourself, be assured that you are not alone! Many people are in touch with their own inner resources. Young children often speak of imaginary friends, and many adults describe inner voices that help them solve problems.

HOW PEOPLE RECALL IMAGES

People recall their past images in many different ways. Some people describe their recall of visual images as a quick flash in which they "see" the total picture in their mind's eye. Others "see" the image clearly first from the center of it, with the edges slowly filling in. Still others speak of "seeing" their images come into focus as if there were a lens in their mind's eye. Recall of sound images is similarly varied. Some people "hear" the sound faintly at first and then describe it getting louder. Others "hear" background noise from which they hone in on the sound to be recalled. All that can safely be said about image recall is that it is as diverse and individual as are the images themselves. Rest assured, however, that your own ability to recall images can improve as can that of all drama participants.

Properties of Images

Two properties are important to recognize about your images: the quality, or how clearly you experience your images, and the quantity, or how many images you can generate. Since mental images are in your head, and since nobody can really disagree with accounts of your imagery, you are the expert.

You can rate your imagery in at least two ways:

- *fluency*—how many images you can generate
- *vividness*—how strong the image may be

Fluency A popular way to rate images is a self-report questionnaire. By answering the eighteen items in the following quiz, you will get some idea of the quantity of images you have in the various sensory areas. (This quiz and those that follow are intended to assist you in becoming familiar with your own imagery. The quizzes can be used as a general measure of images in others as well, but are merely diagnostic and not meant to be used as validated, reliable instruments.)

IMAGERY FLUENCY QUESTIONNAIRE

For each of the items that follow, record the number of images you can generate, spending 15 seconds on each item. Pause between items if necessary. Image fully the sensory experience in each question. If you are asked to image animal sounds, you are not merely to recall that you know a cow makes a "moo" sound, but mentally hear the sound. For best results, have someone time you. Remember, you are looking for as many images as possible, not for vividness of the images.

In 15 seconds:

1. How many different kinds of pens can you see? ____
2. How many t.v. jingles can you hear? ____
3. How many different ways can you feel your leg move? ____
4. How many flavors of ice cream can you taste? ____
5. How many household odors can you smell? ____
6. How many different kinds of fabric can you feel? ____
7. How many different kinds of doors can you see? ____
8. How many kinds of street sounds can you hear? ____
9. How many liquids can you taste? ____
10. How many different objects can you feel yourself toss? ____
11. How many foods can you smell? ____
12. How many living objects can you feel? ____
13. How many makes of cars can you see? ____
14. How many friends' voices can you hear? ____
15. How many objects can you feel yourself lift? ____
16. How many kinds of sandwiches can you taste? ____
17. How many outdoor aromas can you smell? ____
18. How many moist liquids can you feel? ____

The results of this fluency questionnaire will give you some idea of the sensory areas in which you have the greatest storehouse of images. You may have found you can retrieve images in some sensory areas more easily than you can in others. If you retrieved six or more images for one question, you should know that you are above average in imagery fluency in that sensory domain.

There is no limit to the top score of the questionnaire as a whole. If your responses totalled 64 or more, your imagery fluency is above average. After reading the section on improving imagery presented later in this chapter, you may want to nurture some of your own images and retake the questionnaire. Remember, with frequent practice, you can develop your ability to image. You can also assist others in developing their ability to image.

Vividness You can also rate yourself on clarity of images. If you would like to know how vivid your images are, take a few minutes to see how clearly you can form images on the items of the following test.

IMAGERY VIVIDNESS TEST

Read each item. Picture the described object or experience as clearly as you can, then rate your image according to the following scale:

5—Very vivid, as if the real object were present
4—Clear, fine details discernible
3—Moderately clear, most significant parts present
2—Vague and dim, traces missing
1—Incomplete, more missing than present
0—Unable to form any part of the image

1. See a blue, cloudless sky. ( )
2. See a blank sheet of paper. ( )
3. See your bedroom at home. ( )
4. Feel your feet hitting a cold floor. ( )
5. Feel the soft texture of a fur coat. ( )
6. Feel the coldness of an ice cube. ( )
7. Hear the sound of a clock ticking. ( )
8. Hear the sound of screeching car brakes. ( )
9. Hear a friend call you. ( )
10. Smell peanuts roasting. ( )
11. Smell a room full of cigarette smoke. ( )
12. Smell your favorite fragrance. ( )
13. Taste a tart apple. ( )
14. Taste a spicy pizza. ( )
15. Taste warm bread. ( )
16. Image yourself moving a heavy box. ( )
17. Image yourself riding a roller coaster. ( )
18. Feel yourself tossing a beach ball. ( )

As you score this test, you may discover that certain images seem clearer than others. You may have found it easier to retrieve the visual images than the auditory ones. Or, you may have experienced a particular level of clarity throughout the entire exercise and, for example, rated all the images as 3. A perfect score of 90 would mean that you have a very vivid imagery storehouse—one that only a few people are likely to possess. Any rating over 70, however, indicates very well-developed imagery skills. Remember, individuals vary in terms of the types and vividness of the images they remember. Later in the chapter we will discuss ways to develop your own imagic storehouse — and to encourage images in others.

HOW PEOPLE USE IMAGES

Images rarely remain static for more than a fraction of a second. *Imaging* occurs when people begin to move their images and form associations between them and other images. Most people are imaging during simple, everyday activities. Deciding which of two roads to take or selecting a shirt to go with your brown pants involves *imaging strategies*. An important characteristic of imaging strategies is their variety. The strategies you select from your repertoire of strategies can be very different from one day to the next. Your selection may be based on your mood, the time of day, or any other external or internal conditions. Different individuals also favor different sets of imaging strategies. Two people given the very same imaging task usually describe two very different experiences.

Even though people may be imaging and enjoying the results of their imaging every day, rarely do they focus on the technical process involved. Most people pay little attention to their images except when an unusual image or association pops into their minds. But when attempting to solve important problems or when intently pursuing a piece of information, many people have naturally and spontaneously developed ways to encourage image retrieval and/or to manipulate these images.

Ways of Imaging

One way to learn about imaging is to pay attention to your own image-making process. Whether consciously aware of what is occurring or not, you are using imaging strategies daily. Think, for example, about the simple task of placing groceries in a refrigerator. At first you may place the objects randomly about, but as the refrigerator fills up, you begin to select places for your purchases. What can fit on the tall shelf on the door? What can fit on a short, wide shelf? By visually imaging the food placed in a particular area you will have a sense of what will fit where. "If the milk moves to the tall door shelf, and the butter goes in the butter container, then the chicken will fit on its side." This strategy of *shifting and rotating* is just one of several imagery strategies you may use to stock your groceries.

A second imagery strategy is to *expand/contract* an image. While buying a new pair of slacks you may think they need a wider or thinner belt. So you mentally image the belt to be so. You may hear a Mozart symphony and prefer that it be played faster or slower. Just as the images you have stored are in all the sensory domains, so do you use imaging strategies with all these types of images.

Another interesting strategy is to *superimpose* one image on another. While making some zesty spaghetti sauce you taste it several times before it is properly seasoned. Each time you taste it you mentally image the missing ingredient that must be added to the sauce. Before you actually add it, you superimpose the taste of the salt or oregano over the real-life sauce. With patience, persistence, and luck, you eventually produce a good Italian sauce. You may even try to recall the taste of your grandmother's sauce and compare it to yours in order to discover the missing ingredient.

Dynamism of a Dog on a Leash by Giacomo Balla epitomizes the concept of the rotating image. Note how the dog's feet and chain seem to be moving. (Albright-Knox Art Gallery, Buffalo, New York; bequest of A. Conger Goodyear and gift of George F. Goodyear, 1964)

One last strategy we would like to mention is that of *personification*. While this strategy is not as widely used by adults, the idea of embuing an abstract or inanimate object or idea with personality is pleasing to young people. A third-grade teacher may coax her students to write neatly by telling them, "Mr. Pencil is going to help you write neatly on this test." Personification and other imagery strategies often make routine tasks easier and more pleasurable.

Flexibility of Imaging

An important characteristic of imaging is flexibility. *Flexibility* describes the ability to recall images in a variety of categories, to utilize a variety of imagery strategies in manipulating the image, or to change a mental perspective in relation to the image. Fluency relates to sheer numbers of images; flexibility to the ability to move from category to category within those images. When asked to remember experiences from your childhood, you may be able to recall a variety of sound, sight, and taste images — indicating that you have flexibility within sensory categories.

A simple activity can demonstrate the difference between fluency and flexibility of imaging. In fact, if you image that you are participating in this activity, you are well on the road to both fluency and flexibility. Image an empty tin can. Jot down all the possible uses for the can. The more uses you can picture, the higher your fluency score. Now, think of all the categories of your responses: storing things, molding things, holding down papers, and so on. If you have a variety of categories of responses, you have a high level of flexibility in terms of imaging. This skill, plus a few others particular to drama, can stand you in good stead as a creative drama leader.

Controllability of Imaging

Another property of imaging, similar to flexibility, is the ability to manipulate, in the mind's eye, a single image through a series of tasks. This property, called *controllability,* can be improved with practice. The ability to hold and manipulate images can allow people to conduct problem-solving tasks in their mind's eyes. They have enough control over their images that they can, for example, visualize route A and route B and can choose the more desirable route to drive during a rainstorm.

People who have mastered controllability of imaging are able to use this skill in accomplishing a variety of tasks. Controllability of imaging helps young people master math skills. It likewise allows a sculptor to try out a variety of approaches before actually chiseling away at the marble. Certainly the sculptor Michelangelo would have rated high in controllability of imaging.

If you would like to test your imaging controllability, answer the questions in the following test.

IMAGERY CONTROLLABILITY TEST

After reading each item, close your eyes and try to picture what has been described. Check the response that most appropriately describes the image that you formed. Once you have completed an item, do not go back.

Picture yours or a friend's hand, and imagine the following:

	Formed	*Unsure*	*Not Formed*
1. The hand getting larger	( )	( )	( )
2. Getting smaller	( )	( )	( )
3. With long fingernails	( )	( )	( )
4. With clipped fingernails	( )	( )	( )
5. Putting on a blue glove	( )	( )	( )
6. Now the glove turning green	( )	( )	( )
7. The glove disappearing	( )	( )	( )
8. The hand disappearing	( )	( )	( )
9. The hand reappearing	( )	( )	( )
10. The hand wearing a gold ring	( )	( )	( )
11. The hand waves	( )	( )	( )
12. The hand points	( )	( )	( )
13. The hand picking up a red pen	( )	( )	( )
14. The pen turning yellow	( )	( )	( )
15. The hand tapping a pen on a desk	( )	( )	( )
16. The hand touching surface of desk	( )	( )	( )

	Formed	*Unsure*	*Not Formed*
17. The hand picking up a book	( )	( )	( )
18. The hand placing a book on a desk	( )	( )	( )
19. The hand disappearing	( )	( )	( )
20. The hand reappearing and touching a book	( )	( )	( )

Allowing 2 points for every "formed" response, 1 point for every "unsure" response, and no points for a "not formed" response, tabulate your score. A score of 30 or more indicates a good ability to control images. Having good flexibility and control of your imagery gives you an opportunity to try out many situations before they occur.

Theatre artists need to develop controllability of their images too. An actress applying make-up must recall the made-up face of the previous day in her mind's eye, retain those aspects which were perfect, and modify those that were less so. Playwrights must have control of their aural images; actors their kinesthetic images. In modeling their developing skills after similar theatre skills, those participants in creative drama expand their imagery controllability in a variety of modalities. As a matter of fact, research indicates that controllability appears to be the skill enhanced most readily by drama.

IMAGINATION

By far the most complex of all the processes studied by theoreticians and practitioners in the field of mental imagery is imagination. Imagination is both process and product, and in many ways it is the goal of mental imagery. Imagination is often the final stage of the image-making process. Once images are combined and manipulated during imaging, a new, revised imagination image is the result.

Nothing is true if it is not imagined.

Eugene Ionesco

Developing an "imagination image" in the mind's eye constitutes only half of what imagination is. The other half involves putting the idea into action. In other words, imagination is both process and product. You can experience the results of another's imagination by, say, testing the chef's speciality, attending a concert, or viewing a clothes designer's latest collection. As you look around, you can probably see the results of many other imaginations. Nevertheless, the observable result of imagination had to begin as an internal process. **Imagination involves an internal process and an external product.**

Imagining is more complex than imaging. Imaging involves the exploration and manipulation of numbers of possibilities. Imagining involves a similar exploration and manipulation of possibilities, but also includes decision-making and attention to final product. Those people who use their imaginations are able to trust their ideas and give up rigid rules. When they are imaging, people mentally move an image. When they are imagining, images often move themselves!

The imaging process is somewhat like flying a kite. While the kite is on the ground, you must coax it and delicately feed it to the wind. Once the wind grabs hold, the kite is off by itself, often ready to take you with it. When you move from imaging to imagining, your mental processes are similar to the movement of the kite. At first (during imaging) you hope you will find the right wind. Then, maybe seconds later (during imagining), you are airborn in a flight that is controlled by you and the wind working together.

Attend to your imagination while it is at work in the following exercise. Look at the people in the photographs on page 63. Study their faces and the way they are dressed. Can you make up a life story for any one of them? Don't write or make any notes — just let your imagination do the work.

When you first began to look at the picture, you may have quickly passed over the figures until one or two held your interest. You may have experienced an inner dialogue with yourself about the character's financial status, age, occupation, or personality. Perhaps you then proceeded to a deeper level of imagery and made judgments about the character's health and personal life. At this point, the image builds and generates new images that suggest others. Images begin to flow; some you like and accept; others you disregard.

If you have a good imagination, you can spend hours looking at one picture. Or, if you are a writer, you can write a novel based on that one picture; a playwright, a whole play. Anton Chekhov explains that the sound of an ax hitting wood was the image that stimulated the play *The Cherry Orchard*. Imagination is also central to the creative drama experience. Integral to imagination is the initial source — the object, photo, or remembered image.

The full realization of imagination demands product as well as process. Certainly you know many people who are full of wonderfully imaginative ideas, but are unable to put them into practice. In fact, some of them live, Walter Mitty-like, only in their own mind's eye, even though an imaginative one. Inhibitions of many sorts prohibit them from action. Many more people, however, are able to act upon their imagined ideas. As a result, many wonderful inventions, designs, and works of art are produced daily. These people are able to put their ideas into action.

IMAGE/IMAGING/IMAGINATION

Imagination is not linear. The circular shape of Figure 3.1 and Figure 3.2 can help you understand this complex phenomenon. The following system, termed the *iii Framework*, has been developed to clarify two essential aspects of imagination: cyclic and oscillation. The iii Framework is so named because of its three phases: *image, imaging, imagination*. Figure 3.1 depicts the natural and instinctual imagery cycle.

Figure 3.1 demonstrates the way an individual uses his or her memory image to develop an imagination image. **Each person retrieves one or more images, manipulates the images through imaging, and comes up with an imagination image.** Notice that the arrows in the diagram go in both directions; arrows in only one direction would imply that imaging occurs in a consistent, ordered manner. Individuals retrieve images, manipulate them,

At first glance, these photos seems to be of ordinary scenes. A more careful investigation yields details that help reveal specific clues to each subject's character, as well as the situations. (Photos by Pam Rich)

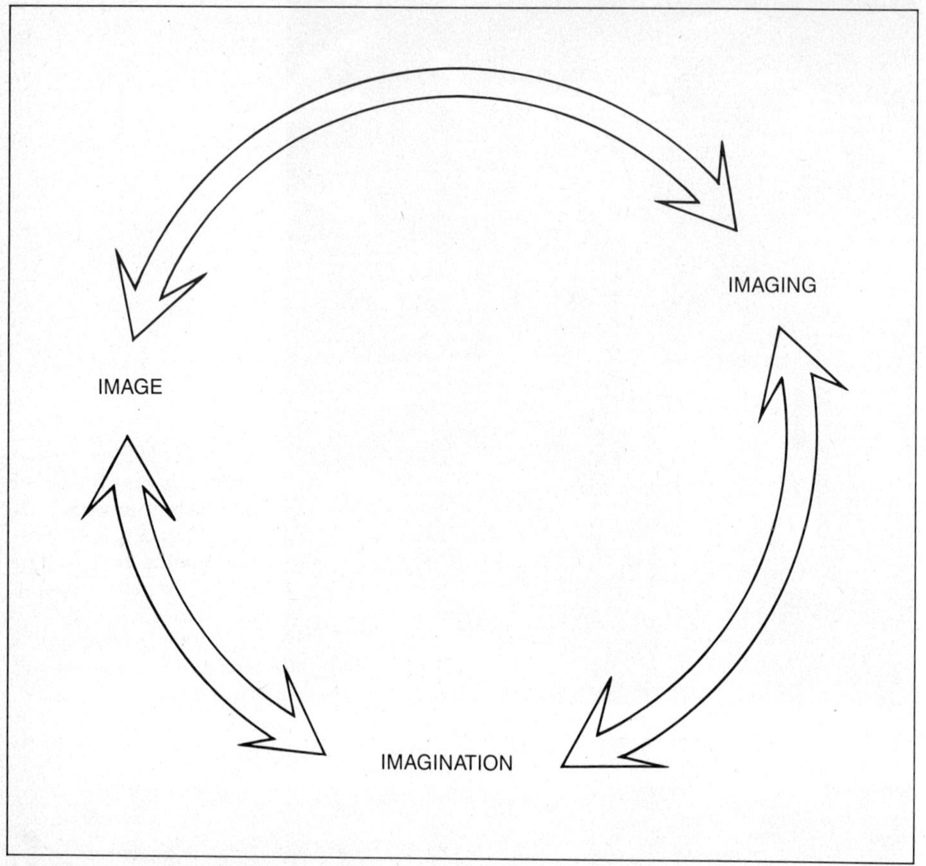

FIGURE 3.1 iii Framework: Cyclic

discard them, get new images, recombine the two, and get an imagination image — all in a flash!

Those who are imaginatively gifted already experience this cycle but may or may not be aware of what they do. Our interviews with artists and scientists suggest that most people undergo a similar three-phase process. Our observations also lead us to believe that individuals who do not use their imagination as readily can learn to develop imagery skills by practicing this natural three-phase process. They must, however, be guided through a wide variety of processes and activities in order to recreate with training what others do instinctively. Remember, when assisting those who use imagery less readily, don't expect or even encourage them to go through the phases one-two-three. They need to be relaxed and comfortable so they can concentrate on learning the natural fluid cycle described by the iii Framework.

Another key factor in successful imagery is the ability to oscillate between the internal world of ideas and the external world of people, places, and things. The critical factor is not the mere existence of both internal and external, but rather a dynamic oscillation between inside and outside. This oscillation occurs naturally and spontaneously or it can be learned and enhanced through systematic training.

Figure 3.2 depicts the oscillation aspect of the iii Framework. A brief look

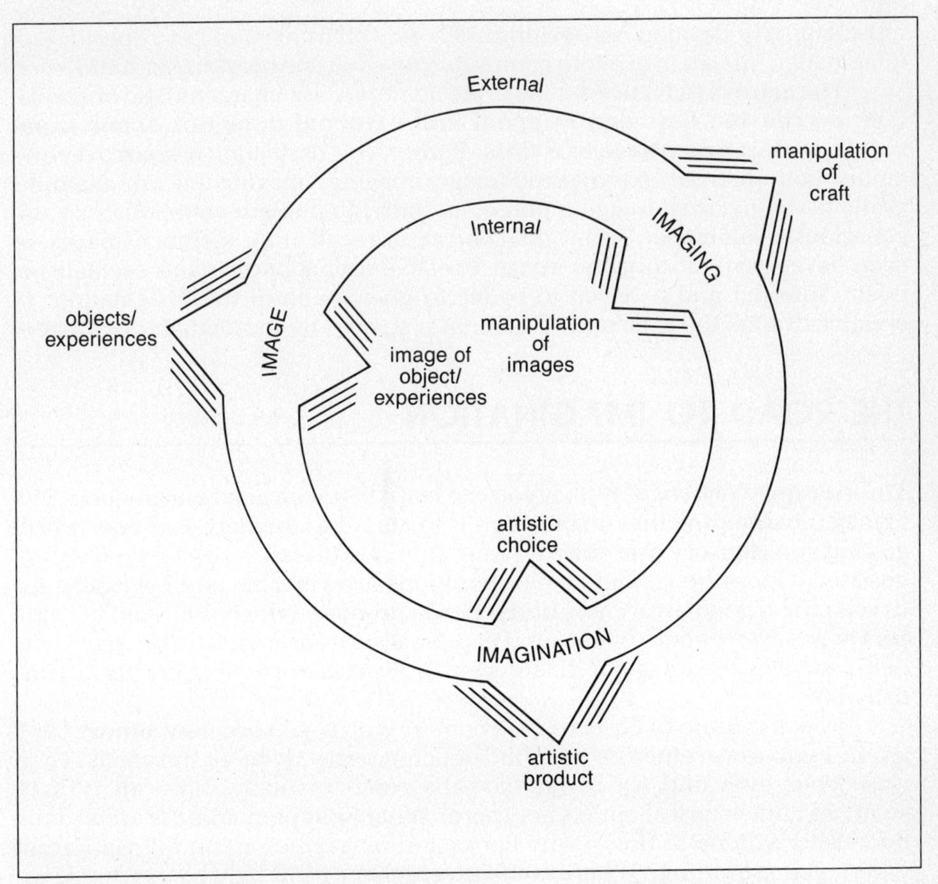

FIGURE 3.2 iii Framework: Oscillation

at this illustration can give you two quick clues about oscillation between the internal and external. First, image/imaging/imagination are still the essential phases. Second, oscillation is extremely complex. The following discussion untangles the web.

The world is the source for anything imaginative. The individual stores people, places, objects, and experiences as images. In the *image phase* this world represents the external component, with the internal aspect being the sensory impression or mental image. **Imaging also has an internal and external component.** Internal imaging involves holding, moving, or manipulating an image in the mind's eye. External imaging is exactly what it sounds like: an individual manipulating self and/or objects in the world at large. External imaging is rearranging the room in a number of potential lay-outs, moving around an intended photo in a camera viewfinder prior to snapping a picture, or trying on various outfits to achieve the desired effect.

In the arts, the external manipulation—imaging—relates to craft elements basic to the art itself. **Imagination takes place both in the mind's eye and in the world.** In order to select the best imagination image source, artists must have experiences with the craft elements of the art as well as know their own inner world of images. A visual artist experiments with color, form, line, canvas, and brushes in order to paint what he sees in his mind's eye. A poet must similarly develop her writing skills as well as expand her repertoire of imagination images in order to communicate what she hears in her mind's ear.

The arrows in Figure 3.2 illustrate an important characteristic of oscillation: **oscillation between internal and external does not occur separately within one phase at a time.** Rather, this oscillation crosses over and among both internal/external and image/imaging/imagination. For example, while in the external imaging phase, an individual might consciously or unconsciously remember the original object, or recall other memory images, or even develop an imagination image. Creative drama participants oscillate between internal and external in order to give shape to the imagination. In creative drama, the external component is shaped by the elements of theatre.

THE ROAD TO IMAGINATION

The iii Framework suggests that you can learn to have a good imagination. The first step in building that imagination is to attend to the here-and-now world around you. Sensory exercises drawing attention to visual, auditory, olfactory, gustatory, kinesthetic, and tactile sensations are valuable and necessary for developing a good awareness of the here-and-now, which will soon become part of your storehouse of images. *Perceptual awareness* and *artistic sensitivity* help you take advantage of the interesting aspects or exciting events in your daily life.

Take a minute to observe the room in which you are now sitting. Look around you as carefully as possible, noticing every detail of the room. Then close your eyes and try to recreate the room mentally. How many light switches and electrical outlets are there? What kind of molding is around the doors and windows? How many books and magazines are in full view from where you are sitting? Where is the greatest source of light in the room?

Once you begin to concentrate on objects of all sensory modalities, you automatically build a storehouse of images from which you may later draw. How accurately you remember each image is directly related to the degree of observation occurring during this state. As you expand your experiences of the world, your imagery storehouse will also expand. As you practice image retrieval, it's important to be in a place free from distractions and physically comfortable. These two conditions will allow you to relax and be receptive to any imagery stimuli. After you have found the ideal location and can relax, you begin to enter a receptive state.

> ***You can't depend on your judgment when your imagination is out of focus.***
>
> Mark Twain

Improving Imaging and Imagination Abilities

People learn to image by practicing imagery. Once you give yourself permission to do so, the sky's the limit in terms of your developing imaging and imagination abilities. You can improve your own imaging ability and stimulate that of others in many ways. Richard de Mille, in the preface to his book *Put Your Mother on the Ceiling*, describes the step-by-step manner by which he taught a group of young people who were low imagers to acquire imagery and imagination skills. Instead of asking them to imagine that their mothers were on the ceiling — a highly unrealistic notion — he asked them to view a here-and-now swing and then image it. Then, he hoisted the swing to the ceiling and had the group image that. After a series of imagery tasks, each one a step closer to the ultimate objective, all the members of the group were able to put their mothers on the ceiling!

Other approaches are less step-by-step. Jean Houston, coauthor of imagery-related books such as *Mind Games,* believes that people can naturally and spontaneously develop their imagination if the activities and exercises are universal and speak to the collective unconscious. Activities that focus on opening doors, floating on water, or walking through forests — more spiritual in nature — can stimulate the imagination. Although they disagree on the optimum method, both groups do agree that imagery can be learned and leads to imagination.

Perhaps the most important characteristic of someone with a good imagination is that person's ability to entertain the possible. Imaginative people don't close doors; they like to experiment; they remain receptive to new ideas; they adopt a playful attitude. Creative drama provides a forum in which playing and experimenting are central. A participant in these activities has the wonderful opportunity to expand his or her imagination, a key component of dramatic learning.

THEATRE GIVES SHAPE TO IMAGERY

The road of imagination can lead to a variety of destinations. The very same initial image and similar imaging strategies can produce a play, an invention, or a piece of music — based on the situation at hand and the inclination and skills of the creator. The inherent nature of the science or art form in which the creator is working gives final shape to the idea. The same sound image of chopping wood may inspire Anton Chekhov to write *The Cherry Orchard,* Samuel Morse to invent the telegraph, and Leonard Bernstein to compose the rhythmic "America" for *West Side Story.* Each creator, having experimented with the nature of the respective final form (a play, an electric device, and a piece of music) puts the image into action.

Artists store everyday experiences to be used as sources for their art-making. This trio of photos depicts the same central image of "family" as interpreted by artists working with three different art forms. On page 68 is Mary Cassatt's painting *The Boating Party;* At the top of this page is Henry Moore's sculpture *The Family Group;* at bottom is a photo of the Group Theatre's production of Clifford Odets' *Awake and Sing*. (Cassatt, National Gallery of Art; Moore, Collection, The Museum of Modern Art, New York, A Conger Goodyear Friend; Odets, Library and Museum of the Performing Arts, Lincoln Center, New York)

The question that has probably popped into your head is, "Where does the road of imagination lead in the creative drama experience?" The answer is not simple, because the final form is not a theatre production in the classic sense. Although the final outcome of creative drama is not the formal presentation of a well-rehearsed play for a paying audience, creative drama does share with theatre many of theatre's elements, principles, and conventions.* These give shape to the imagination. A closer investigation of the theatre model can help you develop understanding of the dramatic behavior that you will expect from participants and of the outcomes you will encourage. Without such knowledge of theatre, you can have no real understanding of the many destinations on the road of dramatic imagination.

The early creative drama practitioners, in developing this new art form, looked to theatre to provide them with a variety of models, techniques, and forms. They did not set out to develop a "junior theatre" method. In their wisdom, they instinctively selected those aspects of theatre that could be emulated by creative drama's participants, including principles of dramatic structure, conventions of theatre production, and artistic processes of theatre's creators.

Unfortunately, almost seventy years later, many of today's creative drama leaders do not understand the importance of creative drama's relationship to theatre. When they assist creative drama participants in developing potentially excellent enactments, these leaders do not have a sense of what makes up simple dramatic action or what constitutes acceptable theatrical conventions. Consequently, these leaders are unable to be helpful in structuring the final enactment. Or worse yet, they reinforce inappropriate behaviors because they think that silliness is somehow "show biz." **A knowledge of theatre is vital.**

The discussion below of those aspects of the theatre model that you must understand before you begin your work as a creative drama leader cannot substitute for theatrical training and experience, or even for consistent theatre attendance. What it does is give you a bare-bones understanding of theatre and its relationship to creative drama. Our intention is to stimulate you to further investigation, so that you develop your own perspective concerning theatre's relationship to creative drama.

ESSENTIALS OF DRAMATIC STRUCTURE

The most obvious similarity between theatre and creative drama is the drama itself—the dramatic action. What we call enactments or final products in the creative drama arena, and plays in theatre, share an essential structure, which every work of art must have.

The term *drama* comes from a Greek word, the verb *dran,* meaning to do or to act. Consequently, at the heart of drama (whether theatrical or creative) is *action.* Following are the essentials for constructing dramatic action:

Plot All plays have plots; all drama enactments have plots as well. The organization of a play is its plot. A plot is different from a story. A plot includes

* *In Chapter 5, we present a more detailed discussion of the relationship of imagination in action for three related phenomena: theatre, creative drama, and dramatic play.*

the story line but refers to the organization of all the elements into a meaningful pattern; it is the framework of the action. A plot is how the story is told—which of the many incidents are dramatized and in which order these incidents are revealed to the audience.

There are two basic kinds of plots: *climactic and episodic*. In a climactic plot, the story is joined later—after much of the conflict has already occurred. A climactic plot begins with exposition, a device by which the audience learns the history of the characters. Complications, crises, obstacles, and discoveries take place during the middle portion of the play. At the end of the climactic plot, these complications are resolved and the plot is unraveled in the *dénouement*. Another name for the climactic plot is the *well-made play*. The plays of Henrik Ibsen, such as *A Doll's House* or *Ghosts,* have climactic plots.

In the *episodic plot,* the story is told chronologically, from beginning to end. Consequently, the story does not have the cause-and-effect structure found in the climactic plot, in which only selected events are portrayed. Episodic plots usually have more characters and scenes, cover a longer period of time, and range over a number of locations. Many of the plays of Bertolt Brecht, such as *Mother Courage and Her Children* and *Caucasian Chalk Circle,* are good examples of the episodic plot.

The first plots developed by creative drama participants are often episodic, filled with many people and events. Although they initially work without much selectivity, participants can be coached to pare away the nonessentials and make exciting and solid dramas with episodic plots. When they are ready, participants begin to develop dramas with climactic plots: ones with murder and robberies! At this point it is the leader's job to introduce concepts of beginning, middle, and end, and to foreshadow the *dénouement*. This information appears in all books on playwrighting and is introduced in many of the activities in the Transformation level of the Rutgers Imagination Method.

Character Character is the primary means by which plots are created and is the major ingredient for the advancement of plot, both for theatre and creative drama. Characters must always ring true. Although they do not have to be people you could meet on the street, characters must be based on these people, so that we feel we do know them or would like to know them.

Within each drama, characters must be individual, yet typical, so they offer members of the audience someone with whom to identify. The audience learns about a character through what he/she says, he/she does, and what others say about him/her. Characters must have strong objectives. Characterization happens not merely through words, but in the way the character talks—tone quality, articulation, regional speech—and how the character moves—locomotion, stance, gesture.

All of these character aspects must be likewise considered by the creative drama participant, particularly as the dramas become more advanced and crafted. It is the job of the leader to help participants see themselves as characters and use basic drama skills to put these images into action.

Characters selected by creative drama participants are often decidedly more unusual than many of the realistic characters popular in contemporary film, theatre, and television. Drama participants often choose to portray nonhuman characters, such as animals, or inanimate objects, such as rocks and rainbows. Drama participants also enact characters who are more like the "stock characters" of the *commedia dell'arte,* the popular form of comedy that flourished in Italy in the sixteenth and seventeenth centuries. These characters often symbolize some particular type of person (the bully or the nerd) or some

At the core of the actor's craft is the transformation of self into character. In this photo actors Gerald Hiken, Skip Lawing, and Pamela Burrell physically transform themselves (with minimal costume pieces) into horses for the New York production of *Strider*. (Photo courtesy of *Strider* production company)

outstanding characteristic of behavior (the person who giggles) to the exclusion of everything else. Playwrights could learn about interesting characters by watching drama participants in action.

Dialogue Dialogue imparts information, directs attention, and tells about character. It is not real-life speech, but a selection and compression of natural speech. Through it characters reveal self and plot. Each character speaks differently from any other, from the actor performing the character, and from the playwright.

In creative drama, the dialogue serves the same purpose and is equally difficult to develop. Early in creative drama activities, much of the dialogue is often rambling and characters speak very much as the performer. Of course, since one of the early goals of creative drama is to encourage the participant to feel at ease speaking in front of a group, dialogue of this nature is acceptable. Later in the process, the participant is coached to listen closely, select carefully, and reproduce stored sound and speech images.

Conflict Dramas must have strongly opposing forces. There are five types of conflicts at the core of dramas: person versus self, person versus person, person versus nature, person versus society, and person versus technology.

Conflict is also at the core of creative drama. Many leaders fear the conflict implicit in dramatic action and try to discount its importance by forcing harmony. Dramas without conflict defeat one of the fundamental benefits of theatre—the strongly cathartic effect when the "bad guy gets it." We certainly don't condone fistfights, but we do encourage conflicts with their resolutions, even if you have to live through several bank robberies and shoot-outs before getting to the real thing!

Drama participants are usually extremely fair in their dramatic realizations of conflict. A large percentage of dramas we have seen have two strongly opposing forces in which these forces are balanced. Nothing is more tedious to the sports fan than a lopsided game. After a few ten-second dramas, nothing is duller to drama participants than a bad guy who conquers everyone or a good guy who never has to struggle against all odds. The conflict as much as the outcome is the source of pleasure. The ritualized activities of drama allow participants to resolve conflicts in a protected environment.

Avant-Garde Forms Many of the less traditional and more recent structures of dramatic action provide models for the dramas of young people. Quite instinctively it seems, young people model their dramas after the non-sense nature and non-sequitur structure seen in such pieces as *The Bald Soprano* by Eugene Ionesco or *Waiting for Godot* by Samuel Beckett. It may be that young people see sense in "nonsense," or that this type of structure closely resembles the seemingly disjointed nature of dreams. Nevertheless, they love to fill their dramas with verbal nonsense and existential characters.

Other forms we have seen resemble ritual dramas similar to those of the performance groups popular in the 1960s and 1970s and the theatrical spectacle and/or performance art of Robert Wilson/Philip Glass' *Einstein on the Beach*. Finally, many dramas are also modeled after the technology of the day. Stop action, fast forward, and instant replay—all aspects of MTV, video, and the television age—appear more and more often in the dramatic forms and structure of the enactments of young people. Probably you and most of your potential drama participants were raised on *Sesame Street*, an extraordinarily avant-garde art form, filled with puppets, humans, cartoons, and filmed action.

THEATRICAL CONVENTIONS SHAPE THE ENACTMENT

Creative drama uses more than the conventions of dramatic structure. Theatrical conventions, which are more production-oriented, also shape the enactment. These "rules of the game" or theatrical devices expedite communication to the audience. Theatrical conventions also assist communication of performer to observers within creative drama. Today's theatrical conventions have evolved over time and are what the audience readily accepts. Only the very basic ones are discussed here.

Acting Conventions Theatrical conventions quickly grasped by even the youngest participant are those that focus on being seen and heard. Speaking loudly and not turning one's back on the viewers are two obviously desirable characteristics of the drama player. Young participants know that in real life not everyone faces front and speaks up, yet they can easily accept these "rules of the game." Most do so naturally, and those who do not usually adopt them with a little encouragement from the leader.

Certain playwrighting conventions also fall within the domain of the performer in the creative drama arena. Some popular conventions that are used instinctively in the creative drama enactment are the soliloquy, the aside, the monologue, and the flashback. A *soliloquy* is a speech in which the character reasons aloud, revealing his or her innermost feelings. A *monologue* is an informative speech delivered by a character, either to the audience or to the other characters. An *aside* is a speech delivered by one character to another, which is supposedly not heard by the characters within hearing distance on the stage. And a *flashback* is an episode performed during the play that has occurred at an earlier time. The flashback is usually seen by the audience through the eyes of the character who is currently onstage; often various technical additions, such as dim lights or soft music, help separate this moment from the rest of the play. All of these devices are popular with participants in creative drama activities. Many of them crop up spontaneously in the work of participants who have observed them in the theatre or on television.

In your imagination hold this stage aship.

William Shakespeare

Production Conventions Contemporary audiences and observers of drama also accept many conventions connected with the physical production, such as setting, costume, and make-up, all of which are eagerly imitated by the creative drama participant and add to the necessary visual component of theatre. Sets may be made of flats (a frame and a canvas wall-like device) and filled with boxes to represent furniture. An everyday here-and-now object, such as a paper cup, may be used to indicate a much more spectacular prop, such as a murder weapon or a spy glass. Scarves and hats used to indicate a more elaborate costume give both the participant and viewer a "handle" to assist them in imagining the character portrayed.

The relationship between the production conventions and the accepted rules of the dramatic play of young people is clear and suggests that the conventions of all three activities—play, creative drama, and theatre—represent the same "suspension of disbelief" that makes these phenomena magically communicative.

THEATRE PRACTITIONERS AS ROLE MODELS

The creative drama participant emulates many theatre artists, not merely the actor, as those outside the field sometimes believe. At various times during the creative drama experience, the participant becomes director, actor, playwright, designer, and critic. Much of the literature on the creative and pragmatic nature of these jobs provides models for procedures and behavioral expectations for participants in creative drama. The following discussion is meant to give you a taste of the theatre artist model used in the development of the Rutgers Imagination Method, and to expand your view of drama's potential to reach participants whose talents are not limited to performing. This background, combined with attending the theatre on a regular basis, can give you a sense of the scope of the human imagination and provide inspiration for your work as a leader of creative drama activities.

The Actor

The actor is perhaps the most familiar of all theatre's creators, perhaps because he or she is most in the public eye. Many people view actors as magicians, in touch with deep and hidden reservoirs of emotion. On the other hand, some people devalue the job of the actor, because the craft seems merely a continuation of the skills of everyday life. In truth, the actor's job, as in any other artistic job, requires mastery of particular skills as well as control of a fluent and vivid imagination.

Central to the actor's craft is an ability to assume a character other than self—to behave "as if" he or she were another person. The actor does not actually become another person, but rather establishes the illusion that he or she is another. For a scripted drama, actors must become the embodiment of the character as created by the playwright. The actor uses a well-trained voice

A classic story has the potential to stimulate uniquely personal imagination images in the minds of its readers. The power of *Alice in Wonderland* also to stimulate the theatrical imagination is demonstrated by these two photos, each of a very different production of *Alice*. Interestingly, each company was intrigued by the theatrical potential of the imagery strategy "growing taller." (Photo left of Dallas Theatre Center's *Alice in Wonderland,* courtesy of designer Irene Corey; photo right of Looking Glass Theatre, Providence, Rhode Island, *Alice in the American Wonderland,* courtesy of Johanne Killeen)

and body, as well as a well-developed theatrical understanding of people, to portray this character. In order to develop an interesting, but believable character, an actor often selects relevant moments from his or her own life to enrich the interpretation of the author's creation. Actors spend much time on vocal work: developing rich tone, wide-ranging inflections, and a clear articulation, so that their voices can be heard. They also must be able to modify their voices and dialects in order to sound as the character they are playing would.

A physically fit, flexible body is also essential not only to assist actors in enduring even the most physically challenging roles, but also to permit them to assume the shape and movement pattern of another. Actor training often includes classes in movement, dance, fencing, and juggling to encourage timing and agility, as well as an understanding of the body's potential and limitations. Actors are often called upon to wear costumes of a different era. They must move as if they belonged in them—no small task for the 1980s actor suddenly encumbered by corset, heels, and wig.

Well-trained actors approach their roles by means of a systematic, developmental method, the mastery of which is often a consuming passion. A variety of methods are taught in drama schools. Some of the most popular are Michael Chekhov's, Constantin Stanislavski's, and Lee Strasberg's. Each of these methods offers actors a set of techniques and a theoretical framework within which to create character. All of these methods focus, to a great extent, on the actor's use of past experience in the development of compelling characterization.

In recent years, actors have also participated in ensembles, which develop their own original pieces of theatre through improvisational methods. Actors are always part of an ensemble creative process, of course, but in an improvisational company of this nature, they must develop story, character, and even dialogue, often without the assistance of a playwright.

The participant in a creative drama experience uses many of the same skills and functions as an actor, particularly the actor in an ensemble improvisational company. Both need a flexible body and a voice that can be heard; both must reach into his or her storehouse of images as sources for drama or as a means to personalize a story; and both need a systematic method to help them connect ideas to action.

The difference between actor and drama participant, however, is that the latter participant focuses more on the connection of ideas and action, while the actor must focus on end result. Time spent on introspection, on working with others, and on communicating through word and action is important for the cultivation of actorlike techniques, as well as daily life skills. Working with imagination and action gives the drama participant an understanding of his or her own personal creative process, both individually and in a group.

It is essential to keep in mind that while the skills required of the drama participant are very much the same as those required of the actor, the ultimate objective for the drama participant is very different from that of actor. The difference has to do, of course, with the final product. The actor must work to develop the very best final theatre production, whether or not that final product and rehearsal process is the best experience for him or her. The creative drama participant uses these skills to develop dramatic learning abilities, not to perform for the public, but to realize his or her potential and to transfer some of these skills to everyday situations.

The Director

The director is a twentieth-century phenomenon. Before this century, the functions of each artist were specific and theatre was ritualized, but the modern era's interest in psychological motivation and complex technological discoveries changed both process and product of theatre. Now, theatre needs directors to organize a complex art form.

The primary functions of the director are interpreting the script and organizing the various aspects of production so that they are in line with this interpretation. The director must work with all theatre artists — actors, designers, and technicians. The director communicates his or her interpretation of the playwright's story by means of the evolving stage picture. In order for the final product to come about, the director must remain in control of the rehearsal process, must communicate well, must be able to retrieve images and communicate them through words to people with a wide diversity of experiences, and must be able to share his or her personal images with all those involved in the production.

The director can provide a role model for both the leader of creative drama and the participant. The leader often assumes many of the same functions as a director. Early in the drama experience, the leader helps build skills and cultivates the imagination of the participants. Later, the leader establishes scenes and objectives and structures evaluation. Participants look to the leader, as to a director, to help merge the group.

Participants in creative drama often need to have some of the same skills as those required of the director. The most important of these is the ability to have a sense of the whole: to chart the progress, to know how to use movement and people to help tell a story, to aid in negotiation of the group, even to affirm the appropriateness of the initial idea. These skills are sophisticated ones and certainly are not instantly acquired by the drama participants. Yet they are skills to be encouraged by the leader.

The Designer

The designer translates the words on the page to pictures on the stage. Color, light, shape, and size speak as clearly to the audience as do the words. Often the design is executed not by one person but by several who individually create set, costumes, props, lights, and make-up. Much collective planning goes into a total design concept. A truly collaborative effort results in a unified stage picture that often pleases or startles the sensibility of the audience.

In plays that are realistic in style, designers often use the world around them as source material for the set, costumes, or props. A real dress or a real room is never transferred directly from life onto the stage; the designer must select and refine the real thing so that it is larger than life. A dress for a character must, for example, be a representation of all the wardrobe of the character. Transforming life into art, in this case, is extremely subtle. For more presentational plays, designers develop imagination images to assist them in creating a fantasy world. Also in presentational plays, designers must establish mood, period, time of day, and even relationships. In *Romeo and Juliet,* for example, the costume designer can help the audience keep all the characters straight by costuming the Capulets in red shades and the Montagues in blue.

The creative drama participant uses many of the skills of the designer in manipulating props, objects, costumes, and set pieces to help make a dramatic enactment. Initially, participants may merely play with these theatrical objects and consciously or unconsciously try to recreate an effect stored in their minds. But they may also work on developing a sense of space that evolves into a more dramatic sense of place. Observation is a tool both for the designer and for the creative drama participant.

As the participants become more skillful, they may emulate designers even more closely, creating specific costumes, props, and/or set pieces with their newly developed imagination images and visual arts/design skills. Many participants who do not excel in the performance aspect of creative drama carve out a niche for themselves in the area of prop, costume, or set design.

The Playwright

Playwrights are unique among theatre artists. They are creative artists as opposed to interpretive artists. In other words, they must make a piece of art "from scratch," using only their own images as sources for action. Consequently, the playwright must be an astute observer of the world: of people and of events. He or she must have an eye for detail and an ear for talk, as well as the ability to combine and recombine all these events and people into an imaginative piece.

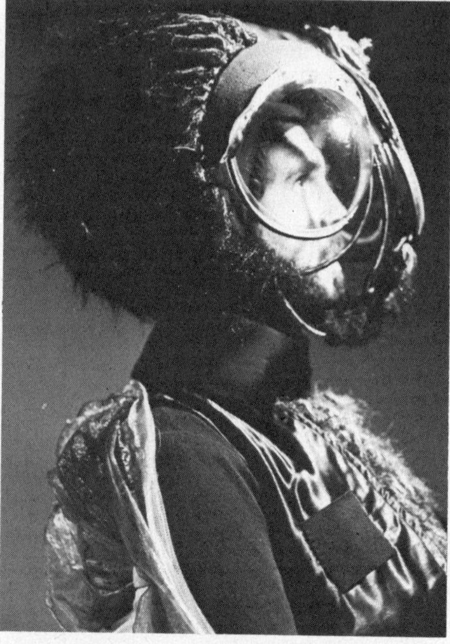

These two photos record two distinct points in the imagination into action process of a gifted theatre artist. Shown here are the design sketch (*left*) and the actual mask worn by the actor playing a fly in Mofid's *The Butterfly*. (Everyman Players, Dallas. Production directed by Orlin Corey and designed by Irene Corey. Photos by Beth Odle courtesy of Irene Corey.)

Eudora Welty, novelist and story writer, describes her active story-making process:

> Long before I wrote stories, I listened for stories. Listening *for* them is something more acute than listening *to* them. I suppose it's an early form of participation in what goes on. Listening children know stories are *there*. . . . My instinct—the dramatic instinct—was to lead me, eventually, on the right track for a storyteller: the *scene* was full of hints, pointers, suggestions, and promises of things to find out and know about human beings.

In emulating the playwright or, in this case, the novelist, the drama participant must be involved in the active observation of the world. He or she must listen *for* stories and seek to observe people and recall events. In this way, the participant will come to know that his or her own life is full of people, events, and ideas that can be valuable sources for drama-making. Intense observation, plus understanding of one's own personal value, are essential life skills, as well as ones important in the drama arena.

The Critic

A theatre critic can evaluate objectively and has developed a consistent way to view theatre and to report what he or she has experienced. People who read the critic's reviews or listen to his or her commentary come to rely on these evaluations. If one is deciding whether or not to attend a specific production, the critic's review can help one make a decision. A gifted critic can make a theatre event survive long after the production has closed. In the published theatre criticism of Brooks Atkinson, for example, long-gone productions of the past still live as part of the imagic storehouse of today's reader.

The evaluation techniques of the critic can be models for the reflection phase of the creative drama process. In early drama experiences, the leader acts as the sole critic, the only one with permission to comment during the drama session. The leader offers clear, objective criticism to help both participant and observer focus on the actual outcome and to compare this result with the intended outcome. As drama skills improve, participants learn to compare the image in their mind's eyes with the here-and-now rendition of it. They learn to ask questions of their peers and assist them in drama-making.

WHAT CREATIVE DRAMA SHARES WITH THEATRE

What drama leaders often forget is that much of creative drama's power is derived from the fact that it is an art form. Like theatre, creative drama provides its participants and observers a catharsis, a means to communicate, and an opportunity to stop the world—for a brief moment. For all its practical educational benefits, creative drama also nurtures sublime experiences, because creative drama is, at its best, an art.

Creative drama is a relatively young art, and theoreticians have yet to clarify what makes it unique as an art form. To understand its artistry more clearly, we have looked to its parent art, the theatre and pointed out characteristics shared by both, in order to explain what attracts participants to the art form of creative drama.

Theatre and Creative Drama Are Ephemeral

The transitory nature of theatre — a quality it shares with all performing arts — sets theatre apart in a significant way from the visual and literary arts. When a painting, a poem, or a sculpture leaves the creator's hands, it is finished, complete. The viewer or reader can go back to it again and again. It will always be there and never change. (Sometimes the viewer changes, but never the work of art.)

Theatre is very different. Each theatre experience happens once and becomes part of the past, never to be recaptured in precisely the same way again by performer or audience. Each theatre event thus exists only in the memories of those present. If the event is sublime, those present have shared a moment that remains sublime. Not even a video of the production can capture the fleeting experience of actually having been there, although it may serve to recall memory images or produce imagination images.

In this photo, these young people are engaged in a creative drama enactment that rivals the pomp and circumstance of many grand theatrical spectacles. Kings, queens, thrones, rituals, and coronations can capture the imagination of children and adults alike. (Photo courtesy of Michael Rocco Pinciotti)

Why participate in an art so transitory? Investigation suggests that a theatrical event's ephemeral nature allows it to be dynamic. Subtle changes can occur in performance as each different audience slightly affects the ongoing art form, for every new audience offers different feedback to the performers, who then respond in a new and different way to every audience.

A certain immediacy is inherent in the theatre and is a direct result of its ephemeral nature. Thornton Wilder called this the "perpetual present tense." Like life, theatre is witnessed in the present, but always with a fresh remembrance of the past and a sharp anticipation of what is to come. Designer Robert Edmond Jones observed that to participate in the theatre is "to be aware of the now."

Creative drama shares this maddening but enticing characteristic with theatre. In no other art experience in schools are participants more aware of the now. Initially, participants take great joy in making art that is so transitory — so like life in its immediacy. (Unlike life, however, participants are able to control exactly what does and does not happen.) After the "honeymoon period," participants may experience frustration in not being able to recreate exactly what they had enacted previously, but it is at this opportune moment that the leader can coach them in *third eye* skills — spontaneous doing and monitoring. One of the challenges of mastering creative drama is working within the limitations of the art form itself.

The Form and Content of Theatre and Creative Drama Focus on Human Action

What distinguishes theatre from other arts is that both theatre's form and content focus on human beings. Live actors communicate to a present audience about the experience of people in relationship to one another. In no other art are both form and content so closely tied to life.

The essence of theatre is human beings *in action,* not human beings merely speaking lines. The words of the dramatic script are only one part of the drama and are only symbolic of the underlying motives and relationships. Because a script is easily recorded, distributed, and studied, it may seem to be the only "stuff" of drama. Scripts are important, but only in that they express the actions — the needs and desires — of human beings. No musical notation, no paper and paint, no photo equipment are available. Human action and interaction is the core of theatre.

Human action is likewise the focus of creative drama. Participants are the form, and their imaginative interpretation of their world and the people and events in it are the content of drama. Participants are simultaneously artistic form and content. They tell their own life stories, directly or indirectly, to others who watch and listen. Daily activities portrayed by one member of the group become part of the whole group's collective storehouse of experiences.

Theatre and Creative Drama Involve Communication in a Direct and Intense Way

Theatre evolved from storytellers reciting myths and legends to listeners, and from ritual ceremonies in which chiefs shared their good fortunes with other tribal members. Plantings, harvests, battles, marriages, births, and deaths were important events that theatre's early performers shared with others. In many ways, these early playwrights share with contemporary ones the need to communicate with an audience who understands.

In a similar manner, the creative drama experience fulfills its participants' needs to make sense of an event by communicating it to others. The exchange between participants and observer — whether verbal or nonverbal, immediate or delayed — is one of the basic encounters of creative drama. With this in mind, you as leader must nurture the communication. Each participant must have an opportunity for input; each observer must learn to respond and evaluate in a way that is productive for the enactment and for the individuals involved.

Theatre and Creative Drama Mirror the Times

Theatre experiences are related to the society in which they are produced. Not only the script but also the entire production reveals the attitudes, values, and life style of those who created it. If only theatre could be preserved (and you have just read how it cannot), archeologists would learn as much from the production as they could from any artifact found in a dig.

The content of creative drama enactments reflects the contemporary society and the socioeconomic class of its participants. Some drama content is, of course, universal. Fairy tales, legends, and myths have been and will always continue to be a mainstay of creative drama. Countless psychologists have tried to explain why these stories are so compelling; all agree that young people respond to them on some deep and subconscious level. Interestingly, the thrust of fairy tale enactments do not change, but details do. Contemporary twists — Cinderella's visit to McDonald's — and socioeconomic turns — Jack's encounter with a man with a switchblade — tell observers much about these young people.

Topical dramas change over time. The Patty Hearst dramas of the mid-1970s are no more; nor do we see the flower children stories of the late 1960s. Unfortunately, nuclear disaster is a popular topic today. Nonetheless, the method detailed in this book is based on the notion that each person's experiences are important sources for drama material. What these young creators select to dramatize is extremely revealing, and they often surprise themselves by what they find inside themselves. Although it may be difficult to coach participants to make dramas about themselves, the ultimate effect of such enactments can equal the tremendous cathartic effect felt by both dramatist and audience in drama's parent art form — the theatre.

Theatre and Creative Drama Are Metaphors for Life Itself

In many ways already discussed, theatre is very much like life. In fact, theatre resembles life so much that it may safely be said that it is a giant metaphor for life. Through metaphor, one person or thing is likened to another in order to point up its nature or meaning more clearly. Everything in theatre — the performers, the action, the props and costumes — mirrors life.

An actor who plays Willy Loman in Arthur Miller's *Death of a Salesman* does not say to himself or the audience, "I am now going to act like Willy." Rather, to the audience and to himself (for that moment in time), he says, "I am Willy." Program notes do not state: "Act 1: An area made to look like the Loman house." Instead the note says, "Act 1: The Loman house." The comparison can continue.

In like manner, creative drama is a metaphor for life itself. By "suspending their disbelief," participants and observers can experience going to the moon, being eighty-nine years old, and sliding down a rainbow. Through practice, participants become better able to image the impossible — in the past, present, or future. Virginia Koste termed dramatizations of these sorts "rehearsal for life." She certainly is on-target in her assessment of the symbolic nature of creative drama!

Theatre and Creative Drama Are Ensemble Arts

Theatre is an ensemble art. Playwright, director, designers, actors, and technical artists all work together to develop theatre's total artistic effect. Both the process and final product reflect the talent, experience, and merged individual points of view of all involved. The success of the whole production is dependent, in part, on how and when the group gels. Often it is the director who develops and communicates a unifying point of view.

Creative drama mirrors theatre in that both are ensemble arts. In creative drama, individuals learn to work together to develop a group performance. Each individual makes a unique contribution, yet modifies his or her desire, based on the unique requirements of a particular group. Unlike theatre, in which all the artists are employed or agree to work together under the generally accepted conditions of the director and a rehearsal schedule, creative drama does not provide such clear-cut structure and leadership. Consequently, it is up to the leader to cultivate the ensemble nature of creative drama, and each participant's task is to communicate a point of view.

The ideal group, whether the creative drama class or the theatre ensemble, must work in a state of mutual support, or *cooperation*. They must also achieve *coordination* through actions synchronized to provide common benefits. Finally, the highest levels of group organization, *collaboration*, produces a melding of individuals and actions into a unified whole.

Of course, each group is different, and each individual is called upon to contribute different skills to each different group. For example, an individual with moderate experience in creative drama who finds himself in an inexperienced group may become the person who builds morale, the *team builder*. He or she may be *the idea person* or *the coordinator*. The same individual who finds himself/herself in an experienced creative drama group may need to listen for awhile before making his or her contribution, or be *the implementer* of others' ideas. People who study group process are well aware of the various ways one individual may work in a variety of groups.*

Another interesting aspect of the group process is how each group gels. Early in their creative drama experiences, individuals new to creative drama have difficulty giving up their autonomy. Often observers see parallel play — individuals working together but not relating to one another. This can create a problem if individuals continue to fail to work as a unit. Development of a working and relatively consistent organizational structure becomes critical, but if the leader takes charge at this time and helps participants see what is occurring, the group can become a working group. If the leader lets the internal bickering continue, the creative drama class can become a free-for-all in which each individual continues to try for center stage. In this case, the drama leader is an essential facilitator of the ensemble aspect of creative drama.

* *These concepts are discussed in more detail in Chapter 11.*

Theatre and Creative Drama Are Combinations of Many Art Forms

Theatre encompasses not only a variety of viewpoints but also various other arts. Theatre is literature in the script; architecture in the setting; sculpture in the three-dimensional forms and the use of light and shadow; dance in the movement patterns; painting in the set and make-up; and music in the sounds, songs, and flow of the language. Artists of diverse talents work together in creating the spectacle of a unified production.

Those who participate in creative drama get a taste of all these arts too. A widely held misconception concerning creative drama is that participants experience only the literary or only the performance aspect of theatre. But a true creative drama experience, in mirroring theatre, gives those involved a chance to discover talents in a variety of artistic modes.

> ***The loveliest and most poignant of all stage pictures are those that are seen in the mind's eye.***
>
> Robert Edmond Jones

The Unique Nature of Creative Drama

Theatre has contributed many of its characteristics to the art form of creative drama. In order to facilitate participants' mastery of creative drama, the leader must be aware of these shared elements. Yet every creative drama leader must also be aware of what aspects are uniquely creative drama's. What is unique is not the imagery processes or the characteristics of dramatic behavior, but, rather, the particular way in which both aspects are balanced in the connection between imagination and action. When leading creative drama, you must focus not only on the development of the internal and external, but also on the unique connection of the two.

The ultimate dramatic learning and mastery of creative drama presupposes the ability to connect both imagination and action, individually and collectively. It is this connection that sparks dynamic dramatic learning and is the ability that transfers from the creative drama arena to the world at large. It is this experience in connecting imagination to action that makes creative drama the ideal rehearsal for life and a prime vehicle for personal growth and development.

CONNECTING IMAGINATION TO ACTION

As you learned in Chapter 1, dramatic learning encompasses internal processes and external behaviors, as well as the connection between imagination and action. It is this connection between imagination and action that permits individuals to do their best work. Within a typical education curriculum, creative arts activities often provide individuals with their only practice in connecting ideas to action. **Research suggests that it is this skill in connecting ideas to action that transfers from the creative drama arena to real life.** Consequently, the nurturing of this connection must be a major focus of creative drama. In line with this idea, Transformations — the second level of the Rutgers Imagination Method — is devoted exclusively to transforming ideas into action.

Chapter 5 is divided into three sections. The first presents three scenarios that describe gifted individuals who connect imagination to action in very special ways. We present these scenarios, all inherently dramatic in nature but not precisely about drama/theatre, because each example focuses on a pivotal connection found also in creative drama. The second section describes examples of the connection of imagination to *dramatic action:* dramatic play, a theatre rehearsal, and a Transformation drama activity. These scenarios illustrate the relationship of these dramatic learning experiences. The final section presents a more practically oriented view of the iii Framework to assist you in nurturing the imagination/action connection in yourself and others.

APPLIED IMAGINATION

The capacity for imaginative behavior is both spontaneous and natural. The ability to remember, plan, and act upon the imagination made early humans essentially different from any other animal and enabled the species to become wise. Only humans have the great gift for imagination — it is species specific. Their capacity for imagination allows people to remember, to plan, and to dream. Behaviors and actions are, consciously or unconsciously, influenced by the ability to imagine. Almost every person, no matter how limited, possesses this ability to apply imagination to his behavior. Imagination and action working together are the means by which people learn, solve problems, and create. The natural, spontaneous ability to connect imagination and action can also be enhanced through training and practice. All people who solve problems or express their ideas, whether homemaker, scientist, artist, or athlete, demonstrate just how closely imagination and action are intertwined. The following principles are true of all situations where imagination is connected to action, including creative drama:

IMAGINATION AND ACTION WORKING TOGETHER

- Imagination and action connect spontaneously and naturally.
- Practice and training can assist people in their connection of imagination to action, as well as help people refine and improve the connection.
- Multisensory memory images provide the best stimulation for imagination and action.
- The connection of imagination and action assists people in a wide variety of everyday situations.
- The results of the imagination/action connection can run the gamut of behaviors — from everyday activities to the original solution of problems or creation of unique works of art.

Among today's role models, three popular heroes are the Olympic Athlete, the Super Sleuth, and the Award-Winning Film-Maker. Individuals who achieve success in these endeavors do so in part because they are successful in connecting their vast imagery storehouses to their equally well-developed sets of behaviors. The Olympic Athlete connects internal processes to the achievement of sublime physical actions; the Super Sleuth wonderfully deduced images to detective problem-solving; and the Creative Artist a compelling vision to a unique work of art.

The following examples of the connection of imagination to action were chosen not solely because they portray actions of gifted individuals but also because they illustrate particular aspects of the connection of imagination and action found within creative drama: **the physical, the problem-solving, the art-making.** As you read these examples, focus on the nature of the connection and the techniques each person uses to achieve the final goal. Those techniques and strategies highlighted in the following examples may already be part of your own imagination and action connection.

> ***Artists treat facts as stimuli for imagination, whereas scientists use imagination to coordinate facts.***
>
> Arthur Koestler

The Physical Connection

CASE STUDY

INNER REHEARSAL Greg Louganis, an Olympic diver, attributes his winning gold medals to his "inner rehearsal" as well as to his incredible physical fitness. Greg explains that he is an expert at mental rehearsal. First, he rehearses his dives from the perspective of an observer—watching someone perform. Then, he rehearses them from the diver's viewpoint—going over the kinesthetic cues as well as the visual ones. Finally, he rehearses them to music—coordinating timing with auditory recall. The images acquired by these strategies connect to his physical action and enable him to earn Olympic gold.

Olympic diver Greg Louganis is an ideal representation of the connection of imagination to physical action. (Photo courtesy Steve Goldstein/Image Bank)

Athletes are perhaps the most sublime example of the perfect connection of imagination and physical action. On a consistent basis, they must strive to match their behavior to an imagination image in their mind's eye. For an athlete, imagination is necessary as a *precursor to action.* In fact, some sports heroes create news by verbalizing their incredible ability to connect imagination to action. The legendary Babe Ruth not only imagined how and where he was going to hit a home run, but was so certain that he could execute the move he gladly told the world before he hit the ball!

Athletes rely heavily on *sensory cues* and *memory images;* the combination of these in imagination provides a stimulus for action. Tennis champions John McEnroe and Chris Evert-Lloyd often speak about hearing the sound of a lob, drop shot, or line drive and positioning themselves to meet it. The real-life sound stimulates an auditory imagination image that helps the tennis player keep fractions of a second ahead of the ball. Athletes also develop a *kinesthetic imagination,* or what they sometimes call a *muscle memory.* Gymnasts, ice skaters, skiers, and divers often speak about how they simultaneously perform and see themselves performing. In this manner the imagination, which includes both previous auditory, visual, and kinesthetic images, assists in *monitoring their performance.* Not only are the athletes developing their bodies but they are also refining their inner resources.

Athletic coaches are also aware of the importance of the imagination/action connection; the best coaches know that they must develop athletes' inner resources, their bodies, and the connections between the two. Such books as *The Inner Game of Tennis* and *The Hidden Skier,* an exploration of the inner and outer world of skiing, describe techniques that can be modified for use in a great variety of physical activities. Both works also discuss imagery's use in reducing stress. Coaches have realized that the stress of competition can overpower even the best athletes. The ability to use imagination for *stress reduction* is important for everyone, but particularly for individuals who must maintain their bodies at an optimum level.

A positive image of success, a multisensory and clear picture of the action to be performed, and the ability to control an anxious attitude enhances the skills of all people engaged in psychomotor activity. Learning a new physical skill or developing an old one requires the connection between imagination and action in the form of mental rehearsal to develop muscle memory, the use of a "third eye" to develop a positive feedback system, and a stress-reduction technique to develop confidence — all strengthen the imagination/action connection.

Creative drama relies heavily on the participants' active physical involvement. Many early drama skills require each drama participant to achieve a certain level of physical expression. Because of the "as if" nature of drama, participants are often involved in learning new psychomotor skills or adapting old ones to express various characters or emotions. They must learn to communicate with their bodies, as well as through their voices. Participants must also control what they do physically and develop their ability to achieve consistent results.

Just as do athletes, drama participants develop the ability to physicalize and to monitor themselves simultaneously. This ability to view self from outside self is often termed in the imagery literature a *third-eye* skill. This third-eye monitoring ability helps drama participants self-correct while they are in the process of creating. It also provides constant information from a variety of perspectives to help them while they are in the act of performing.

The Problem-Solving Connection

CASE STUDY

THE DEDUCTIVE PROCESS Detective Sherlock Holmes seemed intensely caught up in a reverie, as he rocked back and forth in his favorite chair. In his mind, he was reviewing the information he had carefully elicited from his client Helen concerning her stepfather, Dr. Roylott. Holmes was also retracing his tour of the room and grounds where Helen's unfortunate sister had died. Over and over he manipulated the data in his mind. "Ah, ha," he exclaimed, "I have the answer. Come with me, Watson."

Some time later in a small, dark room, Holmes and Dr. Watson saw a gleam of light and smelled the strong smell of burning oil — both sensory sensations reinforced Holmes' notion of what was to happen. Hours passed before they heard a gentle, soothing sound. In a brief instant, Holmes struck a match and lashed furiously with his cane at the bell pull. In actuality the rope was not a rope at all but a speckled snake, which provided the name for the account—"The Adventure of the Speckled Band." In another moment's time, the snake had injected the devious Dr. Roylott with poison from its deadly fangs. Holmes' actions, based on his deductive use of imagery, had saved himself, Dr. Watson, and the innocent Helen.

Sherlock Holmes, a fictional hero created over a hundred years ago by Arthur Conan Doyle, epitomizes the ideal deductive mind. Holmes' imagery-based techniques are beautiful in their simplicity, and at the same time awe-inspiring in the complexity of the data-gathering and deductive processes utilized to solve a problem. If carefully dissected, the solutions provide models for the connection of imagination to problem-solving activities. Everyday, business executives, scientists, and children using computers become detectives of sorts. Several potentially useful strategies appear on a consistent basis

In Wyndham Robinson's *Reveries,* detective Sherlock Holmes is in deep meditation. Interestingly, Holmes' memory images are of characters from the popular drawings of another artist of the time, Sidney Paget. (By permission of the Crown Publishing Group)

throughout the Holmes detective stories. Interestingly, many of the procedures used by Holmes over a century ago are those very techniques stressed in the most recent imagery/problem-solving literature. His famous "reveries," depicted in this illustration, are in fact personally *guided fantasies* in which he turns inward to allow his images of people and places to merge and overlay and suggest possible solutions.

In problem-solving the relationship between imagination and action requires a great deal of trial and error. For a trial-and-error approach to be successful, *fluency, flexibility, and a playful attitude* are necessary. To solve a problem, the generation of many possible solutions—termed fluency—is essential; judgment must often be suspended in the early stages of using images to solve the problem. A playful period of mental and physical manipulation must occur before selection and refinement. Holmes publicly shares his joy in his own ability to play. In almost every story, he captures the trust and admiration of his new clients by telling them what he knows about them through his careful observation of sensory detail as well as how he utilized these details in deductive, imagery-based detection.

Flexibility allows the solver to view the problem from different perspectives and thus explore a variety of possible solutions. This frame of mind encourages a flow of images and ideas that then can be juxtaposed, combined, rearranged, and elaborated upon to find the best solution. When confronted with the fact that his initial image of a large group of gypsies, stimulated by the word "band," was not the correct image, Holmes allows himself to retrieve another image, this time a snake with multicolored bands, that leads him to the ultimate solution. Armed with such flexibility, everyone can make discoveries or solve problems.

What is now proved was once only imagined.

William Blake

Another strategy, often utilized by Sherlock Holmes and one that is wonderfully dramatic, is his "putting himself in another's shoes." After careful observation and precise questioning, Holmes is able to see himself as either his client or as the villain and behave as they might behave. He can then deduce the past of these individuals and project their future actions. This monitoring ability to *view self as other* allows him to deduce the intended actions of Dr. Roylott in "The Adventure of the Speckled Band."

This kind of applied imagination is often considered *discovery.* Upon close scrutiny, however, you can see that very little is left to chance. At each step of the way, the Super Sleuth wonders and acts, visualizes and tries again, reviews the previous steps or clues, and continues with diligence and purpose to solve the problem. David Perkins in his book *The Mind's Best Work* describes this problem-solving process as a network rather than a direct path to discovery. In the end, however, the route to discovery seems rather "elementary."

Creative drama participants, either individually or cooperatively, often must solve a dramatic problem. They are discoverers of their own ideas in action. One very useful strategy, provided by the Holmes model, involves the *oscillation between image and action.* This oscillation helps clarify the stimulus/image and assists participants in realizing the necessary dramatic skills. Oscillation takes place individually and within the group as a whole. The group must develop a similar image, negotiate who and where each person is, and coordinate all ideas and behaviors as they solve the dramatic problem.

Participants, through trial and error, explore a number of dramatic solutions before choosing the best response. In creative drama, they are encouraged to develop a flexible network of vivid, multisensory images, various imagery strategies, and a repertoire of dramatic behaviors from which to choose. Selection, refinement, reflection, and evaluation are then necessary components in the discovery process and in the development of imagination and dramatic behavior.

Masters of creative drama develop a variety of *metacognitive abilities*. They acquire **knowledge about themselves, other participants, the tasks required to accomplish the dramatic enactment, and which strategies produce which results.** Like Sherlock Holmes, they "know that they know," feel confident with this knowledge, and delight in using it whenever they can.

The Creative Arts Connection

CASE STUDY

"I CELEBRATE THE IMAGINATION" Film-maker Steven Spielberg credits both his vivid storehouse of memories and his experience with cameras as essential to his success in the movies. Spielberg explains, "In my films I celebrate the imagination as a tool of great creation. . . ." Many of his real-life experiences and childhood fantasy/nightmares have been imaginatively reshaped into episodes in his films. Spielberg transforms the frightening "tentacle trees" he remembers from his New Jersey childhood into larger-than-life humanlike trees that scare the children in *Poltergeist*. In *E. T.*, Elliot's messy room and fantasy life in his clothes closet, visual aspects that help the audience know and like the boy, are described by Spielberg as part of his own childhood experience. In this case, the connection of imagination and action is easy to spot and clearly illustrates the transformation of life into art.

Spielberg became the "family photographer" at twelve. His first movie was of "my Lionel trains crashing into each other." In all his interviews, Spielberg tells of being unable to stop working on the techniques of films; his addiction to the craft and his obsession with the world of his imagination and his real-life experiences make Steven Spielberg an exemplary Creative Artist, one who is able to connect his ideas to action.

A Creative Artist, and one who reaches a wide and varied audience, is the contemporary film-maker. All creative artists utilize the imagination/action connection for the purpose of **self-discovery, manipulation of craft, and ultimate sharing or communicating of images.** Art, whether it is expressed through movement and gesture, pictures and motion, color and line, pitch and rhythm, is based on and communicates the artist's unique imagination images.

Imagination involves an inner dialogue of observing, planning, recalling, manipulating, and rehearsing that leads to the ultimate artistic product/work of art. Since Creative Artists are concerned with self-discovery, their personal experiences, vivid memory images, and novel imagination images are most important. Such artists are acutely aware of the world around them; they

As a child, Steven Spielberg spent time daydreaming and developing his fantasy worlds and characters. As an adult, Spielberg is able to reach into this rich imagic storehouse and pull out E.T., a creature who has long been within him. E.T. has similarly captured the imagination of countless filmgoers. (Copyright © by Universal Pictures, a Division of Universal City Studies, Inc. Courtesy of MCA Publishing Rights, a Division of MCA Inc.)

purposefully explore the rich sensory images of their world to increase their image storehouse. As painter Pablo Picasso said, "one must have constantly before one's eyes the very presence of life." This *artistic sensitivity* provides them with a potential storehouse of images, ready to be manipulated, arranged, and put into the chosen medium.

The unique expression of imagination/action occurs, in part, because of the idiosyncratic and personal nature of the artist's images and ideas. The material for imagination comes from within artists themselves; they discover that they are the source and resource for their art-making. D. H. Lawrence in his essay "Making Pictures" agrees: "I believe many people have, in their consciousness, living images that would give them the greatest joy to bring out." The artist's creative output relies heavily on a rich storehouse of vivid sensory images and the ability to manipulate and control these images at will, as well as the potential to meld imagination and craft elements. Some artists explain that they can "capture" the internal image only through external manipulation of craft elements.

The Creative Artist must constantly explore the potential and limitations of the medium of choice. The Creative Artist comes to know the medium through practice and repetition, as did the Olympic Athlete and the trial and error of the Super Sleuth. As the artist begins gaining control over the craft within the art form, the images and ideas often become clearer and more defined. The desire to communicate and perfect their images demands that artists continue to explore the medium's potential, which in turn increases the competency level and makes the communication and perfection of the images clearer.

Participants in the creative drama experience are artists too. They explore and utilize many of the same imagination/action connections as do working artists. Through creative drama, participants come to know themselves in a number of ways. They come to trust their inner resources and discover in themselves the variety of images and experiences that can personalize drama. A heightened sensitivity to the world can motivate them to continue both the internal and external search. They also come to know their own external resources as well as the wealth of dramatic behaviors available to them. By manipulating, playing, and replaying, they become aware of the craft of theatre, and where their strengths and limitations lie. Through creative drama, participants learn both process and product as their competency levels grow.

IMAGINATION AND DRAMATIC ACTION

The previous scenarios describe three examples of imagination in action. Each person described possessed tremendous natural, spontaneous abilities enhanced through training and experience. All three were naturals. All three illustrate the essential aspects of the connection and provide you with an interesting perspective on the connection of imagination and action to be found in creative drama.

The next scenarios describe three examples of the connection of imagination to a variety of dramatic activities. Each encompasses aspects of the physical, the problem-solving, and the creative arts connections just described. These scenarios are presented to provide more precise information about the connection of imagination and dramatic action in order to aid you in your role of leader. As you read them, keep in mind that they foreshadow essential elements of the Rutgers Imagination Method. The discussion after each scenario touches on aspects of environment, facilitator, process as it is related to product, and the balance of individual and group.

Dramatic Play

Young children easily transform their everyday world into other places and times.

CASE STUDY

AN IMAGINATIVE JOURNEY Three children, ranging in age from three to six, enter the living room dragging a variety of objects: a flashlight, a blanket, two plastic swords, a bucket, and a stuffed bear. The eldest of the small group commands the others to "climb aboard the spaceship or you will be left behind." Quickly they leap upon the couch. You are most certainly aware that they have transformed this everyday space; you are an observer as they travel to a "galaxy far, far away." Their body posture, facial expressions, and verbalization give you clues as to who they are and where they are going. At times the three are in sync, fighting the forces of evil, capturing Teddy or maneuvering their ship through outer space; while at other times three separate, yet simultaneous dramas seem to be occurring. Times and events become mixed as the three stop and start the action, breaking the momentum as they rush

This drawing of children at play shows the spontaneous, natural connection of imagination to dramatic action. (Drawing by Michael Rocco Pinciotti)

to get a cookie from the kitchen or change the direction of the drama by adding another object or idea. In time and for no apparent reason, the playing dissolves and the drama is temporarily over.

Experience and Environment Our young space enthusiasts demonstrate the importance of a stimulating environment. Young children's play scenarios revolve around what they know, what they see, hear, and feel — the world at large. Quite often they reenact an entire drama with specific characters, pieces of dialogue, and a sequenced story line taken from a recent movie or even what happened at the breakfast table that morning. Just as often, those images become mixed and recombined throughout their playing: Young Luke's mother tells him he has to eat all his oatmeal before fighting Darth Vader. This mixing, rearranging, and combining is what makes young children's imaginative play amusing and sometimes quite comical, but it also serves a special purpose as a learning strategy useful in problem-solving situations.

The ability to manipulate, rearrange, and combine images in imaginative play keeps it interesting, novel, and reinforcing; it is also at the heart of the creative process. Fluency of ideas and images found in highly dramatic play episodes is connected to creativity, divergent thinking, and problem-solving. It is as if the novelty of new images pulls the drama forward, extending both the children's knowledge and their skills through imagination. The connection between imagination and dramatic action is strengthened through their experience.

Objects play a very important role in the development of dramatic play and provide a link in the connection between imagination and dramatic action. The objects in the room were an initial stimulus for the space journey episode: "Hey, let's use the couch for a spaceship!" or the impetus for continued action through the drama, as the ruler becomes a laser gun, "Quick, we must save Teddy, let's zap them." The younger the children, the more reality-bound they are in terms of using the object. Age and experience increase children's ability to transform their world symbolically: the blanket becomes a cape, the bucket a space helmet.

Initially, children explore the sensory aspect and function of any object within reach. Everything from ants to zippers is touched, tasted, squeezed, and dropped to discover the properties and purposes of the object. Children then play with objects, practicing and rehearsing their use in a reality-oriented way. *Repetition* and *replication* are necessary to ensure the correct usage and to develop the necessary motor skills. A toddler can exhaust even the most patient adults as he or she cajoles them into having tea for the twentieth time.

Exploration, repetition, and replication are essential for the next important step to occur, the *transformation* of an object. This happens when a child changes the object in some way and denotes the imaginative potential of that object: "a spoon becomes a workin' man's hammer." Once a child has crossed this threshhold into imagination, he or she is not bound by the reality of object or, in fact, by reality itself. This is the basis of *as if behavior:* a stick can be used as if it were a sword; a child can act as if he or she were a knight; a group of children can behave as if they were on horses without any props at all. As if behavior is basic to the imagination/action connection in drama and lays the groundwork for all dramatic learning.

The Ideal Adult Playmate The importance to a child of an adult who values this type of learning cannot be stressed enough. Through playful interaction with the child, an adult can demonstrate the special connection between imagination and dramatic action. In this situation the adult might have said, "Let's use these rulers for light/energy swords. Zap! Zap!" The role of a significant adult as a *model* encourages dramatic learning and sets a playful, experimental tone that allows the child to entertain the possible in a safe, nonthreatening environment.

A critical adult can destroy even the most imaginative play. In order to participate or observe play, an adult must not think that what is occurring is silly. The ideal adult playmate must do more than merely humor this play. A knowledgeable adult sees play as what it is: a way to learn vital skills and practice connecting ideas to action.

Play as a Group Action The space venture was not a solo venture; it involved a group of children becoming involved in the playing of a unified, albeit spontaneous and disorganized story line. This group enactment is infinitely more complicated than playing a pretend game alone. First, the social aspect of playing together demands that those involved utilize *metacommunicative signals* that say, "This is play." These signals help the players to establish the pretend nature of the situation as well as to negotiate the plan of action and to define the relationships among the various roles. Second, within play, individual needs must meld into the group. Because of the difficulty of establishing a cohesive group, young children may often sustain play only briefly. Or they engage in parallel play, with each person playing a drama that rarely intersects with any other.

As children develop and have more experiences in playing together, they begin to acquire the cognitive, social, and dramatic skills necessary to become a more unified group. These skills are important for young children to master and attest to the essential nature of dramatic play in the lives of young children. In almost no other situation, except when they are engaged in dramatic play, do they have the opportunity to work in the group imagination/action connection. These experiences help prepare children for the creative drama experience. Whether it be sharing an apartment with college friends, working as a team on a new product, or flying with the crew of the Space Shuttle, the individuals in these situations had their basic training in imagination and group action when they played as young children.

A Theatre Event

Again we ask that you participate in this scenario, this time as members of an audience of a theatre production.

CASE STUDY

A SPECTACULAR ANIMAL WORLD Imagine that you are watching a performance of *Cats*. As the lights dim in the auditorium, they come up on the stage. You are transported to a "giant playground for cats," where felines rule. You have a rare opportunity to know these animals on an intimate level as they share their hopes, dreams, joys, and fears with you. You come to learn, through the poetry of T. S. Eliot and the action onstage, that Gumbie Cat is deeply concerned with the ways of mice, Rum Tum Tugger seems like Mick Jagger, Macavity is never there, and Grizabella is sad and glamorous. The Practical Cats come alive through the magic of theatre: the set transforms the space, the movement and music emphasize the unique personality of each cat, the wonder of the spectacle enchants you. You are spellbound.

Theatre: An Art Form Rehearsed for an Audience Perhaps the most obvious difference between dramatic play and theatre is the addition of the audience. The fact that an audience is going to receive the result of the imagination/action connection gives strong impetus to the entire process. It also colors much of the form—aspects not even considered in the imagination/action of young children at play.

For example, the theatre artist must always consider the effect of the product: Can the audience see and hear? Will these actions communicate these ideas? The audience that attends *Cats* needs to know exactly what's happening: who everyone is and where the action is taking place. Particularly since the story line is so meager, the ensemble must work hard on the total visual effect, just so the audience can be a consistent part of the ongoing action. It's not enough for the actors to feel like cats or for the designers to think they have created a place where cats live; they must make sure they communicate their imaginative ideas through action to the audience. The performers and crew must help the audience enter the illusion and see and experience the world of *Cats*. All involved must agree to "suspend their disbelief" in a shared metaexperience.

The second characteristic of theatre very different from the dramatic

This photo shows the acting ensemble transformed into the cat ensemble for the New York production of *Cats*. This spectacular production is the result of director, designers, and actors working together. (© 1983, Martha Swope)

play of young children is the *rehearsal process*. Rarely if ever in the dramatic play of young children is the same scene replayed, particularly for the purpose of perfecting it. Occasionally, if a scene is especially amusing, it may be redone. Children become "hooked" on a specific object or character or story element, but not on perfecting the integrated, dramatic enactment. Because they don't have the ability to separate themselves from the dramatic play—thus developing their "third eye"—the second rendition is very different from the first.

In theatre the rehearsal process is a key factor in perfecting the imagination/action connection for the audience. During the rehearsal process, not only the actors, but also the director and the designers, work together. Negotiation is essential during this process in order to coordinate and strengthen the imagination/action connection.

The Actor Works on *Cats* Let's look more closely at the individual actor's imagination/action connection. First, the actors in the company have been observing every cat they can and retrieving images of past cats they have met. They are watching cats move, sleep, play, and eat. The actors are all probably imagining what these cats would be like if they could sing and dance to music—imagination images certainly! Also, they are imagining what they themselves would be like if they became cats—also imagination images. If they have been assigned a particular cat to play, they are searching for the perfect model for their performance.

Second, the actors are reading the script of *Cats* and T. S. Eliot's *Old Possum's Book of Practical Cats,* from which the play was adapted. The script (perhaps less so than a "well-made play") provides the actors with clues about the flow of action and the nature of their characters. It is each actor's job to make his or her cat come to life. The actors are all playing the music; each one must learn to master the melodies and keep the sound images of the songs in his or her mind's ear. Much of the cat-looking and script-reading occurs prior to the first rehearsal.

During rehearsals, each actor transforms himself or herself into a cat. The human body is very different from a cat's body. The relationship to and size of legs compared to body, the flexibility of the spine, the presence of the balancing tail—all are part of the challenge of playing a cat. Remember, however, that each actor does not become a cat, just *transforms* him or herself into a cat. Each actor must overlay self with the visual, kinesthetic, aural cat image, work to develop the flexibility and stamina necessary to physicalize the image, and acquire the vocal range necessary to actualize the aural image. This calls into play his or her entire repertoire of dramatic behaviors.

During the performance, each actor must be able to recreate the cat portrayed in rehearsal. He or she must recall these images, yet keep them as fresh as possible. Rehearsal images, combined with past images acquired during the performance of this and other plays, coupled with the actors' well-developed sets of techniques are essential aspects of the imagination/action connection. The scenario represents the ideal connection of imagination and action, because both internal processes and external behaviors are equally well developed.

The Group Development of *Cats* Not only must each actor transform himself or herself into a cat, but each cat must be part of the same theatrical world as all the other cats. Each actor negotiates with other actors, with the help of the director, to demonstrate each cat's wonderful uniqueness (we don't want cats that are too much the same) and their commonalities as cats. The members of the ensemble must portray the same degree of "catness." (If all actors but one are 60 percent cat/40 percent human, that actor who is 20 percent cat/80 percent human will destroy the ensemble effect.) An essential aspect of the imagination/action connection is that actors must learn to negotiate and share their images with other actors.

In *Cats,* the director works hard to create a merged ensemble. Throughout the rehearsal, the company members are encouraged to share experiences and learn from each other. **The group focus during rehearsals helps each actor to develop a set of theatrical images in common with other actors.** These images are the stimuli for their behaviors. Actors must negotiate with other actors, learn give-and-take, and subsume some of their individual desires for the good of the company. In *Cats,* actors are part of an ensemble, yet many have solos during which they are center stage. Perhaps this rotating focus helps the company bcome a cohesive unit.

Anyone who has seen *Cats* will vouch for the fact that the designers had much to do with the creation of the ensemble. The costumes are individual, yet blend together to create a total effect. It is as if the costumer had one giant image of the costumes for *Cats* and constructed each costume as one aspect of the whole image — the spectacular glitz of each costume merges yet remains separate from the glitz of the others. No zippered animal suits are apparent in this production! The sets and lights and props also help achieve a unified effect. **Each of these designers worked closely with the director, so that one total image was put into action.**

The Audience Affects *Cats* The audience is an important component in the theatrical product. All through the rehearsal process, the entire cast and design team have in their single and collective mind's eye the image of the audience-to-be. Even when the theatre is empty, the actors play as if the audience were there. The design team develops the set, costumes, and lights for the members of a future audience.

During the performance, the audience has an immediate impact. The laughter, the audible sighs, the cheers, and the applause, as well as the interchange of electrical energy between actors and audience, affect the production in progress. This strong emotional bond — stored as almost a kinesthetic image — keeps theatre artists "hooked on theatre" and audiences returning to rediscover this experience.

Creative Drama

The imaginative play of the young children and the polished spectacle of Broadway's *Cats* is related to the creative drama experience. This relationship is clear if you understand one very important notion and dispel one other very common misinterpretation of the play/creative drama/theatre continuum:

Creative drama is not merely one point on the continuum between theatre and dramatic play. Rather, all three are inexorably tied to a fourth phenomenon: the connection of imagination and dramatic action. Creative drama shares with theatre and dramatic play several essential characteristics in relation to this imagination/dramatic action connection. Also, creative drama possesses some aspects of the connection that are unique to it.

In the previous two scenarios, we pointed out those aspects of the connection found in dramatic play and in theatre that are also in creative drama. Obviously, these phenomena stand as appropriate models. In the next scenario, we note characteristics that are unique to creative drama. Clarifying both shared and unique characteristics can help you carve out a special niche for creative drama, within a larger perspective.

Let's join in progress a creative drama class as the participants work on the Transformation Activity "Family Album" (page 243).

CASE STUDY

FAMILY ALBUM The entire class of twenty-eight fifth-graders has been divided into four smaller groups of seven members each. As we enter, each group is focused on a different snapshot, which, in each case, is being held by the person whose family is the subject of the photo.

Group Two is already on its feet staging "what happened before" the Palone family photo was taken. This photo, brought in by Stuart, was taken during the Palone family's Fourth of July picnic. In the photo Stuart, his father, his younger sister, and the family dog are standing around the grill. During the discussion part of the planning session, Stuart had described the events leading up to the moment the photo was taken. Stuart and other members of the creative drama group, well-trained in RIM methodology through participation in Starter exercises, base their questions and comments on the details of the actual photo at hand. They also look carefully at the actual props and costumes available to them.

Acting as director, Stuart selects George to play himself; Jack, his father; Carolyn, his mother; Susan, his sister; and Ken, the dog. Bob will play the personified grill and also act as recorder. This group plays the scene prior to the photo, as described by Stuart. They embellish the enactment through recalled conversations and recreated behavior, all pulled from their own family holiday experiences, as stimulated by photo.

Stimulus for Drama In this scenario, the stimulus for the drama was a photograph brought from home by one of the participants. In selecting which photo to bring to drama class, all participants had the opportunity to choose from a variety of possible photos. Once chosen, the photo could be the focus of much personal imagery, even before the drama session began. Encouraging participants to attend to actual objects and photos helps provide these participants with something "to hold onto" in an art form in which there are few craft materials.

A creative drama environment filled with interesting objects helps further the development of the enactment. Recall the importance of such an environment in encouraging the dramatic play of young children. The creative drama environment may even include some of the very same props and objects, but it must be even richer and must contain props that are more theatrical and more complex, such as photos, records, sound tapes, art supplies, and props and costumes from actual productions. Participants may even use these objects in combination with a story to enhance and personalize the drama.

Continued concentration on the real world and on the objects at hand gives participants practice in *observational strategies* that enhances their imagic storehouse. In-class work with actual objects helps participants make the connection between internal and external by encouraging imagery manipulation in tandem with actual experimentation with props and objects. No matter what the initial source, the previous personal and drama experiences of the participants give shape, direction, and specifics to the enactment.

Ideas for Drama Many of the ideas for drama, particularly in early creative drama work, come from sources external to the participants, such as poems, stories, television, and even the curriculum itself. These early activities, based on literature or television, may often seem stereotypic and lifeless. Dramas turn out this way not because the initial material is inappropriate, but rather because the participants are not yet able to utilize personal images in conjunction with the story. **Drama participants need practice and encouragement in order to develop trust in their personal images and to work from their imagination.**

The best ideas, of course, come from the participant's or leader's own storehouse of people or events. This imagic storehouse is a wonderful personal source for creative drama's imagination/action connection. Dreams, fantasies, and situations from daily experience are important sources for drama material. Remember, however, that initially participants may be reluctant or unable to begin with experiences from their own lives. For whatever reasons, they do not draw from their own imaginations. Therefore, begin slowly, keeping the imagination/action goal in mind. The case studies we present in Chapter 11 describe many drama situations that began with an individual's idea or was the result of a group brainstorming session.

The Leader's Role The leader's role is as multifaceted as the adult's function in dramatic play and the director's duty in the theatre process. Each position demands a certain amount of flexibility, a sensitivity to those involved, and an awareness of the final product and the goals of dramatic learning. The creative drama leader must understand both child development and the art form of theatre.

These elements of knowledge and flexibility are evident in the various teaching roles the leader assumes. Early in the creative drama process or in the early stages of a drama unit, the leader acts as a *guide and a model* for the imagination/action connection. Through verbal coaching and physical demonstration, the leader introduces the necessary imagery strategies and the required dramatic behaviors—both part of early dramatic learning. The leader must encourage and support the participants' initial attempts at manipulating and sharing their own images and actions. Dramatic learning occurs in this relaxed, nonthreatening atmosphere, which, of course, provides opportunities and challenges less available in more restrictive situations.

As the participants progress, the leader's role changes in order to further dramatic learning. The leader becomes more of a director by giving specific directions or suggestions, helping the participants coordinate images and actions, and evaluating their work. At this stage the leader must facilitate the participants' transition from generic to personal images, as well as encourage their development of imagination images. Through playful experimentation, the leader continues to help participants polish their skills by providing feedback and suggestions in order to strengthen the connection between imagination and dramatic action. The leader focuses the energy on individuals and the group.

Finally, in advanced creative drama classes, the leader becomes the *master teacher*—the one who knows. The participants, now confident in their abilities to recognize, manipulate, and select exciting imagination images and dramatic actions to communicate their stories, rely on the leader as a wise resource. They depend on the leader to question their artistic choices and to channel their self-evaluation. The leader inspires and challenges their choices, fully aware of the unique capabilities, strengths, and weaknesses of this particular group.

The Artistry of Creative Drama The connection between imagination and dramatic action in creative drama involves many of the same processes that occur in theatre and dramatic play. The initial awareness begins with an *artistic sensitivity* to the world around. This sensitivity, which utilizes all the senses, grows to be a conscious attempt to build a storehouse of vivid, multisensory images. Participants also begin to build a basic theatre vocabulary and the elementary behaviors that allow them "to show" their images.

The creative processes of *fluency, flexibility, and elaboration,* evident in the work of the detective and the artist, allow creative drama participants to play with and manipulate both their images and the simple dramatic actions. Through experimentation, participants explore the wide range of possible connections between imagination and action and begin selecting portrayals appropriate to the group and within their own capabilities. In the scenario "Family Album," each participant had time to experiment with his or her part. They could add their own experiences or imagination images to enrich the character.

Experiences that encourage coordination of imagery and action help develop confidence. This confidence is built on trust of one's own ability to negotiate for the good of the final group product. Through interaction with self and others, participants come to grips with the limits of self, of craft, and of other. They learn to develop an understanding of favorite tasks and preferred strategies. They also become aware of their own artistic tastes and the contributions their experiences make to how they view creative drama.

To draw, you must close your eyes and sing.

Pablo Picasso

The special relationship between imagination and dramatic action develops through experiences such as the one described in "Family Album." Participants learn to negotiate with others — to stand up for what they would like to add to the enactment, but also to acquiesce when convinced by other members of the group. These negotiated decisions reflect participants' collaborative abilities, their developing sense of taste as well as their acknowledgement of the audience-to-be — all essential aspects of the artistry inherent in creative drama.

Concentrating on the Learning Process The primary difference between the creative drama situation and the others described in this chapter is that the creative drama situation, initially at least, is an artificial one. Of course, all of them, except perhaps the young children at play, contain some aspects of artificiality. But the Olympic Athlete, the Super Sleuth, the Creative Artist, and the cast of *Cats* were skilled enough in connecting images to action that they could create within the givens of the situation. They had enough practice with connecting images to action that they could "call forth the muse" whenever necessary. On the other hand, creative drama participants may or may not respond as quickly and as positively in a situation in which time and place were selected by another. They must be nurtured through practice in making "artificial situations" natural, so that they feel comfortable and confident enough to connect ideas to action.

The focus of creative drama must be on dramatic learning. The ultimate objectives of this learning are that participants can use their internal processes, develop their behavioral skills, and connect ideas to action — in as natural a way as they possibly can. The creative drama leader plays an important part in stimulating the development of these abilities. The leader's awareness of the dual focus in dramatic learning is essential. Also important is an understanding of the principles that encourage the connection of imagination to action. Establishing a similar lesson structure from one day to the next, for example, can help get participants in the creative rhythm to build on yesterday's work.

Through the creative drama experience, participants develop continuity in their actions in terms of their ability to work consistently from one day to the next. They build the necessary skills to *hold an image, repeat dramatic actions, and recreate the entire imagination/action connection.* The internal imagery skills that are targeted by various exercises include *sensory scanning, image recall, compressed rehearsal, and third eye,* while the external dramatic behaviors emphasize *movement, dialogue, story, and characterization.* Since the focus of dramatic learning is to enhance this imagination/action connection, participants learn and practice those skills so they develop the ability to recreate various improvisations from one day to the next. Bringing in the same here-and-now objects encourages and enables the participants to recall the imagination/action connection from yesterday and helps them to recall today's work tomorrow.

Dramatic learning parallels learning in general. As each drama behavior and skill becomes internalized and more automatic, creative drama abilities broaden until individuals master dramatic learning. Remember, however, that all drama participants do not come to drama at the same stage of development or level of learning.

Recall for a moment the discussion in Chapter 1 on the differences between development and learning. Creative drama operates in the zone of proximal development. As leader, you can help participants learn and also encourage their development. Focusing on the imagination/action connection, which research suggests can be learned, provides all participants, no matter what stage of development or level of learning, with a clear path to mastering dramatic learning.

THE CONNECTION OF IMAGINATION AND DRAMATIC ACTION

The connection of imagination and dramatic action occurs during the dramatic play of young children, the theatre rehearsal and performance, and the creative drama process. It is, in fact, a series of connections between the internal world of ideas and the external manifestations of behavior. These connections involve more than an oscillation between internal and external. As the oscillation paths between internal and external become deeper, the connections become skills in and of themselves. These skills and procedures represent conscious attempts (either spontaneous or learned) to activate the connection and to bring together knowledge, experience, and behaviors from both internal and external.

Figure 5.1, the third and final illustration of the iii Framework, depicts the connection of imagination and action. Unlike the previous two illustrations, which were entirely theoretical in nature, this one includes information of a more practical nature and suggests objectives and procedures for actual drama practice. Figure 5.1 is meant to act as a bridge between the theoretical material of this chapter and the practical method detailed in the second part of the book.

Note that the illustration is divided into three separate, but interrelated parts. The left-hand part includes objectives of imagery work; the right-hand part behavioral aspects suggested by the theatre model. In the center are those procedures, perspectives, and processes that represent the connection of imagination and dramatic action. Remember, it is this connection that occurs spontaneously in the dramatic play of young children and spontaneously or

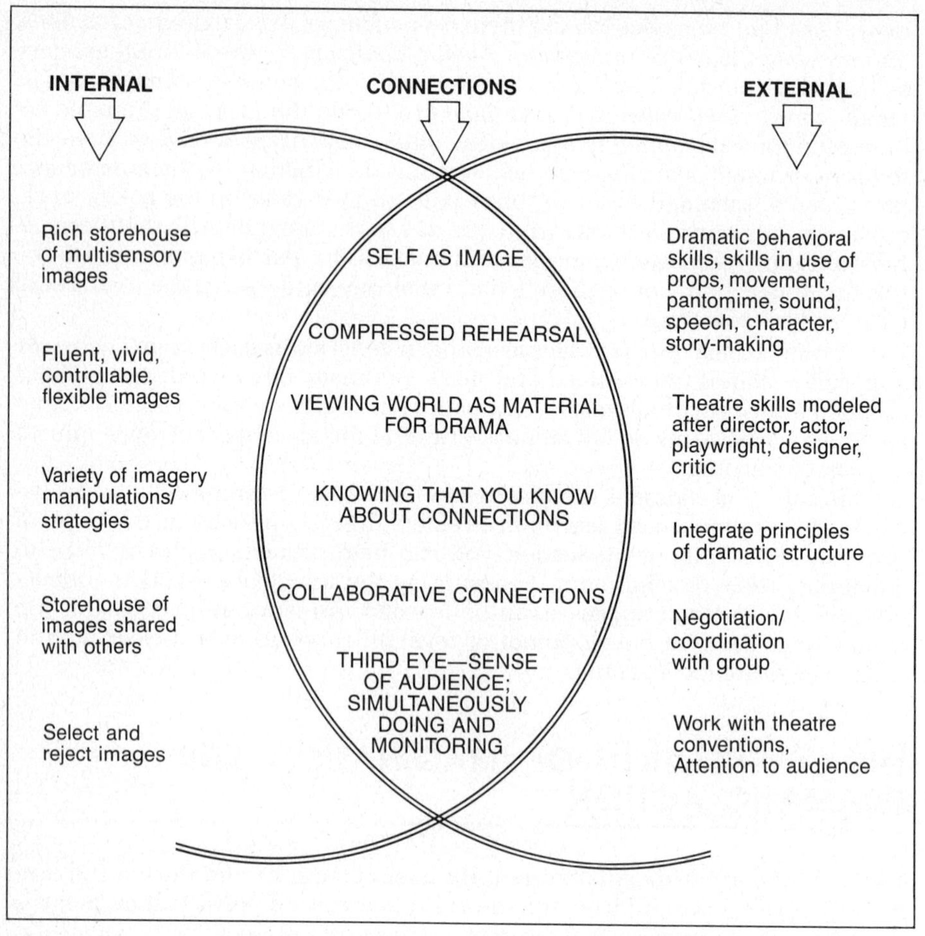

FIGURE 5.6. iii Framework: Connection of Imagination to Action

through training and experience in the work of artists. It is this connection that must be the constant focus of creative drama.

As you study the illustration, note that the internal skills are those internal processes common to many activities, from simple problem-solving jobs to complex art-making tasks. The externals are those behaviors that creative drama shares with theatre, as well as those that focus on group negotiation. The procedures and abilities that appear in the darker area, where the circles overlap, are those that represent the merger of the two. All three aspects—internal, external, and their connection—are equally important:

1. A major goal for internal processes is the development of a rich storehouse of images that are fluent, flexible, vivid, and controllable. Refer back to the information provided in Chapter 3 for suggestions on how to encourage imaging. The resource of bibliographic material on imagery may also contain suggestions. Figure 5.1 depicts simple imagery abilities as well as more sophisticated imagery strategies such as selection/rejection and development of a varied repertoire of imaging strategies. Also important for creative drama are ensemble imagery skills. First, each individual must be able to share his or her

storehouse of images with others in the group. Then, each individual must develop an imagery storehouse he or she has in common with the others in the group.

The leader can never really know precisely what is occurring in the minds of participants. The best way of helping participants develop a rich internal storehouse of images and a variety of useful imagery strategies is to provide an environment rich in objects. Once you know that participants have begun to be active observers of the world, you can introduce the notion of images and provide them with appropriate vocabulary to describe to you and to others what they are experiencing in their mind's eyes. Mind journeys and games in imagery fluency, flexibility, controllability, and elaboration encourage participants' internal development. Research findings in mental imagery lead us to believe that imagery abilities can be learned and improved through training and experience.

2. The behavioral goals are derived from those principles, procedures, and conventions of the theatre, and from information on the group process. What theatre's creators work to accomplish can be models for what the creative drama participant must similarly accomplish. Principles of dramatic structure and theatre conventions give form to dramatic enactments and help establish a framework within which the drama participant can create. Creative drama has a long history of modifying the art form of theatre in developing its own artistic elements and principles. The Rutgers Imagination Method, detailed in the second half of the book, is strongly linked to theatre, as have been all the other drama methods described so far.

The development of a cohesive group — one in which an individual can work in close collaboration with others — is also essential. Your knowledge of group process can help get your group through difficult times. Awareness that individuals test both yours and other's leadership, that rebellion and polarized opinions are common, and that particular group roles as well as drama roles must be filled enhances your function and abilities as a leader. We discuss these group procedures throughout the method as a whole, within the exercises and activities, and most specifically in the introductory material in Chapters 7 and 9.

Providing models for imitation, discussing the structure of dramatic action and theatrical conventions, as well as systematic side coaching, can help participants learn dramatic behaviors. Activities that focus on manageable and learnable skills — pantomime, story-making, characterization — encourage participants in their early attempts at creative drama. Later in the process, participants can combine these basic drama skills into more sophisticated tasks, which often mirror those utilized by director, actor, playwright, designer, or critic.

3. The middle section in Figure 5.1 lists processes that incorporate and integrate aspects of internal and external. The procedures listed facilitate, encourage, and propel forward the connection of imagination and dramatic action. *Compressed rehearsal* is the skill that describes the conscious, internal rehearsal of an external behavior with the intention of perfecting that behavior. If you observe participants in the act of compressed rehearsal, you may see them moving and gesturing in a "compressed" version of the actual task.

Because characterization is an essential aspect of creative drama, the notion of *self as image* encourages participants to overlay internal images of self and the character with personal abilities and necessary traits of the character-to-be. *Third eye skills* encompass simultaneous doing and monitoring and the ability of individuals to see themselves as others see them. Awareness of self and others are precursors to the development of these abilities. These third eye skills are often described as *sense of audience.*

Just as the ensemble nature of creative drama required that participants master group skills and develop a shared storehouse of images, so does this ensemble nature affect the connection of imagination and dramatic action. In one sense, each individual must negotiate with others to resolve personal images and on-going group drama. In another, the participant must similarly resolve the notion of a common imagery storehouse with personal experiences of dramatic behavior. The group connections are intriguing; the complexity of the group connection helps explain the compelling, yet maddening nature of an ensemble performing art.

One exciting result of mastering the connection of ideas and action is the development of *metacognitive skills.* Participants can not only know about the connection but they also begin to know that they know about the connections they make in planning, playing, and evaluating creative drama. Finally, participants begin to demonstrate dramatic sensibility. Perceptual awareness is colored by the knowledge of dramatic structure and conventions and the dramas-to-be. In other words, they begin to view the world as sources for their artistic enactments and consequently shape their observations with dramatic action in mind. When this occurs, the ideas-into-action process has come full circle.

The Importance of Theory

Because the creative drama process is so complex and multidimensional, many leaders become overwhelmed or lose sight of goals and objectives. The iii Framework can provide a tangible handle by isolating key stages and highlighting various processes common to all participants. Figures 3.1 and 3.2 (pp. 64 and 65 respectively) and Figure 5.1 provide a complete picture of how individuals transform imagination into dreamatic action. The three stages shown in Figure 3.1 are experienced by all participants in a creative arts activity. Image, imaging, imagination, viewed cyclically, can assist you in the development of daily, weekly, and unit objectives. An understanding of the internal/external oscillation, pictured in Figure 3.2, can help you attend to what is happening inside the participants as well as what is shown through behavior: the relationship between imagination and action. The oscillation depicted in Figure 3.2 of the iii Framework has colored the development of all creative drama methods and RIM in particular. In Figure 5.1, which teases out aspects of the connection of imagination to dramatic action, goals and procedures are highlighted. These are unique to the Rutgers Imagination Method.

The Theory Is Not Enough

These three illustrations can provide you with a strong theoretical grounding for work in creative drama. They suggest (but in no way detail) the requisite day-to-day activities. The actual activities, presented by a well-trained leader, are what stimulate internal process and external behavior, and also facilitate their connection. What is learned daily contributes to dramatic learning on a cumulative basis. Participants need time to develop these skills and behaviors. The notion of connecting ideas to action must permeate the curriculum, but must be taught step-by-step.

> ***The problems of the world cannot possibly be solved by skeptics or cynics whose horizons are limited by the obvious realities. We need men who can dream of things that never were.***
>
> John F. Kennedy

In order to operationalize this theory, particularly in a creative drama environment, it is necessary to develop daily activities that are part of a long-term plan. This plan can assist those participants who are naturals in developing more sophisticated imagination/action connections, and stimulate those who have not had opportunities or instinctual abilities. These activities must combine a variety of disciplines, yet be consistent with developmental theory. The art form of theatre, the field of mental imagery, and the unique nature of creative drama must merge daily in a special way. In other words, the theory is put into practice through a method.

THE RUTGERS IMAGINATION METHOD

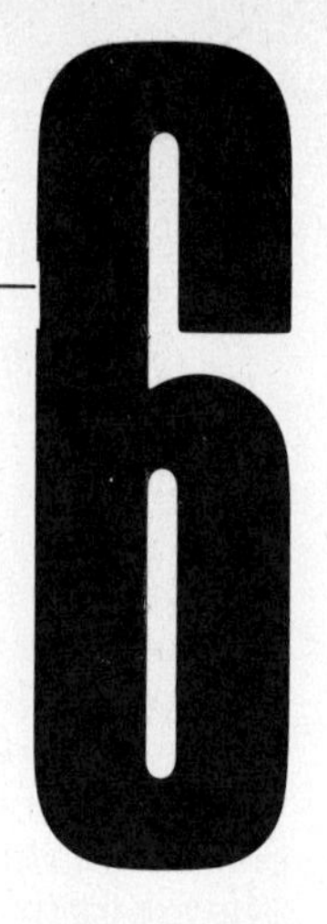

Now you're ready to begin doing drama. Picture yourself standing at the door looking in on a room of more than twenty eight-year olds. Even armed with all the knowledge we have just presented, you probably feel almost as frightened as you did when you first entertained the notion of becoming a creative drama leader. It certainly is important to think about drama, but you must also be aware of how to do drama. As the image of you standing in front of these children becomes clearer and more real to you (you see, you are becoming good at imagination!) a number of questions have popped into your head. In fact, the questions are so immediate that you are unable to believe that you never asked them of yourself before.

"What do I do first?"

"How can I tell if they are learning anything?"

"What activities should work for this age group?"

You might even ask, "Why did I even think I could do this?"

All but the last of these questions are typical and useful.

It's clear that even if you know everything about theory, you still must have an approach — a way that assists you and helps tie together all the theory and connects it to what you are going to be doing — toward leading groups of creative drama participants in a way that is exciting for you and for them. Dividing creative drama into a series of skills can also help you assess what is happening and, therefore, enable you to say with confidence that the participants are learning something!

Following is a developmental method based on the material in the first half of the book. Called the *Rutgers Imagination Method,* it can be the core of your evolving personal approach to creative drama. If you are a novice, you can follow the method with diligence. RIM helps build your skills as a leader as you work through each level. After you have mastered the approach, you will probably add your very own special signature. In fact, that is one of the ultimate goals of this book — to allow you to explore your own world and interests within the creative drama arena. If you are an experienced leader, you can pick and choose from the following exercises. What is more important for you is to analyze the ways in which these exercises and activities have evolved from the theories presented in the first half of the book, as well as to overlay these activities with your own needs and knowledge of children and the drama process.

THE RUTGERS IMAGINATION METHOD

The Rutgers Imagination Method (RIM) is a three-part creative drama approach that focuses on the development of imagination and dramatic behavior, as well as on the connection between the two. RIM was developed from the fields of theatre and mental imagery. RIM activities work toward participants' mastery of specific dramatic behavior and on acquainting participants with a whole repertoire of imagery acquisition and manipulation strategies. RIM stimulates the connection between the two and encourages participants to explore their own ideas, view the world dramatically, organize together with others, and express what's important to them. This approach helps participants master dramatic learning. RIM also gives you, the leader, the confidence to explore your own ideas and images in the drama arena, as you develop leader skills based on a well-organized method.

RIM is much like many other creative drama approaches (particularly those described in Chapter 2). It shares the following characteristics with other approaches:

- Participants plan, play, and evaluate. Although they often merely play in early creative drama exercises, participants (with the help of a good leader) learn to plan and evaluate their dramas as well. The processes of imagine, enact, and reflect are keys to all creative drama, whatever the approach.
- Both the drama process and the resulting product are equal and important aspects of creative drama. Because process and product occur simultaneously, the process/product dichotomy is often difficult to spot. The importance of both, as well as their interrelationship, is an essential characteristic of creative drama.
- Unlike other arts, such as painting or playing the piano, which require paper and paints or music and an instrument, the tools of creative drama are the participant's body, voice, and mind. All other materials, such as props or costumes or set pieces, are merely accoutrements. Creative drama demands that the participant work with self and others; each person contributes himself or herself as the material and instrument of the drama.
- All creative drama approaches are organized in a systematic way—building block, circular, or any other manner that suggests a structure. Structure helps the leader develop an overall curriculum plan and assess progress. Organization is the backbone for dramatic learning. Without a structure, no leader could replicate another's methods; creative drama would be a hodgepodge, based on the leader's whim of the day.

RIM is also different from many of the popular methods in its particular focus:

- **The material for activities comes primarily from the personal imagic storehouse of its participants and/or requires participants to personalize more traditional material.** Its strong relationship to the current life and past experiences of its participants helps make RIM applicable to a wide variety of participants.
- **Here-and-now objects, photos, and drawings are essential to the conduct of RIM, particularly in early experiences.** Locating and bringing in these objects may seem a difficult and unnecessary task, but actually experiencing the present object is a vital aspect of this approach.

Moving in very close to observe an object allows a small, but detailed area to fill the viewer's consciousness. (Photos by James Williams)

The foundation provided by the immediate sensory experience of these objects assists participants in all future dramatic learning.

- **The ultimate goal of creative drama exceeds story drama.** Story drama, a classic activity, remains part of RIM, but is only a part of the second level of activities. The final goal of creative drama is the development of uniquely wrought, well-conceptualized enactments, based on ideas and images suggested by even the youngest participant.
- **RIM offers its participants perspectives other than the acting point of view.** The roles of playwright, designer, critic, and director provide models for exploration. Participants who have skills in areas other than acting are made to feel valuable and important in RIM activities. RIM is broadly developed in this manner to give more "talents" the spotlight and to encourage each group member to make a special contribution to the creative drama experience.
- **RIM has been tested in a variety of situations and with a variety of populations.** Testing provided invaluable information on the activities themselves, on the format of each activity, and on the scope of the method as a whole. We can say with confidence that this is neither an armchair creative drama method nor a method so peculiar to one leader's style that it cannot be utilized by anyone else. Nevertheless, the ultimate goal of the leader should be to develop personal, unique activities modeled on the ones included in this book.
- **Internal processes, external behaviors, as well as the connections between them are a consistent focus of the activities.** Participants work to develop imagination images and dramatic behavior skills, and to realize and explore the connections between the two. Remember, research suggests that the connection of ideas to action is the single most important skill mastered through creative drama.

As you are about to embark on your first "lesson" with second-graders, you are aware, of course, that every drama skill and imagery strategy cannot be introduced at once. You know that skills should be presented in an orderly way and all activities should be grouped. In accordance with these systematic requirements, RIM is divided into three parts so that each level focuses on the particular skills and strategies. Each of the three parts reflects the experience and development of its participants. These activities reflect the changing needs of the participants as they learn to use their imaginations and express themselves dramatically.

The first level of RIM is titled *Starters.* In Starters, participants begin to explore their own world of images and their own ability to do drama. RIM Starters teach theatre vocabulary and present participants with simple dramatic exercises in such basic areas as movement, design, and speech. Each category contains a variety of very different exercises — so you can meet the needs of many groups, as well as cover all necessary aspects of each basic skill.

The action in Starters involves much parallel playing and whole group work so as not to put any individual participant in jeopardy. Dramatic behavior objectives and imagery objectives are often quite separate; the connection comes later. Your goal here involves *fluency* — numbers of images and numbers of attempts at various activities. By the end of Starters, participants know the basics of drama and feel at ease with expressing themselves in this way.

The second level, called *Transformations,* provides the participants with opportunities to coordinate and integrate their skills and behaviors, as well as to communicate their images to the whole group. In Transformations, your job as leader is to encourage participants to connect imagery and behavior and to transform their ideas into actions. The source for materials is personal experience, as well as media, literature, and current events. All the world and each individual can be the subject of a whole drama. Participants learn that their perspectives are unique and valuable to the total dramatic improvisation.

Many of the activities in Transformations are modeled after theatre-making activities. Classics from acting, design, and playwriting have been modified to become part of RIM and have been tailored to enhance the conceptualization of dramatic learning. The important creative processes mastered in Transformations are *selection/rejection, elaboration,* and *flexibility*—the ability to try out a number of ideas within a variety of categories. As leader, you must be the model of what you want your participants to be.

The final level is titled *Mastery*. Unlike the other two levels, which are presented through a series of exercises and activities, we present Mastery in a case study format. In other words, we have documented a number of successful drama improvisations that feature a variety of ages and levels of experience. What these case studies have in common is that one unifying idea or core image sparked each drama and shaped each final product. Each case study represents an ideal integration of dramatic behaviors, internal processes, individual needs, and group goal. Again, as in the previous chapters, we utilize the "You Are There" mode to give you as personal and analytic a view as is possible of the often mysterious forces of artistic creation.

STARTERS

In Great Britain, appetizers before a meal are called "starters." They whet the appetite, give a hint of what is to come, and set the mood for the rest of the meal. The RIM Starters work the same way, stimulating the participants' senses and whetting their appetite for drama. It's easy to think you can skip these exercises because they seem so simple and your participants accomplish them so successfully. Without knowledge and experience in these basic skills, however, participants may ultimately fall back on stereotypic behavior and habituated choices in later activities. So remember, take time now with RIM Starters; they are the "piano scales" of creative drama.

RIM Starters acquaint participants with *drama/theatre skills* and *imagery strategies*. By experiencing the wide variety of exercises contained in Starters, participants develop basic drama/theatre and imagery skills that form the foundation of future work. The overall drama/theatre objectives include the following:

- Observation.
- Vocal and language production.
- Physicalization.
- Characterization.
- Cooperation.

Participants also explore their past experiences (recorded as images), experience and record new here-and-now objects, and play with all these images.

Starters include several overall imagery objectives:

- To experience multisensory images.
- To retrieve images.
- To manipulate images.

Participants also learn the vocabulary of theatre and imagery, so that they can begin to communicate their experiences and intentions to others.

Many exercises found in RIM Starters are similar to introductory activities in other creative drama approaches. One consistent and unique feature of RIM Starters is the constant *dual focus*. Participants learn to focus both internally and externally. You must urge participants not merely to act (without any conscious thought) or merely to plan (without ever doing drama), but to do both and to do both together. Starters introduce the concept that past experiences and current tasks are connected: what's happening inside may be communicated through word and action.

Sometimes, however, in RIM Starters participants can image what they would like to do, but have not acquired enough theatre/craft skills to realize the dramatic enacment. Often participants find their inability to connect ideas to action extremely frustrating. Assure participants that later experiences (particularly in the second level of activities, called Transformations) will provide them with more information on and experience with the dynamic relationship of imagery and action.

Another important aspect of Starters is the *introductory exercises* found in each of the categories of activities. These observation, relaxation, and guided imagery exercises are essential to the later success of RIM as a whole. To the novice, it may seem counterproductive to encourage a relaxed, contemplative mood; creative drama seems such a lively, active endeavor. Research in mental imagery, however, has shown the positive benefits of a relaxed state. Getting in touch with one's own breathing is a good beginning and helps ease participants' transition from the daily stresses so that they may begin drama from a position of calm strength, not frenetic action. So, Starters are quiet and slow starting, but they are foundation building—giving participants a solid base on which to build all their current and future dramatic learning.

All of us collect fortunes when we are children—a fortune of colors, of lights and darkness, of movements, of tensions. Some of us have the fantastic chance to go back to see his fortune when grown up.

Ingmar Bergman

Starters utilize a great many sensory stimuli in the form of here-and-now objects, photographs, pictures, and sounds. The use of the real object or actual sound is important in early work. Participants utilize all their senses to experience the object; through such experiences, participants deepen and expand their abilities to perceive the world and to become aware of its artistic potential. Participants also learn to look for sensory qualities in their remembered images and to make connections between the object and the image of that object in the mind's eye. Starters depend almost totally on *memory images,* although some imagination images will be the source for participants already comfortable with imagery, or for participants who grasp the imagery activities easily. Participants begin to look at the world dramatically, in other words, to

For many people, sight is their primary sense and visual images make up the greatest part of their imagery storehouse. By imaging the eye as an independent agent on a "see" journey, many people have permitted themselves to view the world in a novel way. (Odilon Redon, *The Eye Like a Strange Balloon Mounts Toward Infinity,* Collection, The Museum of Modern Art, New York. Gift of Larry Aldrich)

develop a *dramatic sensitivity.* The current world and their past experiences are the focus. Later on, this world and their lives becomes the obvious choice for material for drama.

In fact, each Starter requires participants to modify only one aspect of the here-and-now. For example, if the Starter requires that the drama space become a grocery store, participants can and usually do remain themselves working or shopping in that store. If the exercise requires that participants change character, usually they become that character, but do not focus on modifying the place. So, for example, participants all may become animals or work on animal behavior, but rarely attend to changing the classroom into a zoo. In Starters, participants focus on only one imaginary aspect at a time. (Of course, a particularly facile individual may be able to utilize more complex imagery strategies. If the individual is not disruptive, allow him or her to continue.) Only after most participants have had many Starter experiences can they begin to combine these skills to form the elaborate characters and complex dramas introduced in the next stage of RIM, Transformations.

Categories of RIM Starters

RIM Starter exercises are divided into seven categories:

- Introduction/Transitions
- Object/Prop
- Movement/Pantomime
- Sound/Speech
- Person/Character
- Sequence/Story
- Design/Environment

Each category focuses on specific drama behaviors and imagery skills, but is organized from the standpoint of drama. Every category but Introduction/Transitions is self-contained; exercises move from simple to more difficult. Introduction/Transitions are not grouped together, but are interspersed throughout the other six drama skill categories.

Introduction/Transition exercises are, as the name suggests, included at the beginning of every new category in Starters. Three basic types of exercises are in this category: *Relaxation, Sensory Awareness and Observation, and Guided Fantasy.* All of these Introduction/Transitions are warm-ups that help participants relax in mind and body, focus on the extensive information available in the here-and-now, and explore their own inner worlds.

The exercises in the Starter drama skill category of **Object/Prop** utilize here-and-now objects as the main stimulus for the exercises. Initially, participants observe and manipulate these props and objects. Your job is to encourage participants to adopt an open and playful attitude toward these objects and to try to think of as many possible ways to use them. These objects are the core of a variety of different kinds of exercises. Often, exercises require that the participants abstract one aspect of an object and then categorize that image. Finally, props begin to be used as one essential element of a simple dramatic improvisation.

The category of **Movement/Pantomime** focuses on the physical development of the participant. This category contains two very different types of exercises, many of them derived from the creative movement field. These exercises focus on physicalization without narrative or character aspects and/or experimentation with the elements of dance — body, space, force, and time. Inanimate objects and photos are often the stimulus for these activities. Pantomime exercises, on the other hand, deal with action without words. This "show-me" physicalization is the mainstay of movement in many older, traditional drama approaches. Imitation and duplication are essential types of pantomime activities within RIM Starters. As leader, you often act as model to be imitated.

Sound/Speech exercises initially focus on simple imitation and duplication of sounds and rhythms. Hearing, listening, and repeating are the basis for early Sound/Speech activities. Imitating, recreating, and discerning patterns are also important skills mastered early in this category of Starters. These exercises are followed by ones in which here-and-now sounds help participants to retrieve previously heard sounds, as well as to create sound intonations. We also include exercises in which participants begin to assign connotations to here-and-now sounds and sound images. Finally, speech-making grows into the skill of dialogue-building and sharing—important aspects of communication.

Person/Character also begins with imitation and duplication. Photos, drawings, and here-and-now objects are the essential initial stimulus. Participants focus on detailed images of people from both recent and distant past. More advanced person/character exercises encourage participants to focus on self, so that they may begin to *overlay self as character*. In other words, participants begin to see themselves in their minds' eye as the character. They also begin to differentiate among characters and between themselves and the character. Ultimately, this overlay of self as image will be the stimulus for sophisticated behavior in Transformations.

Sequencing/Story exercises are one of the least physically active of the RIM Starters. Many of these exercises could be viewed as the precursors to playwrighting. Such concepts as cause and effect; beginning, middle, and end; and climax are explored in Sequencing/Story. Patterns, repetitions, and ordering are important considerations in this category. Participants manipulate photos and drawings and begin to experiment with story-telling skills.

Design/Environment may be the set of exercises usually not included in a drama method. We have included visual art-making exercises because of design's importance as one component of dramatic learning. Perceiving the world in an aesthetic manner and manipulating visual elements to achieve personal aesthetic satisfaction are essential skills for the developing creative artist. Design/Environment exercises focus on experiencing color, size, balance, and shape, through matching, modifying, and changing the aspects of the visual picture. Participants also work on creating a space, as they begin to understand that drama happens in a space. This realization coupled with their developing visual arts skills helps participants work on the idea that dramas are three-dimensional. In many of these exercises, you as leader give directions, then participants work, then you evaluate. This atypical organization is the beginning of the usual plan, play, evaluate organization usually found in RIM Transformations.

TRANSFORMATIONS

Transformations activities are so titled because of the extensive changes they give rise to. *Transform* means to change in form, substance, or appearance: nature transforms a caterpillar into a butterfly; water into ice. The word *transformation* also describes more artistic and seemingly less systematic and inevitable changes: a drama neophyte is transformed into a full-fledged member of a creative drama group; life events are transformed into episodes to be enacted. Extensive, various, and almost magical transformations occur at this level of RIM.

Many new imagery skills and dramatic behaviors are introduced to participants through Transformations. Although these two aspects — the internal and external — are consistent dualities within RIM, activities at this level encourage the *connection* of ideas to action as well. In fact, this connection is so important that objectives for these activities focus on the merging, which is actualized in each Transformation activity.

Imagination images are the primary source for these activities. Memory images are the mainstay of Starters, with only some participants building behavior on imagination images. The very nature of the activities in Transformations encourages the production of imagination images, the kinds of images that research suggests are the more vivid and flexible. Going to the moon, living in medieval times — actions such as these — help participants develop imagination images. These images are the source of new discoveries and inventions, as well as creative works of art. The use of imagination images as the stimulus for dramatic behavior can open up the actual and imagined world as sources for drama-making.

The repertoire of creative processes increases. Fluency is a key process for Starters. Transformations require participants to utilize such additional creative processes as *flexibility, elaboration, selection,* and *rejection* — all essential for success in the problem-solving tasks found in the activities. Within creative drama, flexibility describes the abilities to generate images and actions in a variety of categories and from a variety of perspectives, as well as to connect ideas to action in a variety of different ways. Elaboration describes the ability to complete the execution of idea-into-action tasks with an eye for detail. Selection and rejection imply the ability to let go of an idea after realizing that it doesn't work or because it doesn't gel with the ideas of the rest of the group.

> ***The act of imagination is a magical one. It is an incantation destined to produce the object of one's thought, the thing one desires, in a manner that one can take possession of it.***
>
> John Paul Sartre

Participants experience an expanded view of *theatrical role models.* Activities in Transformations encourage participants to emulate the function of artists other than the actor. Participants have the opportunity to experiment with the roles of director, designer, playwright, and critic. By offering this expanded perspective, we hope to reach participants who may not be performers, but who, nevertheless, can make an important contribution to the group enactment.

Participants also experience a deepening view of theatre. By working on the five categories of activities, participants learn about the various "transformations" that frame the overall dramatic product. Activities in these five categories have been constructed to assist participants in experiencing a variety of modes for transforming life into art.

Theatrical conventions, principles of dramatic structure, and *other "rules of the theatre game"* help shape the creative drama enactment. As you learned in Chapter 4, the parent art of theatre has donated many of its conventions and principles to the art form of creative drama. It is at this stage of RIM that these principles and conventions are introduced. Since Transformations focus on "doing drama," participants need to know what it is that they are doing. Activities at this level systematically provide the necessary information that

George Seurat's *Sunday Afternoon on the Island of La Grande Jatte* represents both the result of an artist's work and a stimulus for future art-making. Almost one hundred years after Seurat transformed his surroundings into this serene painting, Stephen Sondheim and James Lapine further transformed art into new art in the theatre piece *Sunday in the Park with George.* (Courtesy of the Art Institute of Chicago)

shapes the drama-in-progress. Also added in Transformations is the concept of *audience,* another key element provided by the theatre model.

Participants are presented with procedures that incorporate the internal and external, by focusing on the connection of images to action. Three of the major procedures are compressed rehearsal, self as image, and third eye. *Compressed rehearsal* describes just that—a minirehearsal of a behavior or scene in the mind's eye. What is so fascinating about this procedure is that research shows that as many physical and mental benefits can accrue from compressed rehearsal as from the actual action. *Self as image* describes the primary internal process of being able to view oneself as a character accomplishing a task. *Third eye* ability is the ability simultaneously to participate in an action and monitor that action. All three procedures are presented and explored in many Transformation activities.

The *ensemble nature* of drama is an essential characteristic of Transformations. Transformation activities encourage uniquely different individuals to become a merged ensemble without losing the individuality of each participant. Each category of activities has as a major objective the development of a collective: a collective place, a collective plot, a collective spectacle.

Categories of Transformations

Transformations are divided into five categories:

- Self as Character
- Events/Stories into Plots

- Place Becomes Setting
- Adding Conflict
- Creating Spectacle

Unlike Starters, Transformation categories do not divide activities into segments of equal weight. Of major importance are Self as Character, Place Becomes Setting, and Events/Stories into Plots. The activities in these three categories focus on essential Transformation skills and deal with the connection of ideas to action. The other two categories, Adding Conflict and Creating Spectacle, present activities that may be self-contained, but also may be used in conjunction with activities within the other three categories.

Self as Character Self as Character activities focus on individual development of character. Within Self as Character, participants alone, in pairs, or in a group, deal with the internal and external aspects of a dramatic character. No longer is a mere stab at characterization acceptable; character work encompasses consistency, desirability, appropriateness of character movement and gesture, and motivation. Participants expand their experience in vocalization, verbalization, and physicalization to include talking and listening, working with others in character, and relating in character to situation. Much work occurs in pairs. In Self as Character, a major focus is connecting imaginative character images to character behaviors.

Self as Character activities build on Starter exercises in the categories of Person/Character, Objects/Prop, Movement/Pantomime, and Sound/Speech. Participants elaborate on and combine all the drama behavior skills mastered in Starters. They also continue developing such imagery strategies as self as image and manipulating and combining both memory and imagination images. The major question participants ask themselves is, "What if I were someone else?"

Events/Stories into Plots The focus in this category is on telling, communicating, and dramatizing stories. In Transformations, participants see how their own lives, as well as stories from literature, become the material for a dramatized enactment. This category is filled with traditional story dramatization of fables, legends, and fairy tales. Added to this traditional drama material are enactments of personal life events, as well as individual's dreams. Other sources include plots from television and movies and journalists' accounts from newspapers. We even include enactments from sensational tabloids to entice adolescent participants.

Exercises from Starters in the categories of Sequence, Object/Prop, and Sound/Speech are the precursors of Transformations activities. In Transformations, participants explore skills used by many creative artists, including playwrights. *Beginning, middle,* and *end; closure* and *climax* are some of the new ideas. Also important in this category is *negotiating with others.* The individual is less important than the story as a whole, as individuals learn to select aspects of many different experiences, combine them, add imagination details, and then utilize these imagination experiences as the plot of the improvisation. In no uncertain terms, participants begin to see life transformed into art.

Place Becomes Setting The overall objective of activities in this category is making the drama room into a dramatic setting. The focus is not people or events, but totality of environment. Participants must show the observer not only who they are but also where they are, through both action and words.

Settings may be actual places seen by participants, such as beach or grocery store, or fantastical places based on imagination images. Activities in this category introduce the theatrical concepts of *mood, time, period,* and *consistency of place.* Through subtlety of action, participants suggest the three dimensions of setting: time, place, and design.

What is essential also is consistency of setting within the group. In order to have a unified setting, everyone must be in the same place. Implicit are discussion among participants and collective decision-making. Design/Environment, Object/Prop, and Movement/Pantomime from Starters are the participants' first experiments with place. Their sensitivity to place expands as they make selective decisions, merge past images with the here-and-now, and focus on communicating to the audience/observers.

The role of critic is a new concept introduced in these activities. Place Becomes Setting encourages artistic awareness of environment and provides experiences in selecting and rejecting theatrical elements, as well as elaborating detail. Observers, too, begin to make evaluations about setting based on the comparison of here-and-now setting with their own memory images of real places or with their imagination images of fantastical ones.

Adding Conflict Activities in Adding Conflict are of two different types: ones which can be utilized as separate activities and ones which are added to the activities presented in the three previous Transformation categories. Both of these types of activities, however, focus on conflict. Through experiences with activities in this category, participants begin to explore motivation and variations of conflict, constructing scenes that focus on the source, the building, and the resolution of various conflicts. Activities assist participants in learning how to add tension to propel the drama forward.

Conflict is not really a part of the Starter experience, although the skills learned in Sequence/Story, Person/Character, Movement/Pantomime, and Sound/Speech provide a good skill base for these Transformations. The real conflicts, which participants experience in everyday life, and the fictional ones, read about or viewed in movies or television, are the personal sources for the activities.

Many drama leaders fail to realize the importance of conflict and try to discourage its addition to creative drama enactments. These leaders are doing their participants a terrible disservice. As you learned in Chapter 1, the dramatic play in even the youngest child is full of conflict and resolution. In fact, as dramatic learning is mastered, people more readily resolve conflicts on their own, without the assistance of parents or teachers. As you learned in Chapter 4, the very essence of drama is conflict; the purging effect of drama occurs through resolution of this conflict. These Transformation activities give participants knowledge, which is critical to sophisticated dramatic learning, as well as provide insight into the life experience.

Creating Spectacle Creating Spectacle focuses on activities related to theatre design. Participants work on designing and constructing *costumes, make-up, sets, props,* and *lights.* Activities are self-contained, but can be used in conjunction with those from the other categories of Transformations. Also included in this category are activities in which participants add music and dance to the evolving theatre spectacle. Participants learn to consider the total theatre effect. They also experiment with a variety of stage spaces in terms of the performer/observer configuration.

Design/Environment, Object/Prop, Person/Character, and Sound/

Speech from Starters are the basis for these activities. Participants attend to detail and elaborate on their images in their minds' eye. In this category, you can help participants see the connections between the design element in creative drama and the design aspect of theatre. Several of these activities focus, in fact, on theatre-going and the development of their skills as audience members. Experiences in Creating Spectacle complete participants' knowledge of all aspects of creative drama.

MASTERY RIM

Mastery RIM, the third and final level, as its name suggests, focuses on the most complex level of creative drama activities. At this stage, groups become very different from one another. Each participant and each group masters the skills in a way that reflects past experiences, unique perspectives, and prior and current training. Consequently, we cannot present a series of categorized exercises such as those found in Starters or Transformations; Mastery RIM cannot be classified in a precise manner. What we have done instead is to consider the characteristics that warrant classifying participants on this level as "masters of creative drama." Then, we describe a variety of successful lessons that represent the vast diversity of Mastery. This method of reporting and describing individual cases, called the *case study format,* is not uncommon in reporting research in the field of theatre and education and seems a potentially valuable method for creative drama.

In the other two levels of RIM, groups were more like each other; and participants created in ways similar to others of their age and experience. At Mastery RIM, the sky's the limit! Drama work at this level takes on unique characteristics and develops in an infinite number of directions, mirroring the dramatic skills and imaginative ideas of its participants, as well as reflecting some ideal connections of imagination and action. At this stage of RIM, you and your participants are becoming true artists in the manner suggested by the theatre model, yet reflecting the unique aspects of creative drama as well.

In Mastery RIM, participants begin to develop dramas that integrate the dramatic learning stimulated by Starters and Transformations. The various imagery processes, the variety of potential theatre models, theatre conventions, plus the potential of creative drama—all become integrated as part of participants' repertoire. Participants and group begin to pull together their diverse ways of knowing and their personal experiences, in a unique manner. Participants are eager and able to work with personal memory and imagination images that are vivid and controllable, to communicate with one another, and to negotiate for the good of the drama. What is occurring at Mastery RIM are the *cyclic, oscillation,* and *connection aspects of the iii Framework*. What we present are various situations; the sum of each is an ideal and unique portrayal of the iii Framework.

Characteristics of Mastery

Before the idea of ideal creativity frightens you, we must assure you that when your group reaches Mastery Level RIM, the sublime nature of their work will be obvious to you. Be assured also that not every group reaches Mastery, particularly if you as leader see them only once a week for only ten weeks.

Your knowledge of the following characteristics can acquaint you with what occurs during Mastery:

- Knowledge of Theatre as Art and Craft
- Group Dynamic
- Metacognitive Ability
- Originality — the Ultimate Creative Process
- Strong Thematic Image at the Core Knowledge of Theatre as Art and Craft

Knowledge of Theatre as Art and Craft Each individual within a Mastery group has a command of the many elements of theatre, appropriate, of course, to his or her developmental level. The group member can draw from a repertoire of basic Starter skills or more advanced Transformational abilities, as necessary. The core image, the on-going drama, another group member, as well as past experiences provide all the stimulation necessary. The well-integrated body of craft skills, seen in Mastery participants, can be likened to those at the disposal of the improvisational theatre-ensemble member.

As well as demonstrating command of creative drama as craft, Mastery participants enact dramas that show their knowledge of creative drama as art. They know that drama can be a way to communicate experiences — real or imagined — with others and for others. The magical quality of drama, often experienced by drama novices, lost for a time in Transformation work, returns again in Mastery dramas. The craft underpinnings, often the full focus in Transformations, are part of an integrated whole that represents an advanced level of dramatic learning.

Group Dynamic The most apparent characteristic of a Mastery group is that the group can be called a "collective ensemble." This group must work together in a way that emulates the ideal theatre ensemble. First, this group must demonstrate *cooperation,* working in a state of mutual support. Second, the group must show *coordination of images, action, and their connection* — all synchronized to provide common benefits. Third, the individuals must mold what they do and how they do it, and even how they think about putting ideas into action into a unified *collaborative* process, shared by each member.

Also, as you observe the group during planning and even during improvised enactments, you are able to see how ideas and actions come from one person, are joined by another, and refined by still a third. You can almost feel the electricity, as the creative problem is solved right before your eyes. This type of collaborative structure can be classified as decentralized; ideas don't have to go through a pivotal person (the adult leader or even the class leader), but flow freely among members.

Another interesting characteristic of the Mastery group is that all communication roles are filled. By this, we don't mean director, actor, or playwright, or even character roles in the on-going enactment. Instead we describe the roles that research in communication theory suggests must be filled in order to accomplish a group task successfully. A Mastery group of from five to seven members must contain *an idea person, an idea coordinator, an implementer, a critic, a team builder, an inspector,* and *an external contact*. One member may take more than one communication role; all, however, must be filled. The detailed discussion in Chapter 11 provides more information on communication roles, and how you can recognize and stimulate them.

Metacognitive Ability Participants in Mastery creative drama not only develop enactments that are well integrated and often original, but also know

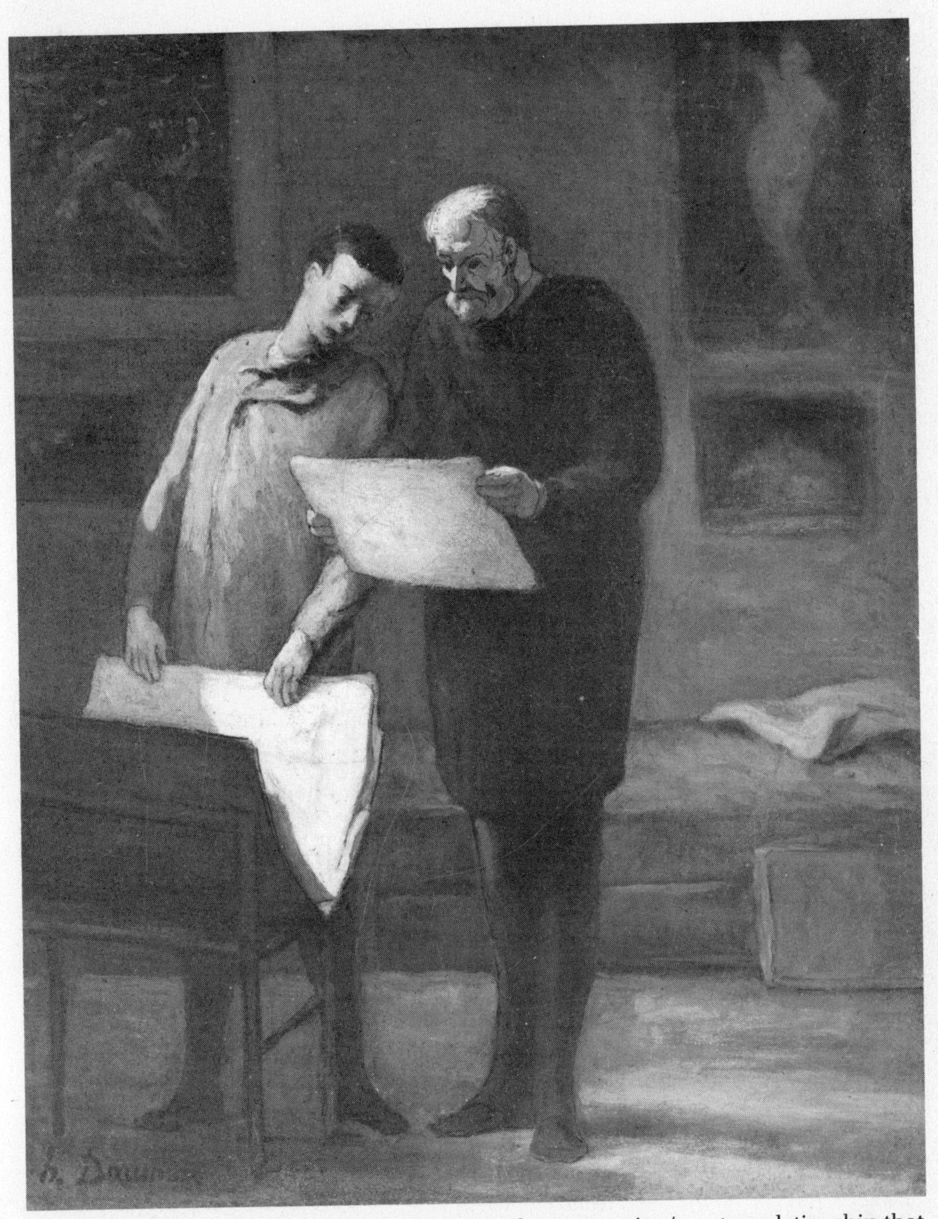

Daumier's *Advice to a Young Artist* illustrates the apprentice/master relationship that has existed in all the arts since medieval times. (National Gallery of Art, Washington, D.C., Gift of Duncan Phillips)

how to think about doing drama. Their enactments benefit, because participants are able to think about creative drama and know themselves and others within the creative drama arena. They possess *metacognition,* a way of thinking about knowledge and thinking. Metacognition in creative drama is that segment of a participant's stored dramatic learning that deals with knowledge of or belief about what factors or variables act and interact in what ways to effect the course and outcome of the process/product.

As participants experience Starters and Transformations, they learn about themselves and others in their group, and what actions and strategies work in what situations. By the time they reach Mastery, individuals are able to develop dramas with an understanding and integration of this stored information. The kind of trust in and knowledge of one's ability to put imagination in action is fostered through continued participation in drama activities. This unique form of knowing — metacognition — makes creative drama more than a mere curriculum frill. It is, in fact, an integral part of each child's learning and development.

A balance must be established between these two worlds — the one inside us and the one outside us. As a result of a constant reciprocal process, both these worlds come to form a single one. And it is this world that we must communicate.

Henri Cartier-Bresson

Originality: The Ultimate Creative Process In Mastery, participants often acquire a perspective that helps classify their dramatic behavior as original. By original we mean statistically uncommon, or demonstrating qualities that are rarely viewed in dramas of other groups of this age or experience level. Often, the core image is the product of original creative thinking. This original image is often further enhanced by unique dramatic choices in terms of character, plot, or place. These choices are not "cute" for cuteness's sake, or novel for novelty's sake, but represent a creatively conceptualized piece of original drama.

Strong Thematic Image at the Core A characteristic shared by almost every Mastery case study is that the activity begins with a particularly evocative image. The source of these images is usually within the group, but occasionally the leader is able to offer an interesting thematic image around which an entire drama can develop. Although the images that seem to spark a group are as unique as the group itself, several types of thematic images reappear on a consistent basis: images that evolve from a Starter, fantastical images, popular axioms, contemporary/societal images, and multidimensional/theatrical images. Examples appear in the case studies in Chapter 11.

RIM IS UNIQUE

As you begin to read the many activities and case studies in the next chapters, keep in mind that each level with its activities is part of a complete method of drama. Too often, in actual creative drama practice, a single day's lesson is unrelated to anything that came before or will come after. This "one-shot deal" quality encourages the leader to think up a lesson on the way to school or pull exercise cards from a shoe-box haphazardly. RIM's greatest strength is that it has been conceived as a self-contained, total method of drama that facilitates and enhances dramatic learning. It can be used in its totality, in part, or as a model. All potential uses are outlined in the next chapters.

The principles below highlight the unique nature of RIM. A discussion of these principles appears in the next chapters, but in a way more particular to operationalizing drama. These principles are included together here as a means of review, and also to provide a compact list to lead you on your way:

- RIM is closely connected to the iii Framework.
- The creative drama leader's role is dynamic.
- Participants explore the functions of a variety of models provided by the field of theatre.
- Imagery and imagination are at the core of creative drama.
- Dramatic learning encompasses both internal processes and external behaviors.
- The major focus of creative drama is on the ultimate connection of ideas to action.

You're ready to begin your detailed study of the Rutgers Imagination Method activities and case studies. Take a breath now and turn the page. In the words of Winifred Ward, "Go Adventuring!"

STARTERS

The following group of exercises begins the Rutgers Imagination Method (RIM). Called Starters, these seven groups of exercises introduce participants to creative drama. Through their work with Starters, participants begin to experience, observe, and record the world around them, as well as use memory images as material for dramatic action. Participants also learn numerous drama behaviors through their experiences with Starters.

I will maintain that the artist needs only this: a special world to which he alone has the key.

André Gide

Starters appear in both Chapter 7 and Chapter 8. Together these two chapters are divided into nine main sections. In the first and the last sections, we present material directly related to the overall conduct of Starters. Each of the other sections contains exercises divided into the following categories: Object/Prop, Movement/Pantomime, Sound/Speech, Person/Character, Sequence/Story, and Design/Environment. Although we discuss Introduction/Transition exercises in a separate section, we have included the actual exercises as opening exercises in each of the other categories. Chapter 7 contains three sets of exercises, Chapter 8 three more sets.

Before each set of exercises, we include a brief discussion of the category as a whole. This discussion deals with goals and objectives, general information, and practical pointers relevant to the exercises. Before and after the entire set of exercises, we also include material of a more general nature, relevant to all Starters. This introductory material helps get you "revved up" to begin Starters. The concluding material, found after all the Starters, helps you form closure on what you have just read and prepares you for the next level of creative drama, Transformations.

TO THE LEADER: GENERAL INFORMATION ON STARTERS

RIM Starters are based on the following assumptions about learning and young people:

• Young people learn at different rates and sometimes in no readily apparent order.
• Each person is his or her own source of imagination, ideas, and dramatic action.
• Each person is unique, with personal strengths, weaknesses, values, and wishes.
• Early learning occurs through personal discovery, typically filled with imitation, and experimentation.
• The space in which people learn, as well as the materials in these spaces, greatly influence the learning that takes place.

You can operationalize your understanding of these assumptions in the way you set up your room for drama — the physical climate, and in the way in which you set up the tone and mood of the drama lesson — the psychological climate. You must establish these climates in a systematic way; haphazard drama environments will most likely produce haphazard creative dramas.

The Physical Climate

Creative drama classes often take place in classrooms, libraries, senior citizen centers, or in a community theatre. You may be fortunate to have your own space or classroom where the participants meet regularly for drama. Some of you may find yourselves meeting in more than one space, or sharing space with someone else on a regular basis. Whichever arrangement is yours, certain physical requirements are necessary to conduct RIM Starters: namely, the physical environment should be adaptable, rich in stimuli, and organized.

An adaptable space is necessary, because you will probably conduct a number of these short exercises in one drama period. You will, therefore, need a space that allows for ease of movement and adapts readily from whole-group work to work in pairs or small groups. This space could be a regular classroom with the desks pushed aside, an empty classroom or multipurpose room, the gym, a stage, or the library. The room should not be too large and overwhelming; you will lose control and the participants may feel self-conscious. There should be some degree of intimacy without overcrowding. Carpeting or an area rug may be helpful to center the whole group and also provide a comfortable place for Introduction/Transition exercises.

The ability to generate many ideas — fluency — and the aesthetic sensitivity to one's world are two of the primary goals of RIM Starters. Research on creativity demonstrates that creative people utilize environmental cues to stimulate ideas and images. Starter exercises capitalize on these findings by providing many opportunities for participants to see, touch, and feel the world around them. The physical climate should be rich in stimuli. The categories of Object/Prop and Design/Environment rely heavily on sensory material to build imagery strategies and dramatic behaviors. Pay close attention to the environmental clues in the existing space you have, so you can point out the specific details, use objects in the space, and encourage participants to make full use of them.

RIM Starters utilize a wide assortment of props, objects, and materials to stimulate images and develop specific behaviors. You must, of course, supply these objects and organize them in some way. If you have your own room, you can keep the various materials in labeled boxes, barrels, or containers. An organized classroom provides the participants with a sense of stability and purpose, and allows them to be responsible for the care of the environment.

Traveling from class to class takes more ingenuity. If you must move from place to place, try to devise some sort of carry-all or drama cart (like those used by many traveling art teachers) to transport your materials. If the school or community center cannot provide a separate space, at least try to secure a closet or corner to store your gear.

The Psychological Climate

Since Starters are participants' first experience with creative drama, the psychological climate is very important. Your attitude toward the children, creative drama, and yourself all contribute to the overall psychological climate. Even though this aspect of the environment is less tangible than the physical aspect, the participants have a special knack of "picking up" your attitudes and intentions. A good psychological climate must start with *you*. Try to be positive and enjoy learning as much as teaching. Since you are obviously interested in drama and theatre, cultivate your "dramatic flair" and use it to capture the participants' attention and focus their energy. You yourself must work toward finding a balance between your playful sense of adventure and your serious belief in the importance of drama.

Stress the importance of freedom: freedom to fail, to learn, and to enjoy success. There must be time to share and think, to work alone and with others, and to act and reflect. The environment must be relaxed, yet still have a sense of purpose. Creative drama requires that individuals take risks, particularly in Starters. You can facilitate this risk-taking by being encouraging and by believing that each participant can accomplish the goals of Starters. You must learn to respect the responses of each participant and encourage them to respect each other. It's your job to encourage participants to share their ideas, to cooperate with one another, and to begin to trust in others, as well as in themselves.

The Leader's Role

Your role as leader is most clearly defined in Starters. Perhaps the most important characteristic for the leader to remember at this level of RIM is sensitivity — sensitivity to the special needs of individuals within the group, to the overall needs of the group, and to the world at large in order to cultivate one's own artistic/dramatic sensibility. As participants work in Starters, novice leaders are building the skills and abilities necessary to be good creative drama leaders. Experienced leaders are fine-tuning their skills by learning to explore their own world of images as they encourage participants to do likewise.

Because Starters focus on basic imagery skills and on simple dramatic behaviors, the leader's role is direct and clear-cut. Starter exercises require that you utilize three main teaching roles:

- Leader as Guide.
- Leader as Coach.
- Leader as Director.

Leader as Guide Your role as guide is contained almost exclusively in the Introduction/Transition exercises. In these, you guide participants through the discovery and implementation of their imagic storehouse. As guide, your responsibilities are twofold:

- To create a trusting environment for relaxation and risk-taking.
- To lead participants through exercises, step by step.

As any guide must, you have to be confident, knowledgeable, and helpful. It's your job, for example, to point out positive aspects of fantasy journeys and even to be the first to share your thoughts. Remember, when you are acting as guide, participants are working on reflection and on voluntary sharing, not on evaluation.

Leader as Coach Your job as coach is to encourage and stimulate the participants to generate images and dramatic actions. Just as an athletic coach pushes and pulls the players to reach their physical potential, so must the leader as coach challenge the participants to realize their dramatic potential. As coach, you must create a playful attitude, so that participants can suspend rules, entertain the possible, and try out a wide assortment of dramatic behaviors.

Four of the Starter categories, Person/Character, Sequence/Story, Movement/Pantomime, and Object/Prop, ask that you be primarily a coach. Sentences you may find useful in this role, and that begin "What if?" or "Show me another way . . ." indicate to participants that there is no one way to imagine.

Modeling plays an important part in these exercises. Feel free to show your students what to do. Don't be concerned if at first they copy you; imitation is an important learning strategy at this level. Provide numerous examples, and demonstrate many ways of solving the dramatic problem at hand. Remember, these exercises are called Starters; as coach, it is you who starts them on the road to dramatic learning.

Leader as Director Your job as director will be to develop participants' ability to plan together and work as a group. In this capacity, you will introduce and explain the exercise, present additional information to stimulate the developing dramatic behavior, and then move through the group, assessing individual or small-group progress. As you develop your directorial skills, you will be able to discern if the group is having difficulty imagining, planning, or negotiating among itself. In Sound/Speech and Design/Environment exercises, using your skills as director, let participants wonder, manipulate images, and replan, as they attempt to coordinate their own images and actions with those of other group members. Starter exercises introduce participants to the classic plan, play, evaluate. As director your role expands considerably when you get to Transformations.

Material on the teaching roles — *Guide, Coach,* and *Director* — are found throughout the Starter exercises. Because Introductions/Transitions are found in each of the other Starter categories, you will be acting as guide within each set of Starters. Other exercises may require that you combine your jobs as coach and director. Remember, a primary goal of Starters is fluency. Participants need to remain open and need to generate numbers of images and ways to solve their dramatic problem. It's *your* job to combine the functions of these roles in any way necessary to help them achieve this goal.

FORMAT OF STARTER EXERCISES

All RIM Starters in this chapter and the next follow the same format. You may choose to follow the format as suggested or modify it by expanding or condensing its scope. But it's important for you to understand the whole exercise fully before making major deletions or additions to it, because each component has been included in the Starter exercises for a particular reason. Following is a discussion of each component within the format of the Starters:

Name of Exercise The name of each exercise describes its main action or primary objective. "Looking at People," for example, is concerned with participants observing people and their characteristics. Names also describe the here-and-now stimulus, as in "Elastic."

Category The category of exercise refers to one of the six major categories of RIM Starters. Exercises are grouped by category. Should you wish to place these exercises in lesson plans, we have included the name of the category to help you keep track of each individual exercise.

Imagery Strategies Imagery strategies are those internal image-related skills that are the focus for each particular exercise: basically, acquisition, retrieval, and manipulation. Other strategies introduced in Starters, but explored in more depth in Transformations, are self as image and allowing image to have a life of its own. Remember, memory images are the main images utilized in Starters. Imagery strategies help participants recall, control, and build vivid memory images. Some participants may also begin to explore imagination images as the source for behavior.

Dramatic Behavior Dramatic behavior describes the particular drama/theatre skill introduced in an exercise. Object/Prop exercises, for example, give participants practice in using objects dramatically. Other types of behaviors include observation, concentration, voice and language production, physicalization, rehearsal, working with others, and simple characterization. Remember, unlike imagery strategies, dramatic behavior is rather easily observed.

Number of Participants The number states not only the maximum number of possible participants, but also the desirable participant configuration. Configurations include individual alone, individuals working simultaneously, pairs working one at a time, simultaneous pair work, and whole-group work. Starter exercises rarely if ever single out an individual or encourage one pair to perform. Rather, exercises focus on simultaneous individual or pair work, small-group work, and whole-group work.

Materials Needed Listed in this segment are specific here-and-now objects that are the stimuli for the exercise. If materials are mentioned, you must use them. We cannot stress enough how essential these are to the conduct of RIM. After you have been conducting RIM, you may even ask your participants to bring objects from home. Some exercises do not have materials listed. These exercises usually focus on sounds or movements performed by you or your participants.

Directions The directions are addressed to you, the leader. They advise you, step by step, how to conduct each exercise. Key words in these directions include "instruct," "coach," "show," and "encourage." These words should clue you into the active nature of your role in RIM Starters.

As you begin to work with Starters, follow the directions carefully. Over time, you will get a sense of what will work for your group, as well as how much coaching they need. In a sense, you will be developing your own storehouse of images about leading Starters.

Guiding Lines Guiding Lines are models of sentences and phrases to use when conducting Starters. These Guiding Lines assist participants in enacting the exercise. Each category requires that you develop unique guiding lines; specifics are presented in the discursive sections before each set. Remember, Guiding Lines are suggestions, not necessarily the specific script. If you are new to drama leading, you may use the lines verbatim, but you will probably find turns of phrase unique to you. The exception may be the guided fantasy exercises. Because these mind journeys are carefully constructed (based on research in psychology), you may wish to use them exactly as they appear.

Notes In this segment we present information that can help you in conducting the exercises. Here, we share research findings, present interesting theoretical parallels (particularly from theatre and creative drama literature), and give examples that might enlighten or assist you.

Modifications In Modifications we suggest various changes that can turn one exercise into many. Modifications do not change the overall thrust of the exercise; they merely suggest slight changes that expand its curriculum potential.

INTRODUCTION/TRANSITIONS

The Starters in this category are not presented in a separate section but are located at the beginning of every other category. These exercises are to be integrated within each category. Introduction/Transitions are integral to the RIM Imagination Method, because they introduce participants to their inner world of images, an essential component of dramatic learning. In Introduction/Transitions, participants practice acquiring, retrieving, and manipulating their sensory images as they develop more and more control over their imagery ability.

> ***Every closed eye is not sleeping, and every open eye is not seeing.***
>
> Bill Cosby

You will find three basic types of exercise in this set of activities: *Relaxation, Sensory Awareness* and *Observation,* and *Guided Fantasy.* These Introduction/Transitions are found at the beginning of each of the other categories. Your job in these activities is to enhance and nurture the sensory modalities that are primary in each of the other categories. The four exercises at the beginning of Sound/Speech, for example, emphasize perceiving, listening, and imitating sounds.

Your role in these exercises is to guide participants through relaxation and guided fantasy and focus their attention on the world at large. Participants will respond not only to your words, but also to the slow, easy pace of your voice during guided fantasies or to your clear tone and precise articulation as you point out objects in the environment. Your words and voice must also be supportive and encouraging to help participants relax and to assist them in seeing how clear or interesting their images are becoming.

Perhaps in no other drama approach are warm-ups so consistently important. You can use Introduction/Transitions in RIM Starters to prepare participants for work in a particular drama skill area or to facilitate an easy transition from one activity to the next. You can also use them in later RIM work.

Relaxation Exercises

Relaxation is one of the keys to successful imagery. A calm mind and body allows participants to retrieve and manipulate images readily. A tense mind and body does not allow for the free flow of images, but rather creates an interference in the imagery process, as a knotted antenna cord creates static on a television and impedes good reception. Relaxation provides a deeper level of awareness and access to more vivid images. The various relaxation exercises teach the participants how to release body tension and focus their energy. The ability to relax one's mind and body is a skill that can be learned.

As you learned in the last chapter, there are four kinds of relaxation techniques in RIM Starters:

- Progressive relaxation
- Autosuggestion
- Breathing
- Counting down

Each technique facilitates a deep relaxed state, with little practice. "Flex and Relax," an example of *progressive relaxation,* requires that participants tense and relax various parts of their body in succession. The exercises and others like it allow participants to feel the tension and then release that tension, thus becoming aware of how tension and relaxation feel in various body parts. Sounds of the sea in "Ocean" and the idea of floating to the floor in "Floating" help participants relax by responding to images in their own mind. When finding other images that work well for *autosuggestion,* try to think of ones with rhythmic movement or sounds. During breathing, participants share with dancers and actors a technique that helps them become aware of their breathing and then slow the pattern to deepen relaxation. After participants have mastered "Breathing" and exercises like it, a few deep breaths before the start of an activity can bring a calmness to each individual and to the group as a whole. The fourth technique, *counting down,* draws the participants into a progressively more relaxed state as they count backwards. As you count down in "Elevator" and other exercises like it, participants will feel more and more relaxed at each descending number.

As guide, you must be acutely sensitive to the tension level of the participants as they begin the exercises. Some classes, or some days, may be more tense than others. You may need to adjust your guiding lines to accommodate such differences. A group arriving after physical exertion, for example, may take a few more minutes to reach a relaxed state than the group who just finished lunch. For the first group, you may begin "Elevator" on the twentieth floor; the second group may only need to begin on the tenth. Also remember that participants will usually improve with practice. Once they have achieved an optimum level of relaxation, they can return to that state more easily.

You must also be aware of any external environmental distractions that may inhibit calmness or make the relaxation process ineffective. Morning announcements or visitors may be distractions that you can avoid by timing your activity differently or by placing a "Do Not Disturb" sign outside the door.

Always consider the temperature of the room and the amount of fresh air. Some participants will be able to reach a relaxed state in spite of any distraction, while others may be sensitive even to the slightest interruption, especially in the beginning.

Be aware of signs of a relaxed body. A limp arm, an unfurled brow, and calm facial features are all signs of a relaxed state. Afterwards, let the participants discuss how this relaxed sensation feels, since it may be new to them. Some participants feel a tingling sensation, a change in body temperature, or a floating sensation. Assure them these are normal sensations, and that relaxation is good for their body. Explain that even in a relaxed state they are always in control of themselves.

The ability to perform at peak level and to concentrate fully are just a few of the benefits of these relaxation exercises. The few minutes it takes to do them are well worth the investment. Before long the participants themselves will request relaxation exercises, and comment on how they used their new-found skill in nondrama situations. Be sure to encourage their developing relaxation skills.

POINTERS — RELAXATION

- Check room for comfort.
- Minimize distractions.
- Be aware of participants' tension level.
- Adjust guiding lines as needed.
- Speak in a calm, even manner.
- Provide positive encouragement.
- Look for signs of relaxation.

Sensory Awareness and Observation

Artists perceive the world differently from the average person. Their heightened sense of perceptual awareness and keen observation skills help them discover a rich assortment of images and ideas to be utilized in art-making. Artists, consciously or unconsciously, record vivid, multisensory images of the world that they can evoke or recall at any time. Everyone possesses the capacity for this type of artistic sensitivity, even if he or she does not possess the talent or desire to become a famous artist. **You must encourage and sometimes even teach drama participants to see — not just look, to listen — not just hear, and to feel — not just touch.**

Sensory awareness exercises demand that the participants actively pay attention to the world around them. These particular exercises include multisensory awareness, memory images acquisition, and integrated arts activities. Participants are guided to discover the multisensory aspects of an object, to find differences and similarities between objects, and to discriminate between various colors, textures, or patterns. They learn to record, make more vivid, and retrieve past images of people, places, and things. Through other types of art-making activities, participants discover alternative ways to view the world and are introduced to basic art principles.

RIM relies on many here-and-now objects to simulate observation and concentration. "Mama" in this illustration is lovingly exploring the color, texture, shape, and size of her flowers given a home in an everyday coffee can. (Robert Carter, *Mama, Sho Loved Flowers,* photograph by D. James Dee)

The sensory awareness and observation activities presented in RIM Starters may be very familiar to you. They may appear too obvious, and thus be glossed over, left out entirely, or used only during the first few classes. Finely tuned senses which perceive the world outside or the world within take time and practice to develop. These exercises offer you ways of working on developing participants' senses and provide a model framework within which you can develop your own unique activities.

As guide in these activities, you cannot assume anything. Such comments as, "You all know what a mango tastes like," or "Remember what a sheep looks like," may leave many a participant confused before you start. Be aware that participants vary in how well developed their senses are, and in the types of images and experiences they have stored. These differences arise from participants' differing sensory abilities and from how each participant views the world, literally. One near-sighted participant may have a strongly developed sense of smell. Another may have an acute sense of color. A third may have an excellent visual memory, but not make clear auditory distinctions. Become aware of each participant's strength and try to capitalize on it. Encourage participants to get the most out of their world, to look again, to dig deeper, to try to record it all! You and your participants will be richly rewarded as their senses become sharper, their memory images more vivid, and their artistic sensitivity more acute.

POINTERS — SENSORY AWARENESS AND OBSERVATION

- Do not assume anything.
- Be sensitive to the modality strengths of each participant.
- Challenge participants to use their senses to reexperience.
- Do these often; observation takes practice.
- Emphasize all the imagery modalities: taste, touch, sight, smell, sound, and movement.
- Vary the exercises.

Guided Fantasy

Guided fantasies are the mainstay of imagery exercise. Dreams, daydreams, creative problem-solving, and guided fantasies all involve the manipulation, connections, and recombination of vivid sensory images. The guided fantasy exercises found in RIM Starters help participants build fluent images that are both vivid and controllable. These exercises build on memory images and add new information, so that rich imagination images may be the result.

Guided fantasies or *mind journeys,* as they are sometimes called, are a set of guiding lines, read or spoken by the leader. Participants, in a relaxed state, listen to the leader and try to visualize or experience the leader's suggestions. Remember, there is not one way to visualize or experience a guided fantasy. In a room of twenty-five there will be twenty-five different fantasies. Some participants may have initial difficulty, but, as in relaxation, will improve with practice. Actually, relaxation and guided fantasy go hand in hand. The more relaxed the participant, the more supple and vivid will be their mind journey.

Generally, guided fantasies require that participants take one of two possible perspectives: either experiencing the journey or seeing themselves experiencing the journey. Participants in the former may be directed to experience the journey firsthand, with such sentences as "Walk down the boardwalk. Smell the salt air. Taste the taffy." Participants in the latter are guided to see themselves from a perspective outside self, such as the ceiling. Guiding words might be, "See yourself walking down the boardwalk. See yourself going swimming. Be aware of yourself floating." Both perspectives offer participants potential opportunities to develop imagery skills — one in actual retrieval of sensory images, the other in monitoring the ability to recall. Usually, participants are not asked to take both perspectives or to switch between them, in a single guided fantasy.

You will find a wide variety of fantasy exercises, from simple activities that require the participant merely to hold an image to complex imaginative adventures. Each one can be used as it is presented or used as a model to adapt and enrich. The following five guided fantasies are representative of the most classic ones, found throughout the literature in mental imagery.

"Write On," a very simple guided fantasy, requires the participant to hold the image in the mind's eye after looking at an object. Participants try to visualize viewing the object from various angles. You can use any object. The goal in this activity is to take a variety of perspectives — rotating the object and self in relation to the object. Often participants will begin this fantasy by focusing only on the object and then create a spontaneous imaginary world, which has been stimulated by the actual object. "Green Meadows" is a classic guided fantasy that focuses on the experience of a tranquil scene. Here you will use many sensory features in guiding the participant to experience the scene. For most participants, the scene is usually a combination of memory and imagination images. You can use any peaceful setting or place in modifying "Green Meadows."

"Up, Up, and Away" focuses on movement, both of the balloon and of the people and things experienced from the balloon. You can modify the balloon ride to travel through time and to view other worlds or dimensions. "Your Place or Mine" allows the participant to explore a safe environment in an unusual way. Using both memory and imagination images, the participants discover windows, doors, and steps — all archetypical symbols. Participants may often see something different each time they experience this fantasy, or may consistently see the same image, because it is so vivid for them. You may modify this fantasy as an exploration of any type of dwelling. "Who Me?" is probably the most difficult one because it requires that the participant take a perspective outside self. You can modify the fantasy by varying the situation or the activity "self" is engaged in, or by adding additional people. One ultimate goal of this and other self-monitoring mind journeys is the development of "self as image" and "third eye" skills, both discussed in future chapters.

As guide, you play a very important role in the guided fantasy. The trusting environment, your voice, and the words you choose all contribute to the overall success of the guided fantasy. As stated earlier, the climate must be nonthreatening and tension-free in Starters. Don't criticize or analyze participants' images. Keep distractions to a minimum. Present these guided fantasies as adventures that all can experience in their mind's eye. You may wish to calm participants with phrases like "I am with you, so you will be safe." Afterwards, sharing the journey is optional; never force participants to share.

Your voice is the magic ingredient in guided fantasy exercises; it should be soothing and nonobtrusive. The participants will create the images. Do not force your own images on them by an overinflected or precious voice, which may conjure up images irrelevant to the journey. Your pace and tone during a guided fantasy is very different from regular talking or even a formal presentation. Your voice should move effortlessly from one line to the next, but you must allow participants time to experience what you are describing. The most common mistake is to speak too rapidly. Participants will become fidgety and annoyed if your pace is too fast, because they will not have enough time to experience the journey. Try practicing the fantasies out loud before you conduct them with your groups. Remember, always bring the participants back to the here-and-now as you conclude the imagination journey.

Guided fantasies are relaxing and enjoyable. Once your group gets the

POINTERS — GUIDED FANTASY

- Maintain a nonthreatening environment.
- Present the journey as an adventure.
- Keep distractions to a minimum.
- Relax the participants before starting.
- Use a soft, effortless voice.
- Practice the journeys aloud.
- Sharing is optional.

hang of them, they will request them, just as they request relaxation exercises. Don't be afraid to make up your own—just keep them simple and don't focus on too much at once. Keep the journey open-ended; your participants will supply the details.

OBJECT/PROP

One of the distinctive features of RIM is the importance placed on props and objects. Even though props, objects, and other stimuli are found throughout RIM, this category is devoted exclusively to exercises in which both the focus and the enactment of the exercises requires specific here-and-now objects. These activities are the foundation for later exercises found both in Transformations and in Mastery. Props are only one, albeit significant, aspect of a well-rounded approach to drama.

To the casual observer, props in the theatre or in creative drama activities may seem like the frosting on the cake. Actors and directors, as well as knowledgeable theatre goers, however, know how significant the props and objects are to the total effect of the production. Acting coaches have also used props in helping actors develop well-rounded characterization.

As a group, creative artists rely heavily on their memory images for material for their art-making. The multisensory awareness of the world around them is vital for their continued development; the image of the actual object becomes the substance from which rich imaginative images flow. Recall for a moment the importance of objects in the development of imagination in young children and how they aid in the growth of imagery ability and creative thinking. Remember also from Chapter 3 the way in which the iii Framework described how a perceived image is manipulated in order to develop the imagination image and action. A key element in both descriptions was the presence of objects in the environment.

Your role as leader in this category is that of coach, aiding participants first to see, feel, touch, and smell the objects around them and then to explore and manipulate them. In Object/Prop, your job is to assist participants in making the connection between the here-and-now object, the internal image, and the external action. Keep reflection to a minimum, with primary focus on expanding the image storehouse and on physically responding to those images. Your work in early exercises is on helping participants hold memory images and retrieve them for use in enacting pieces of dramatic behavior.

One of your goals here is to help participants retrieve many images and try out all of them. Another important goal is to assist participants in making connections between what is in their mind's eye and what they enact in response to this. Maintaining a playful attitude is essential for success. Help participants "throw away" idea after idea, as they use an object in as many ways as they can. Your primary function as coach in this category is to assist participants in using props as a stimulus both for internal work and resulting portrayal.

Initial exercises in Object/Prop encourage participants to explore the sensory qualities of objects, as in "Squish," and their physical properties, as in "Elastic" and "Household Objects." The next set of activities focus on *fluency*. In "Break-Away," "Sticks," "Pass the Object," and "Exploring Objects," participants discover numbers of ways to use everyday objects.

The use of vivid personal images is an important goal in the Starter exercises. Exercises such as "The Ball," "Vacation," and "Empty and Full" require participants to recall and select clear, specific images rather than rely on stereotypic or generic images. These exercises cultivate pantomime skills with props used both as stimulus and integral part of the enactment. Remember, these final exercises are integral to the connection of internal to external and will provide participants with practice in a variety of imagery strategies.

Without giving you a four-page list of possible objects and props to use as stimuli for this category, we would like to suggest types of objects to collect, for use with these exercises and ultimately throughout RIM. First, collect interesting natural and man-made objects with specific sensory features, such as smooth rocks, dried pods, colored glass beads, or gnarled driftwood. Also begin by collecting objects with interesting properties, such as magnets that attract or elastic that stretches. Second, find objects that can be used in many ways. A length of gauzy material, for example, has endless possibilities. An eagle feather, a skeleton key, a feather boa, a small brass box are thought-provoking and dramatic and can be the beginning of an exciting drama. Flea markets, secondhand shops, garage sales, museum shops, and hardware stores are fun places to discover props. Make discovery a challenge, not a chore. Finally, aim for a diverse collection that can be combined and recombined in various ways to demonstrate similarities and differences. Once you begin prop hunting, it's often hard to stop!

POINTERS — OBJECTS/PROPS

- Maintain a playful attitude.
- Encourage participants to attend to sensory detail.
- Assist the participants in generating many uses for an object.
- Help participants make the connection between the object and the image.
- Emphasize the potential of objects and props as a stimulus for drama.
- Collect objects with interesting sensory qualities.
- Find dramatic and thought-provoking props.

Exercise: **Elevator** — Category: Introduction/Transition

Imagery Strategies
Recall the sensation of motion in their bodies; use a visual/kinesthetic image to release tension

Dramatic Behaviors
Prepare for drama work; relate relaxation and motion

Number of Participants: Whole group

Materials Needed: None

Directions: Ask participants to find a comfortable place on the floor. Explain that they are going to play a relaxation game called Elevator. Have participants imagine that they are in an elevator. This elevator is on the sixteenth floor of a tall building and is going to descend *slowly,* stopping to pause on each floor. Explain that the doors do not open; the elevator just pauses on each floor. Explain also that when the door opens on the first floor, they will walk out calm and refreshed.

Guiding Lines: Find a comfortable place on the floor; you are going to take an elevator ride. What is one characteristic of riding on an elevator? Our building has sixteen floors and we will begin at the very top. Lie quietly on the floor. Imagine you are the only one lying on the floor of the elevator. Slowly the elevator descends to the fifteenth floor . . . fourteenth . . . thirteenth. . . . Your body is getting heavier and more relaxed as the elevator descends . . . twelfth floor . . . eleventh. . . . Feel how you relax more and more as the elevator goes down. The doors open and you walk out calm and refreshed.

Notes: Advanced participants may be able to make a relaxing elevator trip in ten or maybe even five floors. Talk slowly and evenly, giving them time between floors to feel their body get heavier and more relaxed.

Modifications: After some practice with the leader's guidance, participants may be able to do this exercise as an individual warm-up/preparation.

Exercise: Write On — Category: Introduction/Transition

Imagery Strategies

Focus on seeing and holding an image; experience an image moving; recall specific details of an image

Dramatic Behaviors

Concentrate on an external image; observe details of an object

Number of Participants: Whole group

Materials Needed: Enough pencils or pens for the whole group (they can use their own)

Directions: Have participants sit comfortably in a circle. Make sure everyone has a pen or pencil to use for this exercise. Have participants look at pencil for 15 seconds, noticing the details, inscription, nicks, eraser, point, etc. Have them hold the pencil at arm's length in front of them and look again, moving the pencil around to see it from all angles. Ask participants to close their eyes and see the pencil in their mind's eye for 30 seconds. Discuss with them what they saw, how they saw the image, how vivid were the details of the pencil and what their penciled name looked like. Have them switch pencils and try again.

Guiding Lines: Sit comfortably. Relax. Hold the pencil in front of your eyes at arm's length.

Look at the details on the pencil. Turn your pencil around (15 seconds). Write your name in the air.

Take a deep breath. Close your eyes.

See the pencil. Notice its shape and design.

See its point. See its color. Notice any inscription, eraser, nicks (30 seconds).

See the pen write your name.

Open your eyes.

Notes: This is an early guided fantasy that adds some degree of manipulation and controllability.

Modifications: This early guided fantasy can be done with any object.

Exercise: **The Feeley Box** Category: Introduction/Transition

Imagery Strategies

Focus on tactile images; complete image when stimulated by here-and-now experience

Dramatic Behaviors

Develop awareness of tactile sensations

Number of Participants: Individual in group

Materials Needed: Prepared carton or box with objects

Directions: Within a medium-sized carton or box, place ten to twenty small objects. Close the box and cut a hole in one end large enough to place the hand and forearm in comfortably. Have participants, one at a time, and for a specific time period, place one hand in the box via the hole. By sense of touch, participants are to identify the objects inside the box. After the time period passes, the participants quickly record what they thought they felt in the box.

Guiding Lines: Close your eyes and *feel* around inside the box. Concentrate on what you feel. Try to record all this information.

Notes: Try to find articles of various textures to place in the box. Find unusual objects, ones that are not easily identifiable.

Modifications: You can make a "theme" box by placing objects from one location in the box—for example, a beach box, a kitchen box.

Exercise: **Household Objects** Category: Object/Prop

Imagery Strategies

Focus on a here-and-now object; reproduce the image in the absence of the original object

Dramatic Behaviors

Focus on the world around; utilize a visual and tactile image to stimulate an action

Number of Participants: Group

Materials Needed: Three household objects: a cup, a teakettle, and a basket

Directions: Arrange participants in a circular seating pattern with your seat as part of the circle. Explain that today the class will look at three objects very carefully with special attention to size and shape. First show the class the cup. Turn the cup slowly so participants can see it from all sides. Ask, "What makes a cup different from a glass?" (handle, size, shape, material). Give each participant an opportunity to hold the cup, to pretend he or she is drinking from the cup. Ask participants to notice how big the cup is and how it feels in their hands. Remove the cup. Repeat the same activity with the teakettle and the basket. When all objects are removed ask participants to recall the cup—the size, shape, and texture. Ask them to drink from the cup. Repeat tasks with other objects.

Guiding Lines: Focus on the cup. Look at the cup as if you have never seen a cup before.

Look at the way the cup fits in your hand. Is it comfortable?

Recall the cup. How big was it? How did you hold it?

Use your image to help you.

Notes: This is a basic imagery activity. Care must be taken to ensure that images *connect* to actual behavior.

Exercise: **Three Chairs** Category: Object/Prop

Imagery Strategies
Experience a here-and-now object; overlay a past kinesthetic image with a here-and-now object

Dramatic Behaviors
Express sitting in a here-and-now chair as if it were a different chair; physicalize different types of behavior

Number of Participants: Individuals within a group

Materials Needed: Three different chairs, in as wide a variety of size and shape as is possible

Directions: Bring into the room three very different types of chairs. (Example: arm chair, director's chair, futon) Have each participant, one at a time, sit in each chair. Make sure each participant has at least a minute to sit in chair. (Several students can sit in all three chairs simultaneously.) Encourage each student to experience the "feel" of each chair.

Now have each participant sit in his or her own classroom chair and try to recreate the feeling of each of the previous chairs. Have group members try to show by the way each sits which chair he or she is sitting in.

Guiding Lines: Use your senses to experience the chair. How does each chair make you feel?

Try to make this chair into the other chair.

Use your image to help you make this chair into the other chair.

Exercise: **Squish** Category: Object/Prop

Imagery Strategies
Recall an object; focus on keeping the image; manipulate the image

Dramatic Behaviors
Communicate activities with props; develop an awareness of props

Number of Participants: Whole group

Materials Needed: Cards with names of various size objects, or pictures of objects

Directions: Direct participants to settle on the floor with room enough to move around them. Give each participant an object picture/card. Spend the first 30 seconds of the activity having the participants quietly image the object. Once you are confident they can do this, have them pantomime how they would use the object. Next, direct them to pantomime the following functions with the imaginary prop: be it, move it, break it, paint it, wrap it, get mad at it, sit on it, put your arms around it, lean against it, and squash it. After they squash the picture/card, hand the imaginary object to the next person.

Guiding Lines: Try hard to see your object in your mind's eye. Show me how you can _________ your object. Can you think of more than one way to do that?

Notes: When working with words on a card rather than a picture of the object, be sure to allow enough time for participants to retrieve the image. Do not rush the activity.

Modifications: Make up your own things to do to the object, but save the squishing for last. It's easier to pass the object!

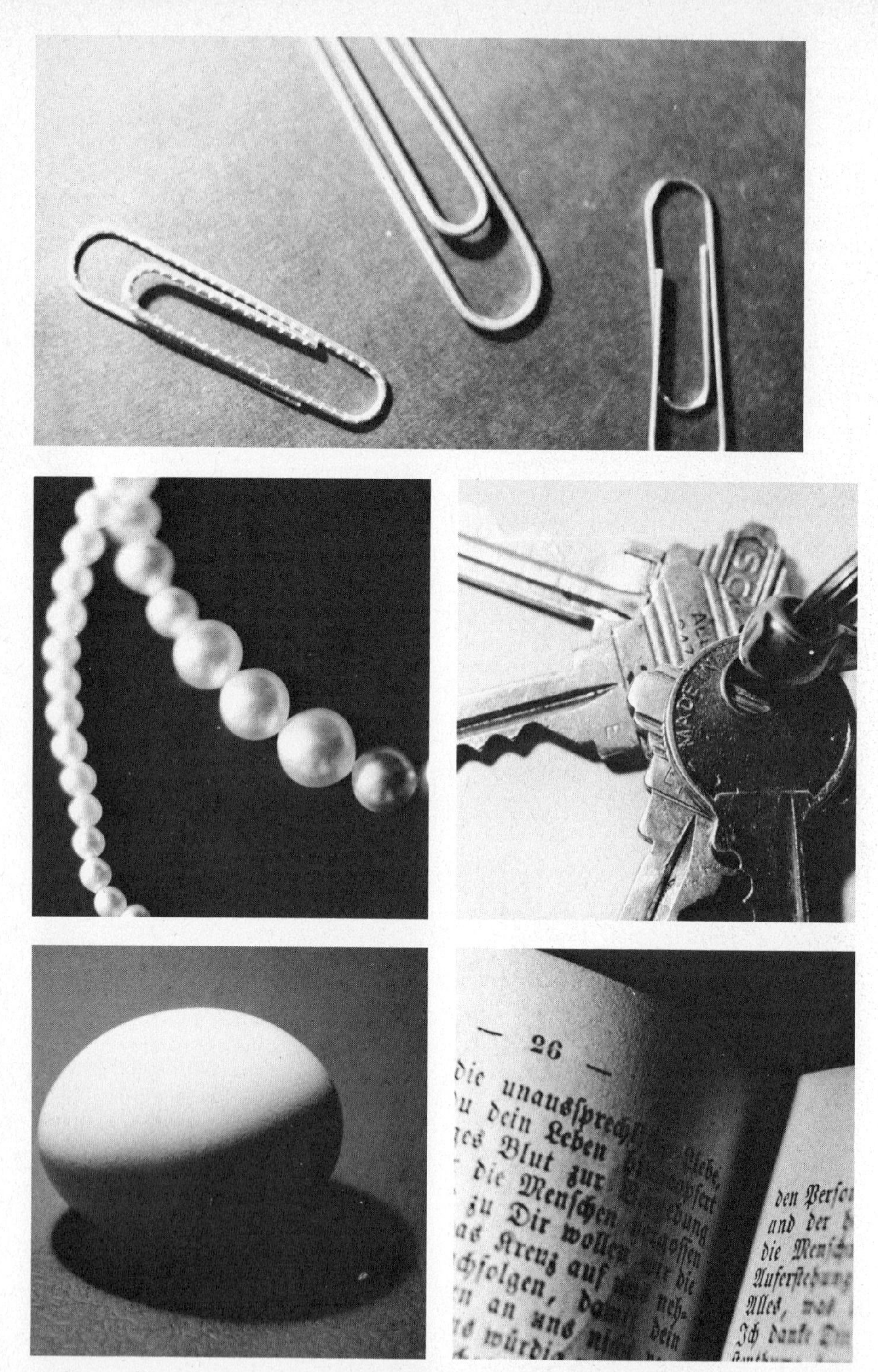

Ordinary objects become interesting when viewed from different perspectives. (Photos by Phyllis Heim)

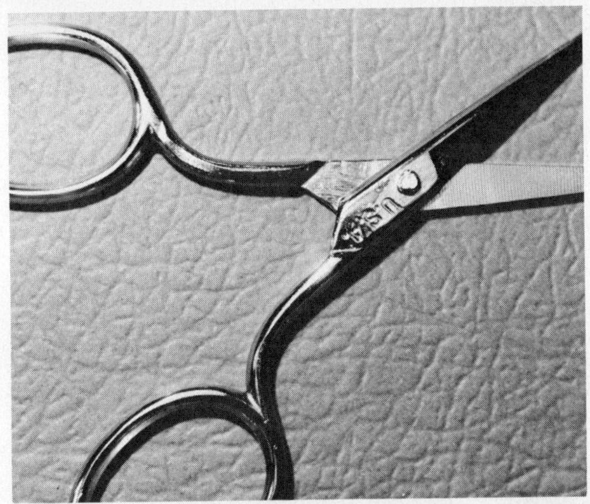

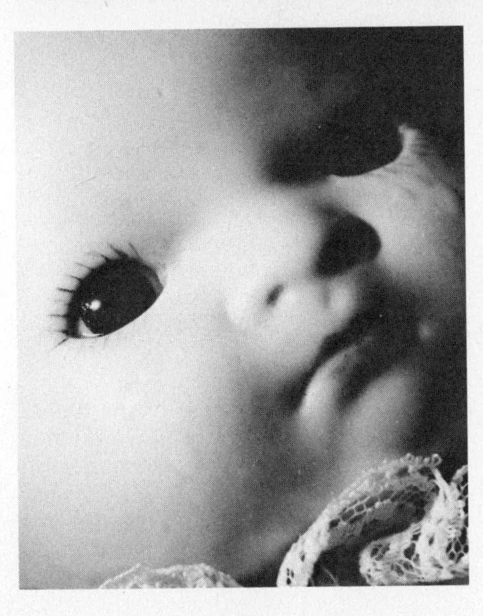

Exercise: Elastic — Category: Object/Prop

Imagery Strategies
Overlay image with self; manipulate elastic mentally as well as physically

Dramatic Behaviors
Construct original prop; allow object to suggest physical shape

Number of Participants: Whole group

Materials Needed: Enough pieces of soft 1-inch elastic (36–48 inches long) sewn together at ends to simulate a large rubber band, so that each person has one.

Directions: With one member of the group, demonstrate how the elastic stretches to many different shapes. Give each participant a piece of elastic, and time to explore. When you are satisfied they have tried a number of ways to use it, have the group spread out to begin making the shapes you suggest.

Guiding Lines: Let the elastic hang around you. Let it stretch from your head to your toes. Let it hold you in tightly. Let it bind your legs. Let it hold part of you tightly, and loop around something else so you can move. Really feel the elastic.

Notes: Your side coaching is the most important part of the activity. As long as the group is making different shapes with the elastic, the activity is successful. Ask them to describe shapes they have discovered.

Modifications: Let two people use one piece of elastic.
Vary the lengths of the elastic and the group configuration.
Try one large group with many pieces of elastic.

Exercise: Pass the Object — Category: Object/Prop

Imagery Strategies
Expand/contract images of real object; recall uses of real objects; overlay shape of here-and-now object on new image; manipulate image

Dramatic Behaviors
Physicalize new use of object; utilize object as a prop

Number of Participants: Whole group

Materials Needed: Objects of various sizes and shapes

Directions: Have participants sit comfortably in a circle so they are able to see each other. As an example, demonstrate how a simple object like a credit card (or one of the objects on hand) can become something else when used differently. A credit card can be a razor, pillow, envelope, etc., depending on how it is used.

With the entire group watching, start one object around the circle having each participant "use" it. When it goes around once, change to another object.

Guiding Lines: Really look at the object. Allow it to stimulate recall of images. Let it become something else. See the image outside you. Let it help you transform this object.

Notes: If participants cannot think of things to use it as, suggest places where they may find many objects of that size. Remember, participants are starting to develop "as if" behavior. They need all the positive comments you are able to give them.

Modifications: The size of the object often determines the size of the pantomime. Try this activity with small objects (one hand objects) and larger ones (as tall as the participants). Finally, use nonrepresentational objects whose shape can be modified.

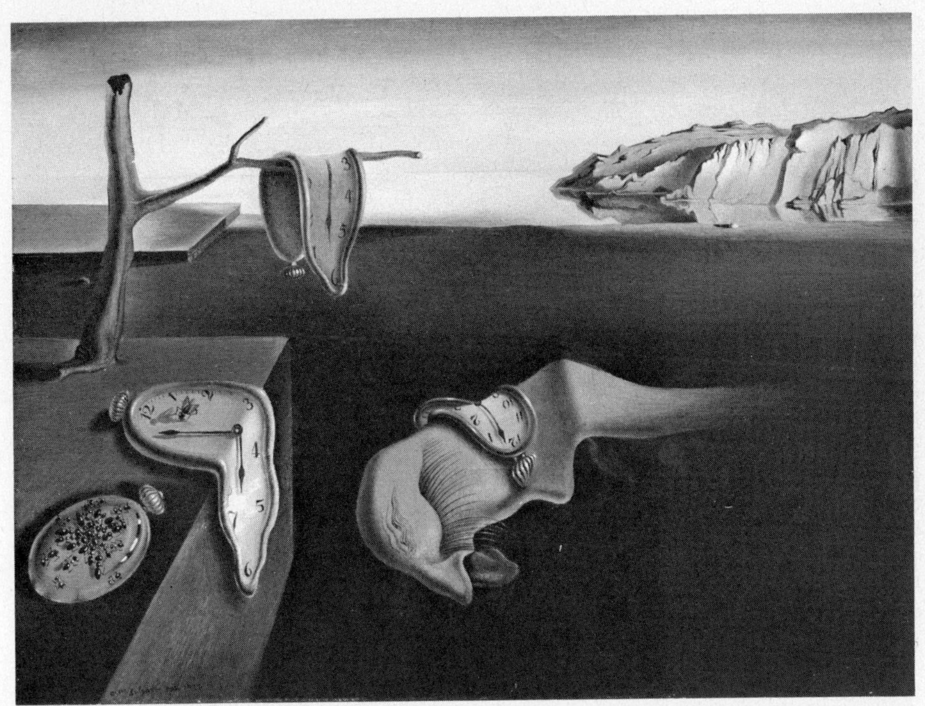

In the *Persistence of Memory,* Salvador Dali is able to break away from the linear, traditional view of time and depict a world in which many times, past and present, exist simultaneously. (Collection, The Museum of Modern Art, New York)

Exercise: **Exploring Objects** Category: Object/Prop

Imagery Strategies

Focus on here-and-now objects; image self using object; recall all possible uses of object

Dramatic Behaviors

Use physical objects to express personal images

Number of Participants: Individual in group

Materials Needed: One prop for each participant. Props should be various-sized objects — compact, pencil, book, broom, stool, ladder

Directions: Place props in various locations on the floor. (Props can be numbered for easier rotation.) Guide participants in viewing all props. Ask participants to image the prop in actual previously experienced contexts. Assign one participant to each prop. As soon as participants are settled with the prop, tell them to examine the prop carefully. On the count of 3, they are to use the prop in as many ways as possible. When you are satisfied they have explored the various uses of the prop, instruct the group to pass their props to the next person. Repeat activity until everyone uses every prop.

Guiding Lines: Look at all the props. Recall the time when you saw these props before, in real-life situations. Can you recall seeing these props in a number of different situations?

Show me how to use the object. Now think of another way you have seen someone use it. Have you ever used it in another way? Explore all the possibilities.

Notes: Before participants receive their props, explain that their first prop is just temporary, and that they will get to all the props in the room.

Modifications: Gather props found in one location — office, kitchen, repair shop as warm-up activity before doing drama set in that location.

Exercise: **Sticks** — Category: Object/Prop

Imagery Strategies
Retrieve images suggested by here-and-now objects; overlay previous image with here-and-now object

Dramatic Behaviors
Utilize a prop "as if" it were something else; monitor personal dramatic behavior

Number of Participants: Whole group

Materials Needed: Enough long dowels for every participant

Directions: Distribute dowels to each participant. Coach them to observe the dowel and move it all around in different positions. Some of the group members may spontaneously begin to use the dowel "as if" it were a more specific prop — a sword, a pin, a hoe.

Ask group members to close their eyes and "see" the dowel in the mind's eye. Ask them to rotate, shift and move dowel around until it becomes a specific object. Then picture themselves using the object. Guide the group to use the dowel as the object.

Guiding Lines: Observe the dowel. Move it around. What does it seem like?

Can you see the dowel? Have you ever seen anything shaped like that? Can you see yourself using the dowel in another way?

Notes: The straight shape of the dowel suggests many other objects with specific functions. In other words, the dowel may stimulate the participants to retrieve previously perceived objects stored in their memory. They then use the dowel and the previous image to stimulate behavior. This activity can be accomplished in a few minutes. Also note that this activity helps to introduce the notion of monitoring with coaching phrases like, "See yourself."

Modifications: Any object of a universal shape can be used for this activity: discs or blocks, for example.

Exercise: **Break-Away** — Category: Object/Prop

Imagery Strategies
Recall/retrieve images associated with object; connect imagination objects/events with real object; explore personal and group imagic storehouse

Dramatic Behaviors
Break through stereotypic behavior; experiment with numbers of ideas; work together as a group

Number of Participants: Whole group

Materials Needed: None — could have actual objects present (clock, hammer, cup, candle, key)

Directions: Ask the participants to sit in a circle. Explain that creative people can generate many ideas about one single object. Show participants an object (for ex-

things connected to the object or what it's made of (for example, gears, hands)

sounds the object could make (for example, tic-toc, bong, ding) ample, clock). Ask participants to think of as many:

images it brings to mind (for example, time, lunch, being late)

places suggested by the object (for example, Switzerland, clock shop, time machine)

Guiding Lines: We want to think of many ideas.

There's no right or wrong answer.

Say the first thing that comes to mind.

Don't think so hard.

Keep up the flow.

Who's got another one?

Notes: This activity can be a verbal or written exercise. When written make sure it is a *group* exercise — not a test of individual memory.

Modifications: First person states an object, next one an image that comes to mind, third one an image that the second person reminded him of. . . . Build the association from the previous one, *not from the original object*.

Exercise: The Ball — Category: Object/Prop

Imagery Strategies

Experience here-and-now objects; focus and concentrate on here-and-now objects; overlay a previous image with a current action

Dramatic Behaviors

Physicalize an imaginary object; communicate a pantomimed prop to a partner (and to audience)

Number of Participants: Whole group and pairs within group

Materials Needed: Balls of various sizes, such as beach ball, softball, basketball, golf ball

Directions: Bring to class a number of different sized balls. Begin to pass around the balls. Ask each person to experience the size and shape and weight of each ball as it is passed around. Now begin to pass around pantomimed versions of each ball. Encourage participants to show shape, size, and weight of each ball.

Divide the group into pairs. Have each pair decide which of the balls they will toss back and forth. Have each pair simultaneously throw ball back and forth. Then have each pair toss a pantomimed ball back and forth.

Guiding Lines: Really feel the ball. See how different the size, the texture, the weight, the shape is.

Now pay attention to yourself and the ball. How do you hold each of the balls? What does your body do when you throw the ball?

Now try to make the ball real to you as you pantomime the ball. Also make the ball real to your partner. Try to recall and recreate your recent past experience.

Notes: Pay particular attention to exploring the *real* objects. Without a good kinesthetic feeling of each ball, participants will find this activity difficult. This exercise also includes an early self-monitoring component. Encourage participants to become aware of "self and object."

Modifications: May be adapted for other objects — cart on box, bucket, etc.

Exercise: Vacation — Category: Object/Prop

Imagery Strategies
Recall images of objects used daily

Dramatic Behaviors
Communicate through pantomime

Number of Participants: Individual in whole group

Materials Needed: Empty suitcase

Directions: Place closed suitcase in center of room with participants seated in a circle around it. Conduct a discussion about things that you have at home that you take with you when you go on a vacation. Discuss what might be in this particular suitcase. After you are sure the group has enough images of things that may be in the suitcase, ask them to individually, but at the same time, open the suitcase and pack. If you think your group is ready, you may choose to encourage them to show packing, one at a time.

Guiding Lines: Really see the objects in your mind's eye. Choose one or two specific objects upon which to concentrate.

Show me, don't tell me, what you are taking out of the suitcase. Make sure you make a difference between a sweater and a shirt. Try to recall real sweaters or shirts.

Be as specific as possible. Show us everything about the object. You may want to take some unusual things with you! Use your images to help you.

Notes: You may want to begin this activity with a long guided-imagery exercise to help participants recall their experiences. Remember, the more specific and personal the item, the better able your participants are to pantomime it.

Modifications: Once the class has experienced the suitcase in conjunction with places they have visited, ask them to pack for places they might only visit in their mind's eye — a safari, the Alps, Hawaii.

Exercise: Empty and Full — Category: Object/Prop

Imagery Strategies
Focus on recording images; recall kinesthetic images; utilize image to stimulate specific behavior

Dramatic Behaviors
Concentrate on pantomime; imitate previous motions; communicate through movement; interpret behaviors of others

Number of Participants: Two groups

Materials Needed: One paper cup for each participant and a bucket of water

Directions: Ask the participants to sit in a circle. Select one person to walk around the center of the circle with the cupful of water. Have participants observe how the person walks slowly and carefully so as not to spill the water. Give everyone a cup of water with which to practice. Once you are satisfied that the participants are aware of walking with water in their cups, divide the group in half. Each group secretly decides on a certain number of cups that will be empty. One group stays in a circle while the other leaves the area, empties certain cups, and returns, pretending all cups are full. The group observing this activity tries to guess which cups are empty and which are full. Reverse groups and replay.

Guiding Lines: Remember how you concentrated when your cup was full. Walk the same way. Don't let your face show that your cup is empty. Recall how you walked when your cup was full.

Notes: Be sure to set up guidelines about having water in the room. Use a heavy cup so observers can't see a water line.

Modifications: Fill other containers.

Exercise: **Strange Encounters**

Category: Object/Prop

Imagery Strategies
Overlay here-and-now object with images; retrieve images suggested by here-and-now object

Dramatic Behaviors
Behave "as if" a prop were something else; pantomime activities

Number of Participants: Whole group

Materials Needed: A very large (dishwasher or refrigerator) box, or a very large table with a covering to the floor

Directions: Present the box to the group. Explain that the box has magical qualities because it can become many things. Ask participants to relate to the box as if it were something else, such as a boat, a house, etc. Before they do the pantomime, they may arrange the box to help it look more like their object. Coach participants into imaging their object. Then, encourage participants to pantomime their activity, one at a time.

Guiding Lines: Really look at the box. What does its shape remind you of? How might you relate to it to make it into a prop or into a set piece? What can it become?

If you can't think of something, let the box suggest the prop. Be confident that the box will help you come up with something.

When you have an idea, go to the box and show us what it becomes.

Modifications: You can also use a newspaper, a desk, a chair, or any other object that suggests other objects.

MOVEMENT/PANTOMIME

Exercises in Movement/Pantomime focus on expressing meaning through movement and communicating images and actions through pantomime. Creative drama is a physical as well as verbal art form. The body, voice, and mind are the basic tools of the participant. RIM also places a great deal of emphasis on the participants' ability to feel comfortable with their bodies, to develop flexibility and agility, and to use their bodies to communicate clearly and effectively. Remember, drama is about action, not words. Help your participants develop skills that are at the very core of the actor's power.

The exercises in this Starter category are of two main types:

- Traditional movement exercises that explore the element of dance, without a narrative or character aspect.
- Pantomime exercises that deal with the "show me" physicalization of various activities.

Both types of exercises are extremely important in developing the participants' understanding of themselves "moving" and "showing." Neither type of exercise involves verbalization. Participants do, however, verbalize when they reflect upon their work and the work of others after the activities have been completed.

The leader's role is primarily that of coach. Since the movement/pantomime exercises occur with little or no participant verbalization, the leader can easily comment and side-coach while participants are working. Guiding lines focus participants' attention on the image or add additional aspects for exploration, such as seeing self become the image. The leader may also act as a model in some of these exercises by providing behaviors for the participants to duplicate or suggesting movement to get participants started. Reflection at the end of the exercises allow the participants to discuss the visual/kinesthetic images that facilitated their movement/pantomime, and to ask specific questions about how to achieve their objectives. During reflection, the whole group, not just the leader, enter into the discussion.

Movement

The movement exercises are based on the exploration of and experimentation with the elements of dance: *body, space, force,* and *time.* In these exercises, you introduce participants to the vocabulary of movement, as well as to the elements of principles of movement. Participants need to use these words to describe how they are moving and what they wish to accomplish. They should be aware, for example, that they are moving at a high level; that they are isolating their torsoes and that they are using staccato movements. These elements are basic to all movements and should be reinforced during guiding lines and during the reflection period.

Body awareness involves an understanding of body parts and body moves. Body parts include the external body parts such as arms, legs, back, or neck; and the internal parts like muscles, bones, or joints, which also aid and influence movement. "Mirror, mirror" is one example of an exercise that isolates specific body parts. How the body moves from one place to another is another important concept. In "Locomotion" participants focus on the various ways to move through space.

Space exercises challenge participants to consider various types of "where" questions. Exercises such as "One to Fifteen" and "High/Low Shapes" provide participants with opportunities to focus on the space around them, and ways to make use of that space.

Force exercises require participants to think about how they move and to consider what happens when they modify the degree of force used. Changes in effort (sharp or smooth), weight (heavy or light), or balance help participants actively learn about force. "Opposites" is an exercise that utilizes force to create interesting new movements.

Time is associated with pulse, beat, accent, and duration, factors that give movement its particular rhythm and pattern. "Metronome" is an example of an exercise that focuses on the element of time.

Most movement exercises follow a format that can be replicated from activity to activity. First, present to the participants the particular element to be explored, often by using a visual aid, prop, or picture. In "Metronome," for example, a metronome demonstrates the idea of fast/slow rhythm. Second, encourage the participants to explore and experiment with the element or concept, first in place, and then through space. Using the metronome, for example, the participants may explore fast/slow with various body parts and then moving through space. Finally, the participants put their movements into some organized form. They start with a beginning shape, move through space focusing on the concept which they have explored, and end with another shape — a basic dance pattern. This simple three-step procedure allows for a thorough and effective experimentation with many elements.

POINTERS — MOVEMENT

- Use movement vocabulary.
- Connect the elements of dance to kinesthetic images.
- Follow a similar format for the movement lessons.
- Encourage experimentation with the element presented.
- Utilize the basic dance pattern to facilitate expression.

Pantomime

Pantomime exercises require the participants to show actions without using words. Early pantomime exercises such as "Small Objects" focus on familiar activities and common memory images. Then, participants explore in pantomime the wide range of possible ways to "show," for example, the everyday action of saying hello in "Greetings." Such classic follow-the-leader pantomime exercises such as "Moving Statues" and "Shadows" require participants to work together as a group or in pairs, either imitating actions or shaping the posture and gestures of another—both important pantomime-related skills. The final pantomime activities deal with important classic theatrical pantomime concepts. "Be a Sport" and "Group Machine," for example, deal with the development of a merged, physicalized ensemble.

Coach participants to visualize the image in their mind's eye and to be aware that images often become clearer through enacting. Also introduce the idea of overlaying self as image by coaching participants to "see" themselves as the person doing the activity. You, as coach, need to emphasize articulation of gesture and movement and matching the action to the image in their mind's eye. Make sure that these pantomime exercises do not turn into party charades. They are not "Guess-what-I'm-doing" games. What they are doing should be obvious. The focus must be on the clarity and exactness of the articulated actions rather than the content of the activity. Always remind the participants to "Show, don't tell." Through these exercises the participants will come to know their physical potential for expressing themselves through movement and pantomime, without the use of words.

POINTERS — PANTOMIME

- Begin with familiar activities.
- Encourage participants to "show, don't tell."
- Provide many opportunities to work in pairs and small groups.
- Strengthen the imagination/action connection by asking participants to reflect on what they have just done.
- Emphasize articulation of gesture and movement.
- Avoid guessing games.

Exercise: **Flex and Relax** Category: Introduction/Transition

Imagery Strategies
Overlay image of relaxation over body tension

Dramatic Behaviors
Focus attention on body parts; develop awareness of ways to release tension; sense the difference between tension and relaxation

Number of Participants: Whole group

Materials Needed: None

Directions: Instruct participants to find a comfortable place on the floor. Ask them to lie on their backs, close their eyes, and rest their arms beside their bodies. You will ask the participants to tense and then relax various body parts until each part of their body has been tightened and loosened and their entire body is calm and tension free. The body parts in sequence are: toes, feet, calves, thighs, buttocks, abdomen, chest, shoulders, arms, hands, neck, face.

Guiding Lines: This exercise will help you relieve the tension in your body. You will feel calm and relaxed after this activity.

First, clench your feet and toes tightly, tighter (for three to five seconds) and let it go. Repeat. Now clench your calves tight, tighter. Now let them go; relax your fists. (Go on to the rest of the body parts as described above.)

Feel the difference between the tightened muscles and the relaxed muscles.

Your body may feel different from when we started this activity. It may feel heavier or lighter, cooler or warmer. . . . Enjoy the feeling. . . . Just relax and let the calm sink into every part of your body.

This exercise will make you feel calm and ready to work.

Notes: Your voice should be smooth and reassuring. There is no right or wrong way to relax; the objective is to relax. The participants will get better at relaxing every time this is done. Check their amount of relaxation by lifting their arm carefully and feeling the looseness and the weight of the arm. Be positive! Be encouraging!

Modifications: Begin with the face and work down.

Exercise: **Up, Up, and Away** Category: Introduction/Transition

Imagery Strategies
Experience the sense of movement; focus on various types of movement in the mind's eye

Dramatic Behaviors
Notice movement in the world; discriminate the kinds of movement of here-and-now objects

Number of Participants: Whole group

Materials Needed: None

Directions: Have the participants sit comfortably in a circle or lie on the floor. Tell them they are going to take a balloon ride today in their mind's eye. While they are floating above the world below, ask them to pay special attention to how things move. Tell them that this is a magical ride and that they will all enjoy their trip very much.

Guiding Lines: Sit comfortably (or lie down) and relax. Take some slow, deep breaths and close your eyes.

Now step into the basket of a large colorful helium balloon. Get comfortable in the basket.

Feel the balloon slowly begin to rise up into the sky. I am with you so you don't have to be afraid.

The sky is clear and there is a gentle breeze.

Direct your balloon above the city.

Look at the people below. See them walking, running.

Look at the cars in traffic. Watch them stop and go at the traffic lights. How else do the cars move.

What else do you see moving?*

Your balloon slowly floats out of the city into the country.

See the birds flying past you. Watch a truck on the road.

See some children on bicycles. How fast do they move?

What else do you see moving?*

Guide your balloon back to the spot where you began.

Now return to this room feeling happy and excited about your magical balloon ride.

When I count to ten open your eyes.

Notes: Remember to pause for at least 15 seconds per line, waiting a minute or more at the starred places (*). Participants need a chance to develop and enjoy their images. In the discussion, talk about what they saw moving (people, bicycles, animals, etc.), the ways they moved (fast, slow, stop–start, etc.), and how they moved (on wheels, legs, etc.)

Modifications: Up, Up, and Away can also be used to get a bird's-eye-view of other things besides movement and to help develop a new perspective or point of view.

Exercise: **Gesture Drawing** Category: Introduction/Transition

Imagery Strategies

Focus on the shape in space; record kinesthetic images through scribbling

Dramatic Behaviors

Observe different shapes; express gesture, posture, shape with ease; develop a kinesthetic awareness of movement

Number of Participants: Whole group

Materials Needed: Crayons (chunky dark crayons), 12- by 18-inch sheets (many) of newsprint

Directions: Explain that the participants are going to draw the person (the model) in the center of the circle. The participants will quickly scribble the posture, stance, and gesture of a model who is posed in the center of a circle. Using loopy circles, the participants scribble the person, trying to get "the feel" of their shape. They do not draw; they scribble! Each picture should take about 20 to 30 seconds. The model (or models) continues to take different poses until the students have done eight to twelve gesture drawings.

Guiding Lines: Today we are going to look closely at the shape people make in space and record that shape in a scribble. Sit in a large circle; give yourself enough elbow room. (Pass out paper and crayons.)

First, let's just scribble to get the feel for it again. When you were little (about two) you used to scribble all the time.

Today we will scribble, but with a purpose.

Okay, take a clean piece of paper.

May I have a volunteer to pose for us? (Select one.)

Stand in the middle and strike an interesting pose. Make sure you can hold it for awhile.

Okay, start with the head and scribble in the shape of the body. DO NOT OUTLINE the body. The body has mass — muscles, bones, etc.

Scribble in the shape . . . the shoulders, arms (big scribble), the torso, legs—relax model.

(Point out the ones who got "the feel" for the shape.)

Next model: shape, scribble, etc.

(Do this eight to twelve times. Encourage the models to take interesting shapes. Emphasize scribbling and the shape the model is in.)

Notes: Many children will begin drawing the outline. Emphasize the mass. Scribbling fills in the shape. Try to capture the "feel" of the shape. Use this exercise often to free up their movement observation.

You may ask various class members to act as models. You can also ask an outsider to be a model.

Modifications: Use newspaper—the printing doesn't matter. Old stumpy crayons work best for scribbling. Use this exercise after characters in a drama have been established to isolate a "psychological gesture" that is specific to that character.

Exercise: High/Low Shapes — Category: Movement/Pantomime

Imagery Strategies
Develop storehouse of images of self moving; select specific images

Dramatic Behaviors
Develop awareness of space; explore various movements; develop awareness of levels

Number of participants: Whole group

Materials Needed: Tambourine or hand drum

Directions: Clear the room as much as possible. Explain to participants that today they will be doing movement. Ask the participants to make a high shape with their bodies. Give them time to experiment with making a high shape. Ask them to make low shapes with their bodies. Give them time to experiment. Have them select two of their highest shapes and two of their lowest shapes. Instruct the group that when you hit the tambourine once, they are to make the high shape and freeze. When you hit the tambourine twice, they make the low shape. Repeat high/low. Vary: high/high/low/low, etc.

Guiding Lines: Really stretch to make that high shape. Remember how that feels. Get as low as you can go. Remember how that feels. Try another shape. Use your whole body. Try yet a different shape. Make them interesting.

Choose your high shape. Choose your low shape. When you hear the tambourine, get a picture in your mind and move. Be in control.

Notes: The participants may select one shape in the mind's eye and execute another. Early in drama, the ability to do what you image is undeveloped. If you go through the exercise one whole time and then repeat the whole exercise, the kinesthetic action will help participants develop images that are their stimuli for future movement decisions.

Modifications: Variations include little and big shapes, crooked and straight shapes, wide and skinny shapes. At this time stick to adjectives that describe body shapes, not feeling ones, like happy and sad.

Eventually have the group consider the flow from high to low shapes or vice versa. Have them work in pairs to develop a dance about shapes.

Exercise: **Mirror, Mirror** Category: Movement/Pantomime

Imagery Strategies
Focus on fine detail in movement; imitate modeled behavior; become aware of body

Dramatic Behaviors
Observe body parts moving; work with partner; learn give and take; observe and physicalize simultaneously

Number of Participants: Whole group/pairs within groups

Materials Needed: None

Directions: Ask the participants to each find their own space. Warm them up by asking them to shake their whole body. "Stretch, swing, bend, twist, and shake again." Explain that they are going to isolate various parts of their body by moving each part one at a time. As a whole group, coach them to explore various body parts (head, shoulders, arms, back, toes, hips, legs, etc.) through movement (swinging, twisting, rolling, shaking, bending, stretching) at various speeds (fast and slow).

After sufficient time for exploration, ask participants to find a partner. Have them imagine that one of them is a mirror (B); the other is looking into the mirror (A). Tell A to begin to make clear, smooth movements with different body parts. B must focus on A's movement and reproduce it exactly. When the activity is progressing, ask the mirror and the leader to switch—with B leading and A mirroring.

Guiding Lines: Slowly! Don't go so quickly that your partner cannot follow. How many shapes can your mirror follow? Change levels. Watch closely! Follow! Mirror exactly. Move your whole body. Isolate one body part. See if the mirror can follow you. Use clear, slow movement. Good!

Notes: This exercise is a classic. Keep the focus on isolating body parts, observation, and mirroring. Allow some giggling and uneasiness, since participants are face to face. This exercise requires concentration. Once participants begin to focus on body parts instead of on the person, they will become more comfortable.

Modifications: For participants who move too quickly, initiate a "mirror" delay.

When the group is ready, divide the class in half and have each half demonstrate its mirror duets.

Exercise: **One to Fifteen** Category: Movement/Pantomime

Imagery Strategies
Image self accomplishing task; expand storehouse of images of self moving

Dramatic Behaviors
Develop a sense of self in space; plan a movement in space

Number of Participants: Whole group

Materials Needed: None

Directions: Clear the room as much as possible. Explain to participants that each must find two places in the room: a starting point (A) and a finishing point (B). Ask each participant to freeze at starting point, to move when you say begin and to freeze at finishing point. Review this activity a few times, then ask participants to move from A to B on the count of fifteen, covering as much space as possible. Before you start, count from 1 to 15, but participants will only image themselves moving from A to B. Then ask participants to move from A to B.

Now, ask participants to image themselves moving from A to B on the count of 15, covering as little space as possible. Then go on to activity.

Guiding Lines: Find a starting place. Remember that place. Find a finishing place. Remember that place.

See yourself moving through space. Make a movement plan. Don't get there too soon! Don't get there too late!

Take an interesting starting shape. Move the way you saw yourself moving. Make an interesting ending shape. When you get there, hold it!

Notes: Often there is little relationship between the activity in the mind's eye and the actual accomplishment of the task. The first time through provides participants with a set of movement images upon which to base the better accomplishment of 1 to 15.

Modifications: This exercise can form the basis for countless others. Asking participants to accomplish it as a character is one way to modify it.

Modifications will make this exercise interesting again and again. Change pathway (direct, indirect). Change tempo (fast, slow). Lead with a body part (head, shoulder, hips, etc.).

Your internal image of yourself and your reflection in the mirror can have similar characteristics and can also be very different. Participation in drama allows individuals to get to know themselves by seeing themselves reflected in and by others. (Pablo Picasso, *Girl Before a Mirror,* Collection, The Museum of Modern Art. Gift of Mrs. Simon Guggenheim)

Exercise: Locomotion — Category: Movement/Pantomime

Imagery Strategies
Overlay self with image; expand storehouse of movement images

Dramatic Behaviors
Physicalize the seven types of locomotion; imitate modeled behavior

Number of Participants: Whole group

Materials Needed: None

Directions: Demonstrate to the group the various ways of getting from one place to the other: walk, run, hop, jump, skip, gallop, leap. Observe and discuss how these movements are different. Ask class to imitate you.

Guiding Lines: Watch me move from one place to another. Focus on what my legs, arms, feet, body is doing.

Imitate me.

Remember how it feels to move this way. Remember what you do to move this way.

Notes: You will be surprised how many participants will not understand the difference between such basic moves as *walk* and *run*. For older groups, ask them to figure it out by themselves before you explain it to them.

Modifications: Let participants watch others to check if everyone is indeed running and not walking.

Possible variations include changing levels (high, middle, low), changing directions (backwards, sideways), or changing speed (fast, slow).

Exercise: Opposites — Category: Movement/Pantomime

Imagery Strategies
Develops kinesthetic images of opposite forces; match auditory and movement images

Dramatic Behaviors
Develop awareness of force; explore the changes force creates through movement

Number of Participants: Whole group

Materials Needed: *Sustained* instruments (triangles, cymbals, gong); *sudden* instruments (drum, claves, wood block)

Directions: Have the participants find a place on the floor. Ask them to sit quietly. Explain that you want them to move their arms until they cannot hear the sound of the triangle any more. Strike the triangle once. Repeat. Now have them move their arms to the beat of a drum, 1, 2, 3. Repeat. Ask the participants to describe the two movements: smooth, flowing, continuous and sharp, sudden, quick, etc. Repeat the sustained and sudden instruments but have the participants move their whole body, first on a spot and then through space. Focus on showing the difference between the two. Finally, ask the participants to create a dance *incorporating* both the sudden and sustained movements.

Guiding Lines: Listen carefully! Keep moving until the sound stops. Use your whole body.

As soon as the sound stops, do the same. Listen! Every time you hear it, move; when it ends, stop.

Change levels. Change direction. Make your moving interesting.

Notes: This exercise lets participants explore one aspect of force. Both the sudden and sustained movements can be used within other activities.

Modifications: Let participants work in pairs with one partner moving with sustained, smooth, flowing movements and the other with sudden, quick, sharp movements.

Exercise: Metronome — Category: Movement/Pantomime

Imagery Strategies
Experience the rhythm kinesthetically; record a particular rhythmic beat; retrieve images stimulated by here-and-now sound

Dramatic Behaviors
Imitate the metronome rhythm in movement; discriminate physically among various speeds; develop rhythmic awareness

Number of Participants: Whole group, small groups within group

Materials Needed: Metronome or drum beat

Directions: Play metronome at various speeds, so participants can see how rhythmic and accurate the metronome is. Choose three different metronome speeds: fast, slow, medium (not so slow or fast that participants can't duplicate it). Play medium rhythm first. Ask participants to move their bodies — in place — to the metronome. Then turn off metronome and ask participants to continue moving in time to metronome in their minds. Turn metronome back on to see how closely movement approximates rhythm. Continue with fast rhythm. Then slow rhythm.

Guiding Lines: Listen to this rhythmic beat (medium).

Stay in place. Move your bodies to the rhythm of the metronome.

Use your whole body, back, legs, hips.

Continue moving to the same rhythm even when I turn the metronome off.

Keep moving. Did you keep the rhythm?

Good.

Let's try another speed.

Notes: At first keep the off time short, especially with younger children. Gradually build up their auditory and kinesthetic memory by increasing the off time.

Modifications: Participants can move in space instead of in place to metronome.

Direct participants to move, in place, at different levels or using only specific body parts. Make the exercise interesting and challenging.

As a follow-up, ask participants to describe past experiences stimulated by metronome sound.

Exercise: Small Objects — Category: Movement/Pantomime

Imagery Strategies
Recall images of specific objects; image self accomplishing task; discriminate between imaging and seeing self image

Dramatic Behaviors
Concentrate on imaginary objects; establish and use an imaginary object in space; monitor and perform simultaneously

Number of Participants: Whole group

Materials Needed: Small cards with activities using small objects

Directions: Direct group to sit comfortably on the floor around the room. Give each participant a "small-object" card. Once cards are distributed, allow the group time to close their eyes and image their small-object activity. When you are certain they can image the activity, have them pantomime these simultaneously. Let the duration of the activity last as long as the majority of the group continues to pantomime. When the activity is finished, tell each participant to pass the card to another person. Repeat until everyone does every activity.

Guiding Lines: Look at the object. See the object in action. Now see yourself using the object.

Now, focus on showing the object. Don't take your eyes off the object.

Again, see yourself using the object.

Notes: Some good activities are: threading a needle, cutting your fingernails, picking up pins on the floor, setting the time on your watch, operating a small calculator, looking for a contact lens, cracking a walnut and eating it, removing a splinter from finger.

In all exercises where participants are to pass a card or object, it is a good idea to establish a rotation pattern for them to follow.

In this exercise you are introducing the difference between doing or seeing self doing.

Modifications: Repeat with large objects.

Exercise: Greetings — Category: Movement/Pantomime

Imagery Strategies
Recall a sound and/or visual image; image self adopting that remembered behavior

Dramatic Behaviors
Work with a partner; use a visual or sound image to stimulate current action

Number of Participants: Individual within the whole group

Materials Needed: None

Directions: Ask the group silently to recall various ways they have seen people greet each other after an absence. Encourage them to recall as many of these reunions as possible. Then ask each participant in the group to focus on the visual and/or sound image that is most clear. Ask each participant to picture him or herself assuming that gesture and greet others in that way.

Have everyone stand up and, all at the same time, go from person to person greeting each in that particular way.

Guiding Lines: Recall how people say hello. Focus on the way each looks and moves and talks.

See yourself greeting others, in that particular way.

Now act on that image. Greet others the way you saw yourself do it.

Notes: This exercise may be used later in the drama process to help participants discover character behaviors.

Exercise: Moving Statues — Category: Movement/Pantomime

Imagery Strategies
Recall and record images; discriminate between current here-and-now shape and memory images of previous one

Dramatic Behaviors
Attend to body shape of others; plan new poses; explore physical space; work as a group

Number of Participants: Individual within group

Materials Needed: None

Directions: Appoint one person in the group as the observer; others around the observer are statues. Tell the statues to strike a pose. Allow the observer a designated time period to observe the statues. Direct the observer to close his eyes, and count slowly to ten. In that time, the statues change position or poses if they wish. On the count of ten, the observer tells the statues to freeze. The observer opens his eyes and trys to identify the statues that moved.

Guiding Lines: Try to make a mental picture of how you see people stand. Concentrate!

Statues move quietly! Some move a lot, others hardly at all.

Compare what you see with what you saw.

Notes: This exercise is more effective if the statues move quickly and quietly so the observer cannot hear. Arrange the space in the room so many participants have to be near the observer.

Modifications: Have statues assume poses at various levels — some standing, sitting, kneeling.

Exercise: Shadows — Category: Movement/Pantomime

Imagery Strategies
Record movement; attend to detail of self and in others

Dramatic Behaviors
Observe another's movements; imitate another's movements

Number of Participants: Pairs

Materials Needed: Flashlight or lamp, darkened room

Directions: Using the flashlight in a darkened room, demonstrate a shadow. Explain that shadows follow behind and are in the same exact shape as the person, hand, or whatever you use to cast the shadow. Divide group into pairs, with one person in each pair designated as the shadow. Have the pair move across the floor, the "shadow" copying every move. Repeat until the idea of "shadow" is clear and everyone has had a chance to do it.

Guiding Lines: Who knows what a shadow is?

Watch closely while I show you a shadow of my hand (move hand). What happens to the shadow when I move my hand? The shadow moves exactly as my hand does; it copies my hand movement.

We are going to make shadows today—you'll work in pairs — one of you will be the shadow. As the shadow, copy the movements of your partner exactly.

Find a partner and line up on this side of the room, shadows behind your partner. When I tell you, move across the room, shadows following. Don't move too quickly; be deliberate and slow. Shadows, copy your partner. Anticipate their moves. You should be moving exactly the same.

Next three pairs. . . . (Continue until everyone has had a chance to be a "shadow.")

Notes: In the demonstration, don't let the shadow get too much bigger than the hand itself. This may distort their understanding of the goal of the exercise. You may need to demonstrate the movement across the room with a student partner so they understand. In this case, you should be the shadow. Make them move slowly at first. If they understand let them move faster, but keep the movements smooth, not jerky!

The woman in this painting uses her arms, hands, and even her head to make a swan. Within this shadowplay, the shadowmaker and the swan seem joined. (© 1985 Lauren Attinello, *Swan*, courtesy of the artist)

Exercise: **Group Machine** Category: Movement/Pantomime

Imagery Strategies
Retrieve previously perceived image; incorporate self image with group image

Dramatic Behaviors
Move as if mechanical object; work as a group

Number of Participants: Whole group

Materials Needed: Several simple machines: an electric can opener, a mechanical motor, a clock

Directions: Demonstrate each machine to the group. Point out the details of the mechanics of the machine: how a switch turns it on, how each part meshes with others. Discuss with the group how mechanical tools move differently from humans. Remove machines and ask participants to retrieve images of these machines or other machines they have seen. Ask them to try to focus on just one aspect of the machine that they might be able to demonstrate with their bodies. Have them picture themselves moving as if a machine.

Then have one person start a machine movement in place. Encourage others to join as another part of the machine until they have made a large group machine.

Guiding Lines: Really observe this machine. See the detail in its mechanics.

Try to recall this or another machine you have seen. See the detail.

Picture yourself becoming the machine.

Merge your image with what is happening with the group.

Notes: In early group drama, you may have to coach participants into joining the activity.

Modifications: You may wish to develop machines which have a purpose — like making a shoe — or you may have pairs or threes recreate a specific machine — a washer or a dishwasher, for example.

Exercise: Be a Sport — Category: Movement/Pantomime

Imagery Strategies
Overlay self and image; select images to be enacted; retrieve images of sports

Dramatic Behaviors
Work in small groups; physicalize whole picture; experience plan/play structure

Number of Participants: Small groups of three to six

Materials Needed: Various sports equipment

Directions: Show various sports equipment from the selected group sport (baseball, basketball, hockey, football, for example). Coach participants into recalling the sports as played or viewed by them. Then ask participants to see themselves becoming part of the sport, playing various positions and using various equipment. After this coaching, divide group into small groups. Ask each group to decide what players are necessary to make a complete picture of the sport. Allow each group to plan the scene, using no props, merely pantomiming the activity without dialogue. After ample planning time, have each small group show whole group their sport.

Guiding Lines: Have you ever seen football? Have you ever played football? Recall the activity. See yourself involved in the activity. See the whole picture.

When you plan, think about what part you play in the whole. Sometimes you must change what you play to make a better group picture.

Notes: This exercise focuses on the individual working to develop the whole group picture.

Modifications: You may also ask the group to pantomime places, such as a playground or a library.

SOUND/SPEECH

The Sound/Speech Starters are built primarily on one sense modality — the auditory. These exercises develop and enhance auditory images, beginning with listening and hearing and continuing on to creating and communicating. Participants may come to you with a keen sense of hearing and a knack for recreating sounds and words. Still others may have difficulty, due to inexperience or to a less well-developed sense of hearing. These Sound/Speech exercises begin with listening and imitating. Then participants create and share sounds, using body, voice, and instruments. These exercises demand that participants attend to the rhythm, tone, texture, and context of sounds before adding speech to them. When they begin to add words in later exercises, participants will have a rich repertoire of auditory images and communication experiences.

In Sound/Speech exercises the leader is more of a director than a guide. The leader introduces the exercise, gives examples, and then allows the participants to discover and explore the world of here-and-now sounds and their own auditory images. Since listening is the basic skill, the leader does not talk as much during these exercises as in some of the other Starters. Fewer guiding lines are suggested. The leader often moves through the group listening to individuals, pairs, or small groups. Evaluation takes place after the exercise has been completed. Many leaders do not feel comfortable with preverbal work and quickly pass by these early exercises to move on to verbal exercises. But, Starters build the elementary imagery strategies and dramatic behaviors that can be combined and enhanced in Transformations. Don't shortchange your participants.

The Sound/Speech exercises can be discussed in terms of three main kinds of skills: *identification, exploration,* and *communication.* Identification exercises develop listening skills that demand that participants really hear sounds and work at recording auditory images, as well as discriminate among sounds. Participants attend to various everyday sounds in "Find-a-Voice" and "Noisy Words" and engage in imitating or creating sound patterns in "Story Sounds" and "Musical Patterns." You can modify these exercises by changing the sound stimulus. The objectives of these exercises is to heighten the sense of hearing as participants work at listening, recording, and imitating sounds around them.

The Sound/Speech Starters that focus on exploration are fun and lively. Using their own bodies, rhythm instruments, found objects, musical selections, and their own voices, participants discover the diverse tonal qualities and auditory textures that sounds can create. Participants work in pairs to develop the basic talk-and-listen pattern in an exercise like "Echo." During the exploration exercises, participants are introduced to the particular way that creative artists use words within a drama to create mood and heighten emotions. "Moody Words" and "Background Music" are two examples of exercises that focus on dramatic sensibilities. The ability to recreate an auditory message or pattern — in sounds, words, or with instruments — is a precursor to work with dialogue. Participants must feel the exchange and the alternating pattern of talking and listening before effective, communicative dialogue can occur.

In the most difficult exercises, participants focus on the specific message to be communicated. They explore the many ways words are used to communicate and to express a feeling in "Oh, Oh" and "Bright Idea." The talk-and-listen pattern is strengthened in "Musical Conversations." Through these Starters, participants learn how to create and communicate using their voices, body, musical instruments, and other here-and-now objects. Participants have the opportunity to discover the importance of dramatic dialogue in these exercises, especially in "Wizard."

POINTERS — SOUND/SPEECH

- Focus initially on listening and imitating.
- View Sound/Speech in a context larger than just verbal.
- Be a good listener.
- Provide a variety of objects, instruments, and music for sound stimulus and creation.
- Emphasize the tone and textural quality of sounds, music, and words.
- Build the talk-and-listen pattern.

Exercise: **Silence Game** Category: Introduction/Transition

Imagery Strategies
Experience silence within; focus on the quiet and calm

Dramatic Behaviors
Develop awareness of self as silent; center energies; develop self-control

Number of Participants: Whole group

Materials Needed: None

Directions: Have the participants sit in a circle on the floor. Explain that you are going to close your eyes, and that they are to get absolutely silent, quieting their bodies and getting very calm. When they are quiet, open your eyes and comment on their silence and readiness to work.

Guiding Lines: Let's play the Silence Game.

I will close my eyes, and I want each of you to get as quiet as you possibly can.

Quiet your bodies by making them very still and relaxed. You can keep your eyes open or close them.

Let your mind be calm and quiet. (When it is very quiet, open your eyes.)

I can see and hear that you are very silent and ready for our drama work today.

Notes: This can be used as a preparation for other listening work or as a transition exercise before beginning drama work, before returning to regular classes, or between drama exercises to refocus.

Exercise: **Green Meadows** Category: Introduction/Transition

Imagery Strategies
Focus on an imaginary setting; recall various sounds; experience the peace and tranquility of the setting

Dramatic Behaviors
Notice specific sounds around them; discriminate sounds in a meadow

Number of Participants: Whole group

Materials Needed: None

Directions: Have the participants lie down or sit comfortably in a circle. Tell them they are going to take a guided fantasy journey to a peaceful meadow near a running brook. While they are there, you want them to listen carefully to the various sounds and noises they are hearing.

Guiding Lines: Sit comfortably (or lie down) and relax.

You're sitting (or lying) in a calm, peaceful meadow.

Feel the cool green grass.

Feel the warm sun and gentle breeze on your face.

Smell the scent of flowers in the air.

Look up and see the blue sky. Small white clouds are drifting by.

See some birds flying by. Listen to them.

Take a deep breath. Listen carefully. Do you hear anything else? a bee near a flower? crickets chirping? Listen.

Hear the babbling brook. Listen to the water flowing, splashing over the rocks.

Walk over toward the brook.

Do something you enjoy.

Enjoy this calm and peaceful setting.

Return to this room.

When I count to ten, open your eyes.

Notes: Remember to pause at the appropriate places, giving the participants enough time to create and enjoy their images. Use a very pleasant, soft voice during the guided fantasy. Give the participants time to return at the end by counting to ten. Participants will be relaxed and calm after this exercise, so plan a low-key activity to follow.

Modifications: Plan guided fantasy journeys to other tranquil places: a beach, a shady tree, a pond, etc.

Exercise: Musical Pictures — Category: Introduction/Transition

Imagery Strategies
Focus on the feeling or mood in a piece of music; allow here-and-now sound to inspire them

Dramatic Behaviors
Physicalize the feelings in music; discriminate between different types of music; respond to sound through movement

Number of Participants: Whole group

Materials Needed: Crayons or chalk and newsprint, record player, variety of music

Directions: Instruct the participants to find a place on the floor where they have room to draw. Pass out newsprint and crayons. Explain that music can make people feel many different ways and that they are to discover the feeling in the music by making designs, while listening to various kinds of music. Choose four to six songs that are very different from one another (classical, marching band, rock 'n' roll, etc.). Try to find a variety of moods and feelings in the pieces. With each song they are to begin a new design. After each song, participants will choose their favorite musical drawing and share them, in a circle, as the songs are replayed. Emphasize the way the song made them feel and how this was demonstrated in their design, the line, pattern, color, etc.

Guiding Lines: Quiet your minds and bodies.

Listen and let your hand respond.

Feel the music in your body.

This song has a different feeling. Listen quietly for a few seconds before you begin.

Notes: Many school libraries have collections of records. Check with the music teacher. You may even want to make a tape of appropriate pieces for further use.

Remember, don't confuse the objective of this exercise with objectives of more complicated activities, which, on the surface, seem to be similar. Your focus is simply to inspire participants to draw to music, not to make a visual record of the music.

Modifications: Focus on inside sounds: the door closing, footsteps, something falling, etc.

Exercise: Find-a-Voice — Category: Introduction/Transition

Imagery Strategies
Focus on texture, tone, and details in sounds; match a here-and-now sound with a sound image

Dramatic Behaviors
Listen to individual voices; become aware of the differences and similarities in voices

Number of Participants: Whole group

Materials Needed: Several copies of simple voice exercises, a poem, or nursery rhymes

Directions: Have the group sit in a circle. Select three participants to read the same piece, one at a time. Then have the participants close their eyes and quietly select one of the three readers to reread their piece. Ask the participants to identify which person had spoken of the three. Redo this a number of times, selecting different readers and making it more and more difficult to discriminate between voices.

Guiding Lines: Listen to the voice, not the words. Hear the sounds their voices make. Listen closely. Which reader just read? How did you know? What was different about their voice?

Notes: Surprisingly, many people cannot match voices, except of people with very distinctive tone or diction. Try not to make this exercise a guessing game, but an exercise of real concentration.

Modifications: If the group has been together for a while, class members may know the voices of their class members. Ask participants to close their eyes for the whole exercise or ask the readers to disguise their voice while reading.

Exercise: Story Sounds — Category: Sound/Speech

Imagery Strategies
Retrieve and select auditory images

Dramatic Behaviors
Physicalize sound; work in group; develop awareness of sound; identify sounds that communicate real-life sounds and mood

Number of Participants: Whole group

Materials Needed: Stories rich with action; sounds of cars, planes, wind, rain, cities, people

Directions: Instruct participants to sit quietly on the floor while you read the story to them. After reading it once, discuss how the story could be enhanced by adding sound effects. Review the story, pausing each time a sound could be added. Ask participants to decide on how to make the sound. When all sounds have been created, reread the story without pausing, while they make the sounds.

Guiding Lines: How can you make that sound with your body? What pitch is the sound? How long should it last? How loud/soft should it be? How can you make that sound?

Think of sounds that are not mentioned. Can sound create mood? Add both sound effects and mood sound.

Notes: Poetry, short stories, fables, and fairy tales are excellent sources of additional material for this type of exercise.

Modifications: Make a sound tape of the story. Listen to the tape and discuss how the sound effects can be modified or changed to enhance the story.

Divide class into small groups. Give each group a story to tell with sound effects.

Exercise: **Noisy Words** Category: Sound/Speech

Imagery Strategies

Recall sounds images; focus on here-and-now sounds; create onomatopoeic sound images stimulated by here-and-now words

Dramatic Behaviors

Observe sound-word relationship; communicate sound words; identify many objects that can make similar sounds when they move

Number of Participants: Whole group

Materials Needed: A set of cards, each listing one onomatopoeic ("noisy") word: plop, bang, buzz, ring, whirl, rumble, stomp, clap, snap, slap, rip, zip, clop

Directions: Seat the group in a circle. Distribute one card to each participant, including yourself. Ask each participant, one at a time, to "say" the word, making the word sound as much like the real sound as possible. Then ask each participant to recall a real experience in which the sound describes the main action. (Example, the clock buzzed.) Ask each person, one at a time, to sit in the middle of the circle. Repeat the sound with as much expression as possible. The other participants must identify as many objects or images that make that sound . . . being as descriptive as possible. (Thick pudding plops; big heavy raindrops plop; golf balls in a pond plop, etc.) When all the images run out, select a new word and continue the exercise.

Guiding Lines: Really hear the sound. Recall an experience in which you heard this sound. Try to see the action and add your action to the sequence. Be descriptive. Let us see and hear the noisy word you describe.

Notes: The focus of this Starter is to generate a large number of images from one noisy word. This allows participants to share personal images and experience idea-hitchhiking.

Modifications: Have small groups work together to create a noisy poem, using one "noisy" or onomatopoeic word as the stimulus.

Exercise: **Musical Patterns** Category: Sounds/Speech

Imagery Strategies

Match here-and-now sounds with sound images; concentrate on musical sounds; focus on musical patterns

Dramatic Behaviors

Listen closely; distinguish among musical instruments; repeat a musical pattern; develop talk-and-listen skills.

Number of Participants: Whole group

Materials Needed: Rhythm instruments (enough for everyone), such as claves, tone block, shakers, rhythm sticks, maracas

Directions: Place a rhythm instrument in front of each participant seated in the circle. Let them discover the sounds their instrument can make, then place the instrument down in front of them again. Explain that they must listen very closely to your instrument. Make a sound pattern with your instrument. Repeat the pattern. Ask the participants to make the exact same pattern with their instruments. After a couple of tries call on participants individually, or a few at a time, to repeat your pattern. Vary the pattern.

Guiding Lines: Listen to the pattern my instrument makes. Try to record this pattern. Hear it in your mind's ear. Listen again. Repeat my pattern with your instrument. Be exact.

Notes: Depending on the age and experience level of the group, adjust the patterns, varying the length and detail of the rhythm. Encourage the pairs to really get a sense of the talk-and-listen pattern. As soon as one "speaks," have the other repeat the pattern until it almost has a rhythm of its own.

Modification: Once the participants feel at ease with a number of lengths and pattern rhythms, divide the group into pairs and have them practice talking and listening with their instruments, taking turns leading the pattern and responding to it.

When participants are experienced, you can lengthen the number of beats in the pattern to be imitated.

Exercise: **Echo** Category: Sound/Speech

Imagery Strategies
Recall/retrieve sound images; develop a repertoire of sound images; focus on listening

Dramatic Behaviors
Imitate a variety of sounds; work in pairs; utilize voice and body in sound construction

Number of Participants: Pairs/whole group

Materials Needed: None

Directions: Begin this activity with a discussion of the many sounds everyone is capable of making with the human body. Explore ways to clap, tap, snap, slap, stamp, knock, etc. Encourage them to find as many sounds as possible and to use their whole body. Use guiding lines. After you have allowed ample time for exploration, divide class into pairs. Designate one person A and one person B. Instruct A to make a body sound. B is to echo A and add another sound. A then echoes B by first saying two sounds, then adding another. Pairs continue echoing and adding a sound until one person cannot remember the sequence. After the first round, discuss how to concentrate on sounds so they are easier to remember. Repeat the exercise, focusing on whether close attention will assist pairs in recording and recalling sound images.

Guiding Lines: Think of your whole body as an instrument. Find another way to make a sound. Explore the possibilities. Make an interesting combination or pattern. Listen. Record. Remember. Duplicate the sound. Add another. Make it interesting. Echo the pattern. Keep the sounds moving back and forth.

Notes: Encourage the students to move the sounds back and forth strengthening the talk-and-listen pattern.

Modifications: The voice is a very supple instrument. Repeat the exercise using nonsense words and a variety of vocal sounds. Allow time to explore what the voice can do before beginning.

Exercise: **How Far Am I?** Category: Sound/Speech

Imagery Strategies
Recall sound images; image someone far away

Dramatic Behaviors
Concentrate on vocal projection; develop awareness of speaking to various distances

Number of Participants: Small groups

Materials Needed: Cards with events such as calling people for dinner, rooting for your favorite team, calling children in from the playground, flagging down a taxi

Directions: Divide the participants into small groups. Explain that there are many times when we talk to people who are at a distance from us. Ask the group to name some of those circumstances.

Give each group a card that has a situation where people may be talking at various distances. Have each participant in the group talk to an imaginary person at a distance decided on by the group. Direct the participants to perform the exercise simultaneously as they try to project their voices various distances. When the exercise is completed once, all the groups are to pass their card on to the next group and repeat the activity.

Guiding Lines: From how far away are you speaking? What do you have to do to make them hear you? Keep speaking until your group knows how far away you are. Make them imagine the distance from which you are speaking.

Exercise: **Moody Words** Category: Sound/Speech

Imagery Strategies
Match sound images and vocal qualities; recall personal images; associate sound images with words

Dramatic Behaviors
Create a total sound picture; explore vocal qualities; discriminate among moods

Number of Participants: Whole group

Materials Needed: None

Directions: Explain to the whole group, seated in a circle, that this exercise explores the sound qualities found in just one word. (Select a subject rich in personal images; one of the seasons, a type of weather, a particular holiday, celebration, or event.) Ask the group to think of and agree upon one characteristic of snow—for example, "white." Have the groups explore all the ways you can say the word *white* (loud, soft, high, low, long and drawn out, short and quick, etc.) Select several ways to say *white* that express the feeling of snow. Use guiding lines. Divide the class into sound groups; giving each group one of the sounds for *white*. Explain to the groups that they are going to create a composition or sound picture of snow. Call on the groups, by pointing, to say *white*. Vary the sounds so sometimes they all speak together, sometimes separately. Record the total effect.

Guiding Lines: Imagine what snow looks like. See it falling softly. How would you say *white?* Sometimes it snows hard: say *white*. Snow can blow and move across a road: say *white*. Sometimes it just flurries, barely snowing at all: say *white*. Find all the ways the word *white* could communicate different snow experiences.

Notes: You may need to give a couple of examples before asking the participants to respond. The goal is to find the vocal potential of one word and to see how, when many renditions are joined, a total sound picture emerges. Remember to use silence as part of the picture.

Modifications: Divide the participants into four groups, each choosing a different word to characterize the image (e.g., white, falling, cold, light). Alternate their moody words to create a sound picture.

Can you image yourself projecting your voice with varying degrees of loudness so that the man in these six different pictures will be able to hear you? (*Yoga*, Photos by Michael Rocco Pinciotti)

$5
ADMISS
$10
DOORS OF
10 PM
Black
13
the stage at IRVING

$5
$10
DOORS OF
10 PM
Black

$5
$10

Exercise: Background Music — Category: Sound/Speech

Imagery Strategies
Focus on auditory images; utilize here-and-now instruments to create a musical effect; discern feeling or mood in a piece of music

Dramatic Behaviors
Discriminate between different types of instruments and sounds; work in groups; construct sound pieces; express feeling through sound

Number of Participants: Whole group

Materials Needed: A wide assortment of musical instruments. Cards with the following words on them: Morning, Storm, Train, Typewriter, Bee, Adventure, Challenge

Directions: In a whole group, listen to some familiar background music. Themes from popular movies are good (e.g., theme from *Star Wars, Rocky,* etc.). Explain that background music creates a particular effect to help listeners feel a certain way.

Divide the whole group into smaller working groups of between four and six children. Give each group a card with a title. The group, using the available instruments, must create a piece of music that creates a particular effect so listeners feel a certain way. Encourage them to try out a variety of sounds before deciding on their musical pattern. Tape the music from each group.

Guiding Lines: Discuss the effect to be achieved. How should this background music sound: Strong or light? Fast or slow? What instruments best fit your sound needs? Should you use similar or contrasting instruments? Work together. Use everyone's ideas.

Notes: Other music pieces that correspond to the titles given include: "Morning" from Peer Gynt Suite by Grieg; "Cloudburst" by Grofe; "The Little Train" by Villa-Lobos; "Typewriter" by Leroy Anderson; and "Flight of the Bumblebee" by Rimsky-Korsakov. You may wish to play these pieces to help participants understand that sound/music creates feelings in its listeners.

Modifications: Participants can create background music for their own dramas.

Exercise: Oh, Oh! — Category: Sound/Speech

Imagery Strategies
Recall/retrieve images; vocalize response, stimulated by recalled experience

Dramatic Behaviors
Communicate responses; express feeling through sound; explore communication through vocal tone and pitch

Number of Participants: Group

Materials Needed: None

Directions: Describe to the participants several situations that usually call for an emotional response, such as receiving a new puppy, watching a frightening movie, breaking an expensive vase, hearing a new song, hearing the ice cream man, falling and hurting their knee. Ask participants to respond with "oh" to each situation in a way that reflects how they feel about the situation.

Now coach them to recall their own real-life situation, to which they responded with an "oh." Ask participants to recall the situation in such detail that they are compelled to respond with "oh." After the recall, ask volunteers to describe situations.

Guiding Lines: How might you respond to this situation. If you could not say anything, just the word "oh," how might you say the word, so we would know how you feel?

Recall a real-life situation, like the one I just described, to which you responded "oh."

Try to remember the situation so well that you say "oh."

How did you feel?

How many ways did people say "oh" to mean many different feelings?

Use your voice. Check the reactions of your listeners.

Notes: You may want to model several oh's before asking individual children to respond. You want participants to realize that *how* something is said communicates as much as *what* is said.

Modifications: Try other responses, such as gasps, applause, screams.

Exercise: **Bright Idea** Category: Sound/Speech

Imagery Strategies
Select words to express feelings; recall/retrieve previous communication

Dramatic Behaviors
Develop awareness of voice inflection; explore various ways of persuading someone to do something; observe others in group

Number of Participants: Whole group

Materials Needed: One light bulb

Directions: Instruct group to sit in a circle while you place the light bulb in the center. The purpose of this exercise is to explore a variety of ways to convince the bulb to light. Begin the exercise by discussing how you ask, coax, plead, beg, order, demand, and threaten people to do things. Then, proceeding around the circle, ask each participant to try his own way to convince the bulb to light.

Guiding Lines: Listen to the ways other people try to get the bulb to light. Can you think of another way? How many bright ideas do you have for getting something you want? Really try to convince the light bulb. Make the situation real for yourself.

Notes: Exercises similar to this one are often found in improvisational acting classes. Sometimes called "jumps" (when one person "jumps" another to reach his/her objective), this exercise forms the foundation for dialogue building for the purpose of achieving objectives.

Modifications: Any object can be substituted for the light bulb.

Exercise: Musical Conversations

Category: Sound/Speech

Imagery Strategies
Match here-and-now sounds with sound images; concentrate on sounds

Dramatic Behaviors
Develop talk-and-listen skills; work on rhythm dialogue; listen for distinctions in expression

Number of Participants: Whole group

Materials Needed: Musical instruments, one for each

Directions: Discuss with the group places where people meet to talk either seriously or for fun. Where may they encounter groups of people talking?

Distribute the various musical instruments. Ask the participants to listen carefully to the different sounds their instrument makes. What type of person would make this sound? Have the participants play their instrument fast/slow, loud/soft. What kind of conversation would you be having when the instrument is played fast, slow, etc.?

Establish the social event. Have the group mill around, meeting various people and engaging in conversations using only their instruments for voices.

Guiding Lines: Listen to your instrument voice. What are you saying? Try to communicate the message.

Listen to the others' instrument voices. Who are they? What are they saying to you?

Use only your instruments to speak. No voices. Talk and listen.

Notes: At first, participants will find this rather humorous. Laughing masks the instrument sounds. Make the exercise short initially and each succeeding time lengthen the conversation time. Participants will learn to concentrate solely on the instrument voices. Allow time to talk about who they were and what types of people they met and conversations they had.

Modifications: Change instruments and repeat.

Exercise: Wizard

Category: Sound/Speech

Imagery Strategies
Recall image of previously perceived objects; select from image storehouse; use a variety of images as source for imagination image

Dramatic Behaviors
Talk-and-listen; communicate desire through dialogue; verbalize a need

Number of Participants: Individuals

Materials Needed: None

Directions: Choose one participant to play the "wizard." Explain that wizards can make almost anything happen. Usually they make good magic, but sometimes they play tricks on people. Then ask each participant to image something to request from the wizard. Coach participants into recalling that image clearly, if it is something they have previously experienced; if the wish is for something they haven't experienced, coach them into making the imagination image real to them.

One by one, the group goes to the wizard and communicates his or her wish to him. Explain that participants must really *convince* the wizard, because the wizard can grant or deny wishes. Also explain that those who are not granted wishes may have another opportunity to ask the wizard in the following round. When everyone in the group asks for one wish, select a new wizard for next round.

Guiding Lines: Really see your request! See the detail! The image is so clear that it compels you to speak! As you talk to the wizard, describe the detail in your image. Communicate the image to him.

Notes: If the wizard has a difficult time with granting or denying wishes, coach him in considering the request and not making snap decisions.

This exercise focuses on an important skill: developing images as the source of verbalization. Many participants merely say words, without considering the source for these words — the image. As leader, you must be able to spot the difference between a participant who is merely talking and one who is strongly stimulated to communicate.

MORE STARTERS

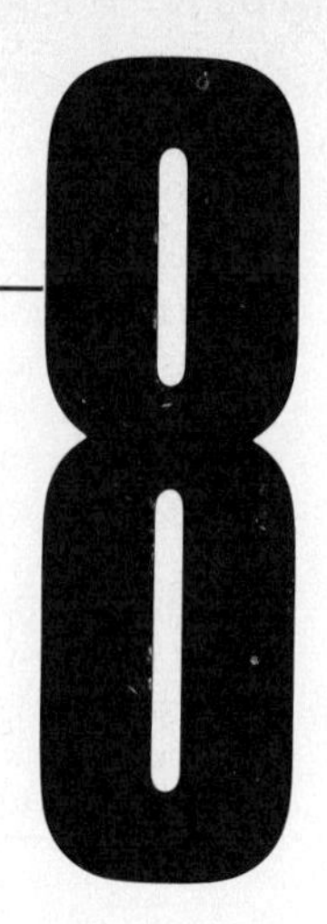

This chapter contains Starter exercises in the categories of Person/Character, Sequence/Story, and Design/Environment. It also contains a section that can help you build a RIM curriculum. As in the previous chapter, we include general information about the category as a whole, before presenting the exercises. The Starter format for each exercise is just like the Starter format for the exercises in Chapter 7.

PERSON/CHARACTER

Dramatic learning occurs when the participants are actively involved in developing specific skills that allow them to think and act dramatically. The ability to create a character, to act "as if" you are someone else is the hallmark of the creative drama process. Person/Character is the drama skill category with which you are probably most familiar, because of its link to actor-training exercises. Most other creative drama methods emphasize exercises that build characterization skills, some to the detriment of other areas. Remember that in RIM, Person/Character exercises are only one set of skills, albeit significant, necessary for dramatic growth.

Person/Character Starters begin with simple imitation exercises that require the participants to observe and attend to the detail in the posture and movement of others. Participants draw on recent as well as distant memory images to recreate characters. They are discouraged from falling back on stereotypic character images. Early characterization exercises help participants explore movements and gestures of both people and animals. Later exercises utilize props to stimulate character images and help create clear, vivid, and interesting characters. Through these exercises, participants develop self-awareness and realization of the uniqueness of others, as they differentiate between self and others.

Sometimes I feel like a figment of my own imagination.

Lily Tomlin

The leader acts primarily as a coach, giving suggestions and support. As coach, you must always remind the participants to visualize themselves in character, doing an exercise. Since Starters are based on memory images, the participants can return to their mind's eye to check on their character image. Remember in Starters participants are asked to imagine only one aspect of an improvisational situation. Thus, their "as if" behavior almost always occurs in the here-and-now. By isolating the specific skills necessary to create a character, participants become grounded in the types of simple behaviors unique to character development. Your main task as coach is to help individuals create their own character, drawing on their physical attributes and unique set of images. In Transformations, these skills are the foundation of the true art of characterization.

Early Person/Character exercises use specific here-and-now objects to stimulate character behavior. "Hats," "Clothes Make the Person," and "Magic Cloth" give participants practice in developing character movement and simple dialogue. Costumes are essential to the conduct of the exercises, for they help stimulate the recall of persons the participants have known and give participants something to "hold on to" as they explore characters.

The next group of Person/Character exercises deals with participants becoming the characters depicted in actual photos. Participants work on animal characters in "Animal Faces" and on people or people/animals in "Picture Freeze" and "Under the Big Top." Participants also explore simple character in the manner of the theatre costumer. In "Fantasy Creatures," participants construct character masks.

The final set of Person/Character exercises are more difficult. Each requires that participants add imagination images to their planning stage and improvise a major portion of the dialogue. In "Group Shoot," participants must add their unique point of view to a traditional Old West scenario. In "Stay in Character" and in "Living Biographies," participants must be so confident of their character and have such specific visual, kinesthetic, and auditory images of him or her that they are able to react in character to unexpected situations and to questions from other group members.

Coaching during Person/Character exercises takes sensitivity and the ability to withhold judgment. You must create a climate safe enough in which your participants will take risks and act "as if" someone else. Be careful not to evaluate too soon, since some participants will continue to use characters that have met with your approval. These exercises will bring out the wide range of individual personality differences in one group — from class clown to shrinking violet. If you keep the initial focus on the internal image rather than on the external action, you can ensure that all are as ready as they can be to begin.

POINTERS — PERSON/CHARACTER

- Develop a keen sense of observation yourself.
- Help participants attend to detail and observe people's unique characteristics.
- Encourage participants to see the character in their mind's eye.
- Emphasize fluency of ideas.
- Steer participants away from stereotypic character images.
- Assist participants in exploring character through prop and action.

Exercise: Breathing — Category: Introduction/Transition

Imagery Strategies
Focus on one's breathing and its ability to be calming

Dramatic Behaviors
Notice one's breathing and the changes that occur at relaxation; develop self-awareness; relax one's body through breathing

Number of Participants: Whole group

Materials Needed: None

Directions: Have participants lie on their backs and take a couple of deep cleansing breaths. Have them attend to their breathing, lengthening their breathing rhythm until they are calm and relaxed.

Guiding Lines: Lie down with your arms at your sides and your legs uncrossed. Close your eyes.

Inhale through your nose and feel your chest expanding. Then release all your breath. This is called a cleansing breath. Repeat.

Lie still and just relax. Notice your effortless breathing rhythm. Don't try to breathe, just relax and let the air flow in and out.

As you relax, your breathing will become easier, your body may feel warmer or heavier.

You are relaxing, your breathing is calming your body and your mind.

You are now calm and comfortable.

You are deeply relaxed.

Notes: If someone's body looks tense, this means they are "thinking" about their breathing. This is stressful, not calming. Emphasize "not thinking"—letting breathing flow. Participants get better at this with practice.

Exercise: Who Me? — Category: Introduction/Transition

Imagery Strategies
Recall specific characteristics of self; match view of self with image; experience looking at self; achieve realistic self-image

Dramatic Behaviors
Develop awareness of self; concentrate on seeing self; notice details about self

Number of Participants: Whole group

Materials Needed: Full-length mirror

Directions: Have the participants view themselves in a full-length mirror. (This may be done at home.) Coach participants to look carefully at hair, eye color, and shape, height, features, and the clothes they are wearing. When they are seated comfortably in a circle, explain to the participants that they are going to look at themselves in their mind's eye.

Guiding Lines: Sit comfortably and relax. Close your eyes. Take a deep breath and let it out slowly. I am going to ask that you view yourself from outside yourself, maybe from above or from in front. Look at you standing in a room. Get closer. Look at your face. See the hair on your head. See the color of your eyes. See the shape of your nose, mouth, cheeks. See your whole body. See the clothes you are wearing. Note the way you look. See yourself doing something you do all the time. See yourself from different angles: the side, the back, the front again. Listen carefully to your voice as you speak. Look at yourself again standing in the room. When I count to ten, open your eyes.

Notes: You must be very encouraging in this exercise, since it is often initially very difficult for some participants. Do this short exercise often so they may get plenty of practice seeing themselves in their mind's eye. This is an important strategy in the evolution of Person/Character and in the next levels of RIM. Encourage participants to learn to develop an objective view of selves, an essential skill for self-monitoring.

Modifications: Have them see themselves in different contexts (school, play, etc.) and doing different activities (playing ball, sleeping, eating, etc.) Can also be used once they have created a character, to see themselves as the character.

Exercise: Looking at People — Category: Introduction/Transition

Imagery Strategies

Record kinesthetic images; focus on self as image; recall the "feel" of a particular shape

Dramatic Behaviors

Observe body posture and shape; notice body details; practice looking at another carefully and being looked at closely

Number of Participants: Whole group

Materials Needed: None

Directions: Explain to the group as a whole that today they are going to look very closely at the body position, shape, and postures of people. They will begin by observing each other in everyday types of passive activities. Divide the group in half; group A will be observers and group B will engage in an activity, standing, seated or lying, without speaking (for example, reading a book, doing homework, listening to the radio, etc.). The observers pick one person to observe. While staying at a distance they look carefully at body/position/shape, trying to feel the posture without initiating the pose directly. After 5–10 minutes of observation, change groups.

Guiding Lines: Look at their posture, not what they are doing.

Notice how they take up space.

Imagine yourself in the same body position.

Try not to imitate; just "feel" the position.

Feel the shape; look at body details, tilt of the head, position of the arms, legs, hands, feet.

Feel your body parts making the same shape.

How does your body "feel" in that position?

Notes: You may need to take a few minutes at the start of this exercise to actually imitate the pose in order to establish the kinesthetic image, especially with younger participants. However, move quickly to this exercise so the participants get practice at making the internal connection.

Modifications: Try observing other classes in the library or study hall. If possible go outside of school to a park or senior center. This can also be assigned as an out-of-class task after it has been done in class.

This drawing, entitled "Bottle People," was made by a student in Elizabeth Eron Roth's art class. Liz asked the class to use everyday objects as the "given" and add details gleaned from personal memory or imagination images. (Photo by Daniel Roth)

Exercise: **Hats** Category: Person/Character

Imagery Strategies
Recall images; connect images of hat with person or person with hat

Dramatic Behaviors
Observe detail in costume; imitate another's walk

Number of Participants: Whole group

Materials Needed: Enough hats for each participant

Directions: Arrange hats on the floor, so they are visible to the participants seated around them. Select one or two hats and conduct a discussion about the characteristics of each hat. Let participants choose a hat. After they return to their seats, coach the participants to recall a remembered image of a hat or a person suggested by the chosen hat. Ask each participant to image a person who might wear this here-and-now hat. When you are confident they have clear images of people to work from, ask each participant to begin to walk as if he or she were the character.

Guiding Lines: Look at the hats. Observe and record every detail. Does this hat look like any other hat? Try to recall someone who has a hat like it. Try to recall what that person was like. If you can't recall a person, try to decide who might wear a hat like that.

Notes: The participants may or may not have a remembered image of someone wearing a hat suggested by this hat. Don't worry. Early in drama activities having a strong memory image may not occur. Probably the here-and-now object will trigger simple behavior.

Modifications: Later in the drama exercise the participants can begin to verbalize as if they are the character suggested by the hat.

Exercise: **Bag Land** Category: Person/Character

Imagery Strategies
Merge self with image; develop early imagination images stimulated by art materials and memory images

Dramatic Behaviors
Move like another character; develop a sense of character as a whole

Number of Participants: Whole group

Materials Needed: One paper grocery bag per person; various art supplies — markers, scissors, colored paper, tape. Examples of different types of bags (suitcases, satchel, purse)

Directions: Show the various bags to the group. Ask them who might they know who would carry a bag like these. Coach them into recalling the person.

Ask group, individually, to make their brown bag into one of these bags, or into a bag that might be carried by someone they know.

When the bags are finished, coach participants to move around the room as if they were the character, doing various activities.

Guiding Lines: Look at these various bags. Who might carry these bags? Think of a person you know who carries a purse, a satchel, a suitcase, a doctor's bag.

Now let's construct the bag. Make your brown bag into the bag you just recalled.

Now that you have made the bag, carry it in the way the character would and begin to move as if you were the character.

Notes: This exercise really has two parts — making the bags and enacting the character. Try not to make the focus of the exercise constructing the bags. Work on making the bags for the purpose of enacting the character.

Initially, there may be little connection between the bag and the character portrayed, because participants may have limited art-making ability. Each time you do this activity, strive to assist participants in seeing the *connection* between the bag and the character. In fact, participants may finally develop a character and then carefully construct an appropriate bag.

Exercise: **Magic Cloth** Category: Person/Character

Imagery Strategies
Expand sensory experiences of here-and-now objects; overlay self with character; allow cloth to suggest character

Dramatic Behaviors
Use a here-and-now object to stimulate behavior; costume a character; move "as if" character

Number of Participants: Each individual within group

Materials Needed: Enough large pieces of cloth for each participant to have one

Directions: Bring in enough pieces of soft material (gauze is best) so every class member may have one. Coach each participant to use five senses simultaneously to experience the material.

Then, ask each participant to drape the material in such a way that it suggests a piece of clothing. Coach them to allow the material to magically become that piece of clothing.

Finally, ask the participants to become the character suggested by the costume piece. Ask them to begin to walk around the room as if they were the character.

Guiding Lines: Use your senses to experience the material. Focus on all the details of this cloth.

Allow the material to take shape before your eyes. Trust that your images will allow this costume piece to develop. You can fold, drape, or tie the cloth. What else?

See if this costume piece calls up a character. Recall a picture of a person you have seen wearing such a garment.

Now begin to move as if you are this person.

Notes: This exercise is designed to be repeated at various stages of creative drama. Early on, this exercise may take only a few minutes. Later, you can break the exercise into its components, and coach participants into deeper involvement in terms of use of character images.

Modifications: The here-and-now experiencing of material can begin to make new theatre images. If participant has not had previous images stimulated by material, the material itself can suggest interesting behavior.

Exercise: Clothes Make the Person

Category: Person/Character

Imagery Strategies
Image self as character; recall images of people

Dramatic Behaviors
Walk and talk like character; physicalize characters suggested by costumes; notice how costumes help build a character

Number of Participants: Small groups

Materials Needed: Several complete costumes

Directions: Discuss with the whole group how clothes make the person. For example, you would not see a policeman wearing a clown costume, nor a nurse wearing a tutu. Center the discussion around the costumes you have for them to work with. Assign one complete costume to each group of three participants. Have one group member wear the costume. Instruct the costumed character to walk and talk like the character, as you side-coach various activities for them to perform. Structure this exercise so that each participant has time to wear a costume at least once. If additional time is available, pass the costume to the next group and begin again.

Guiding Lines: Have your character try on a new pair of shoes, walk down the street on a beautiful sunny day, find a diamond in the street. Have your character look lost, try to talk to another. Have your character ask someone in the group what time it is. Use the costume to help you develop character.

Notes: The focus of the exercise is not the wearing of costumes, but the characters inside. Remind participants that, no matter how many times someone puts on one costume, the character is never the same.

Be sure to evaluate the different types of clowns, policemen, etc., by asking *how* they were different.

Save old Halloween costumes for this activity!

Exercise: **Animal Faces** Category: Person/Character

Imagery Strategies

Record specific images of animals; align image of self with here-and-now photo

Dramatic Behaviors

Notice expressive lines in faces; develop awareness of expressive facial movement

Number of Participants: Whole group

Materials Needed: Close-up pictures of animals

Directions: Instruct group to sit on floor around room. Give each person one of the pictures of an animal. Direct the group to study the pictures of the animal's face and to identify the distinguishing features of the face alone. After the group has had a chance to study the pictures, ask them to do something to their own face that would make them look more like the animal. Call *1-2-3-freeze,* and have them hold their face in that position while you select a few participants to observe the others. Pass the pictures to the next person and repeat.

Guiding Lines: What is it about that [animal] that makes it look a certain way? How can you move your cheeks without your hands to look more like it? Experiment! Raise and lower your eyebrows. Does it feel as if you might look like your animal? Try to duplicate the animal's face!

Notes: It is important to have good close-up pictures of animals. A trip to the zoo would also be an excellent stimulus for this exercise.

Exercise: **Picture Freeze** Category: Person/Character

Imagery Strategies

Shift/rotate a perceptual image; overlay self-as-image

Dramatic Behaviors

Develop kinesthetic awareness of people; imitate poses in pictures

Number of Participants: Whole group as individuals

Materials Needed: Full-length pictures of people

Directions: Bring in an assortment of magazine pictures of people in many different poses. Discuss the various poses and how people bend, stretch, or support their weight. Place the pictures around the room, assigning each participant one picture. Coach the group to study their picture, allowing enough time for careful observation. Begin the picture freezes by slowly counting as the participants recreate the poses in the picture. On the word *freeze,* the participants freeze in the pose. After they have held the pose for a few seconds, tell the group to relax, and move on to the next picture.

Guiding Lines: Recreate the pose, don't mirror it! It might be easier if you stand behind the picture. Try to capture the full gesture of the body. Try to reflect the person's expression. Imagine what the person might be thinking and feeling. See yourself as the person.

Notes: It is best to set up a rotation system where students move to the pictures. Try to find pictures that require students to sit, kneel, and lean on objects, as well as standing.

Modifications: Use photographs, films, or videos of animals moving in natural environments or zoos.

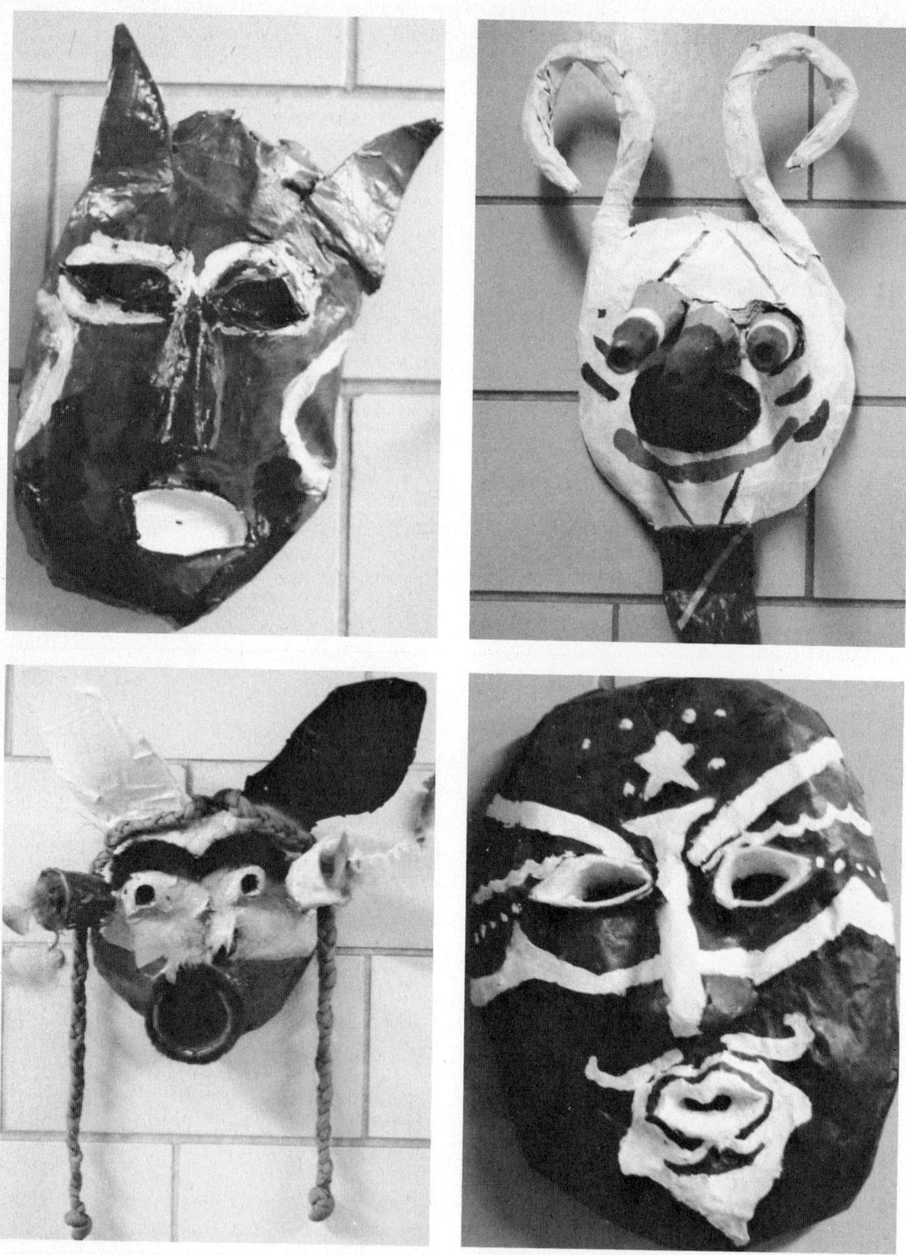

Encourage your students to utilize a wide variety of materials as they create their fantasy creatures. These are some of the final products of young people engaged in arts and imagination workshops in the New York City area. (P.S. 9, New York City, Photos by Michael Rocco Pinciotti)

Exercise: **Fantasy Creatures** Category: Person/Character

Imagery Strategies
Recall previously perceived creatures; select vivid creature characteristics; overlay images with here-and-now materials

Dramatic Behaviors
Construct a mask; plan and design a fantasy creature

Number of Participants: Whole group

Materials Needed: Oaktag, scissors, markers, hole punch, glue, tape, staplers, pipe cleaners, yarn, crepe paper

Directions: Have the participants recall various fantasy creatures from movies *(Star Wars, E.T., Wizard of Oz, Dark Crystal)* or television characters such as the Muppets, Fraggle-Rock, and He-Man. Ask them what characteristics make the creature interesting, scary, funny, etc. Explain that they are going to make a mask of their own fantasy creature. Have them decide what characteristics (eyes, hair, ears, etc.) are going to make their creature interesting. Give each participant a piece of oaktag, which he or she folds in half and then cuts half an oval from the top to the bottom of the folded oaktag. When students open the paper, they have an eliptical mask shape that can be decorated to create a fantasy creature.

Guiding Lines: What will make your creature interesting?

Which characteristic are you going to accentuate? Eyes? ears? hair?

Remember, these are fantasy creatures.

Make them look like something you've never seen before.

Use images from real life, but really exaggerate the characteristics.

Notes: Encourage the students to design a truly fantastical creature. Suggest various uses for the materials, hair, eyes, ears, etc. Since this is the first attempt at mask-making, the emphasis is on exploration and manipulation of materials to create a finished mask.

Modifications: Have the participants create a voice for their creature. Display the masks or use them for further work.

Exercise: **Under the Big Top** Category: Person/Character

Imagery Strategies
Recall images of circus; develop ability to see self as image

Dramatic Behaviors
Physicalize personal images; communicate a character through pantomime

Number of Participants: Whole group

Materials Needed: Pictures of circus performers, animals, and places in the circus

Directions: Instruct group to sit on the floor as you discuss going to the circus. Show pictures of the various characters they might see there. After you feel confident that the group can recall circus images, put the pictures away and ask participants to pantomime a character from the circus. If the group seems ready, encourage the characters to interact.

Guiding Lines: Show me who you are. I see lots of clowns, and monkeys, and elephants. Do I see someone selling cotton candy and peanuts? Show me exactly who you are. You may want to try to be another character now. Show me by the way you are walking and moving. I see some other very interesting animals.

Notes: Many people have personal experiences of the circus. Encourage participants to share theirs with you.

Your side coaching can assist those participants who may have difficulty either in retrieving the image or in connecting the image to their pantomime action.

Modifications: Place can be changed to meet the needs of the age of your group.

Create a Big-Top sound tape to use as background music and direct course of action.

Exercise: Stay in Character — Category: Person/Character

Imagery Strategies
Extend storehouse of images for a particular character; image self as character; expand character image on demand

Dramatic Behaviors
Walk and talk like someone else; concentrate on staying in character

Number of Participants: Whole group

Materials Needed: Cards with personality types or "character cards" (optional)

Directions: Discuss how performers must stay in character. Explain that each participant is to select a character (on his own or by picking one from the "character cards") and image doing tasks the way that character would.

When all the participants have selected characters, coach the group to take off their shoes, write their names, walk to a chair, etc. Continue naming activities that can occur in the room. Then, move the group away from the regular drama area, reminding them to stay in character. You may elect to take them out of the building or into other sections of the building, reminding them to stay in character all the way.

Guiding Lines: Remember who you are and stay as that character. What would your character do in these situations? Don't forget who you are. Think before you move. If you are a character who can't do the task, why not ask for help? Try to be your character all the time. Try to make me forget who you really are.

Notes: Participants may have the image, but are unable to act upon it. Coach them as they are working to make connections between idea and action.

Exercise: Imaginary Friends — Category: Person/Character

Imagery Strategies
Hold and respond to a well-developed imagination image; experiment with an image having a life of its own

Dramatic Behaviors
Work with an imagined person; experience an understanding of two-way nature of dialogue; develop two characters simultaneously.

Number of Participants: Whole group

Materials Needed: None

Directions: Discuss how young children often have "imaginary friends." Point out stories or television plots involving an invisible character in which most people could not see the character, but at least one person could. Ask participants to describe the behaviors of all involved. Emphasize how important it is for one person to behave as if he or she sees the imaginary character. Ask each individual to develop an imagined character and to enact situations with that character. Give participants planning time and then ask several to begin to enact these situations with the imagined character in attendance!

Guiding Lines: Make the person real for you. Listen for the words. See the person move. Behave as if an imagined character were really with you.

Now, communicate to observers that this imagined person is really with you. Hold the image! Respond to the character!

Notes: Initially, participants will portray themselves in response to the imagined character; the focus will be on developing the other character. Once the participants are comfortable, they can also become a character in response to this imagined one.

Modifications: You may wish to use this exercise after participants have developed playwrighting skills. Scenes in which more than one imagined character appears can be the focus of comedy writing.

Exercise: Group Shoot

Category: Person/Character

Imagery Strategies

Recall television shows/movies of a particular action; image self as character

Dramatic Behaviors

Walk and talk like someone else; explore many possible ways to experience and portray a single action

Number of Participants: Whole group

Materials Needed: None

Directions: Begin this exercise with a discussion of death scenes and the variety of ways in which television and movie characters get shot. Discuss recalled death scenes, making sure to point out such aspects as length of death, location of wound, and direction of falling.

Ask each participant to find a place where he or she can fall to the ground without hitting another person. Explain that you will say *"1-2-3 hit."* On the word "hit" they are to get shot by a gun or arrow and begin to die. Vary lengths of deaths, character who is dying, direction of fall, and what part of body receives wound.

Guiding Lines: Show where you are hit. React to the shot. Fall slowly or fall quickly. Does your character cry? Is your character brave?

Notes: This exercise may seem violent or morose, but "bad guys" are the choice of many young people. Instead of encouraging a free-for-all or avoiding the material entirely, use exercises of this type to structure violence for enacting dramatic action. Remember, also, that killing "bad guys" for justifiable reason can be purging. If you feel unable to lead this exercise, wait until you feel confident or substitute another action.

Modifications: When participants have developed playwrighting skills, you may wish to use this exercise to help structure the climax of a mystery scene.

Exercise: Living Biographies **Category: Person/Character**

Imagery Strategies
Use detail of here-and-now photo to stimulate recall of kinesthetic and vocal images of similar people; overlay image of self with image of another

Dramatic Behaviors
Explore the types of characters one would like to portray; add detail to character enactment

Number of Participants: Individuals

Materials Needed: One close-up photograph of people for each person; overhead projector

Directions: With overhead projector, show group photos of faces. Have each participant select a photo that pictures the character he or she is to become. Discuss each face in great detail.

Give each participant five minutes alone with the photo to make up a biography of the person. Each participant then performs an oral biography for a partner or for the rest of the participants.

Notes: When selecting pictures for this activity, include a wide variety of ages, ethnic backgrounds, emotions, and occupations.

This exercise is one of the first ones that encourages participants to make personal selections concerning characterization, based on a rapidly expanding knowledge of self.

Modifications: You may wish to explore, with experienced participants, whether portraying characters who look like self is easier or harder than enacting characters who are very different in appearance.

SEQUENCE/STORY

The drama skill category of Sequence/Story develops improvisational and storytelling skills, both precursors to playwrighting. Each of the skills requires the ability to order ideas and images for the purpose of creating a complete thought, series of actions, or story. Sequencing ability assumes an understanding of cause and effect, time relationship (before and after), and order (beginning, middle, and end). Developmental level and experience facilitate the growth of these skills, but even preschool children have a basic understanding of sequence, especially as it relates to their first-hand knowledge of daily events.

In Sequence/ Story Starters, participants have many experiences in ordering and grouping images, ideas, words, and actions. The stimuli for the exercises include photos, sounds, picture cards, and here-and-now objects. Participants need many opportunities to manipulate the stimuli to create their own stories. Because these exercises emphasize the "plan" phase of the creative drama process more than any other, activities may not appear as physical as those in other Starter categories. The skills learned in this category, however, can be useful to the work in other drama-skill areas, particularly as participants learn to move and speak.

The leader here is most akin to a coach, encouraging and leading the participants step-by-step. Guiding lines include such phrases as "Think again," or "Add another." Sequencing, ordering, cause and effect, and main idea are comprehension skills taught and reinforced in almost every traditional subject area, especially reading and math. Be aware that, even though your participants may understand the concept of sequencing, it may take time for them to develop the skills to express the sequence dramatically. Begin simply and build more elaborate sequences.

In these RIM Starters, the main thrust of each activity has to do with stories: *story-making, story-enacting*, and *storytelling*. Story-making requires participants to organize a series of present actions or objects. The emphasis is on ordering the information to make a story, not on creating a new story. "Follow the Leader" and "From Here to There" provide practice in ordering actions; "Magic Potion" works with time relationships. There is not necessarily a "correct" order. Participants merely choose an ordering that makes sense and that they can justify. Any order of activity cards can tell a true and valid story, depending on the point of view of the story-maker.

These exercises lead naturally to putting ideas into sequenced actions. In story-enacting, participants must show the order of time or events by enacting the story through movement and action. Initially, participants are required to observe and duplicate a series of movements. "Sequence-a-Movement" requires participants to observe and physically recreate a movement sequence. More difficult are "Scramblers" and "What Happened Before?," which give participants their first experience in acting out a complete story through action.

Because Sequence/Story develops so many of the beginning playwrighting skills, storytelling, the final set of exercises, focuses on the relationship among the ideas in a story. These exercises emphasize the storytelling connection as participants tell stories from pictures, sounds, and words. Storytelling involves the creation of a story and can be accomplished with or without words.

Create a storytelling mood or climate by capitalizing on the images often associated with storytelling, such as summer campfires or medieval troubadours. "Story Building," "Story Shuffle," and "Missing Links" are reminiscent of these experiences, in which the whole group partakes in sharing a tale, or creating one. "Three Pictures" challenges the participants to find the story in a set of unrelated pictures. Coach the participants to use vivid language and images and to stop at key places in the story to heighten dramatic action. Also encourage them to try to recall and repeat the same story. You can also tape storytelling sessions and share the tape with the group for a listening activity.

Of course, do not forget your potential as a teller of tales. Television and the electronic media have almost obliterated that special kind of magic between the storyteller and his or her audience. Both younger and older drama participants respond quickly, falling under the storyteller's spell as he or she spins the tale. Start with stories that you have read or ones handed down to you. They need not be long, but they must capture the attention of the listener. With a little practice, you yourself can revive the art form of storytelling for yourself and your listeners. Watch how they learn from your example.

POINTERS — SEQUENCE/ STORY

- Begin sequencing familiar activities first.
- Provide opportunities to tell stories with pictures, sounds, and words.
- Coach the participants to articulate the steps in a sequence.
- Look for the inherent logic in all sequences.
- Develop your own skills as a storyteller.
- Think of these exercises as precursors to playwrighting.

Exercise: **Floating** Category: Introduction/Transition

Imagery Strategies
Focus on particular movements; record differences of similar movements

Dramatic Behaviors
Imitate the floating of object; experience the physical sensation of floating; calm the body and prepare it for drama work

Number of Participants: Whole group

Materials Needed: Feathers, flimsy plastic bag (dry-cleaning type), chiffon scarf

Directions: Have the participants sit in a circle and watch as you let a feather fall from a height, then the chiffon scarf, and then the dry-cleaning bag. For each object, draw attention to its lightness, how it floats down, and its quiet and relaxed resting at the end. Have participants find a self-space and have them float to the floor, first as a feather, then as a scarf, and as a plastic bag. Discuss how it feels to float.

Guiding Lines: Watch closely while I show you three objects.

See how quietly they float to the ground.

See the soft crumpled shape of the scarf.

Watch how the bag collapses and gently lands.

What made them float? (air around it)

Find a self-space and stand very still. Then I'll know you're ready.

Float to the floor, in your own space, as softly and slowly as the feather. Experiment with how slowly you can float down.

Float down as quietly as the scarf; land in a quiet, crumpled shape.

Collapse as gently as the plastic bag . . . slowly . . . slowly . . . until you're calm and relaxed on the floor.

Feel the calm.

Notes: This is a relaxing warm-up that leaves participants with a sense of well-being.

Exercise: Quick Flash — Category: Introduction/Transition

Imagery Strategies
Focus on detail in here-and-now; retrieve detail in images

Dramatic Behaviors
Notice the world; select visual details

Number of Participants: Whole group

Materials Needed: Magazine or catalogue photos picturing "busy" scenes, which have been made into slides or flashcards

Directions: Explain to the group that you want them to learn to be a visual detective. You will show them a slide. Give the group 60 seconds to observe the scene. Coach them while they view.

After you have shown the picture, ask the participants to see the picture in their mind's eye. Encourage them to retrieve as much as possible in their mind's eye.

Guiding Lines: See the picture. Look at the many objects in the picture. Time is running out. See as much as you can and remember.

Now that the photo is gone, try to see as much of it as you can.

Notes: After you have been working with Quick Flash, ask participants to bring photos from home. Encourage them to bring clear, strong pictures.

Early in the exercise, don't stress time limit. When you do, make the observation as unstressful and playful as possible.

Modifications: As the exercise progresses, lessen the time the photo appears on the screen. You can actually intensify the participants' observation powers by shortening viewing time. Always remember to warn participants of time limits.

Cover a number of small objects with cloth. Remove cloth; rearrange objects. This strengthens participants visual awareness and visual memory.

Exercise: Smell as Stimulus — Category: Introduction/Transition

Imagery Strategies
Record images; recall past images; use smell to recall images in another sensory area

Dramatic Behaviors
Remember important past experiences; relate experiences recalled through stimulation of smell

Number of Participants: Whole group

Materials Needed: Five vials of aromas

Directions: Bring in five vials of easily recognizable aromas, such as vanilla, orange, lilac, strawberry, evergreen. Pass each one around, one at a time, to persons seated in a circle. After one vial has been circulated, ask each person *not* to identify the smell, but what the smell reminded him or her of. Finally, ask for volunteers to share the episode recalled to them by the stimulus of the smell.

Guiding Lines: Smell the here-and-now smell. Reach back into your storehouse of images and recall the episode stimulated by this smell.

Notes: This exercise is not like many transitional ones that focus on simple recall of smell. Here, the focus is to use smell to stimulate other sensory domains and other situations. Often smell can be the stimulus for sophisticated story development and character-making in later levels of RIM.

Exercise: **Follow the Leader** Category: Sequence/Story

Imagery Strategies
Select movement images; connect movement images; sequence images; match behavior to movement images

Dramatic Behaviors
Observe leader; imitate leader; remember sequences

Number of Participants: Whole group

Materials Needed: None

Directions: Instruct the group to stand in a large circle. Appoint one person to be the leader for a certain length of time. Tell the leader to perform a sequence of three completely different movements of his or her own choice while the rest of the group observes. Instruct the group to perform the same sequence of movements. Once the group has consistently mastered a sequence of three movements, the leader performs four movements. The leader adds on additional movements, one at a time, until the group is unable to recall and perform the sequence.

Guiding Lines: Observe the leader carefully and remember the sequence of events. Make sure you do everything exactly as the leader does.

Leader, don't try to stump the group. Go slowly. Try to be clear in your movements.

Notes: If there is a great difference in ability within your group, place less able participants together, so they will have an equal chance at keeping up with the group.

Modifications: When the group seems ready, add sounds to the sequence. The sequence of sound/movement/sound can last longer and be recalled after longer periods of time. Try, for example, to ask the group to perform sequences after a few days or even a week. If the group is able to recall and perform, ask them to discuss *how* they remembered—a metacognition perspective.

Exercise: **From Here to There** Category: Sequence/Story

Imagery Strategies
Combine images into a sequence; organize memory images into an imagination image that shapes future behavior

Dramatic Behaviors
Plan sequence of events; develop awareness of sequencing; use objects in a related way

Number of Participants: Group divided in two parts

Materials Needed: Objects of various sizes, such as large carton box, stuffed garbage bag, beachball, tray of glasses, gloves, glass of water, hat, scarf, vest, a dozen golf balls, bucket of sand, stack of plates, handful of paper clips

Directions: Divide the group and props in half on opposite sides of the room. Tell the group that each member's task in this exercise is to move three objects from one side of the room to the other. All three objects must be moved during the same trip across the room. A participant may select any three objects he or she likes, but must plan ahead. Once a participant touches an object, he or she cannot put it down.

Discuss the importance of planning ahead. If hands are occupied holding a beachball, one cannot put on the vest. Instruct the group that one person from each group begins the activity. Once the props are on the opposite side of the room, the other team may use them. Continue the exercise until everyone has had a turn.

Guiding Lines: Remember, once you have touched something, you must pick it up. Plan out what you want to use first. Is there any way for you to carry things inside other things? Think carefully and plan ahead. What do you want to take first? What do you want to take last?

Notes: The more difficult the objects are to carry, the more the participants have to think ahead to plan how they are going to be able to move them. The leader must keep participants on task, using images, so activity doesn't become merely a game. Once the group is able to plan ahead, you can ask the group to develop "the most interesting way, the most unusual way, the silliest way" to carry the objects.

This stop action sequence is an early attempt to show movement and is a precursor to the technology of film making. (Eadweard Muybridge, *"Daisy" Cantering, Saddled,* New York Public Library, Art Prints and Photograph Division Astor, Lenox, and Tilden Foundation)

Exercise: Sequence-a-Picture

Category: Sequence/Story

Imagery Strategies
Retrieve visual images when stimulated by the have-and-how picture; select/reject images on demand

Dramatic Behaviors
Contribute to a group-developed art work; document a group sequence

Number of Participants: Whole group

Materials Needed: 8- by 11-inch white paper; pencils or crayons for everyone

Directions: Instruct the participants to sit in a circle. Pass out paper and pencils or crayons to everyone. Tell them to put their names on the back of the paper. The exercise is to create a picture to which everyone adds on something. The first person makes a mark, line, shape, or object on the page. When you say "switch," they pass the paper to the right. Each one then adds on something to the picture he or she receives. This continues until you say "stop."

When all the pictures have circulated and everyone has had the chance to add on something, ask volunteers to document the development of the piece.

Guiding Lines: Look at the picture.

Add on something interesting.
What do you see?
Make the picture more elaborate.
Look carefully at your add-on picture.
Describe how it got the way it did.
Tell the sequence.

Notes: This exercise stimulates visual image-making, as well as encourages recording and retrieving sequence of events.

Modifications: This exercise can be done in small groups also, especially with older children.

Exercise: Magic Potion

Category: Sequence/Story

Imagery Strategies
Recall sequence of events; incorporate images of past experiences with here-and-now activity

Dramatic Behaviors
Work in a group; focus on sequence of actions; re-create a sequence

Number of Participants: Small groups

Materials Needed: Measuring spoons, containers, and various kitchen utensils; a variety of edible materials to dissolve in such liquids as water, juice, or milk
(Some interesting additions may be sugar, chocolate, spices, ice, food coloring, and syrups. You may want to have such items as celery, carrots, and cinnamon sticks with which to stir the magic potion.)

Directions: Divide the whole group into smaller groups, each with its own set-up for making a magic potion. Explain that a magic potion can make anything happen: it can make them stronger, smarter, or even fall in love. What is most important is that each group record exactly what is going into its potion and in what order, so they can repeat it when they need to make it again. Instruct each group to create its own magic potion, paying careful attention to how much and in what order the ingredients are added. As they add ingredients, they should write the recipe down to share later with the whole group.

Guiding Lines: Remember, your potion is going to be magic! What is on your table that will help you make the magic happen? Remember how much of everything you put in, and be sure to write it down. Do you have to say any magic words or perform any magic ritual to get the potion to work? Remember what you are doing so you can write it down.

Notes: You may want to read a few stories, such as *Alice in Wonderland* or the *Sorcerer's Apprentice,* in which magic potions are an important part. Remember, the making of the potion is not as important as the sequencing and recording of events.

Although the exercise is geared to younger participants, older participants may be enticed to make potions for a *particular purpose.*

Modifications: You may want to try casting a spell (sequence of words) or other such magical events requiring a specific set of sequential tasks.

Exercise:
Sequence-a-Movement

Category: Sequence/Story

Imagery Strategies

Connect movement images; sequence here-and-now movement with movement images

Dramatic Behaviors

Observe movement; physicalize a series of movements; build a movement sequence

Number of Participants: Whole group

Materials Needed: None

Directions: Begin with the group standing in a circle. Direct participants to stand at arm's length apart. One participant starts with a simple movement. The second participant performs the movement of the first participant and adds another movement. Each participant, in turn, performs all the movements observed and adds his or her own movement. For example, if participant A raises his arms, participant B raises his arms and then shakes his arms; participant C raises his arms, shakes his arms, and kicks his foot. After the last participant performs the full series of movements, the whole group together recalls and performs the full series of movements.

Guiding Lines: Focus on the movement. Concentrate on all the movements.

If you forget a movement, look around the circle, think of the person and the movement he or she has performed. Try another level, try another shape, another level, another direction.

Try to think of all the movements as one sequence.

Notes: The first participants obviously have an easier task than the last participants, so you may wish to arrange the participants according to ability to concentrate. Repeat the exercise several times, rearranging the order of participation. Each participant will then have both the easier and more difficult task.

Modifications: This exercise can be done with sounds, gestures, and words.

Many types of sequence cards, commercially available, can stimulate drama-making. (Photo by Michael Rocco Pinciotti)

Exercise: **Scramblers** Category: Sequence/Story

Imagery Strategies
Recall images of a sequential nature; focus on images associated with picture stimulus

Dramatic Behaviors
Imitate a specific action; identify the dramatic order of actions

Number of Participants: Small groups of three or four

Materials Needed: Sequence-activity cards

Directions: Give each group a set of cards, one card for each participant, that depicts one sequence of an action, such as building a snowman or hitting a home run. Instruct participants to practice imitating the action on the card, but scramble the sequence. In turn, each group shares its scrambled set of actions in front of the others. The observers then order the actions to make the sequence correct, by having the players change places until the actions are unscrambled and tell the right story.

Guiding Lines: *To Participants:* Show me what the person is doing on the card. Line your actions up and scramble the order. Freeze your action.

To Observers: In this sequence they are building a snowman. Which action comes first? second? third? fourth? Tell me the story.

Notes: Sequence-activity cards are part of any primary grade's language arts/reading program. Stress that the actions tell a story. Have participants tell the story after unscrambling the action.

Modifications: Participants may like to create their own sequence of actions to use in this exercise. They may also wish to make their own original sequence cards.

Exercise: 24 Hours — Category: Sequence/Story

Imagery Strategies
Recall personal images of time sequences; image self through day; develop self-monitoring abilities

Dramatic Behaviors
Communicate through action; reconstruct one day of their lives

Number of Participants: Whole group

Materials Needed: Large cardboard clock with moveable hands

Directions: Instruct participants to sit on the floor while you discuss with them what they do throughout the day. Point out that not everyone gets up or goes to sleep at the same time, and that there are many different activities that people do in the evening or after school. After you are confident they understand how their schedule may be different from their best friend's, begin the activity.

Starting at 5 A.M. or at a time when you are sure most participants will be asleep, instruct the group to show you through pantomime what they are doing. Slowly move the hands of the clock, stopping at half-hour intervals, each time asking participants to show you what they are doing. Move the hands around the clock until one day is complete.

Guiding Lines: Remember to show me what you are doing at ______ o'clock. How fast do you wake up? Are you hungry for dinner? Show me by what you doing what time it is.

Notes: There may be participants who are unaware of what time they eat, go to sleep, etc. There may also be participants who have a varied after-school schedule. In those cases, have them select *one* activity they enjoy doing at that time.

This exercise is one of the first to encourage self-monitoring. Participants should be encouraged to view their own life as material for drama.

Modifications: Vary lengths of time; expand to a week (by days).

Exercise: What Happened Before — Category: Sequence/Story

Imagery Strategies
Record an imagination/action sequence; use here-and-now photos as stimuli for imagery activity; shift images in the mind's eye

Dramatic Behaviors
Develop sense of sequence in a story; place characters in a specific situation; experience cause-and-effect

Number of Participants: Whole group

Materials Needed: Photos or pictures of people in various situations

Directions: Show each participant the photo or pictures. Ask participants to observe the photo carefully. Ask them to decide who these people are and what they are doing. Then ask them to picture in their mind's eye how these people got to this photo position.

Conduct a discussion allowing all participants time to express how they imagined the sequence of events. Ask participants to describe the actions they see in their mind's eye.

Guiding Lines: Look at the photo. See the detail. What do these people seem to be doing? How are they related to one another?

In your mind's eye see these people before they had this photo taken. What were they doing? See them arriving at this situation in your mind's eye. Record the action carefully.

Notes: Advertisements often depict groups of people and are excellent sources.

Modifications: The photograph can also be used as a record of the beginning of an action. Participants then develop a sequence for "what happened after."

Once participants are experienced, you may bring up the notion that the persons are models for the photo, but themselves before and after. Thus, the exercise can stimulate story-building skills, as well as character-development ones.

Exercise: Story-Building — Category: Sequence/Story

Imagery Strategies
Sequence a series of images; retrieve connecting images; develop early imagination images stimulated by story

Dramatic Behaviors
Build a story; work with a partner

Number of Participants: Whole group, then pairs

Materials Needed: Enough story starters, one for each pair in the group (for example, "The sky was dark and the moon was full . . ."; "I awoke in the middle of the night . . ."; "As I walked down the street . . .")

Directions: Begin by reading a story starter to the group. Ask what could happen next in the story. Accept suggestions that direct the development of the story. When the story appears to be well developed, ask for possible endings to the story. Retell the completed story to the group.

Divide the group into pairs. Give each pair a story starter and tell them to complete the story, giving it a middle and end. When the pairs have completed their stories, each pair shares the story with the class.

Guiding Lines: Listen to the story. Concentrate on what is being said. Try to picture the action in your mind's eye. Before you tell your part of the story, see the action happening.

Notes: The focus of this exercise is to provide story development, calling attention to plot line. Many unexpected tales will evolve, and many will be humorous or grotesque, but they are acceptable as long as you judge them to be in good taste. This exercise opens participants to the many possibilities of sequential development within a story.

Modifications: Select beginning lines or paragraphs from famous stories.

Exercises: **Story Shuffle** Category: Sequence/Story

Imagery Strategies
Connect objects in the creation of a story; develop a sense of shared imagination images

Dramatic Behaviors
Verbalize a story; plan a story within a specific framework; establish the importance of objects in a story

Number of Participants: Small groups—three to five participants

Materials Needed: Watch or clock, glass (any kind), a handkerchief

Directions: Instruct the participants to sit in a circle as you pass around the three objects of interest: a watch or a clock, a glass of any kind, and a handkerchief. Divide the entire group into smaller groups of three to five participants each, with no more than six groups. Give each group a slip of paper listing the three objects in a specific order, making sure each group gets objects listed in a different order, for example: (1) watch, handkerchief, glass; (2) watch, glass, handkerchief; (3) glass, watch, handkerchief. Tell the group to create a story, using the objects in the *specific order given.* You supply the lead-in for the story: "It was raining when I entered the dark house. . . . " After the groups have organized their story, everyone has a chance to share them. Emphasize the order of the objects in each story and how the order changed the direction of the stories.

Guiding Lines: Listen to the words of the story.

What images have popped into your mind?

Add an object to that picture.

Keep the objects in order.

Give your story an ending.

Notes: Remind the groups to end their stories, thus giving them a beginning, middle, and end.

Modifications: You can use different lead-ins for more stories with the same props or let the groups create their own beginning. Once the groups have developed storytelling skills, they can add many more props to elaborate on their stories.

Exercise: **Missing Links** Category Sequence/Story

Imagery Strategies
Sequence related images; merge related/unrelated images

Dramatic Behaviors
Work with partner; understand concepts of simile, metaphor, time; communicate a complete thought

Number of Participants: Pairs

Materials Needed: A set of cards, each listing sentence middles. Examples include "grinned like, wanted nothing, attempted to," and so on

Directions: Distribute one card to each pair. Keep one card to be used as an example. With whole group, read this middle and ask the group for a beginning and end to the sentence. Then divide the group into pairs and give one card to each pair. Direct each pair to supply a beginning and end for their sentence middle. When each pair has planned, ask each to share the sentence with whole group.

Guiding Lines: (Note: These guiding lines are presented prior to the exercise. Unlike many of the other Starters, sequence activities usually involve a planning period and then enactment.)

Think of a time in your own life that you "decided not to" or that you "jumped high." What happened before? What happened after? Share your experience with your partner. Together use both your experiences to construct a whole sentence that describes the action.

Notes: All sentences are acceptable, provided they have logical sequential development. The verb supplied stimulates the recall of images and guides the development of the sentence.

Exercise: Three Pictures **Category:** Sequence/Story

Imagery Strategies

Encourage imagery strategy; use here-and-now pictures to stimulate images; retrieve stored images to assist in here-and-now task

Dramatic Behaviors

Build stories from pictures; develop a story; build skills in sequencing; describe a planning sequence

Number of Participants: Whole group; pairs within group

Materials Needed: Enough copies of three very different pictures (photos from the text may be used)

Directions: Hand out one copy of the three pictures to each participant. Guide participants to view the scenes in picture A, picture B, picture C. Explain that the pictures are in no particular order. Instruct the pairs to place the pictures in an order that makes sense to them. Ask pairs to verbalize the process they went through to make their decision.

Guiding Lines: Look at these pictures in detail. What is happening? Who are these people and what are they doing? Try putting the pictures in different orders. Experiment to see which order you think tells the best story.

Notes: A large part of the success of this exercise is based on the verbal ability of the group. If your group is not immediately successful in this exercise, return to it at a later time.

You may have to give suggestions to help get participants on track. A good connecting device can be that participants are on a jet plane flying over these separate actions, or that participants are in a time machine, or that participants are searching the world for a missing person.

DESIGN/ENVIRONMENT

The Starters in the drama skill category Design/Environment approach the creative drama process from the point of view of designer. As we noted in Chapter 4, designers depend on their aesthetic sensitivity to make interesting visual choices and create a sense of place. Designers communicate to the audience the drama's place, period, and even mood or feeling. Their use of space directs the attention of the audience members and provides a focus for their viewing. Designers have spent many years studying artistic principles, exploring various material, and manipulating different types of spaces to communicate their images. Their keen perceptual awareness, however, is at the core of their creative efforts.

Through RIM Starters, participants share in this artistic decision-making by planning and creating various imaginary and physical environments. Exercises must first begin with attention to the participants' own environment: the colors, textures, shapes, and patterns that surround them. Then they work on numerous visual art projects that emphasize principles of design and spatial awareness. Ultimately, participants work together to create a specific place. To achieve this group end, they must coordinate their images and efforts. They must begin to view the space from the perspective of creator and observer.

Your role in these Starters is primarily that of a director as in Sound/Speech. In the early exercises, guide the participants to perceive similarities and differences and to develop specific images of a variety of places. In later activities, you will use a plan-play-evaluate process, giving directions and demonstrations, allowing participants time and space to work, and then commenting on the joint effort. During the process you may ask questions that help clarify the image and add information or guidance in terms of material or construction. The guiding lines reflect this type of leader interaction.

The Design/Environment exercises fall into three general groups. The first group focuses on the perceptual qualities of the world, with participants asked to discriminate among colors, textures, and shapes. Exercises may utilize all of the sense modalities, as in "Apple," or isolate a specific sense, as in "Colors" or "Textures." Do not rush through these exercises. Some participants will readily discover the perceptual features, while others may take more time to experience them. Participants may not be aware of the differences between a Granny Smith and a Golden Delicious Apple, for instance, but once they have experienced the differences and labeled the distinctions they have these apple experiences on record.

Seeing is an experience. . . . People, not their eyes, see . . . there is more to seeing than meets the eyeball.

N. R. Hanson

The second group of Design/Environment Starters requires that the participant solve an artistic or spatial problem. By manipulating and playing with an assortment of materials (from markers and cardboard to rostrum blocks), the participants explore the design potential of different media. Directionality, movement patterns, and spatial awareness are the keys to such activities as "Treasure Map," "Obstacle Course," and "Blocks."

The third group and bulk of exercises deal with establishing place. Whether it be generating many ideas for place, as in "Magic Stones," or in creating a specific image of place, as in "Grocery Store" or "Jungle," the entire group is involved. Matching individual images to the group goal requires a great deal of negotiation from individuals. As director, you introduce the plan, play, and evaluate the results throughout Transformations.

In working toward creating a group image of place, you must be aware of three ways in which confusion and frustration may occur. The first lies in the participants' inability to "see" the image of place. They are unsure of details because of limited prior knowledge of the specific place, inadequate information, or your poor directions. Their image of place is fuzzy, and therefore they cannot participate fully in its creation. Find out if their image of place is clear by asking them to describe the place. The second problem can occur in realizing the image. The image itself may be quite clear and vivid, but, inexperienced participants often lack the skills to actualize place. Questioning will also be helpful in pinpointing this problem. Quite possibly, participants are unable to enact the place because of lack of space, time, or materials. Make sure their image conforms to the reality of the drama situation.

The final problem can occur if individuals disagree on how to coordinate and integrate their various unique images into one group image acceptable to all. You may need to intervene. Participants need practice in sharing images and negotiating, since they may not have had many opportunities to make group decisions. This skill is extremely important and constitutes one of the major benefits of dramatic learning.

POINTERS — DESIGN/ENVIRONMENT

- Pay attention to perceptual features.
- Provide experiences with the visual arts.
- Develop spatial awareness through manipulation of objects.
- Help participants coordinate their images and actions.
- Ask many questions to help participants clarify images.
- Work toward the group image.

Exercise: **Ocean** Category: Introduction/Transition

Imagery Strategies
Overlay image of a place with a relaxing experience; image while relaxing

Dramatic Behaviors
Develop awareness of breathing during relaxation; develop awareness of verbal/auditory suggestion

Number of Participants: Whole group

Materials Needed: Record player or cassette recorder; sound track of ocean waves

Directions: Ask the participants to find a comfortable place to lie on their backs. You are going to play a piece of music or of sounds that will remind them of lying on the beach. Ask the participants to close their eyes and experience the setting as you play the sounds.

Guiding Lines: Listen to the ocean, the waves flowing back and forth across the sand. The sand is warm. The sun is shining. You are alone on the beach.

You feel calm and relaxed. You are just lying on the beach listening to the waves—not a care in the world. You have nothing else to do but lie here and listen to the ocean.

Be aware of your breathing. Let it get slower and calmer . . . like the waves.

Let the sand on the beach support your calm, relaxed body. Let the tension flow out of your body like the waves.

Notes: This is a more advanced relaxation exercise, since it is more individual and less specifically directed toward relaxing. It can also be an initial guided fantasy because it is very open-ended.

Modifications: You may find a sound track for another relaxing environment (for example, a pasture, woods). Make sure the sounds are consistent and do not suddenly change into a thunderstorm or hurricane.

Exercise: **Your Place or Mine** Category: Introduction/Transition

Imagery Strategies
Focus on details of house in mind's eye; recall previously perceived houses; experience themselves moving through space

Dramatic Behaviors
Develop awareness of inside and outside environments; realize images have a life of their own; recognize the uniqueness of their images

Number of Participants: Whole group

Materials Needed: None

Directions: Ask participants to sit comfortably in a circle or lie down. Explain that they are going to visit a house today in their mind's eye. Maybe it will be a house they have been in before, maybe not. Have them take a deep breath and close their eyes.

Guiding Lines: Sit comfortably (or lie down). Relax. Take a deep breath and close your eyes. You are now standing in front of a house.

Notice the color of the house. Count the number of windows on the front of the house. Walk around to the back door. Notice where the door is. Continue walking around the house until you're back in front of it.

Go up to the door and let yourself in. The day is sunny and clear and the bright light fills the house. Walk through the downstairs. Notice one thing or more in every room. The living room . . . the dining room . . . kitchen. Now stand at the bottom of the steps. Begin climbing the steps.

When you arrive at the top of the steps, notice three doors leading into three rooms. I am with you, so you don't need to be afraid. Select one door to open. Choose the door, open it slowly, and enter.

Once inside, look around you. What do you see? Notice something you would like to bring back with you. Return to the front of the house.

When I count to five, open your eyes. You are back with me in the classroom.

Notes: Allow at least 15 seconds for each suggestion. This exercise develops controllability of images. Remind the children that this is a friendly place, it's daylight, and they may have been here before. This should not have a scary or mysterious tone. The individual images will be very different from one another; stress the importance and uniqueness of each person. Remember to find out what each participant brought back.

Modifications: You can use this exercise format to visit any place, real or imagined.

Exercise: **Blindfold Walk** Category: Introduction/Transition

Imagery Strategies
Focus on detail in here-and-now; focus on kinesthetic images; retrieve images to assist in working in here-and-now

Dramatic Behaviors
Work with partner; become aware of your body in space

Number of Participants: Pairs

Materials Needed: Various rostrum blocks placed around; enough blindfolds for half the group.

Directions: Divide the class into pairs. Designate one person in the pair as A and the other B. Set up the room so that it is as empty as possible, except for four to six rostrum blocks. Have as many pairs as there is enough room to participate simultaneously. Have a walk-through path filled with four rostrum blocks. Have B help A in remembering the path. Blindfold A, and with the assistance of B, have A walk through the path with as much confidence and as quickly as possible. Repeat, reversing the roles of A and B.

Guiding Lines: Remember the path.

How far away is the next rostrum block? Don't count steps! Just feel the distance.

B, don't tell A. Just watch A carefully.

A, use the kinesthetic feelings you have stored. Trust yourself. Trust your partner.

Notes: This exercise is a classic.

Modifications: When your group feels confident, try this exercise in a more densely furnished room.

Exercise: Apple — Category: Design/Environment

Imagery Strategies

Record various sensory images; compare sensory images; experience an object using all the senses

Dramatic Behaviors

Develop awareness of various sensory modalities: touch, taste, smell, sound; discriminate using senses; notice similarities and differences

Number of Participants: Whole group

Materials Needed: Four very different kinds of apples (at least two of each kind), paper plates or napkins, and a knife

Directions: Have the group sit in a circle and place four different kinds of apples in front of you. Ask participants what is the same and what is different about the apples. Pass the apples around the circle, encouraging them to smell and feel the weight, texture, and shape of the apples. Ask them if there are other similarities and differences. Cut open the four apples; look carefully inside and smell each apple. Then let participants sample each apple (in precut chunks). Go back to the four whole apples and discuss the various attributes of each: hard, sweet, crunchy.

Guiding Lines: Look at these apples. What is different about them? What is similar?

Feel the apple — its weight, texture, and shape. How are the apples different? Do they smell the same?

Taste a piece of each apple. How are they different? similar?

What would you now say or tell me about each one of these apples?

Notes: This is a good early exercise because it helps develop multisensory awareness that can be recalled at a later date, enhanced, and developed throughout RIM. It is best done in the fall because of the availability of a wide assortment of apples. Look for differences first, then similarities. Keep challenging participants to find sensory words to describe each apple. Remember, there may be individual sensory differences among the participants; therefore, aim for a consensus.

Modifications: This exercise format may be used to experience any item in a multisensory fashion (even though you may not eat it). The exercise can be done with any natural object — shells, flowers, minerals.

Henri Matisse's *Apples* helps the viewer look at apples in a dramatic way. (Courtesy The Art Institute of Chicago)

Exercise: **Colors** Category: Design/Environment

Imagery Strategies
Record color images; retrieve color images; match a here-and-now color with a recalled color image

Dramatic Behaviors
Develop awareness of color variety

Number of Participants: Whole group

Materials Needed: Two samples each of a variety of colors

Directions: Bring in two samples each of a wide variety of colors. (You may wish to paint paper or get samples from a local paint store.) Show the class each color sample, but do not name the colors. Then show the first color sample to participants. Remove the sample from view. Ask a volunteer to select the color that matches the one they have just seen.

Guiding Lines: Really see the color.

Store this color in your mind's eye.

Try to recall the previous color and match it to these colors.

Notes: Early in drama classes, keep colors very different. Soon make the color matches closer. Then, bring in various shades of red, for example.

Remember that color names are part of a sales campaign and may or may not describe the color. Instead of avoiding this issue, discuss how naming a color is a creative process.

You may also ask the participants to assign their own names to colors. Explain that these names must describe the color as well as be generalizable enough to communicate to others.

Modifications: You may wish to attempt texture match, shape match, size match. You can also see if they can do matches after time has passed, such as the next day.

Exercise: Textures — Category: Design/Environment

Imagery Strategies
Focus on the tactile qualities of an object; record tactile images; match tactile impressions with object

Dramatic Behaviors
Notice different textures around them; discriminate between various textures; explore their world using the sense of touch

Number of Participants: Whole group

Materials Needed: Crayons and newsprint paper; a few objects with different surface textures.

Directions: Explain to the group that they are going to be "touch detectors." Show participants how every surface has a texture. Pass around a few objects and have the participants feel the differences in texture. Show them that one way to record the texture is to make an impression of it by placing the newsprint over the surface and rubbing a crayon across the texture. Explain to them that you want them to detect as many textures in the room as possible by filling their page with impressions.

Guiding Lines: Touch everything first. Make sure it will make a good impression. Rub carefully. Not too hard, not too soft.

Look for interesting textures. Be a detective! Feel them first.

Then record your impression. Try to remember where you found the texture.

Notes: If your room is not very texturally interesting, bring in pieces of sandpaper and/or objects to create interesting impressions. Encourage participants to touch the surface first before recording their impressions. They are "touch detectives"; they should be thoughtful and clever!

Modifications: Take the group outside or through the school to find different textures.

Exercise: Light/Dark — Category: Design/Environment

Imagery Strategies
Focus on images of light and dark; record here-and-now emotions based on light and dark; connect previous visual images with here-and-now reality

Dramatic Behaviors
Observe how light and dark affects a scene; enact a group scene in different ways based on the effect of lighting; develop awareness of how environment is affected by light

Number of Participants: Whole group

Materials Needed: Lights and lamps that can be brightened and dimmed

Directions: Turn on all lights in the room. Coach the class to observe the classroom in this very bright light. Turn off all but a single small lamp. Coach the class into observing the change in what they see. Turn on lamps to make various levels of lightness/darkness.

Turn on all the lights again and ask the group how the room makes them feel. Ask pairs to pantomime an everyday activity (such as handing out papers, putting on coats, washing blackboard) in full light and then in semidarkness. After the enactment, question them how the activity was affected by light/dark.

Guiding Lines: See the room change. How do you feel?

Describe the details of the room in the light/in the dark.

How does this light and dark make you feel?

Do everyday activities seem to be affected by light/dark?

Notes: This exercise calls forth images of remembered experiences that occurred in light or dark rooms. Help focus participants on using these past experiences to shape current behavior.

Modifications: You can add this exercise to scene work. When used in this context, lighting establishes mood for both participants and observers.

Exercise: Obstacle Course — Category: Design/Environment

Imagery Strategies
Image self moving through space; manipulate images to build obstacle course

Dramatic Behaviors
Move through an obstacle course; plan a course that requires various movements

Number of Participants: Whole group

Materials Needed: Chairs, tables, climber tunnel, things to make an obstacle course

Directions: Discuss what an obstacle course is, and tell the participants they are going to build one. Decide where it would and would not be safe to go. Observe the room and locate objects they can go over, under, around, and through. Once the course is built, side coach the group through it.

Guiding Lines: Construct the course. Let what is here suggest what to do. Now, move through the course. The object is to get from here to there. Is there only one way through the course? Be careful not to miss anything. Don't move any objects.

Notes: Experimentation should be encouraged, but students must take care not to move the obstacles. You may have other students hold chairs, for example, if they have a tendency to fall.

The focus of the exercise is building a course and then moving through it. Suggest that participants build a course that seems to be difficult, but is really quite safe. Participants should know that "theatrical effect" can be achieved in a variety of ways.

Exercise: Blocks — Category: Design/Environment

Imagery Strategies
Recall past images; manipulate here-and-now objects into a configuration suggested by past images

Dramatic Behaviors
Express here-and-now objects through pantomime; build a set based on past images and here-and-now objects

Number of Participants: Whole group, then small groups

Materials Needed: Three large rostrum blocks

Directions: Bring in three rostrum blocks. Begin to move them into various configurations. Ask the whole group to state what is suggested by the various configurations, for example, a mountain, an altar, a chair. Then, divide the whole group into smaller groups. Ask each to act out a short pantomimed activity in response to rostrum blocks.

Guiding Lines: Really look at the set.

What other object or place that you have seen could look like this?

Move the pieces into any shape you like.

If you get stuck, keep moving them. Let the shapes suggest things to you.

Image the shapes much larger or smaller.

You are developing your own set. Develop one you like.

Notes: Often the blocks take on a specific form after they have been moved by a participant. It's as if they magically were formed into that configuration. So, if a participant is having difficulty, encourage him or her simply to manipulate the objects and thus stir imagination. Set designers speak of similar experiences in which the set seemed to design itself.

Modifications: Like many exercises in this category, "Blocks" can be expanded. The focus can be on developing a set in which many scenes could take place, one in which *only* this scene could play, or on one that recreates a real-life scene.

Exercise: Treasure Map — Category: Design/Environment

Imagery Strategies

Image a path; experience an everyday pathway in a new and interesting way; develop early imagination images

Dramatic Behaviors

Develop a visual-spatial awareness of everyday space; experience moment by moment reality

Number of Participants: Small groups

Materials Needed: Paper, markers or crayons, small box wrapped in shiny paper (treasure box)

Directions: Instruct the group to sit in a circle around the treasure box. Tell them that you are going to hide the box—in the building, under a table, in the basketball net, on the card catalog in the library.

Take the participants on a guided fantasy to find the treasure, making left and right turns until they reach the place where it is hidden. Discuss how treasure maps are different from regular maps.

Guiding Lines: Treasure maps are not like road maps; they give clues, not specific directions.

Visualize yourself moving through the building. Find the clue.

See the detail. Recall the building in as much detail as possible.

Remember you don't have to walk to each clue; you can fly or just appear anywhere in the building.

Notes: Use brown paper bags for the maps and tear the edges all around to make an authentic looking treasure map.

Don't show participants where the treasure is located; *lead* them from one place to another on an interesting path. Encourage participants to realize that the clue is important at each stop. Participants must try to experience immediacy and live in the here-and-now. Finding the treasure happens by dealing with each clue one at a time.

Modifications: Have the groups choose their own place to hide the treasure in the building. Create a map for others to figure out where the treasure is hidden.

Try using other sensory clues, tactile, olfactory, or sound.

Exercise: **Variations on a Room**

Category: Design/Environment

Imagery Strategies
Focus on detail; retrieve images; shift and rotate here-and-now objects

Dramatic Behaviors
Observe how the same room can look very different; construct a room; develop awareness of the concept of set

Number of Participants: Whole group

Materials Needed: Classroom furniture in a prearranged traditional classroom setting

Directions: Instruct each participant to sit at one of the desks in the room. Discuss the reasons for a classroom to be arranged in very specific ways. Encourage responses from the group to suggest ways to move the furniture, yet maintain the aspects of the room necessary for teaching. As participants suggest various configurations, move the furniture and conduct a discussion about how the room looks and feels different.

Guiding Lines: Observe the room as it is now, and think of the reasons we are arranged in this way. Are there other possible ways of rearranging the furniture? Think about it in your mind's eye. Shut your eyes and picture all the different ways you could set up the room.

Modifications: The various rooms designed by participants can be used as settings for later exercises.

Exercise: **Magic Stones**

Category: Design/Environment

Imagery Strategies
Recall image of place; overlay past image with here-and-now image

Dramatic Behaviors
Establish environment through pantomime; physicalize a character within an environment

Number of Participants: Whole group

Materials Needed: Enough large stones for each participant to hold several simultaneously

Directions: Bring in a whole pile of beautiful stones. Explain to the group that these stones have been imbued with magic power. They will be able to transform the here-and-now into places they have been to before.

Ask the group to name places they have been to and like very much: amusement park, beach, library. Coach each participant into remembering each place.

Ask each person to focus on specifics of one place and remember the details of people and objects around that place.

Ask each participant to decide on a place in which he or she can become a person as part of the setting. For example, in a library, the participant may see a librarian, student, old man reading. In a grocery store, a checkout person, food bagger, or customer.

Coach participants into returning to images in the mind's eye.

Guiding Lines: Remember the place. Focus on the details of the place. Recall who was in the place.

Retrieve these images. Try to make the classroom into that place.

Use the magic stones to take you to this place and explore the things around you.

Notes: To help shake old prejudices (for example, that imagination is not something desirable), assign "magic power" to here-and-now objects. This can become a freeing agent. After participants have found that they are able to retrieve past images and overlay these images with the here-and-now, gradually wean the class from the use of these magic stones.

Once participants have been successful playing places they have been to, begin to utilize imagination images as the stimulus for more complex enactments.

Modifications: Ask participants to suggest a place where there are many living things that are not people, like a zoo or aquarium.

Exercise: Grocery Store — Category: Design/Environment

Imagery Strategies

Recall a previously perceived environment; select most important aspects of an image; overlay previous image with here-and-now environments

Dramatic Behaviors

Establish locale; pantomime "as if" this room were somewhere else; develop group skills

Number of Participants: Whole group

Materials Needed: None

Directions: Allow the whole group to sit comfortably on the floor. Coach the group into remembering a local grocery store. Have them focus on the details of the place (not on people in the place). After each has remembered a grocery store, hold a discussion concerning their remembered images. Come to some agreement about some basic requirements to establish the set-up of the grocery store: shelves for cans, fruit and vegetable area, front door, check-out counter.

Ask the class to place these areas within the area of the current classroom. If participants are having difficulty, you make decision.

Explain that they are going to pantomime themselves within the classroom grocery store.

Have the class enact grocery store.

Guiding Lines: Recall the grocery store in your mind's eye. See the details of the grocery store. Try to recall the grocery store. What did you buy the last time you were there? What parts of the store did you have to go to?

Notes: This is the beginning of a traditional form in creative drama: plan, play, evaluate. Make sure this playing is based on some imagery-based planning. Also remember that the focus here is on establishment of locale only. Don't worry about interaction or subtlety of small behaviors. The experience of standing up and doing drama is the key.

Modifications: Use other public places —beaches, libraries, museums, playgrounds, etc.

Exercise: **Configurations** Category: Design/Environment

Imagery Strategies
Recall past images of places; match a past image to a configuration of here-and-now objects; overlay self and image of place

Dramatic Behaviors
Construct a set using here-and-now objects; establish place through pantomime; develop awareness of world around them as places of drama

Number of Participants: Whole group

Materials Needed: Rostrum blocks, steps, ramps, etc., and any other moveable set pieces (between five and eight pieces).

Directions: Add to the three rostrum blocks used in Blocks other pieces of moveable set pieces: steps, ramps, and other rostrum blocks. When the participants enter the room, they sit around a configuration you have set up. Ask them what place is suggested by these blocks. Try to elicit many appropriate responses. Offer some of your own to get them started or if they get stuck. Choose one suggestion and ask them to imagine who they would be at this place and what would they be doing. Ask them to show this in a freeze position. Then let them move the blocks into a new configuration, the more interesting and unusual the better. Everyone sits around the blocks, suggesting ideas for place, then takes a freeze position to demonstrate one place in pantomime. Continue the exercise until they are readily thinking of places.

Guiding Lines: Really look at the set. What place does this group of blocks suggest?

Look again? Where could we be?

Let's take this suggestion. Who could you be in this place? Take a freeze position that shows me who you are and what you would be doing in this place.

Now let's change the shape of the place. Stand the blocks on end, move them around. Make an interesting shape. Look at the set. What place does this group of blocks suggest?

Notes: Be sure to stress fluency of ideas. No idea is wrong. Some are just more interesting or more appropriate than others. Encourage the uncommon answer through coaching. Places for drama can be anywhere.

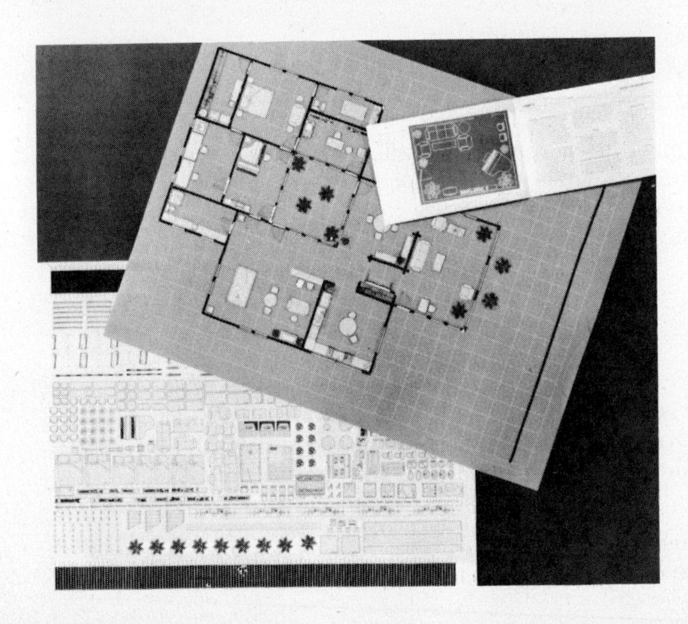

The Plan-a-Flex Home Designer can do more than assist an interior decorator. This kit can teach the concept of creating an environment through space and objects. (Lise Matthews and Bud Brimberg, The Museum of Modern Art catalogue)

Exercise: Jungle | **Category:** Design/Environment

Imagery Strategies
Develop early group drama; recreate a sensory experience with various materials and props; focus on the environmental image of place

Dramatic Behaviors
Plan and create a group environment; design a place to physically be; establish a sense of place; early group negotiation

Number of Participants: Whole group and small groups

Materials Needed: Various art materials: crepe paper, string, cardboard, electrical tape, and other suggestive props, including lights, carpet, and rostrum blocks; also sound effects materials, instruments, and tape recorder.

Directions: Explain that today the class is going to create a jungle in this very room. Ask participants to suggest various types of terrain they would find in a jungle—river, hills, caves, etc. Refer to television and movies, cartoons, and their knowledge of Asian or African or South American jungles. Decide on three to five (depending on the size of the group and space) different physical challenges one would encounter in a jungle: river and waterfall, large trees and vines, etc. Divide into work groups to create the jungle space, giving participants enough time to work. Create a jungle sound tape to accompany the environment.

Guiding Lines: Where have you seen a jungle before?

What is the land like, the plants, the water? What could you see, hear, feel? What physical elements could we choose that say "this is a jungle"?

Keep it simple. Listen to the sounds in this part of the jungle while you work.

Notes: Select basic differences in terrain, keeping the ideas do-able and appropriate to the age level of the group. The focus is on coordinating group efforts to make a whole space. This may take more than one day, or many groups may add to the overall effects of the jungle by creating various aspects of it. Be sure to allow time to "be" in the jungle.

Modifications: Use masks from the Fantasy Creatures exercise to create a story about the creatures who live in this jungle.

GETTING THE MOST OUT OF STARTERS

RIM Starters are organized to facilitate dramatic learning within each drama skill category and also across categories. This organization provides you with a great deal of flexibility in adapting Starters to your particular group or to individual participants' specific needs. The two basic ways to utilize Starters are:

- In-Depth Approach
- Spectrum Approach

Both approaches can be useful in a variety of situations. In order to decide which basic approach is most appropriate for your group, you must assess the needs of your group, your reasons for doing creative drama with this particular group, and the specifics of your situation. You may want to ask yourself some questions:

- What is the age range of the group?
- How much creative drama experience have they had?

- What is the basic temperament or personality of the group as a whole?
- Do any of the participants have special physical, emotional, or mental needs?
- How many lessons will I have with them?
- How much time do I have with them per lesson?
- Is this drama class part of another curriculum area (language arts, visual arts, music)?
- Is there an agenda for this group expressed by someone other than myself (principal, physical education teacher, parents)?

The answers to this quick assessment will help you set realistic goals for yourself and your group and help you select which approach to Starters will be more appropriate.

In-Depth Approach

This approach for using RIM Starters allows you to choose a specific drama skill category and work through an entire sequence of exercises. Participants develop both imagery strategies and dramatic behaviors related to that specific drama area such as Movement/Pantomime or Object/Prop. Initially, you may be more comfortable with this approach until you become familiar with the method and know what to expect from the exercises and the participants. An in-depth approach may be most useful in the following situations:

- If the time you have with the group is limited to only a few classes, you may want to emphasize only one drama skill area such as Person/Character. This allows both you and the group to achieve a certain amount of success and growth in one drama category.
- If the students in your group are young (under seven years old) and you will be seeing them regularly, you may want to acquaint them with each drama area as a whole. Each category is introduced and completed. Behaviors can then be readily assessed and reinforced.
- If your drama class is part of another class, you may be required to address objectives specific to that curriculum area, thus utilizing creative drama as a teaching tool. In a language arts class, for example, you may focus on Sequence/Story; in a visual arts class, you may choose only from Object/Prop and Design/Environment.
- If your group has special needs due to physical or mental limitations, you may need to highlight one category in order to emphasize the specific strategies and behaviors and their connection. A group needing work in the area of language development, for example, may use Sound/Speech exclusively; a group with specific physical needs may work completely within the category of Movement/Pantomime.
- If the group is experienced in creative drama, you may want to return to one drama skill category for a lesson or two for a brief refresher or to give the group further practice in areas in which they need the most work.

Since Introduction/Transition exercises are integrated into each category, each drama skill category provides participants with practice in these important skills. Also particular exercises can be returned to and repeated as the group develops the imagery strategies and dramatic behaviors within the category. This allows the participants to see their progress and reinforces the skills learned. The following example details a four-day plan for dramatic learning in Sound/Speech Starters, using the in-depth approach:

IN-DEPTH APPROACH

Four-Day Lesson Plan for Sound/Speech

Day 1

- Silence Game.
- Story Sounds.
- Musical Patterns.
- How Far Am I?
- Story Sounds.

Day 2

- Green Meadows.
- Find-a-Voice.
- Echo.
- Moody Words.
- Silence Game.

Day 3

- Silence Game.
- Musical Patterns.
- Story Sounds.
- Background Music.
- Bright Idea.

Day 4

- Auditory Pictures.
- Noisy Words.
- Echo.
- Musical Conversations.
- Wizard.

Spectrum Approach

The Spectrum Approach allows you to organize a lesson by selecting various exercises from a number of categories. Instead of working on one category exclusively, you present exercises from two to seven categories during the lesson. The Spectrum Approach is the one most often used in the typical creative drama setting. It works well with beginning or experienced groups, particularly those who participate in creative drama on a regular basis over weeks or months. By experiencing the wide-ranging exercises that develop all the skills which go into dramatic learning, participants get a true sense of the nature of drama and theatre, as well as how to integrate imagination and action. The Spectrum Approach also allows you to assess learning categorically—you can quickly spot areas of strength or weakness in the group. Subsequently lessons can be based on this information.

RIM Starters can easily be organized to meet the group's learning style and changing needs. The exercises are not chosen merely at random, but rather organized to provide a number of drama skill experiences within one lesson. Since the exercises presented in this book are sequenced within a category from simple to more difficult, you can easily select compatible and comparable exercises from different categories.

Remember that, even though you go into the lesson armed with what you feel is a carefully conceived plan, you may still have to modify from day to day or even during the lesson itself. Experienced leaders know that they cannot preordain learning. Some days the group catches on easily and quickly; other classes move more slowly, need more repetition, or take off in an unpredictable direction. Arm yourself with a knowledge of each exercise and its objectives, plan as much as you can, and pay attention to the immediate clues your participants give you.

Variety is the key to the Spectrum Approach. Try to alternate between long exercises and short, between seated and moving, between whole-group and small-group or pair exercise. You also should try to choose exercises in which your role changes. Be sure always to include an Introduction/Transition exercise or two in your daily lesson to help bridge exercises of differing categories, or as a cool-down at the end of class.

Planning for the Spectrum Approach will take some practice and involves continuous assessment of your group. Following is a four-day lesson plan. Don't try to replicate it exactly, merely use it as an example of a successful Spectrum Approach:

SPECTRUM APPROACH

Four-Day Lesson Plan

Day 1

- Flex and Relax (Introduction/Transition).
- Household Objects (Object/Prop).
- Story Sounds (Sound/Speech).
- Quick Flash (Introduction/Transition).
- Hats (Person/Character).

Day 2

- Colors (Design/Environment).
- Who Me? (Introduction/Transition).
- Magic Cloth (Person/Character).
- Gesture Drawing (Introduction/Transition).
- Obstacle Course (Design/Environment).

Day 3

- Twenty-Four Hours (Sequence/Story).
- High/Low Shapes (Movement/Pantomime).
- Blindfold Walk (Design/Environment).
- Green Meadows (Introduction/Transition).
- Pass the Object (Object/Prop).

Day 4

- Elevator (Introduction/Transition).
- Story Shuffle (Sequence/Story).
- Blocks (Design/Environment).
- Looking at People (Introduction/Transition).
- Greetings (Movement/Pantomime).

TRANSFORMATIONS

Chapters 9 and 10 contain the second level of the Rutgers Imagination Method, called Transformations. In Transformations participants learn to transform their ideas into dramatic action. More complex than Starters, Transformations require that participants integrate many imagery skills and dramatic behaviors as they work to connect imagination and dramatic action. Transformation activities encourage the formation of imagination images that can stimulate a variety of end products. Transformations also provide many opportunities for participants to work together to solve a dramatic problem.

The activities included in Transformations closely resemble the drama activities found in other drama methods. Within RIM, however, these activities are only part of the three-level approach. Few participants can achieve success with Transformations if they have not experienced Starters. And, of course, achieving success in Transformations is an essential step toward reaching Mastery Level RIM.

Transformations are divided into five categories: Self as Character, Place Becomes Setting, Events/Stories into Plots, Adding Conflict, and Creating Spectacle. The first three sets of activities appear in this chapter; the next two are in Chapter 10. Each set of activities focuses on one type of Transformation. In Self as Character participants learn to transform themselves into a character. Place Becomes Setting encourages participants, individually and as a group, to transform the here-and-now into another there-and-then world. The activities in Events/Stories into Plot focus on crafting the drama plot. Adding Conflict sheds light on the essence of dramatic conflict and resolution. Finally, in Creating Spectacle participants experiment with props, make-up, costumes, sets, lighting, music, and dance.

GENERAL INFORMATION

Transformations differ substantially from Starters. They are based on the following principles of drama and learning:

- Many young people can achieve success in creative drama by experimenting with roles other than performer.
- Individuals need practice in contributing to the group before they can place the group product above their own individual needs.

• The leader's role and main tasks are to establish the improvisation and lead the evaluation.
• Actual objects, theatre props, and photos are still essential for stimulating drama and imagination.
• Transformations may be the culminating drama experience for a variety of drama participants.

About the Activities

At first glance, the format for Starters and for Transformations seems identical, or at least very similar. There are important differences, however, and they help clarify the uniqueness of Transformations.

In Transformations, we do not state imagery strategies and dramatic behaviors separately, as we did in Starters, nor do we even list a series of objectives for each individual activity. Instead, **every activity within a category has as its objective the particular Transformation described by its name.** For example, all activities in Self as Character focus on each individual, using as many performing skills as necessary, transforming himself or herself into a dramatic character. All Transformation activities retain RIM's dual focus, but all activities within a category have a single objective, emphasizing the connection between internal and external.

Transformations use the classic plan, play, evaluate structure. Starters' *Guiding Lines* and *Directions* are replaced by *Procedures* and *Evaluation* in Transformations. The imagine, enact, reflect structure suggests that participants have more freedom to create, but also more responsibility. During the imagine phase, each participant creates and refines his or her personal imagination images, as well as negotiates with other group members. Planning is modeled on the theatre rehearsal process. During enactment, participants perform the drama for observers, usually other group members or the leader. Reflection focuses on evaluating the past work as well as contemplating the future. Both self-reflection and evaluation of others are key elements in the dramatic learning process.

Transformations provide participants with experiences other than performing. The theatre model suggests other avenues for expressing imagination and connecting ideas to action. **Through Transformation activities, participants can explore and integrate the practices of director, critic, playwright, and designer, as well as refine their skills as performers.** RIM expands creative drama's potential for reaching a wider diversity of participants whose skills may not have been tapped by more traditional approaches.

Group configurations in Transformations are different from the way the group is organized for Starters. Unlike Starters, during which participants all play simultaneously but often in a parallel manner, **individuals in Transformations work in pairs, in threes, in small groups, in large groups, and as a whole group.** Individuals can relate to others within a variety of organizational structures. Consequently, a participant can begin to develop knowledge about self in the group and about other individuals' unique manners of working. This group work, begun during Transformations, reaches fruition in Mastery.

Implicit in Transformations is **the development of a final enactment,** resembling, to a certain extent, the theatre production. Certainly, participants in creative drama expect to perform, but enthusiasm for incompletely prepared enactments must always be tempered by continual emphasis on the process. Evaluation is a tool to keep that balance. Failure to maintain the balance of process and product and internal and external can destroy RIM. Much of the magic of Transformations, however, is the result of a participant's joyful transformation of life into art.

Format for Transformations

Category The category appears in the top righthand corner. The five categories are Self as Character, Events/Stories into Plots, Place Becomes Setting, Adding Conflict, and Creating Spectacle. The category name describes the transformation.

Name of the Activity The name of the activity appears at the left and describes the stimulus or the theatre/imagination premise of the dramatic learning. For example, Person/Animal/Thing (see p. 230).

Theatre Perspective Transformations encourage the development of theatre skills from perspectives other than that of actor. Besides actor, these are director, playwright, designer, and critic. An activity may provide one or several perspectives.

Discussion In Discussion, theories or research findings are suggested that can help the leader place the activity in perspective. Also described are possible responses and potential difficulties of participants of various ages.

Procedures Procedures are step-by-step directions for leading the activity. These directions are addressed to you the leader, not to the participant.

Evaluation Two types of questions you as leader can use in guiding your participants through their own reflection and personal/group evaluation appear under this category. For all activities, we include questions that help participants in self-evaluation. For some activities, we include additional questions to assist observers in their evaluation as audience members.

These are not obligatory questions, of course, but merely models of questions you might ask. Their most important characteristic is that they focus on the specific, in order to counteract such generalized responses as "He was bad." Specific questions encourage participants to explore alternatives and focus on positive aspects.

Extensions Extensions, like the Modifications in Starters, suggest ways to repeat the activity, but not to replicate it. Extensions also suggest ways to embellish an activity.

What's Happening to Participants

Individuals participating in Transformations will experience a wide range of dramatic learning skills, strategies, and behaviors. What will occur for them (internally) and what they will demonstrate to you and their peers (externally) are connected. For ease of discussion, however, we will analyze the internal, the external, and the dynamic connection in separate sections.

Working on Imagination Many new and exciting imagery-related phenomena and creative processes are stimulated by Transformation activities. These new internal processes build on the basic imagery skills learned in Starters and relate directly to dramatic behavior. Transformations rely heavily on the participants' ability to create and use imagination images as stimuli for dramatic action. A large storehouse of images allows the participants to choose a strong personal image as a beginning. This personal image can then be manipulated in the mind's eye in order to create a new image. (Recall the cyclic aspect of the iii Framework.) Throughout Transformations, participants demonstrate *flexibility,* as they generate possible categories of images; *controllability,* as they hold and manipulate personal images; and *elaboration,* as they develop their imaginative ideas.

In Transformations, individuals are not at first able to be selective regarding their imaginative ideas. Their newly created images, evoked from personal experiences and vivid memories, often have a strong affective aspect. The "curtain-going-up" nature of the enactment, peer pressure, and their own confidence in their continued flow of wonderful images allow participants *to select/reject* with ease.

The group focus of Transformations also encourages the development of other imagery-related skills and strategies, both for each individual and for the group as a whole. Individuals become experienced in describing and sharing experiences and imagination ideas, as well as in responding to the images and ideas of others. Idea-hitchhiking is common as participants connect and elaborate upon their images and the images of others. An important group goal is the development of a *unified group imagination image* in which each member "sees" in his or her mind's eye the same imaginary place, set of characters, and story line as do his fellow participants. Images representing this agreement are powerful stimuli that help meld the group and propel the drama forward.

Working on Theatre Skills Transformations are much more theatrical than Starters. The most significant addition to the participants' behavioral repertoire is, of course, the finished product. Many of the activities found in Transformations conclude with a planned enactment. In fact, such enactments help participants understand — through firsthand experience — the essential elements of the theatre model: performer, audience, and message. Because many activities are performed by one part of the class for the other part, who become observers/audience, participants rapidly develop a *sense of audience,* even while planning the enactment. Through trial and error, participants spontaneously or with your guidance begin to use and understand acting, writing, and production conventions. In fact, their dramas contain exciting and interesting characters and plot twists, all of which are based on life as they know it or imagine it to be.

In Transformations, participants emulate a variety of theatre's creative and interpretive artists. Not only do they learn to work as an actor does, but this second level of RIM isolates, integrates, and encourages the creative behaviors of the director, designer, playwright, and critic. Participants continue their work as actors to perfect their voices and bodies, but Transformations also require that participants take other actors into consideration. Transformations also provide opportunities for participants to work as directors — to interpret and unify others' ideas and images, to communicate a point of view, to help others build skills, and to develop a sense of the whole.

Participants also work as designers. The design element, a unique aspect of RIM, expands from early Starters to include more elaborate prop and costume building and to focus on the artistic selection process. As playwrights, participants select appropriate words and actions to communicate a story. Activities in Adding Conflict, for example, sharpen a participant's sense of the dramatic. Finally participants learn to be objectively subjective as they become critics; they view the enactments as informed observers and make critical judgments based upon their knowledge of peer potential and the requirements of creative drama.

Making the Connections At the heart of Transformations is the connection between imagination and action. This connection is pivotal in the participant's development of new and more sophisticated levels of dramatic learning. Just how imagination and action connect for an individual is somewhat particular to that person. Once the individual has made the connection for the first time—has hooked together the internal and external—the avenue is irrevocably open.

The connections learned through Transformation activities are specifically artistic. The activities involve the concrete transformation of life into art. Imagination and dramatic action connect to solve a dramatic problem. Connections such as self as image, compressed rehearsal, and third eye facilitate fluid, flexible image-making connected to a physical repertoire of dramatic actions. Several elements that stimulate the connection are built into the activities themselves. The plan/play/evaluate format allows participants to experiment freely.

The group negotiation aspect of Transformations also facilitates the connection. A word, gesture, or facial response from another group member can stir up the connection. In fact, many reticent participants need only a cue from a trusted peer whose position in the group encourages modeling.

The Leader's Role in Transformations

The second level of RIM calls into play an expanded set of leader behaviors that require you to rely on your own creative imagination to select, tailor, develop, and connect activities as needed. At the same time, the more specific nature of Transformations requires you to know about the theatre. Also, your understanding of how imagination and action are linked in the iii Framework and how the group is involved in this connection will strengthen your leader skills.

As leader of Transformations, your job is to make a conscious attempt to structure participants' dramatic learning through concern for both process and product. Your primary responsibilities are to:

- Model appropriate behaviors.
- Select and plan activities.
- Provide information, directly or indirectly.
- Facilitate the group process.
- Observe, assess, and evaluate the group.

Modeling was an important aspect of your role in Starters. As leader, you modeled specific dramatic actions and behaviors that facilitated the sharing of memory images. In Transformations, the behaviors you need to model are of a more cognitive nature. They include problem-solving skills, group negotiation skills, and the ability to attend to both process and product—the same skills you would like your participants to attain. Each skill involves a set of behaviors and attitudes that facilitate the development of dramatic learning at this level.

When you model creative problem-solving skills, you need to be a good listener, ask leading questions, and demonstrate flexibility in thought and action. Participants should see how you consider all their ideas carefully within the selection process, even the silly ones, and yet always consider alternatives. Learning negotiation skills is not always easy. Some students learn the process instinctively; some groups "click." Others always seem to have difficulty; these groups never click. As a model negotiator, you provide the medium—the drama task—and enough structure to guide participants in their efforts. Transformations are structured to help you and the participants attend to both process and product. Your thoughtfulness, interest, and reflectivity about their work will provide an excellent model for their own self-evaluations, not just at the end but as they work.

In Starters, your role as guide required that you create a trusting, nonthreatening atmosphere to facilitate relaxation, image retrieval, and willingness to try drama. During Transformations, you must have a more organized plan, one that focuses on the drama process and integrates the various theatre perspectives. Your choice of Transformation exercises must connect to what happened in Starters and be based on particular goals. **Continuity is the key here—within the lesson, day to day, and week to week.** Daily, you must make sure that you have allowed adequate time for planning, playing, and evaluating.

What you say to initiate an activity is extremely important. In your presentation, you must clarify the stimulating image, assist participants in their own imagery manipulation, help participants connect image to action, and stimulate compressed rehearsal. In Transformations, you must also introduce potential theatre perspectives and facilitate the group process. In the discussion section of each activity, we have pointed out drama/theatre principles that can enhance your understanding of the activity and prepare you to present it to participants.

As observer/leader in Transformations, try to discern, using your experience in Starters, which participants are using imagination images, which ones need more imagery work, and which need more time on drama skills. Listen to planning sessions, watch enactments and reenactments, and structure evaluations in a way that can help you keep in touch with the participants' level of dramatic learning.

Your assessment of the group's work can give you clues for your next move. You may discover that you need to provide information in terms of technical suggestions or identify a certain theatre convention. You may give the information outright or lead the participants through what-if questioning.

"What-if?" questions—the mainstay of creative problem-solving—allow participants to begin to evaluate and reflect upon their ideas and their work. Your role as evaluator is based not on a rigid set of theatre standards but rather on what you have observed participants need to know now as they acquire dramatic learning skills. Good questions can help participants make artistic decisions, select and reject ideas, and connect imagination and dramatic action. As participants' level of artistic knowledge increases, they will begin to question also. Good questioning is:

- Specific—vague or rhetorical questions waste time.
- Logical—questions must have a purpose.
- Brief—get to the point and be direct.
- Simple—use language related to imagery and to drama/theatre.
- Stimulating—questions should arouse thoughtful responses.

To assist you in questioning well, we have included some model questions in each activity. Through evaluation, your knowledge of the art form of drama/theatre, imagery, and the group process helps participants bridge the gap between process and product as they build dramatic learning abilities to think about as well as to do drama.

As leader of Transformations, you must remember that the group structure—the way that small groups work together—and the group task develop in a parallel way. In other words, how well the group works together greatly affects how well it succeeds at creative drama. Most groups develop in a similar fashion, going through the same developmental phases to reach a new level of dramatic learning. As the group becomes unified, you will function less and less as an essential member of it.

Individuals in a group respond in similar ways as the group evolves and takes on a purpose and identity all its own. In Mastery, the height of group development will occur as participants collaborate with ease to develop an original product. It is in this second level of RIM that participants learn to transform their individual and collective images into a coordinated group effort. Initially, the group is very dependent on the leader as it tries to discern the nature of the situation and the acceptability of behaviors. As the group is *forming*, members discover the drama tasks, the rules and procedures for negotiating, and the unique personalities of the individuals within the particular group.

Sometimes the group will appear to be evolving nicely when you will begin to notice signs of discord: rebellion against the leader, disagreement among participants over the possible solutions to a task, or even resistance to the demands of the task entirely. Take heart: this *storming* phase is a necessary one. Continue problem-solving and developing group negotiation skills, and keep the focus on both process and product. Eventually the dissension will disappear, and cohesiveness will supersede argumentativeness. This *norming* phase represents dramatic growth—a new level in ability to understand self in relation to others and to work together, openly exchanging ideas and feelings related to the drama task.

At this point your job is letting go. But rest assured that before this can happen, you will have time to impart all that you know about the imagination/action connection.

SELF AS CHARACTER

This set of activities focuses on the individual development of character. Participants work on developing both the internal and external aspects of a dramatic character. The transformation of self into character involves a number of dramatic learning abilities initiated in Starters. Observational skills that were begun in Starters and continued in Transformations allow participants to think of characters in flexible, elaborate terms.

In order to transform self into character, participants must develop an imagination image of character. By emphasizing various aspects of the character's behaviors plus his or her thoughts, feelings, likes, and dislikes, participants come to view the uniqueness of character as overlayed on self. This composite character image takes the participants' actions out of the realm of charades and into the art form of the actor. Each participant works at filling in character with personal imagination images.

> ***"First of all," he said, "if you can learn a simple trick, Scout, you'll get along a lot better with all kinds of folks. You never really understand a person until you consider things from his point of view . . . until you climb into his skin and walk around in it."***
>
> Harper Lee

Remember, the primary focus here is on the transformation of self into character, not on the total picture during the improvisation. The dramatic actions grow from the participants' observations, personal and memory images, and knowledge of self. Through compressed rehearsal, the participants select and reject various behaviors as they try on character. By physically rehearsing and extending a wide repertoire of actions, participants come to choose the best actions for their character. **Keep in mind that Transformations involve the connection between specific dramatic actions of character and the unique mental picture of that character in the participant's mind's eye.**

Types of Activities

There are three general types of activities in Self as Character. Each set of activities focuses on a specific aspect of character development. The first deals with breaking down stereotypes and developing unique characters, both in imagination and dramatic action. As participants explore various ages and activities in "Picture Me," "Baby Pictures," and "Golden Years," they develop their concept of personal uniqueness. In "The Line Up" they have an opportunity to create a character of their own choosing.

The second aspect of character development involves creating elaborate, flexible imagination images as stimuli for character behavior. Throughout transformation activities, the development of such images is a goal. Participants have the opportunity to share and build on one another's images and actions. "Person/Animal/Thing" focuses on flexibility of actions as participants transform themselves into people, animals, and objects. Elaboration skills are used in "Oral History" and "Introductions," since these activities require participants to retrieve personal memory images to create character. "Whose Clothes?" involves both flexible and elaborative skills as participants use pieces of clothing to create a character.

Character development, which involves breaking down stereotypes, flexibility, and elaboration in the creation of unique characters, leads logically to the third aspect—*relationships*. Only after participants have had the opportunity to work on individual character development do they begin to see themselves in relation to one another. Even though the relationships they are asked to depict may be mundane, encourage them to develop unique and personal points of view toward it. In "Table for Two" and "Famous Couples," participants have a chance to select actions that communicate the relationship clearly and efficiently, and still maintain a well-elaborated character image. "Split Personality" deals with the relationship between ego and alter ego. Transformations develop the ability to see self from the perspective of a third person. "Ventriloquist/Dummy" requires a small group to work together to create the desired effect.

Theatre Perspective

The majority of activities in this category focus on the perspective of the actor. Taking the perspective of an actor is not the same as training to be an actor. These activities ask the participants to develop observation and communication skills that actors use. Because of the emphasis on elaboration and flexibility in a number of the activities, playwrighting skills are also utilized. Participants must create elaborate scenarios and believable dialogue for their characters. A few activities introduce the directing perspective by requiring the participant to plan and oversee the development of a drama.

Leader's Role

Both you and the participants must develop a basic understanding of the Self as Character transformation. This includes an awareness of how the transformation occurs both mentally and physically; the images, feelings, and information that are recalled or stimulated; and the ways in which participants choose to demonstrate the character through dramatic action. Also the participants should become aware of how they select and reject various images and actions, thus making conscious their own creative process and such dramatic learning skills as compressed rehearsal. These activities also provide opportunity to teach various theatre conventions, such as the aside or the scene within a scene.

Throughout the activities you must encourage participants to create elaborate and flexible images of their characters and communicate these characters clearly with a specific set of dramatic actions. Your verbal encouragement and modeling of this type of dramatic thinking helps the developmental process. By sharing images with others, participants come to see that each person may have a unique point of view. This sharing and acknowledging are the beginning steps in group cohesiveness.

Transformation Tips: Self as Character

- **Encourage flexibility** by stating, "Show me another way" or asking, "What if . . . ?"
- **Encourage elaboration** by stating, "Tell me more" or asking, "How would your character do that?"
- **Point out unique or novel images/action.** Is there a different way of doing that? That's a very unusual solution.
- **Encourage observers to pinpoint specific characteristics.** How do old people walk? Tell me about their speed, body posture, length of steps.
- **Help participants articulate the changes that occur from self to character.** What did you have to do with your body to transform yourself into the character? What gestures did you do differently?
- **Be interested in how participants generated images.** Where have you seen someone like that? Who was your source?
- **Seek out personal images.** How many of you have babies at home? Tell me what they do.
- **Allow for laughs.** A playful, experimental climate helps participants take risks and expand their repertoire more readily.

Activity: **Picture Me** Category: Self as Character

Theatre Perspective: Actor/Director

Stimulus: Recent photographs of participants in action situations.

Other Necessary Props: Additional pictures of young people

Size of Group: Small groups

Discussion: Psychological research reports that children learn through observing and imitating the behavior of other children. They record images of various types of behavior. Because they have spent so much time observing, young people have a rich storehouse of information concerning their peer group. These images can be the stimuli for character work. This activity focuses on the development of characters which are approximately the age of the participants.

Procedure: Divide the participants into groups of four or five, making sure each group has a picture. Instruct the groups to look very carefully at the photographs, concentrating on the young people in the picture. Coach each group to notice the similarities and differences among the young children. Then review each photo one at a time. Ask the person who brought in each picture to provide insight about the characters in the pictures.

Assign the person who brought in the photo to be the director and the other individuals to be involved as performers in the enactment. Explain that each group is to develop a very brief enactment in which participants transform themselves into the characters in the photo. Encourage the group to work on character, not on plot. Give groups planning time. Ask each group to play the enactment, one at a time. Evaluate.

Evaluation: *Actors:* How did the director help you understand what was happening in the picture? Was it easier to get a clear image of your character with that person's help? What did you have to do to transform yourself into the person in the photo?

Director: Did the actors follow your directions? What did you have to do to get them to communicate the characters? How did you feel seeing yourself played by another actor?

Activity: **Golden Years** Category: Self as Character

Theatre Perspective: Actor/Playwright

Stimulus: Pictures of elderly people from a family album or magazine

Other Necessary Props: Assorted

Size of Group: Whole group/pairs

Discussion: Young people often believe that every old person is infirm and lives only in the past. Once they are encouraged to observe senior citizens and talk with them, young people begin to view each senior as an individual. Also, young people begin to realize how many interesting life experiences these old people can share.

Procedure: Begin this activity with a discussion of the various senior citizen/retirement villages in which many elderly people live. Discuss how different individuals age differently. Describe some common ailments: arthritis, memory loss, poor vision or hearing, or emotional problems. Discuss how different individuals try to conquer these difficulties. Encourage participants to view each senior citizen as a unique person, based on his or her life experience and physical health.

Divide the group into pairs. Explain that participants are to transform themselves into old people at one of the following: a bus stop, doctor's office, supermarket, car wash, church social, flea market. Encourage each participant to transform

This photo can dispel the stereotypic notion that old people are infirm. These two senior citizens have just completed two miles in the Senior Olympics. (Photo courtesy of Peter Byron)

himself or herself into a unique character who just happens to be old. Suggest that each old person reveal some aspect of his or her life history during the interaction. Allow each couple to plan how they are going to behave as the elderly pair. Have each pair present the enactment. Evaluate.

Evaluation: *Participants:* What are some of the specific characteristics of your old person? How did you have to modify your qualities to transform yourself into the character? What influenced the qualities you selected for your character? What did you do to generate his or her personal history? How did you choose which memories to share?

Audience: What did each one do to show the specific characteristics? What else could they have added? Were the characters in action like the people in the photo? What personal images are most important to these and other older people? Why?

Extensions: Introduce the idea of a scene within a scene. Have the elderly characters replay the scene, but at the point at which one character recalls a memory have them freeze and have the memory enacted by another set of characters.

Activity: The Line Up — Category: Self as Character

Theatre Perspective: Actor/Playwright

Stimulus: Photos of people in line and/or discussions about waiting in line.

Other Necessary Props: Optional props

Size of Group: Small groups

Discussion: In any public place there are often many different kinds of individuals present. "The Line Up" focuses on people waiting in line in public places.

This activity encourages participants to look for similarities (the fact that each individual is waiting here) and differences (the characteristics and life history) among people. Observing people helps build an increased imagic storehouse and stimulates character imagination images.

Procedure: Divide the participants into groups of three or four. If you have photos of people waiting in line, hand one to each group. If not, assign locales. (Select places like a bank, bus stop, laundromat, supermarket counter, or airport.)

Ask participants to develop unique, well-rounded characters who could be waiting in line. Explain that how they walk and talk and what they say assists in the successful transformation of self into another. Give planning time. Then, ask groups to present the enactments, one at a time, based on people waiting in line.

Evaluation: *Participants:* How did you decide what kind of character you would be? What did you have to do to transform yourself into that character? What details in the photo assisted your transformation?

Audience: Could you think of any other way they could enact the character in the photo? Can you think of any other characters that might fit into their scene easily, perhaps ones who weren't photographed?

Extensions: This activity may also focus on shopping, traveling by public transportation, or talking on a public phone. Each of these scenes may grow into a full enactment.

Activity: **Baby Pictures** Category: Self as Character

Theatre Perspective: Actor

Stimulus: Pictures of participants as babies or infants or young children

Other Necessary Props: Optional photographs of other infants

Size of Group: Small groups

Discussion: Young people often do not recognize themselves in baby pictures because they don't remember being babies or because they feel they look so different today. It is interesting, however, to let them try to recall what they were like at a much younger age, and how they were different from their brothers and sisters or other children. This type of activity is essential for replacing stereotypic images with well-developed imagination images. By focusing on the differences as opposed to similarities of babies, the participants can realize the tremendous variety within characterization.

Procedure: Introduce this activity with a discussion of the variety of behaviors exhibited by babies and young children and the differences among babies. Follow this discussion with a guided fantasy to places where there are many young children—a day care center, shopping with mother, at a playground. Direct the participants to focus on a variety of young children of about the same age and on the similarities/differences in their behaviors.

Divide the group into groups of three or four, directing two participants to be adults and two to be children. Suggest a simple activity, such as celebrating a holiday, eating at grandma's house, playing at an amusement park, which would engage young children. Have each group plan the scene. Coach participants playing children to be aware of one another's actions and avoid using generic images to shape character. Play scenes. Evaluate.

Evaluation: *Participants:* How did it feel to be transformed into a small child? How did you generate ideas for your behaviors as a child? Did you try to remember your own childhood? How did you know what to do in each situation?

Activity: **Oral History** Category: Self as Character

Theatre Perspective: Actor/Playwright

Stimulus: Photographs or pictures of individual people

Other Necessary Props: Optional tape recorder

Size of Group: Individuals

Discussion: Photographs usually give the viewer a moment in time record of the person being photographed. If the photograph is a good one, it may also capture the *essence* of the person and give you additional clues about his/her life. Reading clues from a photo is a valuable communication skill. This activity will encourage participants to look at pictures as a rich source of information.

Procedure: Show various photos to the group. Allow each participant to select one for this activity. Conduct a guided fantasy to assist participants in elaborating upon the character. Focus on having the participants develop a biography of the person in the photo. Immediately following the fantasy, explain to participants that you would like to interview each of them and hear his or her oral biography. Ask participants to volunteer telling their life story in character.

Evaluation: *Participants:* Point out some character clues in the photo. Are these physical or emotional characteristics like your own? different? How did the guided fantasy help you see your character? What else did you see your character do in the fantasy? What did you do to transform yourself into the character you selected?

Audience: Can you think of aspects of this character's life that you would like to hear more about? Did the person walk and talk the way you would have expected from the picture?

Extensions: You may want to tape these biographies for comparison with other groups performing the activity and with the same participants later in their development.

Activity: **Introductions** Category: Self as Character

Theatre Perspective: Actor/Playwright

Stimulus: Photographs or pictures of individual people

Other Necessary Props: None

Size of Group: Pairs

Discussion: This activity is a continuation of "Oral History." Participants use what they discovered in "Oral History" and continue to delve into their image storehouse. The actual one-to-one confrontation of people in a particular place meeting for the first time helps to stimulate imaging and the participants' ability to think on their feet.

Procedures: Show the pictures to the group. Give one picture to each participant. Explain that they are to introduce themselves as that character in a particular place. (Choose a place likely to have many characters, such as an airport waiting room, a playground, a party). Divide the group into pairs. Without giving the pairs planning time, announce that they are at this particular place and they are to begin introducing themselves to the other. When the group begins the activity, walk around the room to spot any difficulties. Focus their work on character in a place by asking: Why are you here? Why do you want to know them? Do you need help? Are you just friendly?

Bring the group back together. Ask pairs to discuss what happened and what could have improved the conversations. Focus discussion on motivation, personal images of the pictures, and appropriateness of action.

Evaluation: *Participants:* Describe what happened when you transformed into the character. Did you have to think up what to do? Were your words and actions spontaneous? Why did you introduce yourself? How did you begin? How did your partner respond?

Extensions: Ask the group to replay the enactment, trying to meet at least five different people at this particular place.

Activity: Person/Animal/Thing — Category: Self as Character

Theatre Perspective: Actor

Stimulus: Photographs of people with animals and objects

Other Necessary Props: A drum or other noisemaker

Size of Group: Whole group

Discussion: This activity forms the basis for all character work. Person/Animal/Thing requires that the participants become a character other than self in a place other than a classroom. It is a continuation of the RIM Starter "Animal Faces." This activity introduces the notion that characterization involves consideration of place.

Procedure: Begin a discussion of the picture you have decided to use for this activity by pointing out the three categories—person, animal, thing—in the photo. Ask participants to image transforming themselves into people in the photo. When you are confident they have completed the imagery task, ask each individual (as a group) to become the person. As you beat the drum, instruct the participants to transform themselves into persons in the photo. Remember, tell the group that they may make sounds *but* should *not* talk.

After the group has enacted people, ask each individual to choose an animal to become. Then enact animals. Then ask them to transform themselves into the objects in the photo. Finally, ask them to select a person *or* animal *or* object into which to transform themselves. If the participants have developed group skills, encourage them to develop the enactment in conjunction with other group members.

Evaluation: *Participants:* What did you have to do to transform yourself into the person, animal, or thing? How did you move your body? Describe the differences in transforming yourself into a person, an animal, and a thing. How did you communicate who or what you were?

Extensions: Choose your own photographs of places that your group might have visited. Later on, you may select photos of faraway places. Just make sure the photos are rich in detail and include people/animals/things.

Activity: Whose Clothes? — Category: Self as Character

Theatre Perspective: Actor

Stimulus: Many pieces of clothing, representational or nonrepresentational

Other Necessary Props: Set pieces as selected by participants

Size of Group: Whole group

Discussion: Early in the drama progression bring in pieces of clothing that are distinctly recognizable as worn by a person engaged in a particular job—a ballet tutu, police hat, clown ruff. These here-and-now pieces assist participants in retrieving some very clear images associated with people engaged in these occupations. These images help participants base character work on strong multidimensional images.

Procedure: Show each piece of clothing, one at a time, to participants. Ask participants to imagine a person, real-life or imaginary, who might wear the piece of clothing you have just shown. Encourage participants to use flexible images and to elaborate upon them.

Ask each participant to choose a piece of clothing and transform self into the character. If necessary, coach participants to see themselves as the character. Explain that all the characters have been invited to a large party, given by the mayor or governor. Encourage characters to mingle and interact with others at the party. Play the activity. Lead evaluations.

Evaluation: *Participants:* Did the clothing help you retrieve an image of someone who wore something like this? Or did you develop an imagination image of a character created by you? How elaborate was your image? Did it grow or change as you mingled? What other pieces of clothing would have helped make your costume more complete? Did you think you needed more props and costume to transform into the character?

Audience: Was the characterization as you expected it to be? What aspects of the costume piece seemed to suggest the character? Was the character stereotyped or almost real-life? How much did you learn about the character?

Interesting pieces of clothing can stimulate rich and detailed characterization. Can you transform yourself into someone who could wear these chic clothes worn by the manequins in this French dress-shop window? (Eugene Atget, *Avenue des Gobelins,* Courtesy of The Art Institute of Chicago)

Activity: A Table For Two — Category: Self as Character

Theatre Perspective: Actor/Playwright

Stimulus: A small table and two chairs

Other Necessary Props: None

Size of Group: Pairs

Discussion: As participants discover character, they must consider their character's relationship to other characters. This activity will give them practice in noticing the way in which people relate to one another. In this and other activities in which participants share their work with the group, make sure the activity does not become a guessing game. Counteract this charadelike drama situation by announcing the relationship *before* the couple presents the enactment to the group.

Procedure: Begin by setting up a table and two chairs. Coach the group in observing the table and chairs. Divide the group into pairs. Explain that each pair will become a pair of people in a restaurant. Assign each pair a relationship, such as mother/daughter, teacher/student, doctor/patient. Allow each pair to plan a scene in which they show their relationship. Participants may make sounds or say words like "uh uh," "oh oh," but not complete sentences. They may modify the position of the table and chairs. Make sure they don't try to communicate, however, with exaggerated movements. Allow ample time for preparation. Ask each pair to show the group the scene that depicts two characters in a relationship.

Evaluation: *Participants:* Describe your transformation. What stimulated your decision on how to walk and talk? Which gestures and other nonverbal behaviors suggested your relationship?

Audience: How did they transform into the characters? How did they show the relationship? Are there other ways to show this relationship? What are the key behaviors that crystalize this relationship?

Extensions: Have the couple engage in other types of activities in which they are able to maintain the integrity of the relationship. You may also allow the pair to speak complete sentences as long as they do not use words alone to communicate the relationship.

Activity: Split Personality — Category: Self as Character

Theatre Perspective: Actor/Playwright

Stimulus: Pictures of famous/infamous characters with a double identity such as Superman/Clark Kent, Dr. Jekyll/Mr. Hyde, Dracula, Batman, Wonder Woman

Other Necessary Props: Various objects that may have transforming power (for example, a rock, a small bottle)

Size of Group: Individuals

Discussion: Many characters in fiction and in film and television possess personalities and/or powers that they must hide from others around them. This activity focuses on establishing a diversity of character traits and on transforming one personality to another—all while remaining a single character.

Procedure: Show a variety of photos that depict aspects of the several personalities of the same person. (If photos are not available, ask participants to retrieve clear images of the various aspects of this person.) Discuss what traits remain consistent and what traits modify as the character moves from one personality aspect to another. Also discuss how the transformation takes place: Is it magical, is the change instantaneous, does the character add or take off a costume piece?

Now explain that each participant is to develop a newly conceived character who is similarly split-personalitied. Each participant is to develop both personalities as well as the manner in which the transformation occurs. Give participants planning time. Have participants demonstrate the character in transformation. Evaluate.

Evaluation: *Participants:* Describe your character. Describe the transformation. What did you have to do to yourself to create the character? What characters did you use for models? What aspects of your character are novel or original?

Audience: Describe two kinds of transformation: the transforming of self in the character and the transforming from personality to personality within the character.

Extensions: Develop a scene in which the split-personalitied character must cope with other people and with difficult situations.

Activity: Famous Couples — Category: Self as Character

Theatre Perspective: Actor/Playwright

Stimulus: Pictures of famous couples such as Tarzan and Jane, The Lone Ranger and Tonto, Batman and Robin, Laverne and Shirley, Smothers Brothers, Johnny Carson and Ed McMahon.

Other Necessary Props: None

Size of Group: Pairs

Discussion: Participants of all ages will enjoy this opportunity to become their favorite television and movie personalities. This activity focuses on the ability to select and recreate the essence of character and of relationships. Participants learn to select character attributes that they are best able to portray and ones that best communicate to observers. Because RIM focuses on personal images, participants must learn about themselves as well as about the characters they play.

Procedure: Have participants choose a partner. Have each pair select a famous pair. Discuss how famous couples have certain ways of behaving that clearly distinguishes them from others. Coach the pair to recall its famous couple in action. Ask participants to identify distinguishing walks or gestures and to focus on the voices and expressions the characters use. Also explain that each participant must select those traits that he or she feels able to portray. Allow time for the pairs to work out a short enactment featuring the couple. Ask each pair to present its couple to the whole group.

Evaluation: *Participants:* What did you have to do to transform yourself into your character? How were you able to select just a few traits among many to communicate your character and your relationship? Did your partner influence your selection process? Did your knowledge of your drama skills also assist you?

Audience: Are there any other character traits that this couple is famous for? What aspects of the behavior communicated the character and/or the relationship?

Activity: **Ventriloquist/ Dummy** Category: Self as Character

Theatre Perspective: Actor/Director

Stimulus: Pictures of famous ventriloquists and dummies, such as Edgar Bergen/Charlie McCarthy, Paul Winchell/ Jerry Mahoney. Also, puppet/person teams like Shari Lewis/Lambchop or Kukla/Fran & Ollie

Other Necessary Props: Cue cards with vaudeville comedy routines, or other optional material

Size of Group: Groups of three (or four if there are three in scene)

Discussion: Successful performance of this activity requires both ventriloquist and dummy to see/hear themselves from the perspective of a third person. This activity helps develop third eye skills.

Procedure: Begin this activity with a discussion about the difference between a ventriloquist/dummy, puppet, and marionette. Point out that it is the ventriloquist who speaks for the dummy, who, in turn, must listen and mouth the words. Point out also that a puppeteer similarly directs the actions of the marionette or puppet. Divide the whole group into groups of three or four.

Appoint participants to play ventriloquist, dummy, and observer or puppeter, marionette/puppet, and observer. Have the observer coach and direct the ventriloquist or puppeter to develop two different voices — one for the self and the other for the dummy or puppet. Direct the observer also to coach the participant playing the dummy or puppet to develop a "mechanical" characterization. Give the groups time to work on performing the routines printed on the cards or to develop comedy routines. Have each group perform. Evaluate.

Evaluation: *Participants:* What images aided your transformation? Were kinesthetic images helpful? Did auditory images shape your voice production?

Observer: Were you able to communicate what you wished the pair to do? What kinds of directions were helpful? What directions were confusing?

Extensions: This activity may evolve into one in which the plot becomes the focus. An entire enactment may focus on puppets or dummies controlling their owners.

EVENTS/STORIES INTO PLOTS

This group of activities focuses on the transformations of stories, poems, and daily events into dramatic plots. Each source provides a wealth of ideas and material to develop exciting dramas. A variety of journalistic and playwrighting techniques have been modified for use in Transformations to assist even the most reticent participant. Remember, the goal here is to transform stories and events into action, not to write a scripted play or to reenact last night's television movies.

As they use classic tales and contemporary literature as the source for enactments, participants develop their dramatic learning skills as interpretive artists. This involves the participant as playwright, actor, and director. From each perspective, participants must select and communicate those aspects of the story that make the dramatic plot crystal clear. Participants make decisions about how to tell the story, what to leave out, what to expand as they transform one art form to the other.

The sources for dramatic plots can be real-life events and situations that

> ***A plot is: The king died and then the queen died. A story is: The king died, and then the queen died of a broken heart.***
>
> E. M. Forster

include the personal experiences of the participants, their inner life of dreams, wishes and fantasies, and information and news from the world around them. Transforming life into dramatic art requires a sensitivity to self and the human condition, while continually asking the question: Can I dramatize this event? Participants work together to elaborate upon and fill in life's happenings to create a dramatic storyline. The give-and-take requires them to talk and listen to each other as artists and as human beings. This type of workshop atmosphere allows participants to share and discuss events important to them and to see their experiences considered, adapted, and performed.

Activities in Events/Stories into Plots also introduce the participants to playwrighting concepts. They learn about climatic and episodic plots; they discover the idea of beginning, middle, and end; they find out what scenes must be depicted by selecting and rejecting ideas as they shape the plot. Participants often begin to acquire a reporters' eyes, always investigating the who, what, where, when, and why.

Types of Activities

Three types of activities are found in this category. Classic story drama activities include "Aesop's Fables," "Poem: Dramatizing the Story," and "Comic Strip Stories." In these, participants are encouraged not merely to enact the story as it appears, but also to modify the plot as they see fit.

The second type of activity focuses on dramatic structure and encourages divergent thinking. The journalist's and playwright's bags of tricks are the sources for many of these activities. Participants approach plot development in "Who, What, and Where," cause and effect in "Before/After," and beginning a scene in "Opening Lines." "Sound Off" requires participants, inspired by music as an artist might be, to create and enact a dramatic plot based on sounds or music.

Transformations rely heavily on the participants' use of personal images. Their experiences, dreams, and observations of the world around them provide the material for these activities. As in "Place Becomes Setting," these activities begin with familiar events, such as "The Big Event" or "Family Album," and move on to more fantastic, magical images, such as in "Dreammaker." Participants transform the problems found in the business world in "Sell It Well."

Theatre Perspective

Certainly, participants learn most about playwrighting and acting from these activities. Several activities also focus on the director's perspective.

Leader's Role

Throughout this set of activities, you need to facilitate the selection/rejection process. Initially participants will try to include too much or emphasize unimportant aspects of the drama. Help them articulate the plot and then put it into action. Allow time for planning and reenactments. Although both you and the participants may be most comfortable with story dramas, quickly move into the other types of activities that focus on transforming events into plots, not merely acting out stories. Since many of the activities require small-group work, during the planning phase move from group to group to assist in the negotiation process. Before the groups share their work, give the audience members various plot structures to look for as they observe.

Transformation Tips: Events/Stories into Plots

- **Encourage idea hitchhiking.** That's a good start. Who could add something interesting?
- **Require participants to put ideas into action.** Show me the story. Use action, then add words.
- **Have participants seek out poems and stories to use.** What's your favorite story? What are you reading now?
- **Encourage personal images through relaxation and guided fantasy.**
- **Ask specific questions about the plot.** How would you end this? What would begin the story differently?
- **Discuss the various stimuli and how they affected the plot.** Which was more helpful, the comic strip or your dream?
- **Have them discuss the distinctions between the real-life experience and the enactment.** Did what was enacted resemble the real events at all? How did you feel watching it happen?
- **Encourage them to articulate the connections between the image and the action.** Did striking the exact game pose help you develop the action?
- **Help them note similarities and differences between enactments.** Which drama held your attention? Why?

Activity: Aesop's Fables — Category: Events/Stories into Plots

Theatre Perspective: Director, actor, playwright, critic

Stimulus: Aesop's Fables — read or told

Other Necessary Props: Theatre props appropriate for each story, as necessary

Size of Group: Whole group or small groups

Discussion: Early in the history of creative drama much dramatic activity culminated in the enactment of stories, fables, poems, and other pieces of literature. Although RIM does not aim for story drama as the final activity, RIM encourages story dramas as an excellent category of culminating activities — one that needs to be explored.

Procedure: Read or tell the fable. Ask participants to list the events and characters in the fable. Discuss which events and characters are necessary for enactment of the story. Discuss what extra characters and events might make the performance more effective. Rehearse the various characters: ask several participants simultaneously to transform selves into characters. Rehearse various scenes in a similar way using small groups. Try to tie the scenes together. As narrator, tell the story as the group enacts the fable. After the enactment, evaluate the drama. Replay with different casts.

Evaluate: *Participants:* Describe your transformation into the character. Describe how you transformed the narrative story into action.

Audience: Describe how the person seemed to transform into the character. Was the dramatized action as you imaged it? What was the same? different?

Extension: This is the basic structure to use with any piece of literature to enact a story.

Activity: **Poem: Dramatizing the Story** Category: Events/Stories into Plots

Theatre Perspective: Actor

Stimulus: Narrative poems which tell a story, such as "The Owl and the Pussy-cat," "Casey at the Bat," "The Midnight Ride of Paul Revere," "Wynken, Blynken, & Nod"

Other Necessary Props: Theatre props as needed

Size of Group: Varies for activities A and B

Discussion: Dramatizing any piece of literature requires that each event be rehearsed separately. When events are performed in order, participants begin to acquire an important sense of sequence—a prerequisite to playwrighting. Participants also begin to understand that important action must be shown, not discussed.

Procedure: There are two ways to approach this activity:

A: Read the poem to the class. Ask the group to list the events and characters. Reread the poem, line by line. Ask the class to discuss the action in each line and as a whole. Divide the class into small groups or pairs, with each group/pair responsible for one line or segment. Allow time for rehearsal in the small groups/pairs. When they are ready, read the poem for their dramatization and have each pair/group act out the line. Evaluate the results.

B: If the poem is short, ask each group to develop the entire enactment. The group may choose to have a narrator or to act out the story without a narrator — through action.

Evaluation: *Participants:* Did the words of the poem suggest action? Did the words stimulate images of previous experiences? Could you see yourself as the character in the poem? Describe your decision-making process.

Audience: Did the performers meet your expectations? How did the performers elaborate upon the action? What did they select to show? What did they leave out?

Extensions: After the group has mastered poems that tell a story, you may choose poems that are more abstract. Check sources for contemporary collections (for example, "Reflections on a Gift of Watermelon Pickle").

Activity: **Comic Strip Stories** Category: Events/Stories into Plots

Theatre Perspective: Actor, playwright

Stimulus: Many episodes of various multiple-frame comic strips

Other Necessary Props: None

Size of Group: Small groups

Discussion: Several generations of Americans grew up with comic strip characters as role models or personal imaginary friends. For many families the Sunday comic page was the most popular page of the paper. Each week another event was added to the life of one's favorite hero, and devotees would have to wait another week to read the next episode.

This activity allows participants to use the stories found in comic strips to stimulate plot ideas. The plots based on action comics will probably be climactic in nature. Plots based on character-oriented comics may be more episodic.

Procedure: Before you start this activity have all comic strips gathered together according to title. For a good selection you should have at least a dozen episodes of each strip. Begin a discussion about comic strips. Ask the participants to tell you about their favorite characters. Discuss whether they have ever developed their own imaginary stories featuring their favorite comic-strip characters. If they have, ask these participants to tell you their stories.

Divide the group into smaller groups of individuals — some who read comics and others who don't. Tell the group they are to select one comic strip series and read all the comic strips you have provided. After they have read the strips, ask them to make up an imaginary scene — one not in the strip but based on the strip — that expands the story of the characters in the strip. Coach them to focus on using the here-and-now strip as stimulus for additional action. After planning time, ask the groups to show you their work. If the characters are unfamiliar to most others in the group, you may want to read some of the strips to the whole group. Evaluate each scene after it is performed.

Evaluation: *Participants:* What aspects of the strip helped you plan imagination/action? Describe the episode.

Audience: Were these dramas extensions of the strip? In what way?

Activity: Headlines — Category: Events/Stories into Plots

Theatre Perspective: Actor, playwright, designer, director, critic

Stimulus: Many newspaper headlines without stories

Other Necessary Props: Assorted props, costumes, make-up, rostrum blocks and other furniture to move about

Size of Group: Small groups

Discussion: Participants often come up with stories worthy of enactment when they are given a here-and-now aspect of the story—in this case, the headline. These headlines often stimulate personal retrieval of images and encourage individuals to begin to communicate their images to one another.

Procedure: Read eight or ten headlines for the whole group and ask participants to elaborate upon several possible stories for each headline. Remember to tell the group that there are no right or wrong stories, only those that are more or less exciting to perform and to watch. (Do not have the real stories attached to the headlines because they may stifle instinctive planning.) Divide the participants into small groups and instruct them that they are to select a headline and create and enact a story. Coach the participants to consider limitations of space, props, costumes, and performance. If necessary, introduce the notions of cause and effect; beginning, middle, and end; and conflict. Allow planning time for set arrangement, costumes, and prop selection. View and evaluate all headlines.

Evaluation: *Participants:* Which headlines stimulated your imagination? What did you have to do to put your images into action? Did you have to modify your original idea once the planning stage began?

Audience: Was this story an interesting episode? If you were a movie critic, what would you say was the best part of the drama? What aspects needed to be changed? What was the conflict? How was it resolved?

Extensions: For a comic twist to this activity try working with headlines from less "reputable" newspapers often found at supermarket checkout counters.

This potpourri of photos depicts people, places, and things. Richly detailed, sharp photos help participants pull from and add to their own imagic storehouse. (Photos courtesy of Michael Rocco Pinciotti)

Activity: **Who, What, Where** Category: Events/Stories into Plots

Theatre Perspective: Playwright, actor

Stimulus: Three sets of cards with types of occupations, familiar places, and common objects. There should be enough cards to repeat this activity four or five times.

Other Necessary Props: None

Size of Group: Small groups

Discussion: Generating ideas is sometimes difficult, but restrictions often help, not hinder. "Who, What, and Where" is a classic creative drama activity. It works because the restrictions provided by the cards focus the image-making process. Participants begin to categorize images, see relationships among seemingly unrelated images, and use the overlay as stimulus for dramatic action.

Procedure: Divide the participants into small groups. Allow each group to pick one card from each set of cards. When they have selected three cards, coach the group to work out a plot that would involve all three elements. After ample planning time, allow each group to perform its drama for the whole group. Remember to tell everyone what three elements the group had to combine *before* the performance begins, thus avoiding a guessing game during the dramas. Evaluate the dramas after each enactment.

Evaluation: *Participants:* Did the word on the card stimulate your images? Could you begin to plan in your mind's eye? What was the hardest aspect of group negotiation?

Audience: Did the combination ring true? Was the enactment similar to or different from your expectations?

Activity: **Before/After** Category: Events/Stories into Plots

Theatre Perspective: Playwright/Critic/Director/Actor

Stimulus: Photographs of people in a variety of situations

Other Necessary Props: None

Size of Group: Small groups

Discussion: Negotiation of one's own point of view with others' is the essence of the creative drama process. In fact, groups that have worked together for some time begin to share theatrical imagic storehouses. But at first, groups have to practice working together. One or two people may emerge as natural directors or observant critics. Your task is to structure evaluation to encourage the development of an evaluating eye. These critical powers transfer to a variety of situations, including becoming a more discriminating audience member.

This activity builds on the Starter exercise "What Happened Before?" but expands the potential tasks of participants and includes more evaluation. Photos of people in situations can be used again and again to stimulate dramatic action.

Procedure: Show the photographs to the groups and explain that the photo was taken at just one moment in time — there is a before and an after to each picture. Divide the participants into small groups, allowing each group to select a photo. Coach each group to plan what might have happened before the photo was taken. Ask each group to show the whole group what happened before the picture was taken.

Regroup and plan what happened after the picture was taken. Have each group enact that scene. After all groups have performed, conduct an evaluation. Be sure to find both good and not-so-good aspects of each performance.

Evaluation: *Participants:* Did striking the pose help you become the character? Develop the action?

Audience: Was the dramatic action appropriate for the photo?

Extensions: As participants become more comfortable with assuming exact positions, you may have them "freeze" into the photo for one moment and run both before and after, with the picture "freeze" in the middle.

Activity: Opening Lines — Category: Events/Stories into Plots

Theatre Perspective: Actor/Playwright

Stimulus: Index cards with opening lines, such as "Pardon me, but aren't you . . ."; "Could you tell me where ______________ is?"

Other Necessary Props: None

Size of Group: Small groups

Discussion: When trying to make the transition from pantomimed activities to ones with dialogue, some participants have difficulty getting started. This activity shifts the focus from having to generate opening lines to allowing the given line to stimulate other images and resulting plot and dialogue. Emphasis can then be placed not on how original the dialogue is but on how well the action proceeds.

Procedure: Divide the participants into small groups of four to six. Read several opening-line cards to the group and discuss the situations in which people use a similar opening sentence. Instruct the group that one person, the first to speak, will have the opening-line card and will address one other participant. Each participant will then join in as he or she "reads" the here-and-now situation. Encourage participants to observe carefully and to try to go along with, not change the direction of, the plot action. Make sure all participants have some role in the drama. Allow groups to experiment simultaneously.

Evaluation: *Participants:* Did the line stimulate remembered experiences of a similar nature? Could you hear yourself or others saying that line in real life? Did the line suggest action?

Activity: **Sound Off** Category: Events/Stories into Plots

Theatre Perspective: Playwright/ Designer

Stimulus: Sound tapes with three sound effects on each tape

Other Necessary Props: Tape recorders for each group

Size of Group: Small groups

Discussion: This activity develops a variety of skills with auditory imagery. It requires that the participants not only identify sounds and delve into stored auditory images for images that match, but also retrieve remembered situations to be used in conjunction with these sounds. This activity forms the basis for a variety of other sound-related activities.

Procedure: Divide the participants into small groups. Explain that the task of each group is to develop a scene or a story that utilizes the sounds in the order presented on the sound-effect tape. Encourage the group to base the scene or the story on situations stimulated by listening to the sound tape. Allow the groups time to plan the story. Have each group enact the scene while the tape plays the sounds. After each performance, conduct an evaluation.

Evaluation: *Participants:* Describe your planning period. How did the sounds suggest action? Were the sounds used literally or for mood?

Audience: Did the action fit the sound? Was the sound incorporated into the action?

Extensions: After you have conducted the activity as described, allow the groups the freedom to change the order of the sounds on the tapes, or make other modifications for repeating the activity.

Activity: **The Big Event** Category: Events/Stories into Plots

Theatre Perspective: Actor/Playwright/Designer/Critic

Stimulus: Photographs of people in important or once-in-a-lifetime activities

Other Necessary Props: Assorted, as needed

Size of Group: Whole group

Discussion: Certain events in a lifetime stand out as most important: a wedding, the first day of school, the Little League Championship game, leaving for an extended vacation, going away to school are all significant occurrences. In this activity, these events become the basis for a group drama, one in which all participants contribute in some way to the drama. This activity expands playwriting skills, particularly in terms of plot development.

Procedure: Show the whole group pictures of these significant events—many of which are so memorable that they are recorded by family and friends. Discuss how those events stimulate strong emotional response. Explain that, although television sitcoms usually make jokes of these events, most people respond seriously. Ask the group to select one such situation as the event to be enacted. Select actors for the drama and, as a group, with your help, plan out the drama. Stress cause and effect; beginning, middle, and end; and other playwrighting tools. Or help the group develop an episodic drama. Discuss style, character. Explain that the goal is to make a serious drama. Evaluate.

Evaluation: *Participants:* Could you incorporate the photo, your own experiences, and the new skills of playwrighting? Which was harder, imaging drama or enacting it?

Audience: Was the drama true-to-life? What elements were selected to be enacted?

The activity in this painting charmingly captures a festive yet hectic holiday atmosphere. An actual holiday photo can also stimulate drama-making, but it can also be more "emotionally loaded" for the person whose family it depicts. (Doris Lee, *Thanksgiving*, Courtesy of The Art Institute of Chicago)

Activity: **Family Album** Category: Events/Stories into Plots

Theatre Perspective: Director/Playwright

Stimulus: Pictures from the participants' family albums

Other Necessary Props: Assorted, as needed

Size of Group: Various

Discussion: Family photographs are powerful stimuli. The here-and-now photos stir memories, encourage people to talk to each other, and often provide the beginnings for a shared group image.

Procedure: Have pictures from the participants' family albums arranged on a wall, so the group can walk around and look at them. After the participants have observed the photos, assemble the group for a discussion about the pictures. Ask questions about the events taking place in the pictures. Select several pictures that could stimulate potentially interesting dramas. Encourage participants to base their selection of photos on dramatic potential — can the locale be enacted? Can we transform ourselves into these people?

Once the photos are selected, ask the owners of those chosen to provide a detailed account of the event captured by the photos. Divide the group into smaller groups, taking care to assign one owner to each small group. Explain that the owner is to become director and cast the participants as persons, animals, or objects in the photo. Give the director time to work with the small groups in developing a drama based on the event in the picture. Show the dramas one at a time.

Evaluation: *Directors:* Did what was enacted resemble the real event at all? Were you able to direct your actors? Could you elaborate on the photo to make the event clear to the others?

Participants: Did the director's image of the character and the action fit the image you had? Were you able to modify your initial images so that you could work with the director and with others?

Extensions: If you have an instant camera available, you can begin to snap photos of the group which are the beginning of the drama group's "Family Album." These photos can, in turn, provide the stimuli for future drama work. Dramatizing photos taken months before really captures the fancy of drama participants.

Activity: Dream-Maker — Category: Events/Stories into Plots

Theatre Perspective: Actor/Director

Stimulus: A dream related by one participant in each group

Other Necessary Props: Enough hats so dream-maker in every group can wear one

Size of Group: Small groups

Discussion: This activity, in modified form, originated in the fields of drama therapy and psychodrama. The thrust here is, of course, educational, not therapeutic. It is important for participants to realize that dreams (both day and night) are rich resources for drama. Early in the conduct of this activity, note that good dreams often are better than bad dreams as sources for material. Also note the inclusion of the "magic hat," which often helps the reticent participant share his or her dreams.

Procedure: Discuss the topic of dreams with the whole group. Explain that everyone dreams, but some dreams are remembered and some are not. Explain too that many people's dreams are similar and that people may have dreams that are unique. Divide the group into small groups (five to seven). Ask a volunteer to relate a particularly vivid dream to his or her group. Explain that he or she is in charge today and that his or her dream will be enacted by the group.

Give each dream-maker a hat, which is to be viewed as endowed with "magical properties." Explain that each dream-maker is to cast the roles and to direct the enactment of the dream. Focus the groups on plot, as well as on character. Encourage the director to narrate during enactments, necessary to ensure that the plot flows as intended. Have the groups present the dream enactments, followed by evaluation.

Evaluation: *Dream-maker:* Did your dream become clear to you as you told it to the group? Did they perform it in a way that resembled your dream? Did you communicate what you wanted to the performers? Were you realistic in your expectations? Did the group drama stimulate you to remember more elements of the dream?

Participants: Could you see the dream? Have you ever had a dream like this one?

Extensions: When the group is experienced and confident, nightmares provide a good source.

Activity: Sell It Well **Category:** Events/Stories into Plots

Theatre Perspective: Actor/Playwright/Critic

Stimulus: Television, radio, newspaper, or magazine advertisements

Other Necessary Props: Cards with names of fictitious brand names (Quackettes, Big-T's, Go-Go Beans)

Size of Group: Small groups

Discussion: Commercials are often better theatrical productions than the programs they sponsor. Without their even being aware of the power of commercials, many participants have stored jingles and punch lines. This activity encourages participants to dissect how commercials make their impact.

Procedure: Begin a discussion about favorite and not-so-favorite television commercials that appear on your local station. Discuss the memorable aspects of favorite commercials.

Ask the participants to decide *who* is the intend purchaser of the product and *how* the sell is made. Focus the evaluation of existing commercials on plot: Does this commercial tell a story? Does this commercial portray an event? After the discussion, divide the participants into small groups. Let each group randomly select one product card. Instruct the group they are to decide what the product is and how to advertise it. Encourage them to use the existing commercials/advertisements as models. After planning time is over, ask each group to show its commercial. Remove those cards from the pack and repeat the activity with new products.

Evaluation: *Participants:* Did you combine aspects of several commercials or use one as a model? What was your objective in the commercial?
Audience: How was the commercial similar to existing commercials? different? Did the commercial remind you of other products?

Extensions: If you have video equipment available, you can expand this activity into a full-scale spectacular. The focus can then be on developing all aspects of the commercial and videotaping it—very much like many of the activities in Creating Spectacle.

PLACE BECOMES SETTING

The third set of activities deals with transforming the available place into a set. A dramatic set can include any or all of the following elements: *where,* a place to be (a bus stop, living room, spaceship, France); *when,* time of day (morning, night, late afternoon) or time period (1920s, twenty-first century, Middle Ages); and *mood,* the feeling you get from the place (festive, sad, scary).

Initially, participants use familiar images to change the space for a drama, by physically rearranging furniture pieces, props, rostrum blocks, or other objects to create the effect of a particular place, or through pantomime. In the former case, the rearrangement may be merely a suggestion of place (two chairs and one table to suggest a café) or a more elaborate set with levels and designated rooms (a cruise ship). In any case, a shared image and "as if" dramatic behaviors are essential ingredients to facilitate the transformation of place to set.

Types of Activities

Activities to transform place into setting fall under the three elements of where, when, and mood. Establishing where begins with public places most familiar to the participants such as school, home, library, or restaurant. In "Get Away" and "On Location," participants are required to retrieve personal images of the place and show where they are through dramatic action. Be sensitive to the specific ethnic, cultural, or geographic places of importance for the participants. Adjust the activities to fit their personal images and experiences. "Have a Seat" demands flexible thinking and elaboration as the participants continue to create a new set from four connecting chairs. The final where activity takes participants to a new place aboard ship in "Ship Ahoy." In each activity, participants must plan and create a new place with other members of the group. They must show where through specific actions and a variety of props and objects.

Establishing when may include time of day (or year) or particular time periods. Time of day requires participants to pay particular attention to detail, since the distinctions are often subtle. "Diner" and "Main Street" both deal with various hours of the day as determined through dialogue and action among the characters. "Medieval Times" and "Roaring 20s" take the participants into another era. These activities rely heavily on props, objects, photos, music, and information provided by the leader. Since participants may have no knowledge of these time periods or only stereotyped views of them, it's important to begin with vivid objects.

Mood describes the feeling created by the setting. The mood may be created any number of ways by using lights or music, changing the speed or tempo of a scene, or accenting incongruities. "Dinner Music" and "Found Sounds" use music and sound effects to enhance a drama. Being "Out of Step" in a place can also change the mood from seriousness to comedy. Changing the speed or pace of a drama can provide some interesting mood swings, from a fast-paced automation scene to a sleepy, drowsy feeling, both discovered in "Metronome Mood."

Theatre Perspective

Transforming Place into Setting covers a wide range of theatre perspectives. As actors, participants work together to create a group image. This job requires time to share the unique images and plan the course of action — selecting, rejecting, and melding images into a cohesive whole. Designers utilize sounds, objects, and props to create both familiar and novel environments. As directors, individual participants work with small groups to create an interesting dramatic set. A number of activities require the participant/audience to critique the work observed by looking at the specific transformation and how it was accomplished.

Leader's Role

As leader you need to focus the participants' drama work on the necessary steps needed to transform their playing area into a set for drama. This requires a clear understanding of the three elements — when, where, and mood — as well as of all the possible combinations. Participants should be guided to recall clear, vivid, personal images of everyday places before going to work. They should share images and decide upon a group image. Specificity of image and attention to detail are necessary to communicate when, where, or mood.

As evaluators, both you and the observers need to look carefully at what the participants did to transform the space and convey the change. Help participants reflect on the specific images or props that stimulated the set design and their course of action. When evaluating mood activities, ask participants to focus on their feelings. If you listen to what they tell you, you will be able to sense when they understand the transformation.

Transformation Tips: Place Becomes Setting

- **Adjust activities to accommodate the unique ethnic, cultural, or geographic features of the group.** Where do you go to meet friends? Where does your family get together? Where do you buy things, clothes, food? Where do you and your friends go for fun?
- **Encourage them to show, not tell.** How much can you communicate just with your body? Where are you? What time of day is it? Is it a particular month? What year?
- **Emphasize the importance of details and specific actions.** Don't you wear a hat in winter? What do you need to check out that book? How many groceries did you buy? Anything breakable?
- **Encourage flexibility from the familiar to the fantastical.** How would you brush your teeth if you were camping? on the moon? in slow motion?
- **Allow time to plan so all members of the group "see" the set.** Plan out the space, not your actions. Decide where everything goes.
- **Encourage the use of props and objects to create the set.** What would help you show us more clearly? How could that have been done more efficiently?
- **Check the group's feelings as you manipulate mood.** Responses vary. How would you feel if we speeded up the scene? Can we go even faster? When should we stop?
- **Focus evaluation on how they negotiated the group image.** Where did this idea come from? Whose ideas were similar? How did you choose this one?
- **Help the audience become active observers.** How did they divide the space?

Activity: **On Location** Category: Place Becomes Setting

Theatre Perspective: Actor/Designer/Director

Stimulus: Participants' own imagic storehouses

Other Necessary Props: None

Size of Group: Whole group

Discussion: Several important imagery skills are reinforced through this activity. The initial participant must retrieve a remembered image of place and self in place and enact the behavior of self in place. By also being aware of the importance of communication, this participant must make a selective decision—to enact a behavior that is particularly representative and communicative. The other participants must "read" the enactment, match the here-and-now behavior with their remembered or imaginative image storehouse, see themselves in that particular locale, and select an equally communicative behavior to enact. This seemingly simple, classic activity actually requires some very complex, yet basic connections of imagination and action.

Procedure: Ask participants to recall images of and experiences in public places—library, beach, restaurant. Ask each participant to select one aspect of place to enact to communicate that place to the rest of the group. Ask one person to begin establishing the transformation. As

Help children dramatize settings by using photos or paintings of places that are of interest to them. This candy store offers participants an exciting locale in which to develop a drama. (Richard Estes, *The Candy Store,* Collection of Whitney Museum of American Art, New York)

other participants identify the place, each joins and also transforms the room into that place. Remember, tell participants that at no time is there to be any discussion or questioning concerning place; participants must "read" the behavior. Continue until the whole group is participating in the transformation of the room into a particular locale. Continue until all participants have established a place.

Evaluation: *Participants:* How did you select the initial action for your place? Was the image clear or did you have to work at it? How many of you went to the center to begin without any idea of what you would do? When you decided to join in, how did you know the locale? How did you decide to add to this place?

Extensions: Choose a location that is interesting for the whole group. Ask smaller groups to enact dramas that take place in this place, but that focus on unusual circumstances. Focus evaluation on the *differences* among dramas occurring in the *same* place.

Activity: Get Away — Category: Place Becomes Setting

Theatre Perspective: Actor

Stimulus: Pictures of people engaged in leisure-time activities

Other Necessary Props: Assorted, representational or nonrepresentational

Size of Group: Pairs

Discussion: This activity focuses on a vacation place as a setting for a drama. The design of the activity pairs participants for an extended time. The pair must make decisions together and play opposite each other during the drama. Consequently, paired participants begin to share and to elaborate upon body images —an essential characteristic of a theatrical collaboration.

Procedure: Begin this activity with a discussion about where participants have actually gone on vacation and where they might like to go. Ask questions about what they did or could do at those vacation spots. Explain that even imaginary vacations can be based on real-life experiences. Divide the participants into pairs. Explain that each pair represents two friends going on vacation. Suggest that the pair agree on a place both would like to see. Allow planning time as you mingle among the pairs. After ample planning time, ask for volunteers to show you what might occur at their vacation spot.

Evaluation: *Participants:* Was it easier or harder for you to work with just one other person? How did you decide on your vacation place? Did you see yourself in your mind's eye before you began? Or did you just make up your activities as you went along?

Audience: What did these participants do to show you where they were vacationing? Did they establish the place in the manner that you expected? What could they have added to help make their vacation place more complete.

Activity: Have a Seat — Category: Place Becomes Setting

Theatre Perspective: Actor/Playwright/Director

Stimulus: Four portable chairs

Other Necessary Props: None

Size of Group: Groups of four

Discussion: A seating arrangement in one location can often stimulate kinesthetic images or visual images of other places where the same seating configuration exists. A church pew, movie seats, stadium bleachers, and sofa all require that people sit side by side, facing the same direction. The here-and-now seating arrangement, currently being experienced by participants, can stimulate remembered images or act as the impetus for the production of imagination images. These images (kinesthetic and visual) help participants modify other aspects of the here-and-now locale or behave in a particular manner that helps transform place into setting. This activity provides simple experiences in the connection of imagination and action.

Procedure: Divide the participants into groups of four. Arrange the four chairs in any configuration in the center of the room. Coach participants to try to recall places in which the seating arrangement resembled the here-and-now arrangement. Instruct each group to decide on one specific location suggested by the seating. Ask each group to develop a short improvisation that establishes the place. Allow groups to plan their episode. Encourage participants to show the image in their mind's eye through specific, clear action. Have each group present the locale. After each group presents its work; change the configuration of the chairs. Repeat.

Evaluation: *Participants:* How many different places were suggested by the configuration of chairs? How did you decide which locale would be enacted? Describe how you worked together.
Audience: How did they transform this place? Point out specific actions and specific words. What additions would have helped in the transformation?

Extension: The chairs can also suggest chairs in vehicles. Dramas then can take place in trains, planes, stagecoaches, ships.

Activity: Ship Ahoy! Category: Place Becomes Setting

Theatre Perspective: Designer/Actor

Stimulus: Pictures of different kinds of sailing ships, military ships, tankers, fishing boats

Other Necessary Props: Chairs, rostrum blocks, ladders, and things with which to construct a ship

Size of Group: Whole group

Discussion: Nonrepresentational objects can be transformed into objects with very specific functions. In activities in Transformations, participants learn to classify objects and images by color, size, and shape to aid them in accomplishing the transformation. Participants work together to construct a place in which they feel comfortable enough to dramatize.

Procedure: Show photos and objects to the group. Point out details in the photo. Ask group members if any of them has seen a boat in actuality, in photos, or on television. Encourage those who have actually been on a large boat or ship to describe the vessel. Once participants have explored their images, explain that they are to transform the room into a ship (using the props and objects in the room) —first in their mind's eye, then in actuality. Give the whole group time to image, then help them negotiate their images, and then put them into action. After the set is complete, ask participants to enact a short scene in which they transform selves into people on the ship.

Evaluation: *Participants:* Did the here-and-now objects help you transform the room into a ship? If so, in what way? What stimulated the connection of ideas and action?

Extensions: Choose interesting and exciting places to visit—like the moon—as a variation. Remember to base activity on specific here-and-now information.

Activity: Diner — Category: Place Becomes Setting

Theatre Perspective: Actor/Playwright

Stimulus: Counter and three chairs lined up

Other Necessary Props: Assorted coffee mugs, salt and pepper shakers, etc.

Size of Group: Small groups

Discussion: Time of day can be determined by what people say as well as what they do. In a twenty-four hour diner people stop in for breakfast, midmorning coffee, lunch, afterschool snack, dinner, and late-night dessert. As playwrights, participants must attend to subtleties of words and phrases.

Procedures: Divide the class into groups of three to four participants. Give each group a different time of day. Let the groups plan who they will be at that time of day. Encourage them to choose time-appropriate characters. Begin with one group and proceed around the clock, allowing each group to enter the diner one after the other. Coach them to show time of day through dialogue. After the evaluation, replay the scene.

Evaluation: *Participants:* What images did the time of day bring to mind? What key phrases or words did you feel were important to designate time of day? How did the time of day influence your choice of character? Were the stimulating images memory or imagination ones?

Audience: How did they show time of day? What did they say that clued you in to the time of day? What are some other key words or phrases? How did the characters fit the place and time of day?

Extensions: Create a continuous flow of time at the diner with participants moving in and out in a particular order. Participants may stay through more than one time frame, depending on their character.

Activity: Main Street — Category: Place Becomes Setting

Theatre Perspective: Actor/Designer

Stimulus: Photos or books with pictures of Main Street(s)

Other Necessary Props: Rostrum blocks or other pieces to designate place; cardboard and markers

Size of Group: Whole group

Discussion: Main Street, U.S.A., is slowly being replaced by urban centers and shopping malls. In small towns and cities of long ago, Main Street was the center of activity for the whole community. All along Main Street, people conducted business, shopped, and visited friends. This activity focuses the participants on a range of actions found in a specific space. As designers, participants learn to work with a variety of givens and to integrate their own imagination images into the creation of a place.

Procedures: Show the participants pictures of Main Streets of long ago or in today's smaller towns. Discuss how a main street is the hub of the community.

Ask participants to decide what types of businesses or shops they would like to find on Main Street. Encourage participants to consider each small location as well as to create the setting as a whole. Allow time to create a Main Street using rostrum blocks and other props. Let participants create a detailed setting.

After Main Street is in place, choose a time of day, day of the week, season, or holiday. Explain that participants are to transform this place into setting in terms of specific season or time of day. Evaluate and replay or choose another time frame.

Evaluation: *Participants:* Have you chosen the appropriate businesses and shops for the setting? How did you know what was needed? How did the time frame change the activity on Main Street? How does the set provide a focus for character, action, and dialogue?

Audience: Have you ever been here? Describe the transformations you see. Did the performers seem to connect their ideas to their actions? Or did you see only chaotic activity? Or were ideas apparent but not fully realized?

Activity: Roaring 20s — Category: Place Becomes Setting

Theatre Perspective: Actor

Stimulus: Photos of people of the 1920s; recorded music of that era.

Other Necessary Props: Any clothing, film of the times, or artifacts showing the life-style of the 1920s;

Size of Group: Whole group

Discussion: This activity focuses on using here-and-now props as stimuli for generating other images as a basis for work on a time period. Specific props and photos suggest other specific remembered images or encourage imagination images. These images then stimulate the behavior of participants. The imagination/action connection focuses on the period of the 1920s. Participants work to establish the mood of that time.

Procedure: Show participants the photos, clothes, and magazines of the 1920s. Ask them to focus on the details of the 1920s. Discuss the period while you play music of the 20s in the background. Explain how much of the mood of the time was exuberant and positive! Coach the group to close their eyes and try to imagine themselves back in the 1920s wearing some of this clothing. Play the music of the period to assist them.

Ask each participant to select a prop or costume piece to aid in the transformation. Again play the music and ask the group to turn the here-and-now room into a 1920s place. Insist that participants work for specifics of place and mood. Generalized exuberance, for example, is inappropriate.

Evaluation: *Participants:* How did this music make you feel while you were listening? Did it help create the mood of the 1920s? What other objects do you think could have helped you get into the mood of the 1920s? Do you have an image in your mind's eye of what the 20s was really like? Can you see yourself in the 1920s?

Activity: Medieval Times — Category: Place Becomes Setting

Theatre Perspective: Actor

Stimulus: Props suggesting knights and ladies (shield, helmet, sword, pointed hat with scarf)

Other Necessary Props: Photos of real medieval encounters or fantastic objects/events (for example, fire-breathing dragons)

Size of Group: Whole group

Discussion: Props or costumes suggesting a particular country or historic period are an efficient way to generate images for creating setting or period. By having here-and-now props and good photographs of the period, participants may be stimulated to develop rich and exciting dramas. Generating images from here-and-now props/costumes is a traditional activity used by actors, playwrights, and directors. This activity also encourages participants to catalogue and categorize new and old images, as well as to communicate these images to others.

Procedure: Show the various props and photos to the group. Spend time on each, asking the group to observe the detail. Pass each prop, one at a time, around the group. Discuss its possible use. Remove props and ask class to retrieve images of each. Also encourage participants to retrieve images from books or movies that seem to be similar to the ones just experienced.

Then return props. Ask participants to transform themselves into people who might live in medieval times. Because this space and time is transformed into a single medieval locale, encourage the whole group to negotiate among members. Ask the whole group simultaneously to transform today into medieval times.

Evaluation: *Participants:* How did the prop help transform you? Did you imagine that you were wearing other clothes or carrying additional props besides the ones you actually had? Describe your negotiation process.

Extensions: The group of young children, described in Mastery, developed an entire fully realized enactment based on this activity. You may wish to use this or another period as the *pivotal* focus for a more theatricalized enactment.

Activity: Out of Step — Category: Place Becomes Setting

Theatre Perspective: Designer/Critic/Actor

Stimulus: Participants' own imagic storehouses

Other Necessary Props: Asssorted, as needed

Size of Group: Small groups

Discussion: This activity introduces the comedic notions of incongruity of actions and inconsistency of place and time. Many comedy writers use inconsistency of period (telephones in 1776) and incongruity of action (a telephone that sprays water in the face of the person answering it) to create a humorous setting. Participants can view early television tapes such as those of Ernie Kovacs or Milton Berle to see the masterful use of these devices.

Procedure: Begin this activity with a discussion of what people expect to see in a certain place or in a certain period. For example, a polar bear might be out of place in Miami; a cave man would look strange driving a Mercedes; a telephone ringing in medieval times would seem silly. Discuss how incongruities and inconsistencies affect the viewer. Point out why the incongruity or inconsistency must be carefully planned.

Divide the group into smaller groups and assign each a location for its drama. Ask the participants to plan a drama with an inconsistency or incongruity in terms of place. Have all groups simultaneously plan and rehearse their dramas. Before asking for groups to show their dramas, tell the audience that they are to observe closely what is happening, somewhat like a critic would. Suggest that some incongruities may be very minor and difficult to detect; others may be very obvious. After each incongruity or inconsistency has been discovered, discuss the effect of the incongruity.

Evaluation: *Audience:* Did you see anything that was out of place in this drama? How did this event affect the characters, mood, setting? If you were a theatre critic, how would you review the enactment?

Activity: Metronome Mood — Category: Place Becomes Setting

Theatre Perspective: Actor

Stimulus: A metronome

Other Necessary Props: Assorted, as needed

Size of Group: Determined by activity selected

Discussion: An important element of dramatic behavior is the pace with which a scene takes place. The pace of an activity can be so much the focus that it establishes the mood of the piece. As the pace quickens, an enactment may become decidedly more frenetic. As the pace slows, the established mood becomes calm and possibly even boring. In fact, the very same enactment, played at differing tempos, affects the audience very differently.

This activity will help participants become aware of the pace of a drama as well as sharpen many imagery/drama skills. The metronome provides a here-and-now sound to help participants understand pacing and resulting mood.

Procedure: Select any previously performed scene, or make up a simple task (like setting a table) that can be performed at various speeds. Ask participants to play the scene once, the way they typically enact it. Explain that the pacing of the scene, because it is as we expect it to be, does not seem important.

Show the whole group the metronome and explain its function. Tell the group they played their scene somewhere in the middle range, at around 104 (the metronome range is 40–208), and they are to think of moving and talking at various speeds. Play the metronome at 80 and instruct the group to image the scene played at that speed. Ask for volunteers to play the scene. Coach the group to observe how the pace sets the mood. Discuss the results of this pace change. Repeat at various speeds.

Evaluation: *Participants:* Did the sound of the metronome affect your action? How did you feel when the action was fast? slow? Did the speed assist or restrict your transformations?

Audience: Did the pace change anything besides the mood? Describe the different versions of the same scene.

Activity: Found Sounds   Category: Place Becomes Setting

Theatre Perspective: Designer

Stimulus: Objects that make interesting sounds or noises

Other Necessary Props: Tape recorders and blank tape, one for every pair

Size of Group: Small groups

Discussion: This activity focuses on two ways sounds may enhance a drama: by suggesting object-related or natural sounds (such as thunder) and by establishing mood. The continuum of sound use, then, moves from the representational (a clock ticking) to presentational (eerie noises played by a synthesizer).

Procedure: Demonstrate some of the sounds the various instruments can make. Discuss with the group how the instrument's sound can suggest other sounds. For example, timpani may also sound like thunder; a small triangle like the chiming of a small clock.

Then ask the group *what mood* is suggested by the sound. Explain that the sounds can be used to enhance drama in at least these two ways: by adding specific, easily recognized representational sounds and by establishing mood.

Ask participants to recall a previously enacted drama. Instruct them to enact the scene, this time adding sound. Divide the class into small groups. Give the group time to plan. During performance, one or all of the performers may play the background sound. Remember, explain that the sound, not the instrument, is present in the scene.

Evaluation: *Participants:* What made you select the sound you used? Did the sound help set the mood for you? How did you decide when the sound should be added? Did your own sound images help you in your selection?

Audience: Did the sound help establish mood? Did the sound clarify action? What made the sound? What other sounds available today might have further enhanced the scene? Did the realistic sounds help you recall sound images or even past experiences? Did the more presentational sounds do the same?

Activity: Dinner Music   Category: Place Becomes Setting

Theatre Perspective: Actor/Playwright/Designer

Stimulus: Recordings of different kinds of music, tape recorders

Other Necessary Props: Two tables, chairs, and other props as needed

Size of Group: Small groups

Discussion: Almost every public place has music of some kind playing in the background. In the United States today 92 percent of all eating establishments have music (live or recorded) for their patrons' enjoyment. Since the kind of music helps create the full effect of the setting, restaurant owners select music with the same care and consideration used by sound designers. Through this activity participants learn to see and record the total sensory effect of places around them. Participants also retrieve sound images and experiment with the various effects of putting auditory ideas into action.

Procedure: Ask the participants if they are aware that music is being played in public and private places, such as in elevators, waiting rooms, and dining areas. Discuss the various sorts of media (live music, tapes/records, "canned" music like Muzak) and classifications (classical, pop, country, rock). End the discussion with a consideration of the effect of the music.

Divide the participants into small groups. Give each group a tape recording

Renoir creates an intimate and casual mood in *Rower's Lunch.* Advanced students will be able to read the mood of this painting; beginning students can respond to the interesting people and unusual dining locale. (Courtesy of The Art Institute of Chicago)

with various types of music. Instruct the group to develop a restaurant scene in which the music you have provided could be played. Encourage the group to establish the place through behavior, dialogue, and seating arrangement as well as through the music being played. Encourage the group to focus on establishing place and mood. Warn them not to depend entirely on music or on dialogue but on a combination of behavior, set, and music. Give groups time to work out the drama. Then have each group, one at a time, perform the scene. Evaluate.

Evaluation: *Participants:* What were some of the first visual images you had after you heard the music the first time? How did you decide on the exact setting for your enactment? Did anyone in the group ever eat in a place like that? How did the music affect the way you behaved?

Audience: Were you able to know the type of restaurant portrayed? Do you agree that the music and setting were compatible? Is there anything else that you might have added to this scene?

Extensions: Once participants understand the concept of establishing mood through music, they can develop enactments in which the music is incongruous and/or causes the behavior to change.

MORE TRANSFORMATIONS

The Transformation activities Adding Conflict and Creating Spectacle extend and shape improvisations into drama. Both groups of activities are essential to the second level of RIM. Participants come to understand the structure of dramatic action and the roles of all the theatre models. These activities can be particularly motivating, especially for junior high students. Don't save these exercises until the last drama class but intersperse them throughout to deepen the drama or add an interesting twist. Ideally, participants will begin to add spectacle and conflict to all their drama work.

> ***The poet's eye, in a fine frenzy rolling, doth glance from heaven to earth, from earth to heaven; and, as imagination bodies forth the forms of things unknown, the poet's pen turns them to shapes, and gives to airy nothing a local habitation and a name; such tricks hath strong imagination.***
>
> William Shakespeare

ADDING CONFLICT

By adding conflict to an improvisation, the images and the dramatic action take on a new shape. The motivation for the drama then becomes the need to resolve the conflict. Unfortunately, conflict is sometimes left out of creative drama work. For dramatic learning to continue, participants must understand the importance, the role, and the types of conflict found in drama. Typical participants in a drama group are not unfamiliar with conflict situations. Daytime television dramas, the nightly news, and even Saturday morning cartoons abound with conflicts laden with violence, aggression, and fear.

In Transformations, participants learn to view conflict as a separate entity, a phenomenon in and of itself. The activities in Adding Conflict take their cue from dramatic literature which depicts a wide range of conflicts and their consequences. The conflict may elicit comical behaviors and situations as in *Comedy of Errors* by Shakespeare, tragedy for Cyrano de Bergerac, or heartwarming results for the family as in *I Remember Mama*.

Through the course of these activities, participants come to realize that there is no dramatic story without conflict. Conflicts may arise from interactions with others, within self, with nature, society, or technology. The conflict often unifies the various aspects of the drama and allows the characters to show their relationships to others and to their world. Both actors and audience members derive pleasure and satisfaction from the conflict's resolution and the tension's cessation.

Types of Activities

Adding Conflict activities are organized according to the dramatic movement they involve. The direction may be either vertical or horizontal, but the core of either is a specific conflict.

Activities with a vertical direction, such as "Not Enough . . . Space" and "Guard" allow participants to experience the dramatic potential of the conflict. In these dramas, the story is not important—the event or situation occurs for its own sake. In the Transformations "Jump" and "Hooked" the tension created is the high point. In "Obstructions" and "Three's a Crowd," participants work together to create an imaginative drama, both in the conception of the idea and in its performance.

The horizontal movement of the second group of activities requires a causal structure. The plot, characters, and set evolve from the conflict and create a connected whole. In "Construction" and "Trapped," the participants use imagination images to create a story line with a beginning, middle, and end. In this type of conflict, the motivation of the characters, as in "Fairy Tales" and "Thriller," is critical. Audience members must see the plot unfold in a logical order. The climax is the peak of interest in these dramas. Participants are required to connect images and actions in a series, with one event causing another. This is the type of development needed in "Forces of Nature."

Theatre Perspective

Adding Conflict covers all the theatre viewpoints. The majority of work is done by actors, who experience and enact the dramatic conflict. Many of the horizontal dramas, however, involve playwrighting skills and enhance the directing perspective. Designers and theatre critics are also roles the participants assume as they view the drama with the third eye.

Leader's Role

It may take a few activities before your participants realize that "conflict" is not always a shoot-'em-up television show. Since adding conflict is a pivotal concept in dramatic learning, you must be patient and continue to engage participants in a wide range of dramatic conflicts. Quite by surprise, one of the activities will "click," and the participants will be able to demonstrate their new understanding. When you introduce conflict to a previous activity, for example, participants enjoy and add a new twist, a new ending, or another character. This way they can build their understanding of conflict, climax, and tension through manipulation of a familiar scene. On the other hand, if a particular conflict activity hasn't caught participants' fancy, go on to another one. Sensitivity and flexibility are your guiding rules.

Transformation Tips: Adding Conflict

- **Pinpoint the conflict direction.** Are you creating a story line here or is the tension more important?

- **Ask participants to articulate their motivation.** Why would you do this? Who would it hurt? make happy? scare?
- **Encourage divergent ways to show the vertical conflicts.** What if . . . ?
- **Be sensitive to the range of feelings expressed.** This drama has created a lot of excitement. What was it about the enactment that saddened you?
- **Explore the range of conflicts.** What's a conflict you could have within yourself? What kind of conflict could you have in a subway? in an airport? at a museum?
- **Encourage participants to consider conflicts in simple situations.** What could be the difficulty in wrapping a present? walking the dog? cutting the grass? buying food?
- **Have participants exaggerate the climax or tension.** Maybe the bomb will go off *now,* before you think it will. What if the bad guy became twelve bad guys?
- **Remember, conflicts are not always tragic or violent.** How could you add a twist to make this situation funny? What other way can someone be scared?

Activity: Not Enough . . . Time

Category: Adding Conflict

Theatre Perspective: Actor/Critic

Stimulus: Buzzer/timer

Other Necessary Props: None

Size of Group: Small groups

Discussion: Many daily tasks must be accomplished in too little time. This activity focuses on how "not enough time" changes behavior.

Procedure: Sound the buzzer. Point out how ugly and annoying the sound can be. Also point out that knowing in advance that the buzzer may sound can affect the way that people try to finish a task to avoid hearing the buzzer. Divide the whole group into smaller groups. Explain that each is to develop a scene in which the members of the small group (transformed into characters other than themselves and in a room transformed into a setting) are to prepare something—a meal or a surprise party, for example. Each group is to perform the scene twice with no time limit, then with an unspecified time limit. Explain that you will sound the buzzer when the group has only thirty seconds left.

Give each group planning time. Have each group perform both scenes and then evaluate.

Evaluation: *Participants:* How did "not enough time" affect your actions? Did the time element transform your relationship to other group members from scene one to scene two? Did you image the sound of the buzzer?

Audience: Describe the difference between the same scene played with and without the buzzer.

Extensions: This scene can grow into an enactment in which the participants are able to structure the activity to build toward the conflict and its resolution. In other words, "not enough time" is the core, and the scene builds from that premise.

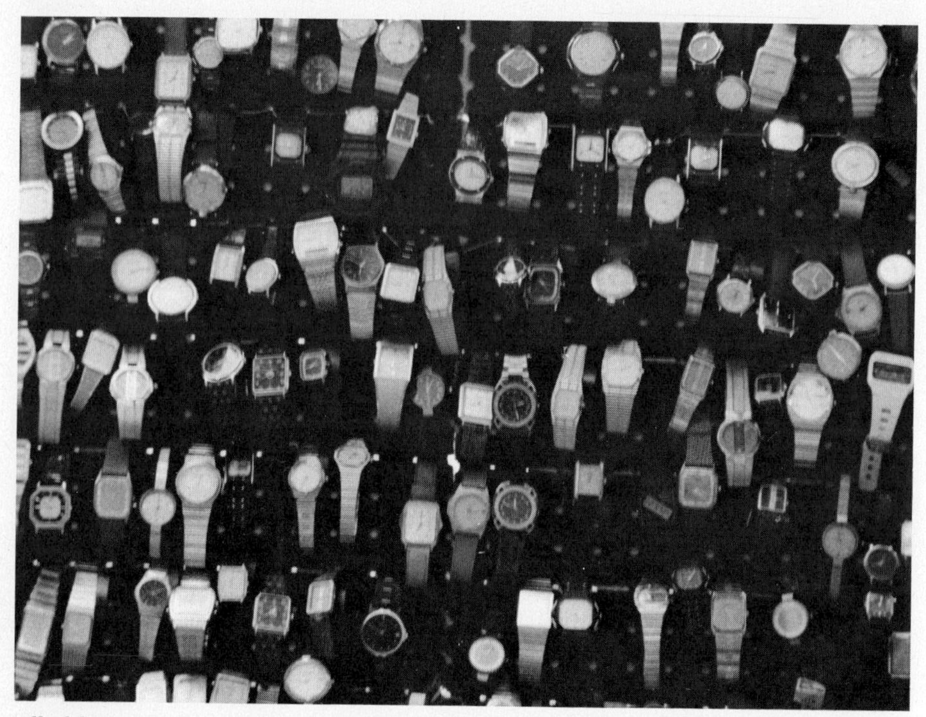

All of these watches, grouped together, suggest that time is a valuable commodity, both for the watch buyer and for the seller. Real time, dramatic time, and imagination time are important issues for dramatic artists. (Photo courtesy Michael Rocco Pinciotti)

Activity: Not Enough . . . Space — Category: Adding Conflict

Theatre Perspective: Actor

Stimulus: Several pieces of lumber (two-by-fours)

Other Necessary Props: None

Size of Group: Whole group

Discussion: The focus here is on the conflict itself, not on the addition of the conflict to an existing activity. This activity helps participants view conflict as an essential element of drama.

Procedure: Clear the whole room, if possible. Ask participants to take up as much space in the room as necessary to be completely comfortable. Then place a few two-by-fours so as to divide the room in half. Explain to participants that they must try to get comfortable in half as much space. Continue to reduce the size of the space; ask participants to adjust to it. Continue halving the space until participants cannot cope with the limited amount of space.

Evaluation: *Participants:* How did the smaller space change the way you were able to behave? Did the smaller space bring about conflicts in your relationship to others?

Extensions: The reduction of space can be accomplished in two ways: you can take away space or add people. Try adding people to a specific playing area so that participants must try to adjust to that type of space conflict.

Activity: **Guard** Category: Adding Conflict

Theatre Perspective: Actor

Stimulus: The leader and a double row of chairs placed back to back in the center of the room

Other Necessary Props: None

Size of Group: Whole group

Discussion: This gamelike activity helps participants, particularly those under ten, experience the immediate consequences of being seen moving—a specific and very real conflict situation.

Procedure: Prepare the participants by discussing various periods of history when danger made travel difficult. Then, transform the participants into characters other than themselves and the room into a setting: they are travelers in a place in which conflict was present, such as the South during the Civil War or the West during the Gold Rush. The objective of this activity is to get from one side of the setting to the other. Both you and the chairs stand in the way. Explain that you are the sentry. If any participant is seen moving, he or she is eliminated and must become part of the chair barricade.

Move across the width of chairs. Allow time for the participants to move slowly from one side of the room to the other. Turn around at various points. Continue activity until at least one participant reaches the other side of the setting.

Evaluation: *Participants:* How did the guard change your movement? What other aspects of your character were changed through the addition of conflict? Did you work alone or together? Did participating in this activity inspire the spontaneous recall of a past experience? Did the memory affect the enactment?

Activity: **Jump** Category: Adding Conflict

Theatre Perspective: Actor/Playwright

Stimulus: Everyday objects and storehouse of personal images

Other Necessary Props: Assorted, as necessary

Size of Group: Pairs

Discussion: A jump is a classic improvisational exercise used to assist actors-in-training in learning the concepts of objectives and obstacles. The focus in this activity is on achieving the objective through a variety of means. For the most part, this activity works best with participants ten and older.

Procedure: Divide the whole group into pairs. Designate one person A and the other B. Distribute one stimulus object to each A. Ask each B to try to get the object from A. Explain that B can use any way to get the object. Encourage B to try a wide diversity of actions to get the object: to wrestle the object from A's hands, to beg, to browbeat. Also encourage A to give B the object if so persuaded, or not if not persuaded.

Have all pairs plan and work simultaneously. Have each pair play the scene, one at a time. Evaluate. Then, switch partners and plan and play again.

Evaluation: *B:* Describe the three ways you tried to get the object. When and if A put up resistance, how did you respond? Have you ever experienced a real-life situation of this nature, which you recalled as you planned and played this activity?

A: Why did you resist? Why did you give the object to B? Did playing this scene help you recall a real-life situation of this nature?

Audience: Could you spot the three ways B tried to get the object from A? Describe the development of the conflict. How did the partners resolve the conflict?

Extensions: Once the group is successful in working with objects known to both partners, have jumper try to get an objective which is not known to jumpee prior to enactment.

Then encourage jumper to request behaviors, not objects, from jumpee, such as leaving the room, giving jumper a hug, or standing up.

Activity: Hooked — Category: Adding Conflict

Theatre Perspective: Actor/Director/Playwright

Stimulus: Very long pieces of elastic

Other Necessary Props: None

Size of Group: Small groups of three or four

Discussion: Constructing activities in which the conflict is built in eases the participants' transition into work with conflict. This early conflict activity, fun and easy, also introduces elements of physical comedy and encourages participants to reach the objective, not play up the obstacle.

Procedure: Divide participants into groups of three or four. Ask each group to develop a task that can be accomplished by three or four people, such as making a bed or playing a game. Explain that now you will add an element of conflict to the scene. Give each group a long and sturdy piece of elastic. Each group is to hook themselves together and explore ways to complete the task. Encourage the group to remember the focus is on getting the job done, not on messing up or acting silly.

If the group is not able to add a conflict, conduct a guided fantasy in which you develop the potential hazards of the elastic. Coach participants to explore their own imagic storehouses for images of impediments and to overlay the image on the here-and-now elastic.

Evaluation: *Participants:* How did the elastic change what you did? How did you conquer the elastic? Were other group members helpful or a hindrance?

Activity: **Obstructions** Category: Adding Conflict

Theatre Perspective: Actor/Playwright

Stimulus: Memory and imagination images of conflict situations

Other Necessary Props: Assorted, as necessary

Size of Group: Whole group divided into two groups

Discussion: Daily life presents many obstructions, some of a personal nature (a mother refusing to allow her daughter on a date), others of a more physical nature (an unexpected detour in a familiar road). Physical obstacles can create the same emotional response as human obstacles. This activity focuses on confronting both human and physical obstructions.

Procedure: Divide the group into Group A and Group B. Explain to Group A that they are to plan a journey that is to take place in the classroom, which they have transformed into a setting, and that they are characters other than themselves. (They may, for example, be explorers charting the North Pole region.) Group B is informed of Group A's premise. They are to transform themselves into characters who present an obstacle, physical and/or personal, to Group A's objective. (Group B might also be explorers who hope to be the first to chart the North Pole.)

Give each group separate planning time. Allow Group A to begin. When Group B is ready, they set up the obstacle.

Evaluation: *Group A:* Describe the changes you had to make to cope with the obstruction.

Group B: Describe how you constructed your conflict so as to obstruct Group A.

Extension: Have Group A and Group B establish their identities and locales independently. When they confront each other, the obstruction will be "as if" two different worlds, with two different logic frameworks, are colliding. Such conflict is the essence of many science fiction films and dramas.

Activity: **Three's a Crowd** Category: Adding Conflict

Theatre Perspective: Actor/Playwright

Stimulus: Storehouse of personal experiences

Other Necessary Props: Assorted, as necessary

Size of Group: Groups of three

Discussion: Many dramatic and life situations involving triads (groups of three) provoke conflict. Such scenes can begin with two people who are initially in agreement. Then, the addition of a third person causes conflict. Young people often have interesting stories of friendships of two people that are changed when a third person becomes part of the interaction.

Procedure: Discuss participants' experiences or observations of situations in which people are interacting well until a third person arrives. Such scenes may be task-oriented (such as playing a game, preparing a room for a party, or packing a suitcase) or merely interactive (agreeing on a movie to see). Ask participants to relate such experiences.

Divide the whole group into groups of three. Designate the two participants who were already engaged in the activity as A and B. C is the participant who enters.

Allow each group planning time to develop a scene of the nature discussed above. Remember, the focus of the drama is not only on the conflict but also on its resolution. Perform. Evaluate.

Evaluation: *Participants:* Did you use a personal experience or one of the scenarios? If you used a scenario, did you add any personal aspect to it?

A and B: What was your response to C? Could you observe the transformation of the scene while it was occurring?

C: Did you experience how you changed the scene?

Audience: Describe how the scene was transformed. What was the conflict? How did the participants resolve it?

Activity: Construction   Category: Adding Conflict

Theatre Perspective: Actor, Designer, Critic

Stimulus: Various building materials: blocks, dominoes, sand, two-by-fours, rostrum blocks

Other Necessary Props: None

Size of Group: Groups of four

Discussion: Even young children can develop and resolve conflicts within a creative drama enactment. This activity focuses on a very specific, physicalized conflict.

Procedure: Begin this activity with a discussion of how people build structures—from snowmen to skyscrapers. Explain that in this activity three members of each group will construct something (within a room transformed into a setting) with the materials provided. They are the builders. The fourth member is a wrecker, who will provide the conflict by trying to prevent the construction. Divide the participants into groups of four.

Within the group, each member is to transform self into a character; the whole group is to transform the place into a setting. The three builders work on building a sturdy structure. The wrecker tries to stop construction in as many ways as possible, through words and through action. Give each group time to plan. Perform the scenes one at a time. Evaluate.

Evaluation: *Builders:* How did you make the building strong so it couldn't be wrecked? Did the knowledge the wrecker was coming change your behavior? Were you able to stop the wrecker?

Wrecker: How did you try to stop the construction? Could you do anything besides fight?

Audience: What kind of scene did you enjoy the most? Why? Which scene had the most exciting conflict? Why?

Activity: **Trapped** Category: Adding Conflict

Theatre Perspective: Actor/Playwright

Stimulus: Storehouse of personal experiences, or images from television or movies

Other Necessary Props: Assorted, as necessary

Size of Group: Pairs

Discussion: Many people have felt trapped—by teachers, by friends, or by parents. This activity focuses on retrieving images of being trapped, modifying them for the purpose of transforming them, and putting these imagination images into theatrical action.

Procedure: Divide participants into pairs. Ask them to develop a situation that focuses on being trapped and getting untrapped. Encourage pairs to construct the scene in four segments: establishing ordinary, everyday activity; getting trapped; getting untrapped; resolution.

Allow planning time. Perform each scene, one by one, followed by evaluation.

Evaluation: *Participants:* How did each of you contribute unique aspects to the trapped scene? Did you use memory or imagination images in the Transformation? Did the intense focus on being trapped and on getting out cause you to lose any of the other aspects of the enactment, such as character or place, for example?

Audience: Describe the conflict. Did the participants work together to solve this problem? Did watching this scene remind you of any real-life traps you have experienced?

Extensions: This activity can be expanded to include the whole group. Many of the popular weekly tabloids contain tales of trapping, being trapped, and escaping—these journalistic tales can be the stimulus for large-scale enactments about being trapped.

Activity: **Fairy Tales** Category: Adding Conflict

Theatre Perspective: Actor/Playwright

Stimulus: Fairy tales

Other Necessary Props: Assorted, as necessary

Size of Group: Small groups

Discussion: Most of the world's best-loved and most popular fairy tales contain conflicts between people and situations. The protagonist must almost always overcome some person or situation to arrive at the "happily ever after" ending. This activity challenges the participants' abilities to focus on the essential conflict and its resolution. Drama participants of all ages can understand the purging effect of good conquering evil.

Procedure: Begin a discussion with the whole group about characters in fairy tales (such as Little Red Riding Hood, Cinderella, Jack and the Beanstalk) who have had to overcome adversity. Point out that the story wouldn't seem as wonderful if we the reader or we the audience did not view the conflict and, more importantly, its resolution.

Divide the whole group into smaller groups. Assign each group a familiar fairy tale. Ask each group to work on three segments of the whole story: the opening (which sets up the conflict between the "good guy" and the "bad guy"); the middle (the actual confrontation scene); and the situation after evil has been beaten (the "happily ever after" ending). Allow time for planning. Perform each scene. Evaluate.

Evaluation: *Participants:* Describe how the focus on the conflict affected the planning.

Audience: Describe the three segments of the drama. Did the participants add any personal experiences to help develop the conflict?

Extensions: This activity may grow into a longer, full-class enactment. Developed to full capacity, it provides an excellent opportunity for advanced work in all theatre perspectives.

Activity: Thriller — Category: Adding Conflict

Theatre Perspective: Actor/Playwright/Critic

Stimulus: Examples from popular television shows, movies, or plays

Other Necessary Props: Assorted, as necessary

Size of Group: Two groups

Discussion: A maniac is often thought to be a person with a neurotic disorder. The word "maniac," however, can refer to someone who has excessive enthusiasm or desire for something. In the various episodes of this activity, the maniac (either sane or insane) is the cause of three aspects of conflict. Also introduced in this activity is the theatrical device which allows the audience to know the fate of the characters while the characters don't. Movie-maker Alfred Hitchcock was a master of this theatrical device.

Procedure: Discuss with the whole group how frequently the movie or theatre audience knows that a maniac has entered the scene, even when the character does not. Discuss popular movies, plays, or television shows in which such a phenomenon exists. Divide the whole class into two groups; select the participant who will portray the maniac.

Present the participants with the premise that someone or something has entered their neighborhood (each participant must transform self into a character in the neighborhood; they as a group must also transform the room into the setting of the neighborhood). Instruct the participant who is to play the maniac to establish a character and plan a situation without informing the rest of the group. Explain that the rest of the group is to try to go about normal daily activity until confronted by the maniac. Conflict will arise at three points: as the maniac performs his or her deeds, when the maniac is apprehended, and when the town decides what to do with him or her.

Allow a long planning period. Advise as necessary. Play. Evaluate.

Evaluation: *Participants:* Were you able to retrieve images of people who frightened you? Did this maniac seem in any way like that person? Discuss what in the here-and-how was able to frighten you.

Observers: Could you see the conflict begin before the performers did? How did the actors' not knowing create a kind of conflict in you?

Extensions: This activity can build into a full-scale extravaganza.

Activity: **Forces of Nature** Category: Adding Conflict

Theatre Perspective: Actor

Stimulus: Storehouse of personal experiences, or photos from newspaper or magazines depicting natural disasters

Other Necessary Props: Assorted, as necessary

Size of Group: Small groups

Discussion: Many plays focus on simple everyday life transformed and forever changed by the forces of nature. Disaster films often begin with scenes of regular life, add a natural disaster, focus on people dealing with the forces of nature, and end with a resolution and a changed everyday life.

Procedure: Discuss how one natural event can cause conflict of person against nature. Ask volunteers to relate such personal experiences. Point out that conflicts may occur when the natural force is very small — a light rain can ruin a picnic — or when it is large and life threatening — an earthquake can destory buildings and kill people.

Divide participants into small groups. Ask participants to plan a scene (such as a wedding, a camping trip, an airplane ride) that would be strongly affected by the forces of nature. Encourage them to plan the enactment both with and without the conflict. Give them planning time. Have groups, one at a time, play the scene both ways: with and without the addition of a natural disaster. Encourage discussion focusing on the effect of the conflict.

Evaluation: *Participants:* How did you use your personal experiences? Describe how the addition of conflict changed your behavior. What aspects of the drama were transformed by conflict?

Audience: Describe the difference between the two scenes. How were the scenes the same? different?

Extensions: This activity can expand to include a full class, all involved in developing a large-scale drama based on the small-group work. Create a sound tape to accompany drama.

Many newspaper photos show terrible misfortunes and are consequently good stimuli for dramas about conflicts and crises. This photo depicts a natural disaster: a flood has made this bridge impassable and people are trapped! (Monroe Country, Pennsylvania Historical Society)

CREATING SPECTACLE

In the Creating Spectacle activities, participants learn that theatre is not life; it is an illusion of life, an artificial medium in which characters, wearing costumes and make-up, appear on a constructed set to share their dramatic story with an audience. Drama transforms life into art in both the verbal and visual mode. In order to grasp the theatre model, participants must experience that which makes theatre so spectacular.

Today's sophisticated moviegoers are well aware that movie-makers use many special effects to enhance the visual aspects of the film. Although creative drama participants will realize that they cannot recreate the spectacular effects of movies, they will be eager to try to integrate visuals into their enactments and experiment with the spectacular.

In order to do this, participants must have a knowledge of all aspects of the drama and of a variety of visual principles and technical skills. The integration of all components requires a great deal of group cooperation and planning. It's exciting to see the progress a drama group can make as it creates other worlds. The activities included within the category can be used as they stand, or in conjunction with other Transformation activities.

Types of Activities

These activities fall into two broad categories. The first deals primarily with the accouterments of theatre. Participants explore visual effects in "Highlights" and "Special Effects" to discover how they can heighten the action. In a drama the actor needs to consider how he or she will be viewed by the audience. "Masks" and "Painted Faces" expand participants' visual realm by using theatrical make-up and various mask-making techniques. "Silent Movie" utilizes music to shape the dramatic action. Any of these activities can be added to dramas stimulated by other Transformation activities.

In the other group of activities, participants work to integrate all the aspects of the drama to create a total picture. Participants take into account costumes, music, sets, lighting, story, and characters as they build a complete world in "Carnival" and "Wild Wild West." Any one of these could evolve into an elaborate dramatic episode. "Local News" and "Happy Holidays" involve participants in elaborating personal images to create behind-the-scenes intrigue. The whole-group involvement can often be overwhelming. To help facilitate group negotiation, specific production jobs are allocated to subgroups in "Big Green Walking Machine" and "Haunted House." These activities may take more than one drama period; give your participants plenty of time to plan and organize their materials before starting.

Theatre Perspective

These activities rely heavily on the designer's viewpoint. This may tap some special talents in individuals who may not excel as actors. An important benefit of these activities is the development of the third eye, an integral component of Mastery level RIM. Also included throughout Creating Spectacle is the point of view of the actor, director, and playwright.

Leader's Role

Those of you who enjoy big parties and can tolerate noise and chaos will find these activities exciting. Even those of you who prefer libraries to rock concerts can have fun as your participants create theatrical excitement. The key is organization. These are not the kinds of activities to choose to do on the spur of the moment. Plan ahead. Check on room availability and the possibility of working more than one day in the same space. Assemble all the materials before you begin. Allow plenty of time for planning (possibly on another day), set up, and clean up. It is a good idea to have a camera ready, since the visual effect is worth preserving.

Transformation Tips: Creating Spectacle

- **Always consider the audience.** Can they see from where they are sitting?
- **Plan ahead.** Next week, we need fourteen brown bags. Who can bring some in?
- **Think big; you can always pare it down.** How can we fit that box in here?
- **Encourage elaborate, original ideas.** These costumes could use some sprucing up. How can we make them look like circus costumes?
- **Encourage flexible problem-solving.** We have no green paint, only blue. What shall we do?
- **Clarify images often.** Have you talked to the group that is working on lighting?
- **Check to see if the actual creation matches the image.** What would you change? Keep the same?
- **Help participants keep in touch with their feelings.** Did the mask help or hinder your creation of the character?

Activity: **Highlights** Category: Creating Spectacle

Theatre Perspective: Designer

Stimulus: Previously enacted dramatic episodes from earlier Transformations or RIM Starters

Other Necessary Props: Costumes, assorted props, various forms of lights ranging from small flashlights to lamps, photo studio lights, floor lights

Size of Group: Determined by previously enacted dramas

Discussion: Theatrical lighting has four main functions: to help the audience focus on what is on stage, to illuminate the actors on stage, to add mood to the set, and to enhance the overall theatrical stage set. Although stage lighting is one of the most technically sophisticated elements of theatre, simple experimentation with lighting can produce interesting results.

Procedure: Review with participants a creative drama episode they created earlier in the creative drama process. Discuss how they have learned about many theatrical elements since enacting their first drama, and how these elements may enhance the effect of their dramas. Replay the selected creative drama episodes. Discuss how the addition of various lighting techniques would enhance aspects of the drama.

Begin a discussion about the natural light in the drama room. Ask participants to find ways it could be manipulated. Examine the additional lighting you have provided. Experiment with the ways it can be used to light various places in the room. When the group has had ample time to experiment with the lighting, replay the drama, adding lights. Evaluate and replay as necessary.

Evaluation: Did the addition of light help focus on the characters? Did it heighten the actors? Did light help set the mood of the drama? Did it blend well into the area of the room where we were working?

Extensions: Consider dramas from the standpoint of light. Let participants explore the possibilities of moonlight, street light, lightning, etc.

Activity: Painted Faces — Category: Creating Spectacle

Theatre Perspective: Designer/Actor

Stimulus: Photos of actors with fully made-up faces. Photos of make-overs from beauty magazines.

Other Necessary Props: Make-up kits for each group

Size of Group: Small groups

Discussion: How a person looks can influence how he or she behaves. Also how a person feels toward life can modify his or her appearance. A person who feels mean may begin to look mean. A person who feels unhappy may develop an unhappy look.

Actors attend to the outside appearance, as well as to the internal characteristics of the person they are portraying. One essential aspect of characterization is the transformation-of-self face into character face. Make-up is part of this transformation and is the focus of this exercise.

Procedure: Show the whole group the pictures of the made-up faces. Discuss how make-up helps change the way someone looks and feels. Divide the participants into smaller groups, giving each group the appropriate make-up. Instruct each group to create with make-up a face for each participant, as one of the characters in the story. Read the story and discuss the characters. Allow each group time to make-up their faces. Encourage each make-up to be a collaboration. Circulate around the groups and help participants apply make-up. When all faces are designed, evaluate the transformations.

Evaluation: Describe the part make-up played in the Transformation. How did the participants use their self faces as the basis for the character faces? Describe how the group negotiated while working together. Were your expectations concerning the face met?

Extensions: Once participants have experimented with make-up, add wigs, hair, and prosthetics to the make-up kit.

Also, once participants have experimented with make-up they can use it as an important aspect of character development in the completion of the more complex enactments found throughout Transformations.

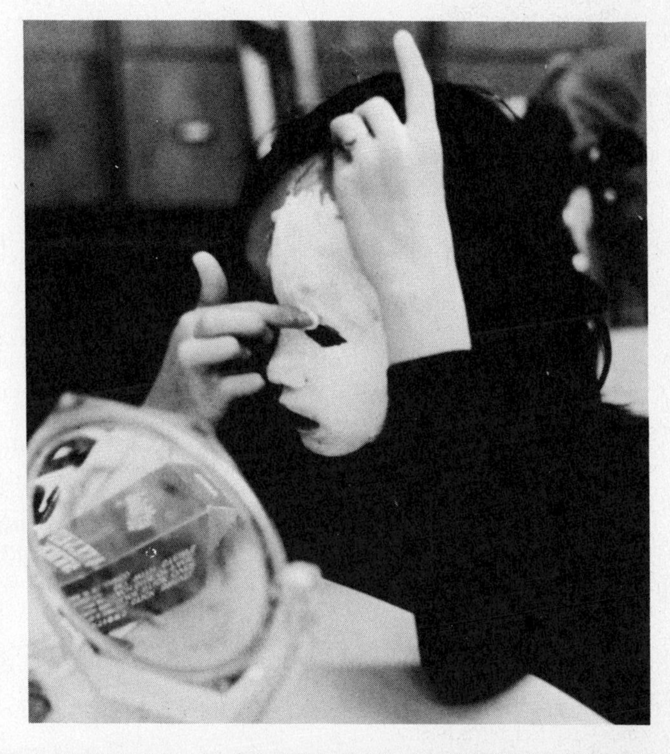

Theatrical make-up can be used to enhance a characterization or to add to the dramatic spectacle. This young girl is in the process of calmly transforming her persona. (Photo courtesy of Jan Pendergast)

Activity: **Special Effects** Category: Creating Spectacle

Theatre Perspective: Designer/Director

Stimulus: Participants' own images of thunderstorms or videotapes of movie scenes showing tropical storms

Other Necessary Props: Large electric fans, tape recorders

Size of Group: Whole groups

Discussion: The planning of special effects helps contribute to the magical effects of theatre. Although some theatrical effects require physical structures and sophisticated equipment, the effects of this activity are achieved through simple machinery. Participants of all ages will enjoy working on these dramas.

Procedure: Direct the participants to sit in the center of the room as you show them videos of a storm. If videos are unavailable, conduct a guided imagery journey to a place where a fierce storm is ravaging the land. Immediately following this activity, conduct a discussion about the elements of a storm. Ask the participants how, if they were movie directors, they would create a storm in this room. Coach participants to identify objects that would help create the wind, lightning, and thunder. As each item is mentioned, allow participants to experiment with how to achieve the desired effect. Ask participants to suggest sounds that may resemble thunder and a driving rain. Tape these sounds as the group performs. When the participants think they have identified and are able to recreate all the elements of the storm, play the sound tape and start the special effects. Evaluate and repeat as necessary.

Evaluation: Did the elements you created feel and sound like the elements in a real storm? What other elements could have been added to make the scene more complete? Were all the elements in the proper balance with each other?

Activity: Masks — Category: Creating Spectacle

Theatre Perspective: Designer/Playwright/Actor

Stimulus: Real masks or photographs of masks

Other Necessary Props: Paper, cloth, trimmings, scissors, glue, staples, pins, buttons, and any other mask-making material available

Discussion: Masks are make-up carried to the next theatrical stage. Masks transform the human face into one that is larger than life. Masks allow the actor to perform extraordinary characters. Designers can also use masks as one essential aspect of the costume of an extraordinary character. This activity focuses on using imagination images as the stimulus for a visual arts creation.

Procedure: Place mask-making materials in a central location in the room. Show participants actual masks or photos of masks. Discuss why masks are used: for disguise, for amplification, to establish style.

A: If this activity is used independently, allow participants to make masks. When the masks are completed, show each mask one at a time. Have the group suggest a character, story, or previous enactment for which the mask might be appropriate. If possible, use the masks in the ways suggested.

B: If the activity is used in conjunction with another, decide what characters need masks. Construct appropriate masks. Replay the enactment with the use of the mask.

Evaluation: *Participants:* Describe how you transformed your image into the actual mask. If you wore a mask, how did it assist you in transforming yourself into character?

Audience: Did the mask aid the effect of the scene? Describe how the actor changed. Did the mask meet your expectations?

Activity: Silent Movies — Category: Creating Spectacle

Theatre Perspective: Playwright/Actor/Designer

Stimulus: Videos of silent movies, or videos with sound turned off

Other Necessary Props: Assorted props, one background music tape for every group of participants, tape recorders

Size of Group: Large group with observers

Discussion: Before the invention of talking pictures, silent movies were shown with live background music. This music served to forecast the mood of the film as well as enhance events in the drama. "Silent Movies" is an activity that requires participants to let the music help tell the story.

Procedure: View several silent movies with the group, pointing out the changes in music as the plot, characters, or set change. If you don't have silent movies, merely turn down the sound on one at hand and add some music. Discuss how the music helps enhance the story and establish mood.

Divide participants into small groups, giving each group its own tape and recorder. Inform participants that each tape contains several changes of background music and no two tapes are exactly alike. Point out that while silent movies are enhanced by the music, it is equally possible to work backwards and create a story from the music. Instruct groups to separate around the room and quietly listen to their tape several times. Coach participants to discuss the story possibilities with their group and plan an enactment using their tape as background music. Participants are to work in complete pantomime, as they observed in the silent movies. Allow time for planning and rehearsing, then view the episodes and evaluate.

Evaluation: *Participants:* Did the music help you retrieve images? Did the sounds dictate character or events?

Audience: How did the music enhance the story? How did it dictate the events and sequence of the story?

Activity: Stunts — Category: Creating Spectacle

Theatre Perspective: Actor/Director

Stimulus: The idea of doing stunts realistically in a drama

Other Necessary Props: Tumbling mats, teacher resources on acting stunts

Size of Group: Whole group and small group

Discussion: Theatrical stunts have been a part of the theatre from its very inception. The actor, with limber and flexible body, has always been required to act as if he or she were dying, tripping, falling, fighting. Mysteries, comedies, and high-action melodramas all involve a certain amount of physical know-how. Drama participants delight in learning the actors' tricks and can use these to add excitement to a lifeless improvisation.

This activity has particular appeal at the junior high or middle school level. Surprisingly, participants may find that they can transform themselves into intensely physical characters more easily than into characters who appear to be more like their actual selves. The glamour of the stunt person may capture these reticent performers.

Procedure: Explain to the participants that actors take classes in combat, dying, falling, and other stunts. Knowing how to carry out such actions correctly keeps the actor from being hurt. (This is not unlike the athlete who learns the proper way to perform a sport.) Begin by modeling simple actions—tripping, fainting, or pratfalls. Always use a tumbling mat for safety. After demonstrating the move, have the students imitate your actions individually.

After they have mastered some simple moves, divide participants into groups of three. Choose a scene done previously in another Transformation and add the stunt. Evaluate.

Evaluation: *Participants:* Was the stunt performed correctly? safely? Did it contribute to the action? Was the timing appropriate? Did it feel natural?

Extensions: If the stunts capture their excitement, expand their repertoire of skills.Teach combat fighting, etc.

Activity: **Carnival** Category: Creating Spectacle

Theatre Perspective: Actor/Playwright/Designer

Stimulus: Pictures of old-fashioned carnival/circus events; background music for circus or carnivals

Other Necessary Props: Tape recorders, tapes, make-up, costumes, circus props, spot or floodlights

Size of Group: Whole group

Discussion: Many young people have strong images of a carnival or a circus. This activity requires participants to share their circus/carnival images with others and ultimately transform the drama space into a complete spectacle. This activity requires an integration of many of the aspects found in the earlier transformations.

Procedure: Several days prior to this activity ask participants to bring in costumes or props that may add to your collection of paraphernalia. As various objects/costumes arrive, show them to the whole group and discuss the various characters that would use/wear them. Begin to build a cast of characters around the costumes and props you collect.

On the day "Carnival" is to take place, discuss the possible ways the room can be transformed into a carnival spectacle. Begin making those changes. Allow time for participants to change into costumes and apply make-up. Assign several participants to be in charge of selecting background music and working whatever lights are available. Have the whole group, in costume, sit in the center of the playing area as you coach them to think of aspects of the carnival that are missing. When they discover certain sounds are missing, assign a group to make a sound tape. Continue with other aspects of the circus. Work until the carnival spectacle is created.

Evaluation: Describe the Transformation. Did what you created match your initial image of it? What else could have been added to transform this room and you into the spectacle of a carnival?

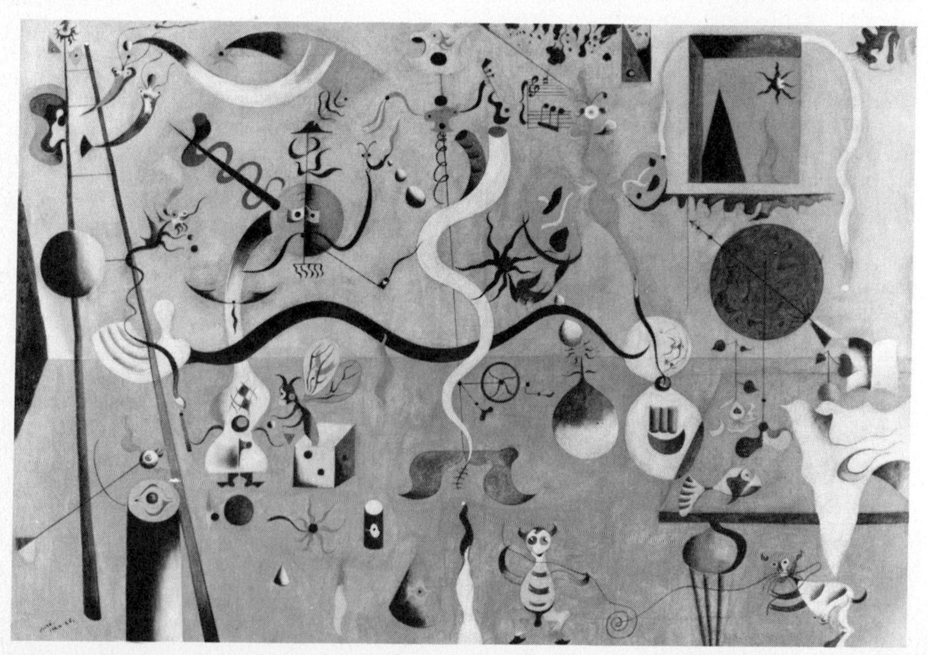

Miro's *Carnival of Harlequin* demonstrates how many events can be separate, yet part of a unified whole. (Albright-Knox Art Gallery, Buffalo, New York)

Activity: **Wild Wild West** Category: Creating Spectacle

Theatre Perspective: Designer/Actor

Stimulus: Videos of Western television shows or documentary of the Wild West or photos of the West; country Western music of the Wild West days.

Other Necessary Props: Assorted props appropriate for that period and other materials provided by the participants

Size of Group: Small groups

Discussion: Most Americans have experienced the West either directly or by viewing movies and photos. The success of the activity is based in part on whether the stimulating images are based on actual experiences of the western United States and on the careful observation of actual photos, or only on viewing fictionalized television shows. Yet an activity based on the American Western has great appeal for a variety of age ranges. This activity requires that participants integrate many of the skills introduced in earlier Transformations.

Procedure: Several meetings before you plan this activity prepare the participants for a drama set in the Wild West. Ask them to supply some piece of costume or props to enhance the drama. (Many participants will have toy guns, cowboy hats, Indian headdress, chaps.) Also, encourage them to bring in photos and stories.

Begin the activity by showing the Wild West videos, if available. View the props the participants have brought in and discuss their functions and importance. Tell the group that they are going to turn the room into a Wild West spectacular.

Divide the group into smaller groups. Explain that each group is to transform the room into a Wild West spectacular. Each group is to integrate character, plot, place into the spectacular. The group can use any available objects or construct their own. Give planning time. Play. Evaluate. Replan and replay, if desired.

Evaluation: *Participants:* What here-and-now objects stimulated the transformation? Describe how you integrated the dramatic aspects and negotiated with group members.

Audience: What aspects assisted the transformation of character, plot, room into the spectacle? What aspects were important? less important?

Activity: **Local News** Category: Creating Spectacle

Theatre Perspective: Actor/Director/Playwright

Stimulus: Videotapes of local news programs

Other Necessary Props: Various chairs, tables, and rostrum blocks; costumes, assorted props

Size of Group: Individual, pairs, and small groups

Discussion: Producing a television news show is the integration of journalism, theatre, and television. Without all three elements the evening news would be boring, inaccurate, and poorly produced. In this activity, the emphasis is on integrating the elements of good theatrical presentation and journalistic reporting to produce the evening news show. The group must work together to transform the classroom, the events, and the participants into a news show.

Procedure: View a videotape of a recent news show from your geographic area. Instruct participants that they are going to have the opportunity to create their own news show with news from their local neighborhoods. Discuss the personnel and set necesssary to conduct such a show. Assign roles for the production. Instruct anchor people, sports, weather, and movie reviewers to plan their own news. Assign smaller groups to be "action" reporters and people interviewed by them. Allow all groups time to plan and rehearse their roles. If costumes or props are needed for their news event, direct participants to design their own costumes/sets. When ready, perform "Local News" several times, making changes suggested by the participants during the evaluation.

Evaluation: Describe the transformations: of the room, the participants, and the story. Was the effect complete? What additional elements could be added to assist the transformation?

Extensions: If the group has had enough experience in working together as a group and has developed activities the purpose of which is to entertain the audience, take this activity a step further: Ask the group to develop a "take-off" of the local news.

Activity: Happy Holidays   Category: Creating Spectacle

Theatre Perspective: Actor/Director/Designer/Playwright

Stimulus: Participants' own imagic storehouses

Other Necessary Props: Costumes and props supplied by the participants, additional props, costumes, make-up as needed, rostrum blocks, chairs, tables, assorted furniture, musical tapes.

Size of Group: Small groups

Discussion: The American way of celebrating holidays makes each one a special occasion. With media attention on pre- and post-holiday sales, greeting cards, holiday-theme party supplies, fireworks, and home decorations, no holiday passes unnoticed. Participants may have a vast storehouse of "holiday" images. In this activity, participants are asked to transform the drama room into a spectacular rendition of a holiday event. This activity focuses on incorporating a variety of skills into a single enactment.

Procedure: Select a holiday several days ahead of the activity and ask participants to bring in props/costumes that may be associated with the event. (Try to conduct this activity in season to ensure the best assortment of props.) On the day of the activity, place props/costumes in several places around the room.

Begin this activity with a discussion of personal experiences of the holiday selected. Also, discuss the origin of the holiday and its contemporary celebration. Divide the group into smaller groups. Explain that each group is to transform the room into a holiday spectacular. Each group is to focus on sets, props, and costumes, as well as story line. Reinforce the notion that "generalized activity" will not suffice. Rather, the group should focus on one episode or a variety of episodes woven together. Allow planning time. Play each drama. Evaluate. Replan and replay, if desired.

Evaluation: Did this drama capture the atmosphere of the holiday? Point out specific props, costumes, set pieces, dialogue, character, and story that helped communicate the spectacle. What additions may have enhanced the transformation?

Activity: Big Green Walking Machine — Category: Creating Spectacle

Theatre Perspective: Designer/Director

Stimulus: Pictures of monsters, large machines, or space fantasy characters

Other Necessary Props: Long lengths of green materials; assorted props and decorations for the machine; tape recorder and blank tapes

Size of Group: Participants divided into designers, sound engineers, actors, and choreographer/directors

Discussion: The spectacle to be created in this activity is the construction of the Big Green Walking Machine. Participants are involved in all aspects of its design and execution and experience everyone working together to create one product. For best results the activity should be repeated several times so participants may experience each phase of the activity.

Procedure: Assign participants to work as designers, sound engineers, actors, and choreographers/directors. Review the responsibility of each role and discuss how the designers must work with the choreographers and sound engineers. Examine the props for the activity. Coach designers to think of various ways of incorporating them into the machine. Instruct the sound engineers to find sounds that may represent the sounds of the Big Green Machine. Ask actors to move in mechanical ways so as to suggest movement to the directors/choreographers. Once each artistic unit has made final decisions, bring the whole group together to work on incorporating into a whole. Coach all participants to create the Big Machine by collaborating with each other.

Evaluation: Describe how each group worked within the artistic unit: the designers, the sound engineers, the actors/movers, and the choreographers/directors. How did all four groups work together to form one artistic spectacular unit? Can you describe the imagery strategies and how you put these images into action?

Extensions: Once they have constructed this monster, participants can develop a complete enactment featuring The Big Green Walking Machine.

Activity: Haunted House — Category: Creating Spectacle

Theatre Perspective: Designer, Actor, Director

Stimulus: Pictures of haunted houses from movie sets or amusement parks

Other Necessary Props: Material for costumes, make-up, various pieces of furniture to be moved around the room, tapes and recorders for sound

Size of Group: Small groups

Discussion: The mystery and intrique of a deserted mansion or haunted house is steeped in personal images and fears of the unknown. This activity allows participants to share their images in a way that may lessen the frightening impact. Also, the group negotiation can help participants realize that others share their fears, or their delight, of haunted houses. By establishing the objective of the development of the ultimate scary haunted house, the leader can help participants use the drama arena as a place in which to grapple with personal fears.

Procedure: Begin this activity with a discussion about amusement park haunted houses and how they are similar

The owners of this fruit stand create an environment to entertain and stimulate their customers. Who would not buy a pumpkin here? (Photo courtesy of Peter Byron)

or different from ones participants have seen in the movies. Allow participants to relate personal haunted house stories to the group. Explain that the group is going to transform this room into a haunted house.

Through a group discussion, decide what physical features are needed to create the ultimate haunted house. List the kinds of activities and characters they would like to include and the roles necessary to create this spectacle (actors, designers, sound technicians). As they work in individual groups, coach the designers to construct a set and the actors to create their characters with make-up and costumes. Call the group together several times during the planning time so they may share their work with others. Continue planning until the spectacle is complete. Invite several members of the group to walk through the haunted house to enjoy the spectacle they have created.

Evaluation: How did the props, costumes, make-up, and sound help create the illusion of the haunted house? Did you feel the characters and haunted house matched your images and dreams of a haunted place? What did you have to do to make this place haunted? Did you find that working together you were able to get new ideas from working with each other?

GETTING THE MOST OUT OF TRANSFORMATIONS

Transformations, unlike Starters, should be coordinated in a more structured manner. Since many groups go only as far as Transformations, the goal is to explore the full range of creative drama experiences within Transformations. Adding Conflict and Creating Spectacle should be incorporated as you go along, not saved until the end. They are not frills, but integral to the growth of dramatic learning as a whole. Planning therefore is essential, especially since some of the activities require advanced preparation by you or the participants.

Getting a handle on how to utilize and integrate Transformations into your RIM drama curriculum can be fairly simple. The following discussion overviews the two ways to get the most out of Transformations — by connecting to Starters and by building with Transformations.

Connecting to Starters

There is not a one-to-one ratio of Starter and Transformation activities. Transformations combine and reintegrate many of the imagery strategies and dramatic behaviors learned in Starters. Some of the Starter categories, however, relate more directly to the Transformation sets than others. The following table designates the relationship between the two RIM levels:

	TRANSFORMATIONS				
	Self as Character	Place/ Setting	Events/ Plot	Adding Conflict	Creating Spectacle
STARTERS					
Sound/Speech	x		x	x	x
Movement/ Pantomine	x	x			x
Sequence/ Story			x	x	
Object/Prop		x	x		
Design/ Environment		x			x
Person/ Character	x			x	

Starters can be used in a number of ways to enhance dramatic learning in Transformations:

- **As a warm-up.** Many Transformations begin with relaxation exercises, guided fantasies, or observational tasks which are extensions of Starter Introductions/Transitions. You can choose specific Starters to reacquaint participants with the imagery strategies or dramatic behaviors necessary to complete the Transformation.
- **For a transition time.** Starters may also be used to refocus the group's energy after an exhilarating Transformation, or as you shift from one type of Transformation to another.
- **For further work.** You may return to a Starter category if you feel the participants need more work on basic drama skills. The group may need a few exercises to recall the behaviors or even a few classes if they never fully developed them during Starters.

Feel free to return to the Starter exercises during Transformations as frequently as you think necessary. Starters form the basic foundation and include a wide range of imagery strategies and dramatic behaviors.

Building with Transformations

Initially, both you and your group will find it easier to stay with one set of activities per class and alternate categories for each class meeting. Often you will have time for only one activity per class period (thirty-five to forty-five minutes). If you have time to lead more than one activity, try to choose the second activity from the same category as the first. You may also try one of the suggested extensions, presented at the end of many Transformations.

Once you become familiar with the breadth and depth of Transformations, you will be able to develop a plan that is interesting to you and meets the dramatic learning needs of your participants. Here are a few suggestions:

- **Story Clincher.** You may find younger participants warm up quickly to dramas using stories or poems. Find literature that deals with the different types of Transformations and use it as a stimulus.
- **Power Image.** Some images or ideas become so enticing that they pull the group forward. Go with it. Let participants develop the image fully by moving across categories to get the full benefit of this motivating idea.
- **Change Partners.** Participants should have opportunities to work with different people in the group. Changing the members of the groups to redo a scene or develop an alternative can be helpful. If participants perform well in the same subgroups, however, you may wish to keep these divisions constant. Often these balanced subgroups move quickly to Mastery level.
- **Hook-ups.** After participants have ample opportunity to understand the individual types of Transformations, try hooking together two activities from different categories. This allows the participants a chance to stretch their creative thinking and integrate one or more sets of drama skills.

Remember to give time for planning and evaluation. If time runs out before all participants who wish to participate in the evaluation have had an opportunity, begin the next class with the evaluation. The evaluation can give continuity to the drama lessons and help get participants back in the mood for doing drama.

MASTERY

This chapter focuses on the third and final stage of the Rutgers Imagination Method — Mastery. Instead of outlining a series of activities, we present several case studies that illustrate how various groups have mastered dramatic learning. As you read this chapter, you will soon discover that Mastery RIM cannot be achieved by replicating a step-by-step series of activities. **Because creative drama is a group art, each group as it reaches Mastery achieves a Mastery level unique to that group.**

In the preceding chapters, we provided a series of general activities that have the potential to promote a desirable outcome for various groups; in this chapter we do almost the reverse. To help explain Mastery, we describe the dramas of several specific groups, pointing out essential details that characterize a Mastery drama, noting particular behaviors of the individuals involved, and tracing the group development of the enactment.

We've chosen the case study format for a variety of reasons. First, the text of the case study continues the "You Are There" focus, an imagery-inspiring format established in Chapter 1. Second, these case studies viewed together can give you a sense of the infinite variety found at Mastery, representing all ages, socioeconomic levels, and degrees of past experience. What's so interesting about these five examples is how different each is, yet how all can be classified as Mastery. Finally, each case study has been selected because it is true to life. False starts, actual dialogue, and leader input are included to show you how these young people, very much like your potential participants, have become Masters of creative drama. Just remember, however, that these case studies are not presented as activities or lessons to be replicated. Rather, they are examples from which you can derive inspiration for your own work, and that will give you a sense of the powerful ideas and enactments to be found at Mastery. Hold in your mind's eye the images inspired by reading these case studies. When your own group is able to master creative drama, you'll know.

Participants in Mastery demonstrate three kinds of learning:

- **Cumulative learning of skills and behaviors presented in Starters and Transformations.** In Starters, participants learned the basic skills of drama through experience with exercises in such areas as movement, speech, and story-making. In Transformations, participants learned more complex skills and behaviors in activities that focused on transforming life into dramatic action. Also in Transformations, participants learned to take a variety of perspectives, derived from the jobs of various theatre artists such as director, playwright, and designer. In Mastery RIM, participants demonstrate that they can use these many skills separately or together.

- **Learning abilities unique to Mastery RIM.** Participants at Mastery demonstrate learning in areas that are uniquely Mastery. They develop consistent ability to work as an effective group member in close collaboration with peers. They often create dramas that offer a unique or original solution to problem-solving in the connection of imagination to dramatic action and that revolve around a strong thematic core. These individuals also begin to demonstrate metacognitive abilities: they are able to perform and monitor simultaneously; and they have developed and have access to a stored set of knowledge and beliefs about drama in terms of self, others, tasks, and strategies.
- **Reintegration of skills from all three levels of RIM.** Participants develop behaviors that demonstrate a reintegration of knowledge, usually in terms of the connections they make in imagination and dramatic action. They view drama differently; they operate differently in the drama arena on a daily basis. These participants have made what psychologists call a *developmental leap.* All the work they have done "ahead of themselves" (to paraphrase Vygotsky) now allows them to meet themselves. We don't suggest that all Mastery groups are at the "ultimate" stage of development, merely that Mastery often occurs when a participant group experiences a new way to integrate information and focus on the connection of imagination to dramatic action.

> ***The response we make when we believe a work of the imagination is that of saying: "This is the way things are. I have always known it without being fully aware that I knew it. Now in the presence of this play or novel or poem . . . I know that I know it."***
>
> Thornton Wilder

FROM STARTERS TO MASTERY: THE CUMULATIVE ASPECTS

Participants who reach Mastery level have learned their craft step-by-step. Your carefully structured exercises and activities have provided them with a knowledge and understanding of internal processes, external behaviors, and the connection of imagination to action. This well-grounded knowledge and experience base provides the participants with the ability and confidence to solve dramatic problems in creative ways.

Participants are experienced in all aspects of imagery. They demonstrate the ability to retrieve images, use a variety of imagery manipulations, and develop imagination images. Participants have both memory and imagination images at their disposal, as well as fluent, flexible, vivid, and controllable images. Also, they can both describe and demonstrate the ability to select and reject from images in their vastly expanding storehouse. They are able to overlay and elaborate on these images.

Participants are able to achieve success in the categories of dramatic behaviors presented in Starters and theatrical skills presented in Transformations. They can, for example, grasp the concepts and work well with movement, props, story-making, character, setting, and spectacle. They are able to take the perspective of the various theatre jobs. Also, as participants end their apprenticeship, they are able to coordinate and integrate thinking and expression. After working with Starters and Transformations, participants are able to perform more than adequately in creative drama situations.

The connection of imagination and action is also emerging as a well-developed ability. Both the process and product of these participants reflect fluency, flexibility, and elaboration. In practical terms, participants work through numbers of ideas and behaviors, change categories of ideas and behaviors, and elaborate on their images and actions. They are able to demonstrate continuity from one exercise to the next and from one day to the next, because they have acquired a storehouse of creative drama images and remembered drama/theatre behaviors large enough to enable them to classify and categorize experiences and consequently to draw upon them. Participants even begin to view the world as providing potential sources of material to be dramatized. Another interesting process, demonstrated early in this approach, is compressed rehearsal, the ability to try out and rehearse a myriad of connections.

UNIQUE ASPECTS OF MASTERY

Most drama participants' drama experiences go only as far as Transformations. The reality of many creative drama situations is that participation in creative drama is a short once- or twice-in-a-lifetime experience. Because they have other academic requirements to fulfill, most are not able to develop higher-level drama skills, nor can most groups emerge as truly unified ensembles. But, reaching Transformations is quite an accomplishment and must not be undervalued.

Some groups, however, do reach Mastery. They perform dramas that are unique and that seem to outshine even the enactment performed yesterday. In fact, these enactments are often far better than artistic pieces offered commercially and often far more exciting than enactments of groups with more creative drama exposure. The most striking characteristic of Mastery RIM are the dramas themselves. The enactments described in the case studies attest to this fact.

As well as representing sublime examples of fine dramatic enactments, these case studies also illustrate four other distinct features that are always characteristic of Mastery RIM:

- The group as a whole works as a cohesive unit.
- Each individual within this group demonstrates metacognitive abilities.
- The dramas themselves emerge from a strong, unifying, thematic image.
- The group process, the individual behavior, and the dramas exhibit originality— statistically uncommon processes and results.

The Nature and Dynamics of the Drama Group

Group Behaviors The *cohesive group* is essential to Mastery. For a group to work together, cooperation, coordination, and collaboration must be present. Initially, the individuals must understand that they are working in a state of mutual support, termed cooperation. Often in trying to reinforce individual achievement, a leader encourages competition, the reverse of cooperation. Groups often demonstrate sporadic cooperation, even as early as Transformations, when the group task takes precedence over individual accomplishment. Forming and storming behaviors (discussed in the introductory material of Transformations) give way to norming behaviors, during which you as leader sense a feeling of mutual support and observe group cooperation. This cooperation among members, only intermittently present in Transformations, is a prerequisite for Mastery.

Second, a group must achieve coordination, the existence of actions and imagery strategies synchronized to provide common benefits. Cooperation implies that two duplicate behaviors may occur parallel to one another, with each individual pleasantly permitting the overlap to occur. As the group begins to make decisions about final product, it begins to demonstrate selection and evaluation for the group enactment and to coordinate the behaviors of its members. Individuals learn they cannot always have the plum role, that another may even do a better job, but they can make a unique and important contribution to the drama. Coordinating actions is not always easy. In fact, many disagreements may occur before final decisions can be made. But in Mastery, the group is usually able to resolve conflicts itself or with some assistance from the leader.

Finally, a higher level of organization that produces a molding of individuals and activities into a unified whole that represents a sublime collaboration is the achievement of a Mastery group. This collaboration of the group implies that each individual's skills have been uniquely integrated within the group. Each member's connection of imagination and action abilities merge with the collaborative whole. Never static, a collaborative group is in a constant state of flux, yet can achieve dramas that represent far more than the sum of its members.

This collaborative group also balances its two essential Mastery communication behaviors: accomplishing the group task of developing a drama and maintaining the group. The primary task of a Mastery group is to put its collective imagination into some form of dramatic action. Maintenance behaviors preserve and facilitate the interaction within the group itself. Both types of behaviors are necessary for group effectiveness. Usually thought of as a by-product of creative drama, group maintenance — the essence of social interaction — is intrinsic to higher level dramatic learning.

Group Structure Within Mastery, the large group as a collective whole, as well as small groups that are assigned or spontaneously subgroup, develop a relatively consistent pattern of interaction among its members. Patterns emerge when these groups, often through trial and error, create a general structure to maintain itself and to accomplish the task at hand.

One of the largest and best-documented bodies of sociometry literature (concerning the effects of structure on communication) has been obtained from studies of micronetworks — groups of three to seven. The organizational structure of these small groups can be divided into two types: *centralized and decentralized.* Centralized structures are those in which most planning flows through some pivotal person (the leader in a creative drama activity) as illustrated by a Y, a chain, or a wheel. Even in Mastery, the leader may remain the pivotal person.

More typical, however, is the decentralized group structure, as illustrated by a circle. The decentralized structure allows more of a flow of ideas and drama skill sharing among individuals. As you read the case studies in the second part of this chapter, note whether the networking seems to be centralized or decentralized.

Communication Roles The interpersonal communication that occurs among group members is affected by and affects the various communication roles the individual performs. A person's role in a group consists of the behaviors that he or she has exhibited, feels comfortable with, and are expected by others in the group. Certain individuals may have different perceptions concerning the role of a particular person; a person's primary communication role may vary as he or she moves from subgroup to subgroup; and group roles emerge for every group member as the subgroup's mutual expectations become established.

Recent research suggests that seven different roles should be present in a small group to achieve balance in task and maintenance behaviors. The seven communication roles in Mastery level, modified from industrial-training research, are:

Ideas person— one who comes up with the initial idea.
Coordinator—person who helps link the various images, ideas, and stimuli; facilitator of idea hitchhiking.
Critic— evaluates the ideas and the action during the process; stands outside the developing drama.
Implementer—helps facilitate the specific improvisation; the skills person who evaluates the practicals.
Team builder—person who negotiates and works on keeping up morale.
External contact— one who checks with the leader and goes to outside sources for relevant material.
Audience/inspector—person who evaluates the job once it has been completed. (In creative drama this role is most often taken either by the leader or by other class members not in the subgroup.)

Although the nature of these seven patterns of behaviors is obvious from the names, even without the brief description, the manner in which these roles are "cast" varies from subgroup to subgroup. Though any individual may from time to time fulfill each of the seven roles, most participants can be effective in only two or three of the roles. Each Mastery group develops strategies for filling each role.

The principle source of communication problems results when there is a duplication of roles or an absence of one or more roles. Based on careful observation and monitoring, the leader must carefully assign individuals to a group and rearrange groups until the ideal mix results. Groups need not consist of seven members, but can range in size between five and twelve. (If the large group is working as a unit on a group project, it may be advisable to break the members into subgroups who each work on separate parts of the whole.)

The Individual: Demonstrating and Monitoring Expertise

Drama participants not only know how to think about drama and how to do drama but they also know that they know. This set of beliefs about themselves stands them in good stead in solving current and future drama problems. This expertise is termed *metacognition,* a knowing about knowing. When drama participants know that they know, they are able to solve dramatic problems more efficiently and creatively, work well with others, and monitor their progress while in the throes of the dramatic enactment. This ability to know about what factors and variables work to enhance the drama, as well as to act upon them, is an important aspect of Mastery creative dramas.

As used in this discussion, metacognition* encompasses:

- Metacognitive knowledge.
- Metacognitive experience.
- Cognitive monitoring.

Metacognitive knowledge is that segment of a person's stored world knowledge, as well as knowledge of the creative drama arena, that focuses on people as cognitive/creative creatures and how they solve cognitive/creative problems. *Metacognitive experiences* are best described as items of metacognitive knowledge that have entered consciousness and can be connected to dramatic action. Both metacognitive knowledge and metacognitive experience can have a strong effect on creative drama. They can lead the participant to select, revise, and abandon behaviors or theatre perspectives in light of the dramatic problem, the ability of others in the group, or even the mood of the day.

The third element of metacognition is termed *cognitive monitoring*—the ability to monitor one's own memory, comprehension, and other cognitive enterprises. Within creative drama, cognitive monitoring also expands to include aspects of dramatic behavior, imagery strategies, and, of course, the connection of imagination and action. This cognitive monitoring notion parallels the imagery-related notion of the third eye. When used in discussions of creative drama, both terms describe the ability to do and to monitor simultaneously.

Metacognitive knowledge focuses on three variables: person, task, and strategy. An example of a metacognitive creative drama knowledge of personal self is an individual's belief that he or she can portray a nonhuman character better than a human one. Metacognitive knowledge of another person may be an individual's belief that another group member seems to do well in a large group, but is not helpful in small-group work.

Metacognitive knowledge of tasks within creative drama most often deals with the demands or goals of the task. An individual may come to know that some drama activities are more demanding or difficult than others, even given the same information. It is easier, for example, to enact just three episodes of a story that has been told by the leader than it is to portray the entire story of ten episodes. Other metacognitive knowledge of tasks within creative drama focuses on understanding what information supplied implies for how the drama problem can be managed. A participant in creative drama comes to know, for example, that the leader supplying only a little information about a story may mean that he or she will have difficulty developing a plot, but that such information is sufficient to develop a strong characterization.

In terms of metacognitive knowledge of strategy, an individual quickly learns there is a great deal of knowledge to be acquired about what strategies are likely to help achieve what goals. An individual may learn, for example, that a good way to recall images of relevant past experiences is to shut one's eyes and breathe deeply. Remember, cognitive strategies are invoked to make cognitive progress, metacognitive strategies to monitor it.

Creative drama exercises and activities give participants opportunities to put metacognitive knowledge into action. The Rutgers Imagination Method in

* *The discussion on metacognition and creative drama is derived in part from the work by John H. Flavell of Stanford University. Although his models do not focus on drama, Flavell's research provides valuable insight.*

particular encourages the development of self-monitoring skills—the self-correcting techniques that are the underpinnings of higher-level imagination in action. These novel situations, structured to draw upon personal images, expressly demand careful introspection and conscious reflection, together with spontaneous action. The organization of creative drama—plan, play, and evaluate—is, according to researchers, the epitome of an organizational format for stimulating metacognition.

In Starters and Transformations, participants develop creative, cognitive, and metacognitive building blocks that are the foundation for the more sophisticated metacognitive abilities apparent in Mastery. An individual suddenly knowing what to do in the middle of a scene is quite typical; this "knowing" may result from divine inspiration, but more certainly it is the result of a metacognitive piece of information, stored in the unconscious and triggered by the similarity of this situation and the stored knowledge of the previous one. When this "knowing" becomes conscious (metacognitive experience), it allows the participant to both change and monitor behavior.

Starters and Transformations systematically stimulate careful, highly conscious thinking and can require almost simultaneous action and decision. Drama work in the first two levels of RIM provides many cognitive and creative experiences with self, other, task, and strategy that contribute to a metacognitive knowledge base. First attempts at cognitive monitoring also occur during these activities.

By the time participants reach Mastery, they are masters of metacognition. They are able to select, evaluate, revise, and abandon dramatic tasks, goals, and strategies in light of their relationships with one another and with respect to their own abilities and interests. Metacognitive knowledge and metacognitive experiences help give participants confidence; **they know that they know and know that they are able to monitor themselves in action.** The well-developed third eye can help participants interpret the meaning and implications of the experience at hand. They can, for example, perform and monitor such aspects as their own role, their own contribution in relation to others, others' roles, how the audience is receiving the performance, and what needs to happen. Certainly, metacognitive knowledge and experience can be useful not only in helping participants master dramatic learning but in helping them learn to make wise and thoughtful life decisions.

The following statements are gleaned from actual transcriptions of creative drama sessions. They illustrate high-level metacognitive knowledge:

IMAGINATION—Begins with Awareness of World

Self: I know that my smell images are particularly vivid.
Others: I know that his images of place are a good source for drama.
Task: I know imagination images are more detailed than memory images.
Strategies: I know that image recall requires relaxation and concentration.

DRAMATIC BEHAVIOR—Begins with Awareness of Self

Self: I know that I juggle well.
Other: I know he is good at characterizations of old men.
Task: I believe good dramas require hard work.
Strategies: I know that historical dramas require research and specific knowledge of period.

GROUP—Begins with Awareness of Others

Self:	I know that this group values my judgment.
Other:	I know that he likes to be in charge.
Task:	I know that this group does funny dramas.
Strategies:	I know that this group needs a lot of time to finish.

CONNECTION—Begins with an Awareness of Creative Drama

Self:	I know that I use third eye skills.
Other:	I know that he has difficulty with Self as Other.
Task:	I know that Self as Character demands two equally strong components: knowledge of self and understanding of character.
Strategies:	I believe that compressed rehearsal is an efficient strategy in refining enactments.

Originality: The Sublime Group Drama

The originality seen in the planning, playing, and evaluating of dramas is a complex, yet compelling, phenomenon within Mastery RIM. In the scientific sense, the term *original* is defined as statistically infrequent. In creative drama, then, "original" behavior would be that behavior that is highly unusual. Similarly, an "original" drama might be a drama that demonstrates a novel response to a dramatic problem. Of course, novelty for novelty's sake alone is not an appropriate goal for creative drama. And, of course, as you guide drama, it's difficult to know (and to care) just how infrequent is this particular response. In fact, constant comparison of this group to other groups will certainly undermine the drama in progress. Consequently, the term *original* must be made operational.

Within RIM, we use the term *original* to describe at least four sorts of originality:

- The selection of dramatic behaviors and theatrical conventions.
- The collaboration within a particular group.
- The personal nature of the stimulating image.
- The connection of imagination and action.

Many Mastery creative dramas contain unusual pieces of behavior and reflect theatrical choices that are indeed novel. "The World Turned Upside Down" is an example of a drama we classified as original because of these highly unusual theatrical choices made by a group of this age and experience. In contrast, we classify "Castles and Dragons" as original, not because the dramatic behaviors are themselves so unusual, but because this young group has developed a drama the scope of which is highly infrequent in groups of this age.

"Russell Revisited" is an example of a drama classified original because of the intensely personal images that are at its core. Cowboys and Indians are typical characters in creative dramas, but this group has gone further and evoked highly personal, vivid imagination images that stimulate powerful dramas. "Dream-Maker: The Drama" is similarly original. "Einstein's World" demonstrates perhaps the most exciting originality: a novel connection of imagination and action. In this case, both planning and playing demonstrate the ability to develop an abstract idea from concrete sources and to connect this abstract idea to concrete movement skills.

> ***The ingenious are always fanciful, and the truly imaginative never otherwise than analytic.***
>
> Edgar Allan Poe

Thematic Image at the Core

The case studies also demonstrate how essential a powerfully stimulating image is to the success or failure of the Mastery enactment. A discussion of an abstract notion concerning relativity crystallized into a very specific movement piece entitled "Einstein's World." "The World Turned Upside Down" began with an analysis of that popular axiom — one that grabbed the attention of the group. More traditional creative drama stimuli are the sources for the other three: a story, a painting, and a dream. Although other approaches often revolve around similar thematic wholes, in this approach the transformation of the stimulus into a central image is the first business at hand.

Other types of images that seem to encourage success are images that evolve from a Starter exercise or images that are inherently artistic/theatrical in nature (such as those that might evolve from viewing the photos included in this book). Another strongly evocative category of images, often effective with adolescents, is central images that focus on personalization of current, societal issues. News stories, from tabloid-style to evening broadcast, stimulate this often difficult-to-reach participant. What you as leader must remember is that almost any idea can be the source of a Mastery drama as long as it is transformed into a vivid, controllable, and multidimensional image that speaks to the group as a whole.

DEVELOPMENTAL CHANGE

The Mastery work often reflects what developmental psychologists term a developmental leap. Through planning, playing, and evaluating, participants demonstrate a *reintegration* of a variety of imagery skills, dramatic behaviors, and knowledge of connections. Because they know that they know, participants feel confident. Because they have had experiences in communicating within a group, and the group contains all necessary communication roles, participants are able to frame communications on a sophisticated level. And because they have mastered drama/theatre skills and behaviors, participants pull from their experience and reintegrate abilities as the drama situation demands.

At Mastery level, imagery strategies, drama experience, and social understanding come together in a new, always efficient but nevertheless artistic manner. This reintegration propels the drama to new heights. Creative drama participants seem to view their work with "new eyes." They have come full circle. Their dramas are as fresh as were their first earnest attempts, yet reflect a real understanding of what they must do to communicate to others in all three stages of creative drama: imagine, enact, and reflect. They also demonstrate a developed sense of audience because they understand how to communicate effectively to a real or imagined observer/audience.

It is this reintegration that signals a developmental leap. And indeed, it is this consistent ability to integrate and continuously to reintegrate the vast storehouse of images, experience, and knowledge of others and audience that the world calls talent. Of course, working in RIM does not make participants talented. RIM encourages participants to view themselves in a new way. RIM enables participants to cultivate their own natural skills and achieve their own potential level of integrated abilities. This dramatic sensibility and well-developed set of craft skills allows participants to think and to act as creative drama artists.

THE LEADER'S ROLE IN MASTERY

The leader's role in Mastery is very different from the jobs required in Starters and Transformations. No longer are you the teacher, the guide, the source of all wisdom (although you will always remain "the one who knows" in your group members' collective mind's eye). Your job becomes more of an overseer or foreman.

It may be helpful to view your function in light of the unique features of Mastery:

You may assist the development of metacognitive abilities by discussing and positively reinforcing those participants who demonstrate high-level functions. (Although you want to encourage metacognitive thinking, do not overmonitor at the expense of the drama.)

Facilitating the group in Mastery is more difficult than in Transformations because much of the negotiation must happen within the group. Probably your most important strategies at this time are to stay as uninvolved as possible, assess the ongoing drama, supply the missing element if necessary, and encourage group collaboration.

Whatever tickles your fancy and the fancy of the group can be an appropriate stimulus. By the time you and your group reach Mastery, you are probably aware of what kinds of ideas they like to trace and what kinds of images they find compelling. Don't be afraid, however, to try an image that failed earlier or even to redo a past success. At this point, participants realize the dramatic potential of any idea or image, so make the idea presentation interesting—their imaginations will do the rest!

Before this discussion discourages you, be assured that the wonderful idea is not too difficult to find. Objects can stimulate dramas, as can stories from literature or items from the newspaper. Figures of speech, abstract notions yearning to be made concrete, music, and the visual arts also have the potential to stimulate. Dreams are always a good source. As you read the case studies presented in the second part of this chapter, note the diversity of central images.

CASE STUDIES

Following are five case studies, a representative sample of the many examples we have seen in our work with advanced creative drama. Although each case study is unique, all are presented in a similar format. The kinds of enactments vary. They run the gamut from classic story drama to dramatization of sophisticated, abstract concepts.

The five case studies presented here provide a picture of the breadth of

Mastery dramatic learning. They represent a diversity of age and experience level and a variety of lesson contents. Yet each case study describes an in-depth knowledge, on both the individual and group level, personalized and integrated internal processes and external behaviors. In these examples, both learning and development have taken place. Mastery, as its name suggests, deals with mastering creative drama.

"Title"

PRELESSON INFORMATION

The Group This section contains relevant social and economic information. Also in this section are such data as male/female ratio, length and type of previous drama experience, and academic achievement in other curriculum areas.

The Leader The leader's drama and other arts training and experience are noted, as well as his or her particular views concerning drama's place in the curriculum.

The Project The project describes the history of the project, as well as the intended scope of this particular lesson. Included in this section may be the leader's diagnostic or prescriptive justification for the work described.

The Stimulus Stimuli may be the concrete object, artwork, figure of speech, Starter activity, or idea that sparked the group. Also included in this section are the initial leader and participant interactions that established the Mastery lesson.

WHAT HAPPENED

The Group Activity (This category may be further broken down into *The Planning* and *The Drama*.) The case studies are described in a variety of ways: an overview of the group as a whole; a discussion of several small subgroups; a detailed analysis of one subgroup; a discussion of a day in depth; a review of several days; or an overview of the project as a whole.

Questions or Notes These questions are addressed to you the observer and appear at various intervals within the body of the case study. They are not rhetorical but require answers. They are included to keep you on target and to assist you in seeing the essential masteries in the activity. The notes focus on specific aspects of the lesson.

Discussion Aspects of the imagination/action connection, the group dynamic, the metacognitive skills of the individual, the integration of craft elements, the nature of the stimulus, and the leader's function that were not previously mentioned are discussed here. Also discussed are future goals for the group and ways to modify this activity for use by other groups.

"Einstein's World"

PRELESSON INFORMATION

The Group The class is composed of eighteen fifth- and sixth-graders (ten girls and eight boys) who have been classified as gifted and talented and placed in a special program. They have experienced a different arts activity three times weekly for a year-and-a-half as part of their arts enrichment experience. The group is especially bright and creative — any leader's dream.

The Leader The leader, Andrea Elkind, is a member of an integrated arts team, a group composed of artist/teachers with various arts specialties. Andrea offers both drama and movement expertise, as well as an interest in conceptual issues.

The Project "Einstein's World" came about after Andrea and her team had diagnosed that the group needed more work in the Starter drama skill area of movement and the Transformation category of Place Becomes Setting. The group, often praised for their intellectual skills, were physically inhibited. Andrea realized that they needed to work on movement. She presented and explored concepts of body, space, force, and time. Also, she felt that the group was locked into concrete dramatizations of place. They needed to practice connecting their rich and vivid imagination images to dramatizable actions, particularly in terms of setting.

The Stimulus Andrea obtained a *fresnel,* a large theatrical lighting instrument, and aimed it on various objects and people in the room.

Andrea: See those shadows? Those shadows are two-dimensional shadows of three-dimensional objects. The objects have volume, but the shadows are flat. Let's imagine a shadowing that is more complex. Suppose our three-dimensional world, the one we are living in now, is a shadow — a shadow of a world that has four dimensions. What would that world be like? What might be the fourth dimension? What would be the relationship of the three-dimensional shadow to the four-dimensional world? Show me through movement the four-dimensional world and its three-dimensional shadow.

The stimulus here is provided by both the visual and the verbal. Andrea hopes to reach as many of the group as possible through use of words and pictures.

Because the group had been studying the theory of relativity, its members responded immediately. The drama participants were very charged up by the idea; the excitement was electric.

The class had a collective "ah-ha" response to the stimulus.

To know that we know, and that we do not know what we do not know, that is true knowledge.

Henry David Thoreau

WHAT HAPPENED

The Planning Andrea divided the whole group into three smaller ones of six each. During the planning time, she moved from one group to the other. We'll present one group's planning in depth.

Group 2 is made up of six children: four girls — Vivian, Janet, Susan, and Jessica — and two boys — Jeremy and Gary.

Janet: Let's do the light beam. It's like in science, but we'll leave out the scientific part and just keep the humanity. We'll have each twin on different beams and one will stay here and the other will move into space—the four-dimensional world. Then they'll get back together and one will be old and the other won't.

Gary: That won't work. How can we show that idea through movement?

Susan: Let's think about space, body, force, and time—which can we show best through movement?

Jessica: Force, we're good at being strong.

Gary: Yeah, but we feel it and the audience doesn't.

Janet [looking at Gary]: *You* can't do movement at all.

Vivian: Wait a minute, I have a wonderful idea. Let's double everything—force, time, body, space! Two people moving in the three-dimensional world. And in the four-dimensional world have four people doing the pattern faster, with more extra in-place movement.

Jessica: Great! The boys can hold the girls on their shoulders.

Gary: It won't work. How are the two worlds related if they have nothing in common?

Susan: I know. Let's connect the world by having each world do the same pattern—a triangle shape in space.

Jeremy: Let me find the books on Einstein. I'll be right back. *[He runs over to the bookshelves.]*

Gary: You know, this sounds like it could be okay.

Observe how Janet is an idea person, Gary is a critic, Susan has extensive movement experience and helps implement the enactment, Vivian is the coordinator, Jessica is the team builder, and Jeremy is an observer who volunteers his skills when needed. Notice how flexible each group member is when working on the product of the whole. Their focus is on the ideas and the enactment.

Janet: Okay, let's try some movement!

Can you trace the development of three ideas? How has the group combined the image from the science class with their kinesthetic images from previous movement classes?

Concentrating on developing two mirror worlds, the group begins by developing a movement piece that contains two identical worlds. Gradually, they add more people, more in-place movement, a whole extra locomotion pattern, and quicker overall motions to the world that the three-dimensional world shadows.

The Movement Piece The final piece of this group depicts two worlds. The three-dimensional world contains two people (Jessica and Vivian) who move lyrically in a triangular pattern. They are holding hands, crossed like ice skaters', and sway from side to side.

The other group forms a pyramid of bodies with Gary and Jeremy holding Janet, swaying rapidly and locomoting in a triangle pattern. Moving around them in a ferocious circle is Susan. All four people have an expression of high intensity. In terms of concept, their movement piece, depicting the

Notice the many levels and spinning motion of the children moving in *Einstein's World*. (Drawing by Michael Rocco Pinciotti)

four-dimensional world to be shadowed, rivals a professional, contemporary dance company's.

The Discussion When we visited this group six months later, we were again struck by their Mastery level of expertise. Andrea described activities similar to the one we just described in which the group developed a drama stimulated by abstract/expressionist works of art by such painters as Kandinsky and Picasso. She explained that the group didn't just perform a story based on a painting, but really delved into how the elements of visual art could be transformed to the dramatic art, affecting the viewer in the same way as had a specific painting.

Even if your group is not classified as gifted and talented, you certainly can use innovative, abstract ideas such as this as the focus of a drama. In our observations, we have found that most leaders underestimate rather than overestimate the Mastery potential of their group.

"The World Turned Upside Down"

PRELESSON INFORMATION

The Group The group is composed of thirty seventh-graders (seventeen girls and thirteen boys) in a suburban community with an ethnic mix: 70 percent white, 10 percent Oriental, 20 percent black. This intact group has had drama three times a week for almost two years. For many of the children, drama has been a part of their education since first grade. The school's approach focuses on a holistic, integrative approach to teaching.

The Leader The leader, Jeffrey Williams, is trained in and has taught other traditional creative drama approaches. Mr. Williams learned the Rutgers Imagination Method three years ago and has slowly evolved a new personal creative drama approach using much of RIM's theoretical base. When questioned, he stated that the internal/external aspects of the method, plus the strong imagery base, gave his recent drama activities a specificity that marks a radical departure in the way he and his classes view dramatic learning. In his spare time, Mr. Williams is an active member of the local community theatre. In fact, many of his lessons reflect this theatrical interest.

The Project Mr. Williams diagnosed the dramas of this group as becoming too obscure; the group needed to return to traditional story drama and to investigate further the theatre model. He also felt the group was ready to do a drama based on their collective passion — science fiction. Instead of trying to compete with the group's increased interest in science fiction movies and television programs, Mr. Williams hoped to capitalize on it.

"The World Turned Upside Down" represents a traditional story drama with a RIM focus. The project objectives are threefold: to construct a well-made drama piece, to include personal aspects in the development of plot, and to experiment with the theatrical form of comedy. This project took place over five separate drama sessions.

The Stimulus The stimuli were the figure of speech "The World Turned Upside Down," and the NASA photo shown on page 297. The class discussion focused on analyzing the meaning of the phrase. The class rejected its usual meanings (that is, that the world could suddenly change for everyone in it) for a more subjective one. The interpretation that captured the imagination of the group was that one person could perceive that the world had "turned upside down" while others were unaware of it. Mr. Williams asked the class to compare this idea with other renditions on a similar theme such as *Invasion of the Body Snatchers* and tell how this drama would be the same and how it would be different.

The class also had been collectively captured by the lecture on comedy. The group hope to utilize the information on what is funny and incorporate it in conjunction with "The World Turned Upside Down."

WHAT HAPPENED

More than the planning sessions, what is outstanding in this Mastery example is the final product, three scenes of which we describe in detail. "The World Turned Upside Down" is composed of five scenes. Each scene builds in intensity; gradually more and more unnatural phenomena occur, beginning with a talking dog and ending with supernatural forces invading the earth. One class member, Benny, a particularly charming boy who is one of the class leaders as well as excellent at creative drama, is the protagonist. He appears in all scenes and unifies the drama. All the others in the group play a variety of human, subhuman, animal, and object characters.

Scene One: Breakfast at Benny's Benny sits at the breakfast table. Around the table are his mother, father, sister Lola, and brother Bobby. The family eats breakfast and chats about their planned activities for the day. Very slowly the dog, Flash, played by Jennifer, crawls on all fours to the table. Then Flash sits on a chair at the table and begins to eat with a knife and fork.

The comedic aspect is suspension of natural laws; the class knew that observers would laugh at a dog who behaves as if she were a person, thus suspending the natural laws of dog behavior as we know them.

Benny: Hey, Flash, get down.
Flash: Wrrrrong, you rrrruffian. I'm hungrrrry.
Benny: Hey, what? Flash, did you . . . ?
Flash *(barking and wagging her tail; she's got a sausage in her mouth):* R-r-r-r.
(Mother tells Flash to leave the table, but doesn't notice that she is using silverware. The meal and animated conversation resume. Flash again sits at the table.)
Flash: Grrrreat sausage. I'd like some brrrread and butterrr.

Notice that Flash's dialogue is developed to resemble the growl of a dog. These participants have no difficulty playing nonhuman characters.

Benny: O.K. Here. Wait a minute. You did talk. Mom. Dad. Listen. Flash! Say something. She talked. Really.
Flash (back on the floor, she wags her tail): R-r-r.
Dad: Son, you seem to be losing it.
(The scene continues. Everyone but Benny ignores Flash, who begins preparing a meal for her doggie friends who also walk on two legs and talk. Benny, cleaning his glasses, leaves for school.)

Scene Two: The Flying Bus This scene takes place at the bus stop and in the bus. While waiting for the bus to arrive, Benny describes to his best friends, Emmett and Kiko, what has happened. They believe him and come over after school to see Flash themselves.

Many of the participants contributed real-life experiences to the development of this scene. Often they felt that their best friends would understand them, even if their family couldn't.

As they enter the bus, their bus drive Mr. Sartoni seems extremely remote and doesn't greet them. All three boys comment on the change in Mr. S's personality. The bus ride continues until all the class is picked up. (Each of the bus riders has developed a unique character and stays in role.)

Suddenly, the bus begins to fly. (All the performers show this fact by swaying and moving in unison.) Benny tries to get Emmett and Kiko's attention and points out that the bus is flying. Emmett and Kiko laugh at him. The scene ends with Benny realizing that he alone seems to be aware of what's happening.

Scene Three: Automatic Classroom The group has arranged the desks and chairs to suggest a traditional classroom seating arrangement. A math class is in progress. Mr. Williams, the teacher, played by Joseph, is explaining the complexities of multiplication. His movements and speech seem jerky and get progressively more so as the scene progresses. He delivers a funny monologue about math.

This NASA photo acted as a stimulus for the Mastery Drama. Astronaut Edward H. White II, outside the Gemini 4 Spacecraft, certainly sees a "World Turned Upside Down." (NASA)

The class has enough confidence in their leader's good humor that they satirize him in the drama.

Benny: Hey, Mr. Williams. Want to hear a good joke?
Mr. W: No, I do not.
Benny: Knock, knock.
Mr. W: I do not understand knock, knock.
Benny: Hey, quit kidding. That's not funny.
Mr. W: I do not understand kidding. Speak in words I understand.
Benny: You're not Mr. Williams. You're different. I know that everybody seems to be.
(The class rises and each member, robotlike, converges on Benny.)
Benny: Oh, this is what Mr. Williams meant when he described "A World Turned Upside Down."
(Benny escapes the onslaught of robots.)

The comedic element in this scene is people acting mechanically — part of every comedian's repertoire.

Scenes Four and Five The last two scenes focus on the major conflict and its resolution. In scene four, the forces from outer space try to capture Benny — a person versus technology conflict. Scene five depicts a world in which everything is turned upside down. Animals act like people, and robots rule the world. All the regular people are gone except Benny, who is put on display in a cage with a sign reading, "A Right-side-up Person."

Discussion The above drama represents a reintegration of theatrical and imagery skills. What is also gratifying for the leader is that it is original and exciting to watch.

"Dream-Maker: The Drama"

PRELESSON INFORMATION

The Group The group is composed of creative arts college students who are being trained in RIM so they can lead creative drama activities with young people. This group of twelve has only been together for fifteen weeks, but all have had either teaching or arts training. The group members clicked with each other immediately and performed several Mastery improvisations over the semester.

The Leader Dr. Caryl Smalser, the leader, is one of the first doctoral students trained in RIM at Rutgers. She has now returned to her college teaching job and is training the second generation of students to know RIM. Because she was instrumental in early modifications, Caryl understands RIM both practically and theoretically.

The Project "Dream-Maker: The Drama" had its beginnings when the class enacted Dream-Maker, a Transformation activity. That enactment led to this discussion about the relationship of arts education to arts therapies. The class discovered that this activity had evolved from a drama therapy exercise in which the client relates, casts, and directs the performance of his or her dream. The group decided that they might get to know each other better if they could act out each other's dreams and nightmares. Also, a doctoral researcher was visiting the class that day; the group selected an activity they "knew" they could do well in order to make a good impression.

The Stimulus "Everyone has dreams that are significant and recurring. Each of you concentrate now and retrieve a dream to share with others in the group. [Caryl allows them time to retrieve images.] Okay, everyone, come back to Campbell Hall from your reverie. Now, in your small groups, share your dreams. Decide which one you would like to enact. The person whose dream you have chosen will be director and playwright."

Notice that Caryl sets up the Mastery enactment in a manner almost identical to the way she would a Transformation activity. Directions themselves have no magical power; the power is in the stimulating image.

WHAT HAPPENED

Luckily, the researcher was in one of the small groups and could document what occurred. Her documentation provided a detailed study of a group made up of individuals with well-developed metacognitive abilities. The small-group members were John, Bill, Angeline, Bob, and Jeremy.

The Planning Each member of the group related his or her dream. Then, around the circle, each member gave his or her opinion of the best dream to enact. All agreed that John's dream was best.

Each group member "knew" without having to enact each dream that John's dream provided the best potential for the group. When questioned, four said they just "knew" that John's would be best. The fifth, Angeline, described a "sudden flash" concerning the appropriateness of John's dream. All exhibited metacognitive knowledge — the knowledge or belief about what factors or variables act and interact in what ways to affect the course of the enterprise.

John's dream is about being drafted, for the second time. John had fought in Vietnam until an injury required that he return to noncombat duties. John's fear is that he will be drafted again. His dream focuses on that dread.

John began the planning with the statement, "It's better if I don't play myself." He proceeded to cast Bill as himself and Angeline as his wife.

John acted upon his stored knowledge concerning a metacognitive experience. John "knew" that he did not have the skills necessary to direct and act the major role (metacognition of task and of self). He also knew that of all the group Bill was the person to play him, because Bill had the most skills and a personality most aligned with his own (metacognition of others).

The group discusses which scenes to enact to achieve the full effect of the drama. John senses that five scenes are essential: John and his wife receiving the draft notice, the train journey to the post, meeting the sergeant and bunkmates and establishing friendships, and the bitter confrontation between John and the sergeant. The planning of the first scene begins. At first, John tries to tell Bill and Angeline every line to say. Angeline stops him: "Let us try it. It's always better if we just do it and don't talk too much about it."

Angeline also exhibits a high metacognitive ability; she knows which drama strategies work for her and Bill.

Angeline and Bill enact the scene; their performance meets with John's approval. They move to the second scene — the train journey — in which Bill verbalizes his fears aloud. The third scene focuses on meeting the sergeant. John, playing the sergeant, plays him too broadly. Bob says, "If you start out at that intensity, you'll have nowhere to go for the end of the drama."

> ***I think we are well to keep on nodding terms with the people we used to be, whether we find them attractive or not. . . . We forget too soon the things we thought we could never forget.***
>
> Joan Didion

Bob's statement is based on his ability to monitor the drama's progress and assess its current state — a metacognitive ability.

John tones down the performance. Scene four focuses on the bunkmates. As the scene is enacted, Jeremy says: "I'm not sure I understand what I'm to do. You didn't tell me enough about your friend Sam for me to enact him."

Jeremy seeks clarification; he knows that he will not be able to continue unless he has more information about his character and the objective of the scene. Jeremy monitors his progress, a metacognitive skill.

This scene and the final one are rehearsed to John's satisfaction and pleasure. The group senses it is ready and performs a chilling rendition of John's dream.

Discussion This case study details an ideally matched group, all of whom have high-level metacognitive skills. Although the drama itself is a Mastery enactment, the examples of metacognition are especially illustrative of a Mastery group.

"Castles and Dragons"

PRELESSON INFORMATION

The Group The group is composed of eleven five-year-olds (six boys, five girls) in an after-school drama program that meets for an hour a week. These students are participating in their third ten-week term. The content of the first ten weeks was primarily Starter exercises built around various images (shape, movement, story, collage—a potpourri of many short activities). The second ten sessions involved Starters as warm-ups and led to Transformation activities. During these sessions, the group exhibited strength in Self as Character and Story into Plot. By the end of the second ten-week sequence, they began to demonstrate a great deal of independence, indicating they could handle more. During the third ten-week session, the group showed Mastery potential. Their goal was to present a drama at the end of the third session to an invited audience of parents and friends—something they had never done before!

The Leader Joan Rizzo has a B.A. in Theatre and an Ed.M. in Creative Arts. She has been Education Director at the theatre for six years. During that time, she has developed a strong creative drama/theatre program with satellite programs throughout the surrounding area. In her teaching, Joan stresses the connections between creative drama and theatre.

The Stimulus For the third ten-week session, Joan decided to focus the group's creative energy on one theme or image. She chose "Medieval Times," because it was rich in adventure and the information was new to the participants. She used as her primary stimulus *The Time Traveller Book of Knights and Castles* that begins with a guided fantasy in which the participants travel back in time.* Working together in the same group on variations on the same theme helped propel the young participants into Mastery.

Every week Joan focused on various aspects of medieval life. For eight weeks the participants worked on various Transformation categories, all focusing on medieval life. Joan brought in props, costumes, and drawings.

The here-and-now stimuli are all based on one central image. This focus helps explain why this young group reached Mastery.

Joan tailored activities to capture the attention of her young dramatists. Examples of activities included knight training for the category of Self as Character; the hunt for Story becomes Plot; investigation inside and outside the

* *Time Traveller books are a series of books that take young readers back to everyday life long ago. They are originally published in England by Osborne Publishing Ltd., and in the United States by Hayes Books of Tulsa, Oklahoma.*

Even though the children are preschoolers, they are able to participate in an intense planning period. It is with the assistance of a good leader that these young children, pictured here, are able to develop necessary clear images. (Photo courtesy Pam Rich)

castle for Place Becomes Setting; dragons for Adding Conflict; and costume-building and weapon-making for Creating Spectacle. Each weekly hour would end with a story-making session and short enactment. By the eighth week the young people were contributing easily to the story and connecting much of what they had learned. Also, each week, more young children spontaneously brought in from home objects and stories dealing with medieval times.

WHAT HAPPENED

Prior to the ninth lesson Joan carefully developed a story in which all the various Transformation elements could be combined.

Day 9 On the ninth day Joan began to tell the children a story about a friendly but fire-breathing dragon that plagued the village. All of the various characters — the knights, the ladies, the townspeople — were featured. The story focused on scenes that had been previously enacted, such as daily life in a medieval town and knights dueling. As Joan told the story, she observed the children seeing themselves in the various activities. For example, Claire stood up and curtsied during the scene when the ladies met the knights; Jason wielded an imaginary sword during the dueling part.

When Joan got to the climax of the story — how the villagers were to deal with the dragon — she opened the discussion:

Joan: Why were the villagers upset?
Rachael: They were afraid of the dragon!

Joan: What should they do?
Jason: Kill it!
Lisa: But it was friendly!
Aaron: But the fire was scary!
Joan: What could fire help the villagers do?

Notice how Joan structures the discussion to assist problem-solving. She has mastered several questioning techniques that work.

Sara: Cook food.
John-Paul: Keep them warm.
Ayana: Light the stoves.
Joan: What kind of food needs to have heat?
Cabral: Hamburgers.
Claire: Hot Chocolate.
Zak: Popcorn.
Joan [With a happy laugh]: Popcorn?

Joan demonstrates her own metacognitive ability at this time. Immediately she knows that popcorn is a wonderful choice, because popcorn will work theatrically and because the group is fond of it.

All kids: Popcorn!
Matt: The dragon could make popcorn for everybody.
Joan: Would you like that?
Kids: Yeah!!!
Joan: How would the king and queen discover the dragon could pop popcorn?

In a group as young as this one, the group dynamics do not equal those of an older Mastery group. Although the group has developed a working pattern, the leader acts as an essential, ever-present member of the group.

Kids (after a heated debate): He could be sent from the castle and go out to the fields and be sad and the corn starts popping and everybody is happy and the children find him surrounded by popcorn.
Joan: OK, let's retell the story and keep in mind the fear of the people and the sorrow of the dragon and their joyous discovery at the end. Try to think about possible ways of doing the drama. We're going to perform it next week.

The impact of the stimulus was so strong that children, even at this age, contemplated its power and related how they performed individual enactments at home during the week.

Day 10 The group had an hour to prepare the drama before the arrival of an invited audience of parents and friends. During that time, the group, with Joan's assistance, decided on roles and went through the various scenes. During the rehearsal, they added props (brought in during the previous weeks), wore costumes (made earlier), and utilized sets of rostrum blocks to create a castle setting.

The enactment went better than had the rehearsal. The children worked together as a unit; they helped classmates who had lost track of what was to happen; they paused for a laugh as the audience reacted; they spoke louder and more intensely as the drama built to a climax. They showed an integration of imagination/action skills and a group cohesiveness that far exceeded the expectations of a group of their tender years and limited experience.

At the end of the drama, they joined the audience in eating the popcorn, popped by the helpful dragon. The popcorn had been brought in by Claire, who felt that, "We should share our drama and our food with our friends and family."

"Russell Revisited"

PRELESSON INFORMATION

The Group The group is a third grade living in a small midwestern town near the Canadian border. Mostly whites of Scandinavian descent live in the area, with some Native Americans attending the local schools. Also, within the last two decades, black children, whose parents are stationed at the local air force base, attend the school. This class is 75 percent white and 25 percent Native American. The pioneer spirit, demonstrated by many of the early settlers to this area, is present in the parents of these children, as well as in the children themselves. Parental support of arts activities helps keep drama a daily activity within the curriculum.

The Leader Jim Larson is a tall, handsome, charismatic physical education teacher. He is loved by his students and has recently added creative drama to his repertoire of specialties. While working toward his master's degree in developmental psychology, Jim took a general course in creative drama and attended some workshops on RIM. Prior to attending the workshops, Jim had been aware of his own and others' imagery abilities. He was so impressed with imagery's potential that he has incorporated it into his physical education curriculum and into his drama activities.

The Project This case study documents a group's development from Starters through Transformations to Mastery. The three activities, condensed here, took place on three separate days, months apart: the Starter in September; the Transformation in February; and the Mastery lesson in June. Two of the many continuing spontaneous themes within Jim Larson's drama class are violence and history, particularly of the region, and these are woven into the three lessons.

WHAT HAPPENED

This case study documents the activities of Shawn, Henry, Ingrid, Nina, and Andrew, members of the subgroup discussed in Mastery. Henry, Shawn, and Ingrid are of Norwegian descent; Nina and Andrew are Native Americans.

The Starter Activity On one of the first days of drama class, Jim leads Group Shoot. The first time through the exercise, he comments on various children who pantomime notable "dying" behavior: "Good, Henry, I can see you dying as if you were an old man."

As early as Starters, Henry demonstrates well-developed dramatic behavior skills.

The group likes dying so much that they ask to do "Group Shoot" again. Ingrid suggests that half the class "shoot" and half "die," then change roles.

Early on in the drama exercises, Ingrid demonstrates her creative drama potential as an idea person. It's important to remember that many drama participants, even the ones to reach Mastery quickly, are late bloomers. In fact, within this group, Nina and Shawn do not distinguish themselves until well into Transformations.

First, Jim talks the group through the reenactment, so that participants can clarify in their mind's eye who they are and how they will die. Then, they enact the Starter again.

Observers can see that the class is responding well; their enthusiasm is high, and as they "die" again, their pantomimes reflect even more characterization and specificity than before. Jim makes a mental note that the class has responded to this exercise. In fact, it is his diligence in working for continuity and developing meaningful activities that contributes to the group's reaching Mastery.

When Jim presented the first Adding Conflict activity, the group had already spontaneously sensed that their dramas, to be truly dramatic, required conflict and resolution. On the day before the session we are going to document, Jim had asked the group to image and write down words that threaten and words that calm; physical positions that threaten and physical positions that calm; and actions that threaten and actions that calm.

Jim's Transformation activity focused on conflict with horizontal movement. Entitled "Stop It," the activity's objective was for one pair of participants to try to stop another pair from accomplishing a particular deed or task. Each pair was permitted to use words, physical positions, or actions to try to stop the other pair.

Pair one is Nina and Shawn; pair two is Andrew and Ingrid. Together they develop an elaborate conflict-laden situation of a bank robbery in the Old West in which the criminals — Ingrid and Andrew — try to rob a bank owned by Nina and Shawn.

During Transformations these two pairs naturally gravitate toward one another. Jim does not separate the pairs. In fact, he encourages this group configuration, which helps to propel these participants to Mastery.

The improvisation works well, although the transitions from words to positions to action are somewhat stilted. The characters, the dialogue, and the actual climactic moment, however, reflect a clear integration of a number of skills and a well-balanced group.

These participants are trying to integrate Transformation skills. Time and experience are lacking, but not understanding of what the final product needs to be.

The whole class responds positively to the Wild West improvisation. The Western motif is obviously quite compelling to this group. Jim ends the class with the comment, "I bet all of you would like to go back in time and experience the excitement of the pioneer West!"

Mastery RIM Lesson: *Day 1* Jim brought in a Charles M. Russell painting entitled *Lost in a Snowstorm — We Are Friends*. The painting, with its stark

This painting challenged the students to develop their own version of a traditional conflict. (C.M. Russell, *Lost in a Snowstorm — We Are Friends,* Courtesy of Amon Carter Museum, Fort Worth, Texas)

setting and vivid details, captured the attention of subgroup four, made up of Nina, Henry, Ingrid, Shawn, and Andrew:

Nina: Look at the Indians and the settlers helping each other.
Henry: They really need each other.
Ingrid: Probably there were many situations when Indians and settlers had to help each other.
Henry: Yeah, when the cowboys and Indians were friends.
Ingrid: Then we can make a painting of it.

Notice how each member builds on what the other has said and how the required group roles are filled. As the case study continues, you will see that Henry is both implementer and coordinator, Ingrid is the idea person, Andrew the team builder, Nina the critic, and Shawn the external contact.

Nina: We don't have time for a painting. I don't think we can even paint a painting, even if we had the time.
Henry: What else could we do that's like a painting.
Ingrid: I know! A new art. We can take a picture. Mr. Larson said that photography is a new art. We can take a picture of the way we finish the story.
Shawn: I like to take pictures. I'll bring in my Polaroid that I got for Christmas. I'm good at pictures.
Ingrid: Bring in the camera tomorrow. You'll take the picture. Then we'll do the scene that leads up to the picture. Like in the activity. . . .
Nina: Like "Group Shoot," only better. Combined with all the good stuff from "Wild, Wild West."

Both Nina and Ingrid are demonstrating high-level metacognition. Ingrid "knows" that a photo will help focus the task. Nina "knows" that the group can develop a strategy that utilizes previously successful ones.

A heated discussion ensues. The group agrees that they can't decide and will make decisions about specifics tomorrow, after they have the photo.

Again, this decision demonstrates high metacognitive knowledge. The group members realize that they don't know how to resolve the scene and that further discussion is fruitless. Tomorrow, when the ideas seem fresh and the photo is at hand, they feel they will be able to work better.

Day 2 Shawn has brought in his camera and takes photographs of Indians (played by the two real-life Native Americans) and cowboys helping each other in different situations. The group likes two photographs, both of cowboys and Indians making friends. Shawn shows Jim the two photographs and ask him to select his favorite. He does not select, but asks questions that help focus the group on a decision.

The group selects a photograph that they feel best represents their perspective of the Wild West. Just as Russell offered his artistic point of view about the situation, this group feels that this photograph and the drama resulting from it represents its collective viewpoint.

The subgroup of five works hard on planning, enacting, replanning, and reenacting the drama. They use costumes, props, and sets, with their final objective to portray the situation depicted in the photograph. They call their drama "Russell Revisited."

The first three dramas of the other subgroups are typical confrontation scenes, well done but clearly not Mastery level dramas.

In a large group, some small groups may achieve Mastery level, while others do not. Whether they do or not depends, to a large extent, on the group make up, as well as on the power of the image for that particular group. Variations occur from group to group and from day to day.

The group's drama "Russell Revisited" is extraordinary—a clean, simple enactment of cowboys and Indians who resolve their conflict, help each other, and become friends.

EXPANDING CREATIVE DRAMA

So far throughout this book, we have asked you, as a prospective drama leader, to travel with us in your imagination to a variety of drama sessions, back in time, and even through your inner world of ideas. We have urged you to personalize drama for yourself and for your participants. In this chapter we ask you to image yourself *outside* the drama experience, to begin to distance yourself in order to observe and evaluate the dramas. To assist you, we provide you with a variety of methodologies for looking at the drama process and product objectively. At the end of the chapter, we will ask you to "travel" with us to the future to view the creative drama field as it might be in the twenty-first century.

> ***The act of imagination is the opening of the system so that it shows new connection.***
>
> Joseph Bronowski

ASSESSING DRAMA

Three of the biggest problems faced by creative drama leaders relate to evaluation and assessment. Situations arise in which the leader must evaluate the individuals' progress at the end of a series of creative drama experiences. Or the leader must assess the level of a group in order to select exercises and activities appropriate for the participants. Too, a leader may question when to move from Starters to Transformations. All three situations require that the leader step back from the process and use a systematic, objective measure that is as unobtrusive as possible.

As drama leader, you may feel ambivalent. On the one hand, it may seem anticreative to you to assess artistic development, particularly when it is in progress. On the other hand, if you believe participation in creative drama increases dramatic learning, it must follow that this learning can be measured, or at least described. Besides, outsiders, such as administrators and parents, often ask you for some kind of evaluation. And participants, too, are eager to know "how they did" during the year. In fact, participants are often positively influenced by an evaluation that is systematic, humane, and objective.

The terms *assessment* and *evaluation* are often used interchangeably. For the purpose of this discussion, however, there are two essential distinctions between assessment and evaluation: *what* and *when*. **Assessment measures the progress of students; evaluation focuses on the merits of a program.** Assessment takes place during the phenomenon; it answers such questions as: How far along in Starters are the participants? Should we move to Transformations? What aspects of Transformations seem to be mastered? What needs work? **Assessment focuses on the ongoing phenomenon; its purpose is to measure or describe progress** so that some changes in current and future activities and methods can more appropriately suit the particular needs of the participants.

Evaluation occurs after the fact, when the drama activities are over. Although we like to think that a participant's drama work is never completed, we do acknowledge a time when evaluation is necessary. Evaluation may be used to answer such questions as: How well did the individuals do in mastering movement? How does the preprogram evaluation compare with the postprogram evaluation? Evaluation provides information about a particular set of exercises; this information can assist in developing future activities or in restructuring the curriculum.

When to Do Evaluation/Assessment

Although the reasons behind conducting assessments and providing evaluations may be different, the techniques are similar. The following methods all are based on the theory, detailed throughout the book, that drama has value in and of itself—particularly to assist in stimulating the imagination/action connection. As you study the following measurement devices and procedures, also remember that none of them, taken singly or together, can really capture the "essence" of the drama activity. Each of the measures has its strengths and weaknesses; each can provide a systematic way of looking at drama, as well as some important information. Temper your enthusiasm to overassess the drama phenomenon. Always remember the fact, stressed so often in this book, that drama is an elusive, personal, and magic process. You may observe it or stimulate it in innumerable ways, but you can never know precisely what will spark it.

Assessments occur before, during, and after conducting some portion of drama activities; evaluation almost always occurs after activities. The most traditional time to use these measures, for the purpose of evaluation, is when you have to give a grade or present some kind of final comments to participants, parents, or school administrators. Another typical time to use the following methods, for the sake of assessment, is prior to starting the drama activity as a way of establishing how many aspects of creative drama the group is familiar with or has mastered.

The third most common time to use these measures is when a leader must decide what tactics to use for the duration of the creative drama experience. Decisions about when to continue activities of the same type or at the same level and when to move on can only be made by assessing the current situation. Trying to know when participants may have had enough work on movement, for example, is almost as difficult as knowing when a painting is completed or how long a poem should be. The following methods can assist you in making these decisions, but you must, of course, use your common sense as well.

Rene Magritte has painted his concept of simultaneous doing and monitoring. Certainly the man in this painting seems to know that he knows; he would score high on metacognitive ability! (*The Thought Which Sees,* Collection, The Museum of Modern Art, New York. Gift of Mr. and Mrs. Charles B. Benenson)

What to Do for Evaluation/Assessment

Since most of you will be conducting the assessment and evaluation of your own drama classes, the most obvious choice for material is to recreate a typical creative drama class. If your group is working in Starters, you may measure a set of exercises as described in the In-Depth Approach in Chapter 8 (p. 213) or utilize the exercises in the model of the Spectrum Approach discussed in Chapter 8 (pp. 214–215). Or you may hand-select a potpourri of exercises from Starters.

If your group is working in Transformations, you may select exclusively from one Transformation category or use a particular Transformation plan, as suggested in Chapter 10 (pp. 278–279). You may also hand-select your own potpourri of activities that focus on specific skills or behaviors you would like to assess.

You may also wish to use improvisations different from a typical RIM Starter or Transformation. For instance:

- Outside environments — beach, playground, zoo.
- Inside situations — supermarket, airport, department store.
- Social scenes — fast-food restaurant, pizzeria, museum.

Finally, as you set up your assessment, you must make logical decisions concerning:

- Length of time of whole observation.
- Length of time each participant is observed.
- Configuration of individual/group during observation (whole group, small group, threes, pairs, or individual).
- Recording method, such as simultaneous note-taking or recording after the fact.

Not much data exist concerning the above variables. We urge you to make choices that serve the practical needs of your current situation and give each participant an equal opportunity to exhibit what he or she knows.

The Checklist

A checklist is the simplest method of assessing and evaluating drama. The procedure for using this or any other checklist is straightforward. Familiarize yourself with the items on the list. As each occurs, check off that item. Tabulate the items, and you will have a general, though scanty, assessment. Two issues to consider, when using this or another checklist, are:

How good is the checklist? Is it measuring those aspects of drama that I think are important? The following checklist measures the milestones in creative drama in four important categories: imagery, dramatic behavior, group negotiation, and connection of imagination and action. It has been particularly developed to evaluate progress in the Rutgers Imagination Method.

The second issue is, how do I know that the participants are accomplishing these items? Of course, if the item describes a behavior, then the answer is to watch. If you have many participants working simultaneously, your job is to observe each participant, singly and for about the same amount of time. You must try to be as objective as possible. The situation becomes trickier when the item describes an internal process. Then, you must try to observe outward signs of the behavior—such as eye movements or small physical gestures during compressed rehearsal. You can also listen to what the participant says during the planning and evaluation stages. Finally, you may have to elicit such information through informal conversations or through formal interview.

RIM CHECKLIST

Imagery Abilities

STARTERS

Participate in and use guided fantasy.
Recognize images.
Retrieve images.
Hold images.
Manipulate images.
Use memory images.
Use personal, as opposed to generic, images.
Control images.
Develop vivid images.
Acquire fluency of imaging.
Get in touch with personal storehouse of images.

TRANSFORMATIONS

Develop imagination images.
Manipulate and integrate memory and imagination images.
Use flexibility within imaging.
Able to select/reject/elaborate upon images.
Develop simple group image.
Modify, retrieve, and combine many characteristics of images when necessary.
Incorporate a variety of elements within one stimulating image.

MASTERY

Know that one "knows" about imagery.
Know how one "knows" about imagery.
Develop ability to recognize significance and appropriateness of stimulating image.
Develop dramatic sensibility in terms of recording images.

Dramatic Behaviors

STARTERS

Work with objects and props.
Execute simple creative movement skills.
Imitate/pantomime behavior.
Imitate sounds.
Remember and initiate simple dialogue.
Perform simple character walking and talking skills.
Remember sequences.
Tell simple story.
Use art-making materials.
Match and modify color, size, balance, and shape.

TRANSFORMATIONS

Take perspective of actor, director, designer, playwright, critic.
Understand role of observer/audience.
Transform self into character.
Transform place into setting.
Develop and perform plot and stories.
Use conflict as part of story if necessary.
Explore, develop, and integrate visual aspects into drama.

MASTERY

Demonstrate and reintegrate a full range of drama skills.
Develop novel or original enactments.

Group Process

STARTERS

Participate in parallel play.
Become aware of other group members.

TRANSFORMATIONS

Develop a variety of group negotiation skills.
Participate in idea/image hitchhiking and brainstorming.
Work in a variety of group configurations, including pairs, threes, small group, and whole group.
Experiment with other group members.
Work in a state of mutual support—cooperation.
Coordinate and synchronize actions.

MASTERY

Become a vital member of cohesive, integrated group.
Balance drama and social goals within collaborative process.
Fill necessary communication roles.
Know that one "knows" about group process.

Connection of Imagination and Action

STARTERS

Perceive/observe world.
Become aware of sensory qualities/details in nature, experiences, people, and art.
Develop ability to relax, concentrate, and focus.

TRANSFORMATIONS

Explore connection between imagination and action: physically, through problem-solving, and artistically.
Describe self-as-other transformation.
Demonstrate compressed rehearsal.
Develop ability to select, reject, and elaborate upon within framework of imagination/action connection.
Function within plan/play/evaluate structure.

MASTERY

Demonstrate ability to monitor and to enact simultaneously.

	Describe personal third eye ability. Know that one "knows" about imagination and action in terms of self, other, task, and strategy. Develop a personal sense of audience.

The Rating Scale

The second measurement tool, the rating scale, is also an observational device that is analytical and categorical, but it is much more specific in its delineations. The statements included in the following rating scales describe individual and/or group behavioral or situational characteristics. The descriptions are specific and enable the rater to identify more clearly the characteristic to be rated. Instead of deciding whether the individual's ability to work in the plan/play/evaluate structure is outstanding or above average, for example, you may find it easier to decide between "Always demonstrates four categories of reflection: spontaneous, leader-led, individual, and group" and "Usually demonstrates three categories of reflection: spontaneous, leader-led, and group."

Rating scales have several limitations. Initially, it may be difficult for the rater to understand precisely what quality is to be evaluated, particularly in terms of his or her own internal thinking processes. Thus a rater may tend to carry a qualitative judgment over from one aspect to another. In other words, the rater may have a tendency to rate a person who has good movement skills as good in other traits, too, such as image retrieval or story-making. Another limitation of rating is the tendency to be too generous. When using rating scales, keep in mind that you should omit the items you cannot observe and observe only for short periods of time. Remember, if in doubt, stop observing or leave it out.

Rating scales for Starters and for Transformations constructed to reflect the desirable outcomes of participating in the Rutgers Imagination Method are found on the next pages.

STARTERS RATING SCALE

	IMAGERY
	IMAGE RETRIEVAL
5. Outstanding	Always able to recall detailed memory images of a personal nature. Usually able to identify and retrieve personal images within all sensory domains. Always able to discriminate between vividness of images.
4. Above Average	Usually able to recall with some detail memory images of a personal nature. Usually able to identify and retrieve personal images with two or three sensory domains. Usually able to discriminate vividness of personal images.
3. Average	Sometimes able to recall with some detail memory images of a personal nature.

	Describes retrieved images that seem equally balanced: half detailed and half not detailed. Acknowledges existence of a variety of sensory images, but sometimes has difficulty distinguishing among them. Usually classifies own images as always very vivid, or not vivid at all.
2. Below Average	Rarely able to retrieve personal images. When questioned about personal images, usually describes generic images. Rarely demonstrates fluency in imagery.
1. Far Below Average	Never able to retrieve memory images. Fails to acknowledge existence of personal images. Never demonstrates fluency in imagery.

HOLDING IMAGES

5. Outstanding	Always demonstrates success in holding images within all sensory domains. Always retains images from class to class. Always able to take up the drama from where it was left, even if the elapsed time was a week.
4. Above Average	Almost always demonstrates success in holding images in three or four sensory domains. Retains some images from class to class.
3. Average	Usually demonstrates success in holding images in two or three domains (visual and/or auditory). Usually retains images from beginning of drama session until the end. Occasionally holds images from one week until the next.
2. Below Average	Rarely able to hold images, except in visual domain. Rarely able to retain images within the drama session.
1. Far Below Average	Never able to hold images, except for some in visual domain. Unable to hold images within the drama session.

MANIPULATION OF IMAGES

5. Outstanding	Verbalizes that always has controllability of imagery strategies in all five domains. Always able to utilize a particular strategy in imagery manipulation of all five sensory domains. Always able to combine images from all five domains within one activity.
4. Above Average	Verbalizes that almost always has controllability of imagery in three or four sensory domains. Almost always able to utilize a particular strategy in imagery manipulation in at least three or four domains.

	Usually able to combine images from three or four domains within one activity.
3. Average	Verbalizes that sometimes has controllability of imagery in two or three sensory domains. Usually able to utilize a particular strategy in imagery manipulation in two or three domains. Sometimes able to combine images from two or three domains within one activity.
2. Below Average	Verbalizes that rarely has controllability of images except in visual domain. Rarely able to utilize a particular strategy in imagery manipulation in two or three domains. Rarely able to combine images from two or three domains within one activity.
1. Far Below Average	Does not verbalize about controllability of image. Almost never able to manipulate images.

DRAMATIC BEHAVIOR

	USE OF SPACE/BODY MOVEMENT
5. Outstanding	Always uses whole body freely. Always able to imitate movements of leader or other group members. Always adapts movement to available space. Effectively able to work with concepts of movement: space, force, body, time. Always attempts and demonstrates success in pantomime.
4. Above Average	Often uses whole body freely. Often able to imitate leader and others. Often able to adapt movement to available space. Often able to work with concepts of movement: space, force, body, time. Often demonstrates success at pantomime.
3. Average	Sometimes uses whole body freely. Sometimes able to imitate leader and others. Sometimes able to adapt movement to available space. Sometimes able to work with concepts of movement: space, force, body, time. Sometimes demonstrates success at pantomime.
2. Below Average	Rarely uses whole body freely—just moves arms and legs. Rarely able to imitate leader and others. Demonstrates little variety in space, force, body, and time. Pantomimes activities that are difficult for viewer to discern.

1. Far Below Average	Sits or stands in same spot for duration of an activity that encourages movement — shows little locomotion. Almost never attempts pantomime. Demonstrates much habituated small arm, leg, or head movements.
	USE OF OBJECTS
5. Outstanding	Always uses here-and-now objects. Always attempts to use objects in diverse ways. Always uses objects to assist in communicating dramatic elements, such as character or dramatic locale. Often searches out interesting objects.
4. Above Average	Usually uses here-and-now objects. Usually attempts to use objects in diverse ways. Usually uses objects to assist in communicating dramatic elements, such as character or dramatic locale. Occasionally searches out interesting objects.
3. Average	Sometimes uses here-and-now objects. Sometimes attempts to use objects in diverse ways. Sometimes uses objects to assist in communicating dramatic elements, such as character or dramatic locale. Sometimes searches out interesting objects.
2. Below Average	Rarely uses here-and-now objects. Rarely attempts to use objects in diverse ways. Rarely uses objects to assist in communicating dramatic elements, such as character or dramatic locale.
1. Far Below Average	Fails to use here-and-now objects. Ignores the existence of objects.
	VERBAL/VOCAL EXPRESSION
5. Outstanding	Always demonstrates variety in volume, tone, pitch, and voice quality. Always describes activities with appropriate and colorful vocabulary. Always likes to communicate. Always communicates easily.
4. Above Average	Usually demonstrates variety in volume, tone, pitch, and voice quality. Usually describes activities with appropriate and colorful vocabulary. Usually likes to communicate. Usually communicates easily.
3. Average	Sometimes demonstrates variety in volume, tone, pitch, and voice quality.

	Sometimes describes activities with appropriate and colorful vocabulary. Sometimes likes to communicate. Sometimes communicates easily.
2. Below Average	Mumbles. Speaks without variety in tone, pitch, and voice quality. Uses little appropriate vocabulary when describing activities.
1. Far Below Average	Little or no verbal or vocal response.
	STORY-MAKING
5. Outstanding	Always recalls and repeats events in a sequence. Always eager to relate story to others. Always comprehends implication of events in sequence.
4. Above Average	Usually recalls and repeats events in a sequence. Usually eager to relate story to others. Usually comprehends implication of events in sequence.
3. Average	Sometimes recalls and repeats events in a sequence. Sometimes eager to relate story to others. Sometimes comprehends implication of events in sequence.
2. Below Average	Rarely recalls and repeats events in a sequence. Rarely eager to relate story to others. Rarely comprehends implication of events in sequence.
1. Far Below Average	Fails to remember sequences. Fails to understand implication of before and after or cause and effect.

CONNECTION OF IDEAS TO ACTION

	FOCUS ON IMAGES AND ACTION
5. Outstanding	Consistently engrossed in activity and/or imaging. Questions leader only when real clarification is needed. Rarely imitates others.
4. Above Average	Almost always engrossed in activity and/or imaging. Questions to leader are seeking attention as well as asking for clarification. Occasionally imitates others.
3. Average	Moves in and out of action and/or imaging — more in than out.

	Occasionally engages in irrelevent dialogue with others or with leader. Stops activity for no reason. Often imitates others.
2. Below Average	Moves in and out of action—more out than in. Engages in irrelevant dialogue with others and leader. Poses self-consciously. Seldom does activity without imitating others.
1. Far Below Average	Laughs and giggles. Works on nondrama-related tasks. Tries to distract others.
	FLUENCY OF IDEAS
5. Outstanding	Always comes up with numbers of potential ideas. Always able to add personal episode to group discussion. Always eager to try simple drama or imagery task.
4. Above Average	Usually comes up with numbers of potential ideas. Usually able to add personal episode to group discussion. Usually eager to try simple drama or imagery task.
3. Average	Sometimes able to generate ideas. Sometimes eager to participate in activities. Sometimes eager to contribute to discussion.
2. Below Average	Occasionally able to generate ideas. Occasionally eager to participate in activities. Rarely contributes to discussion.
1. Far Below Average	Never able to generate additional ideas within a category. Never able to contribute within a group discussion. Always dislikes participating in fluency activities.
	RELAXATION SKILLS
5. Outstanding	Always able to achieve almost total relaxation. Always aware of tension with attempts to alleviate it. Eagerly participates in physical and vocal relaxation exercises.
4. Above Average	Usually able to achieve almost total relaxation. When tension is pointed out, can often do something to relieve it. Very often happy to participate in vocal and physical relaxation exercises.
3. Average	Sometimes able to achieve almost total relaxation. Unable to recognize or alleviate some tension in various body parts. Likes to participate in most relaxation activities.

2. Below Average	Occasionally able to achieve partial relaxation. Tension in back and shoulders always present. Has jerky voice and body. Occasionally desires to participate in relaxation activities. Often tries to get focus while others are participating in relaxation activities.
1. Far Below Average	Never able to relax body or calm mind. Shows much tense, habituated body movement. Demonstrates conspicuous tension in back, face, hands, and voice. Laughs and giggles, as well as disrupts others, while relaxation activities are occurring.

GROUP SKILLS

	AWARENESS OF OTHERS/PARALLEL PLAY
5. Outstanding	Always acknowledges participation of others. Always able to concentrate on self while others work at same time. Always able to work in small groups or in pairs. Always demonstrates give and take.
4. Above Average	Usually acknowledges participation of others. Usually able to concentrate on self while others work at same time. Usually able to work in small groups or in pairs. Usually demonstrates give and take.
3. Average	Sometimes acknowledges participation of others. Sometimes able to concentrate on self while others work at same time. Sometimes able to work in small groups or in pairs. Sometimes demonstrates give-and-take.
2. Below Average	Rarely acknowledges participation of others. Rarely able to concentrate on self while others work at same time. Rarely able to work in small groups or in pairs. Rarely demonstrates give-and-take.
1. Far Below Average	Always ignores and disrupts others. Fails to work with others, or is able to work only with single, trusted friend.
	ATTENTION TO LEADER
5. Outstanding	Always responds equally well to leader in his/her role of guide, coach, or director. Always listens to directions. Always considers, attends to, and incorporates side coaching comments.
4. Above Average	Almost always responds equally well to leader in his/her role of guide, coach, or director.

	Almost always listens to directions. Almost always considers, attends to, and incorporates side coaching comments.
3. Average	Responds to two of leader's roles more than to leader in third role. Usually listens to directions. Usually considers, attends to, and incorporates side coaching comments.
2. Below Average	Responds to one of leader's roles more than to leader in other two roles. Rarely listens to directions. Rarely utilizes or even hears side coaching comments.
1. Far Below Average	Ignores leader. Fails to participate as directed by leader.

TRANSFORMATIONS RATING SCALE

IMAGERY

	ADVANCED IMAGING ABILITY
5. Outstanding	Always able to develop flexible imagination images. Always able to select and reject from imagery repertoire as needed. Always able to incorporate a variety of elements within one stimulating image. Always able to modify, retrieve, and combine many characteristics of images when necessary.
4. Above Average	Able to develop flexible imagination images. Able to select and reject from imagery repertoire as needed. Able to incorporate a variety of elements within one stimulating image. Able to modify, retrieve, and combine many characteristics of images when necessary.
3. Average	Often able to develop flexible imagination images. Often able to select and reject from imagery repertoire as needed. Often able to incorporate a variety of elements within one stimulating image. Often able to modify, retrieve, and combine many characteristics of images when necessary.
2. Below Average	Rarely able to develop flexible imagination images, uses memory images instead. Still developing fluency skills. Rarely able to select and reject from imagery repertoire as needed. Locked into the same imaging strategies for a variety of situations.

	Not yet able to demonstrate integrative imaging ability.
1. Far Below Average	Rarely able to develop personal imagination images. Fails to personalize images. Unable to develop imagination images. Unable to demonstrate flexibility of imaging.

DRAMATIC/THEATRICAL BEHAVIOR

PERSPECTIVE OF VARIETY OF ROLES

5. Outstanding	Always able to perform activities that encourage a variety of perspectives. Always able to demonstrate success in five different theatrical perspectives: actor, director, critic, playwright, and designer. Always able to select perspective that best fits own ability and the needs of the drama.
4. Above Average	Almost always able to perform activities that encourage a variety of perspectives. Usually able to demonstrate success in five different theatrical perspectives. Almost always able to select perspective that best fits ability and drama's needs.
3. Average	Usually able to perform activities that encourage a variety of perspectives. Sometimes able to demonstrate success in at least three different theatrical perspectives. Usually able to select perspective that best fits ability and drama's needs.
2. Below Average	Rarely able to perform activities that encourage a variety of perspectives. Occasionally able to demonstrate success in at least two different theatrical perspectives. Rarely able to select perspective that best fits ability and drama's needs.
1. Far Below Average	Never able to perform activities that encourage a variety of perspectives. Never able to select perspective that best fits ability and drama's needs.

CONSIDERATION OF AUDIENCE/OBSERVER

5. Outstanding	Always able to integrate, in both planning and playing, dramatic conventions that are necessary for communicating to an audience. Always able to balance the need to make a personal statement with a sense of how the action is to be or is being received. Always able to objectify opinion when evaluating work of others and never interjects nonrelevant information.

4. Above Average

Almost always able to integrate, particularly in planning, dramatic conventions that are necessary for communication to an audience.

Almost always able to balance the need to make a personal statement with a sense of how the action is to be or is being received.

Almost always able to objectify opinion when evaluating work of others and rarely interjects nonrelevant information.

3. Average

Usually able to integrate, particularly in planning, dramatic conventions that are necessary for communication to an audience.

Usually able to balance the need to make a personal statement with a sense of how the action is to be or is being received.

Usually able to objectify opinion when evaluating work of others, but often interjects nonrelevant information.

2. Below Average

Rarely able to integrate dramatic conventions that are necessary for communication to an audience.

Rarely able to balance the need to make a personal statement with a sense of how the action is to be or is being received.

Rarely able to objectify in evaluating others and almost always tries to take stage when evaluating.

1. Far Below Average

Almost never able to integrate dramatic conventions that are necessary for communication to an audience.

Almost always allows personal viewpoint to take over.

Fails to grasp the concept that drama is to be viewed by others.

When able to evaluate, does so entirely to interject a viewpoint unrelated to drama at hand.

INTEGRATION OF VISUAL ASPECTS

5. Outstanding

Always incorporates the accouterments of theatre — sets, props, lights, costume, and make-up, if necessary.

Always demonstrates a well-developed aesthetic sensibility.

4. Above Average

Almost always incorporates the accouterments of theatre — sets, props, lights, costume, make-up, if necessary.

Almost always demonstrates a well-developed aesthetic sensibility.

3. Average

Usually incorporates the accouterments of theatre

	— sets, props, lights, costume, make-up if necessary.
	Usually demonstrates a well-developed aesthetic sensibility.
2. Below Average	Either becomes obsessed with accouterments of theatre or rarely utilizes them.
	Rarely demonstrates a well-developed aesthetic sensibility.
1. Far Below Average	Fails to attend to visual projects.

CONNECTION OF IMAGINATION TO ACTION

	OVERLAY OF SELF AND CHARACTER
5. Outstanding	Always able to transform self into character.
	Always able to communicate character's physical attributes, vocal and verbal aspects, and role within the drama effectively and in detail.
	Uses elaborate, flexible, personal imagination images in character development.
	Always able to relate in character to others in character.
4. Above Average	Almost always able to transform self into character.
	Almost always able to develop three essential characteristics of character somewhat effectively and with some detail.
	Uses mostly flexible personal imagination images in character development.
	Almost always able to relate in character to others in character.
3. Average	Sometimes able to transform self into character.
	Sometimes able to develop at least two essential characteristics of character.
	Uses personal imagination images in character development.
	Usually able to relate in character to others in character.
2. Below Average	Rarely able to transform self into character.
	Rarely able to relate in character to others in character.
1. Far Below Average	Never able to transform self into character.
	Fails to communicate in character to others as selves or in character.
	TRANSFORMATION OF PLACE INTO SETTING
5. Outstanding	Always able to transform here-and-now place into setting, or another time period.
	Always able to create mood through tempo, speed, and pace.

	Always able to utilize set pieces and objects to establish place.
4. Above Average	Almost always able to transform here-and-now place into setting, or another time period. Almost always able to create mood through tempo, speed, and pace. Almost always able to utilize set pieces and objects to establish place.
3. Average	Usually able to transform here-and-now place into setting or another time period. Usually able to create mood through either tempo, speed, or pace. Usually able to utilize set pieces and objects to establish place.
2. Below Average	Rarely able to transform here-and-now place into setting or another time period. Rarely able to create mood through tempo, speed, and pace. Rarely able to utilize set pieces and objects to establish place.
1. Far Below Average	Almost never able to transform here-and-now place into setting or another time period. Never able to create mood through tempo, speed, and pace. Almost never able to utilize set pieces and objects to establish place.
	TRANSFORMATION OF EVENTS/STORIES INTO PLOT
5. Outstanding	Always able to act out story drama, as well as personalize it with imagination images. Understands and always utilizes dramatic structure conventions such as beginning, middle, and end. Always contributes to developing plot. Comprehends and is always able to utilize both horizontal and vertical direction in plot development.
4. Above Average	Almost always able to act out story drama, as well as often personalize it with imagination images. Understands and almost always utilizes dramatic structure conventions. Almost always contributes to developing plot. Comprehends and is sometimes able to utilize both horizontal and vertical direction in plot development.
3. Average	Usually able to act out story drama and occasionally add personal images to it.

	Understands and sometimes uses dramatic structure conventions. Sometimes contributes to developing plot.
2. Below Average	Occasionally able to act out story drama. Occasionally able to contribute to developing plot.
1. Far Below Average	Often disrupts story drama. Tries to monopolize plot development or fails to participate at all.
	WORK WITHIN PLAN, PLAY, EVALUATE STRUCTURE
5. Outstanding	Always demonstrates equal success with each of the three stages. Always able to make connections between the three stages. Within planning, always demonstrates artful, efficient balance between taking time to plan and realizing the need to enact. Within evaluation, always demonstrates four categories of reflection: spontaneous, leader-led, individual, and group.
4. Above Average	Usually demonstrates equal success with each of the three stages. Usually able to make connections between the three stages. Within planning, usually demonstrates artful, efficient balance between taking time to plan and realizing the need to enact. Within evaluation, usually demonstrates three categories of reflection: spontaneous, leader-led, and group.
3. Average	Usually demonstrates success with planning and playing, less so with evaluating. Sometimes able to make connections among the three stages. Within planning, sometimes demonstrates balance between taking time to plan and realizing the need to enact. Within evaluation, sometimes demonstrates success with leader-inspired and group evaluation.
2. Below Average	Usually has difficulty with planning and reflection. Usually has difficulty in making connections between the stages. Within planning, rarely able to strike a balance. Within evaluation, rarely able to demonstrate success except in leader-led situations.
1. Far Below Average	Rarely demonstrates success except in playing. Cannot make connection between stages.

	SELECT/REJECT ABILITY
5. Outstanding	Always demonstrates ability in selecting some stimulating imagination image while rejecting another. Always demonstrates ability to work at selecting and rejecting of individual behavior through trial and error, self-reflection, leader comments, and peer evaluation. Within group, always able to select and reject self and others' images and behavior for the good of the improvisation.
4. Above Average	Usually demonstrates ability in selecting some stimulating imagination image while rejecting another. Usually demonstrates ability to work at selecting and rejecting of individual behavior through trial and error, self-reflection, leader comments, and peer evaluation. Within group, usually able to select and reject self and others' images and behavior for the good of the improvisation.
3. Average	Sometimes demonstrates ability in selecting some images and rejecting others. Sometimes demonstrates ability to select and reject behavior, usually through trial and error and leader comments.
2. Below Average	Rarely demonstrates ability to select and reject images. Rarely demonstrates ability to select and reject error, and only through trial and error. Often unable to make selective decision to limit one's own ideas and behaviors.
1. Far Below Average	Fails to grasp the concept that some ideas and behaviors may be more appropriate than others. Always unable to moderate behavior.
	FLEXIBILITY AND ELABORATION ABILITY
5. Outstanding	Always able to demonstrate flexibility and elaboration within internal processes. Always able to demonstrate flexibility and elaboration in dramatic behavior whether stimulated by personal experimentation, here-and-now objects, others in group, leader, or drama in progress.
4. Above Average	Usually able to demonstrate flexibility and elaboration within internal processes. Usually able to demonstrate flexibility and elaboration in dramatic behavior whether stimulated by personal experimentation, here-and-now ob-

jects, others in group, leader, or drama in progress.

3. Average
Sometimes able to demonstrate flexibility and elaboration within internal processes.
Sometimes able to demonstrate flexibility and elaboration of dramatic behavior, usually stimulated by here-and-now objects, leader, or personal experimentation.

2. Below Average
Rarely able to demonstrate flexibility and elaboration within internal processes.
Rarely able to demonstrate flexibility and elaboration of dramatic behavior, except occasionally when stimulated by here-and-now object and leader.

1. Far Below Average
Unable to demonstrate flexibility and elaboration in internal processes or in behavior.

GROUP SKILLS

WORKING IN VARIOUS GROUP CONFIGURATIONS

5. Outstanding
Always works well in pairs, small groups, or larger groups.
Has found several ideal team members with whom can feel especially comfortable.
Always shows respect for other's opinions.

4. Above Average
Usually works well in pairs, small groups, or larger groups.
Is experimenting with finding ideal subgroupings.
Usually shows respect for other's opinions.

3. Average
Usually works well in at least one organization structure.
Occasionally shows respect for other's opinions.

2. Below Average
Can only work with particular other individuals or in particular configuration.
Rarely respects other's opinions.

1. Far Below Average
Demonstrates little or no ability to work in any group structure.

GROUP NEGOTIATION BEHAVIORS

Note: This category assesses the group as a whole.

5. Outstanding
Always demonstrates cooperation (state of mutual support).
Always demonstrates coordination (synchronized actions).
Always attempts to work in decentralized structure.

	Always attempts to fill all seven communication roles.
4. Above Average	Usually demonstrates cooperation (state of mutual support). Usually demonstrates coordination (synchronized actions). Usually attempts to work in decentralized structure. Usually attempts to fill all seven communication roles.
3. Average	Individual moves in and out of working in cooperation or coordination. Usually demonstrates centralized structure. Usually attempts to fill at least four communication roles.
2. Below Average	Individuals often work at cross purposes. Individuals often monopolize conversations. Some small groups achieve a tenuous working relationship.
1. Far Below Average	Group has not gelled. Individuals work in tandem, not together.

Descriptive Evaluation/Assessment

A descriptive assessment describes and interprets behaviors that are being demonstrated, processes that are going on, effects that are evident, or even trends that are developing. Your primary objective in using this measure is to describe the phenomenon of creative drama as you see it. You may wish to collect your comments over time and provide a selected chronicle of the development of the individual/group/dramatic enactment over a semester's work. Or, you may wish to develop a detailed narrative of one day's activities.

The major strength of this type of measure (as it exists ideally) is that it is *descriptive,* not prescriptive. The more specific the guide or measure is, the more value-laden it is, because the rater has been presented with a preconceived notion of what should occur. A descriptive assessment, in contrast to the checklist or rating scale, allows observers to describe a myriad of aspects within the phenomenon and enables them to capture unique creative drama situations.

A lack of guidelines may be freeing for observers who are naturally systematic, but it can spell disaster for less experienced or less objective observers. Given no objectives, descriptions, or tangible clues about what to focus on, novices may become overwhelmed and be unable to write anything about what they see. On the other hand, observers who have made their judgments prior to the assessment see only what they want to see. The nondirective nature of the pure descriptive assessment reinforces their prejudices concerning particular participants and exercises or activities.

A type of descriptive assessment, ideal for novices and prejudgers alike, is the *modified descriptive assessment guide.* This modified assessment guide still permits observers to write comments in their own words, to include some dramatic aspects and exclude others, and to follow their instincts. Yet the addition of a particular category system provides the necessary focus, without being too prescriptive.

No assessment should be haphazard. On the contrary, descriptive assessments must be just as systematic and focused as the two previously discussed types of measures. To utilize this modified guide, observers must know what to look for and be careful and accurate in recording what they see. Following are three category systems, modified from a diversity of theatre/drama taxonomies, that can provide just the right amount of focus. Select one to help you begin your assessment. Within the categories in each guide, you are free to write about anything you choose.

Characterization as a Focus

Time spent in improvisation.
Space traversed through locomotion.
Dramatic episodes.
Elaborative movement in place.
Interactions with others.
Character enacted.

Enactment as a Focus

Awareness of theme.
Role-taking and playing.
Creation of plot.
Use of physical space.
Evaluation and reflection.

Characters in Relationships as a Focus

Focus.
Completion.
Use of imaginary object.
Elaboration.
Use of space.
Facial expression.
Body movement.
Vocal expression.
Social relationship.

Inherent in this category system is both a bias and a guide. As you write your comments, try to avoid jargon and clichés. Take care to be as objective and as accurate as possible. And, once you have done a few assessments, you may wish to develop your own category systems. Your assessments can reflect your personal, program, and participant goals.

THE FUTURE OF CREATIVE DRAMA

Earlier in this book, we suggested that to understand the current state of creative drama, you must know its history. As you finish this book, it is also imperative that you assess the future of creative drama — where it seems to be heading. The 1980s finds creative drama poised on the brink of making some internal changes that can influence how those outside the field view it.

> ***Yet in focusing on the arts, we may bring to light capacities and properties which have been hitherto neglected, and may discover as well that such aspects play a significant role outside the arts.***
>
> Howard Gardner

Historically, creative drama has been an educational chameleon. During its early years, creative drama practitioners seemed content for the field to be a sideline, a frill, but a frill on a par with the visual arts and music. Its chief benefit, its proponents claimed, was that it assisted personality development and stimulated creativity.

As school curricula grew more science- and achievement-oriented in the 1960s, creative drama became a vital addendum to learning in general and to basic skills in particular. Creative drama was touted as a *methodology*, particularly in the language arts classroom, to teach nondrama skills. Then, as the arts moved back into educational favor, creative drama evolved into "creative theatre," or was replaced by theatrical activities in which only a select few participated. As trends changed, chameleon creative drama reflected the changes, and quite logical questions have been asked about it by those outside the field. For instance, if creative drama is so extraordinary that only a few can do it well, then why include it in the curriculum? If creative drama is merely a creative method without its own unique characteristics, why use it instead of more precise methodologies to facilitate the educational process? If creative drama is the natural response of all children to their psychological and aesthetic urges, won't the academic restraints of "school" stultify this instinct?

Recent developments within the field of creative drama are providing answers to these and similar questions. As the 1980s draw to a close, arts education (not merely drama, but visual arts, music, and dance) is moving in a new direction. The literature is filled with articles, researched and written by psychologists and educators, that suggest not only that the arts make unique contributions to the cognitive maturation of young people, but that through participation in the arts, young people acquire access to their own inner words of ideas and learn techniques and skills for communicating them to others.

Creative drama, again chameleonlike, is mirroring this trend. Researchers are discovering and reporting the distinctive strengths and significant characteristics of creative drama, as well as those characteristics it shares with other arts. Today's research confirms what creative drama practitioners have long known instinctively, but have also long needed to verify: **Creative drama provides a unique way for individuals to put their imaginative ideas into action.** It is the only art form in which individuals, alone and together, mold idiosyncratic content into a form that communicates to others.

> ***To piece the curtain of the future, to give shape and visage to mysteries still in the womb of time, is the gift of the imagination.***
>
> Felix Frankfurter

Creative Drama as an Answer for the Future

The Rutgers Imagination Method is strongly attuned to recent findings in arts education. RIM is a way for you to be a pioneer — to connect the present to the rapidly expanding future. Perhaps the single most essential notion upon which RIM is built is that drama is based upon certain internal processes and external behaviors that resemble those of the child at play and the artist at work. RIM isolates these components, orders them, and establishes a three-tiered method that allows you to focus on and stimulate them independently and in conjunction with one another. Through participation in drama, individuals master dramatic learning.

The whole of drama, of course, is greater than the sum of its parts; each participant's holistic process and product is uniquely different from every other participant's, but all share a similar array of craft skills and behaviors. It is these components, shared by all drama participants, that you can teach and that they can master. Participation in creative drama demands discipline, rigor, and personal engagement. A systematic approach to creative drama can help you and those outside the field understand that creative drama is not merely performance, not merely a way to stimulate learning in other curricular areas, but a method that focuses on personal understanding and discovery, on working and sharing with others, and on developing skills that put ideas into actions that communicate. To meet the challenge of the 1990s and beyond, RIM offers experiences in conceptualizing the possible, in doing and simultaneously in monitoring that doing, and in inventing a personally defined structure to communicate ideas to others.

The Big Questions

Although creative drama practitioners and researchers are making tremendous strides in understanding the field, several essential issues need further investigation. As we close this book, we pose the following questions for your consideration.

The first set of questions focus on *development and learning:*

- What are the essential developmental stages for creative drama?
- Within each developmental stage, what broad set of skills are being mastered?
- What are the effects of training/learning on development?
- Can researchers/psychologists address the learning and development interrelationship?

The second set of questions focus on the *phenomenon of creative drama itself.* Researchers must seek to clarify a variety of internal issues:

- What is the relationship of the individual to the group and the group to the individual?
- What type of activity—subject, length, scope, group configuration—works best for what type of participant?
- What dramatic behaviors are due to what factors?
- What teaching techniques influence what aspects of creative drama?
- Can we offer a detailed analysis of the relationship of dramatic behavior, imagery ability, group socialization, cognitive processes, creative problem-solving, and the connection of imagination to action within creative drama?

The third set of issues focuses on the delineation of *how creative drama is both like and unlike other phenomena, particularly theatre and the other arts, as well as other cognitive experiences:*

Marc Chagall has achieved a sublime realization of imagination in action as demonstrated by this final product (*above*). Fortunately, we are also able to see examples of his work in progress. The sketch (*facing page*) is a record of the intermediate imaging phase, one that shows how internal and external merge and shape the final outcome. (*Birthday, 1915,* Collection, The Museum of Modern Art, New York. Sketch gift of the artist; painting acquired through the Lillie P. Bliss bequest.)

- What characteristics do theatre and creative drama share, and what is unique to each?
- What characteristics do creative drama and other creative arts share, and what is unique to each?
- What cognitive process does creative drama share with other disciplines, and what processes are unique to creative drama?

2001: A Drama Odyssey

We ask that you come with us on one final imagination journey. (At this point in the book, you are probably taking imagination journeys quite readily.) This time we're moving to a time that has yet to be, to a fantasy world that has compelling powers for all of you who are convinced of the magic of creative drama. We ask that you recall the "magic moments" that introduced this book.

This time, see yourself as the drama leader in one of the magic moments. Now double the image and then triple it and multiply it again, so that this drama activity or ones very similar to it are taking place as far as you can picture in your mind's eye. You are not leading all the drama activities, of

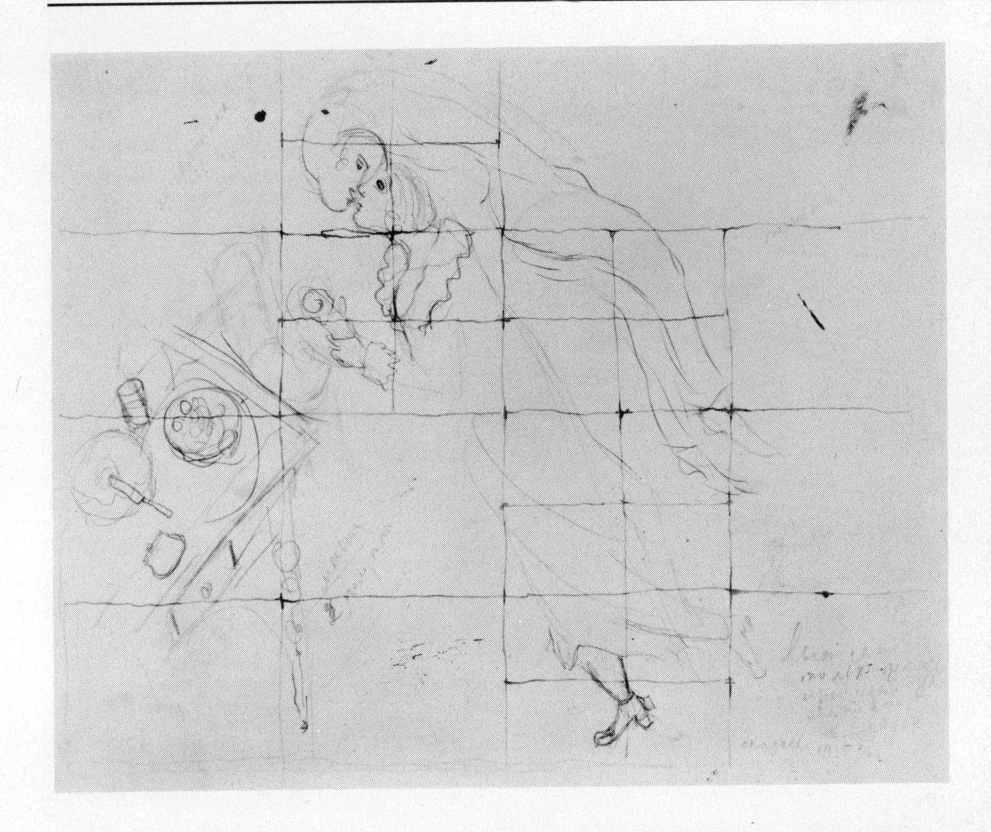

course, but you share with your colleagues the notion that creative drama makes an essential contribution to each participant's inner and outer life in a way no other experience can. Within as many drama rooms as you are able to picture in your mind's eye, leaders are conducting drama activities that have a shared objective: cultivating the potential of the human mind.

BIBLIOGRAPHY

CHILD DEVELOPMENT AND LEARNING

Cole, Michael, Vera John-Steiner, Sylvia Scribner, and Ellen Souberman, eds. *L. S. Vygotsky: Mind in Society*. Cambridge, Mass.: Harvard University Press, 1978.

Furth, Hans G. *Piaget and Knowledge*. Englewood Cliffs, N.J.: Prentice-Hall, 1969.

Gardner, Howard. *Art, Mind, and Brain*. New York: Basic Books, 1982.

Langer, Jonas. *Theories of Development*. New York: Holt, Rinehart, and Winston, 1969.

Singer, Dorothy G., and Jerome L. Singer. *Partners in Play*. New York: Harper & Row, 1977.

Singer, Jerome L., and Dorothy G. Singer. *Make Believe*. Glencoe, Ill.: Scott, Foresman, 1985.

CREATIVE DRAMA

Behr, Marcia W., Alice B. Snyder, and Anna S. Clopton. *Drama Integrates Basic Skills*. Springfield, Ill.: Charles C Thomas, 1979.

Burger, Isabel. *Creative Play Acting*, 2d ed. New York: Ronald Press, 1966.

Courtney, Richard. *The Dramatic Curriculum*. New York: Drama Book Specialists/Publishers, 1980.

Heinig, Ruth Beall, and Lyda Stillwell. *Creative Dramatics for the Classroom Teacher*, 2d ed. Englewood Cliffs, N.J.: Prentice-Hall, 1981.

Koste, Virginia Glasgow. *Dramatic Play in Childhood: Rehearsal for Life*. New Orleans, La.: Anchorage Press, 1978.

McCaslin, Nellie. *Creative Drama in the Classroom*, 4th ed. New York: Longmans, 1984.

Schwartz, Dorothy T., and Dorothy Aldrich, eds. *Give Them Roots and Wings*. Washington, D.C.: American Theatre Association, 1972.

Shaw, Ann M., and C. J. Stevens, eds. *Drama, Theatre, and the Handicapped*. Washington, D.C.: American Theatre Association, 1979.

Siks, Geraldine Brain. *Drama with Children*, 2d ed. New York: Harper & Row, 1983.

Slade, Peter. *Child Drama*. London: Hodder & Stoughton, 1954.

Spolin, Viola. *Theatre Game File*. St. Louis, Mo.: CEMREL, 1975.

Wagner, Betty J. *Dorothy Heathcote: Drama as a Learning Medium*. Washington, D.C.: National Education Association, 1976.

Ward, Winifred. *Playmaking with Children*. New York: Appleton-Century Crofts, 1957.

Way, Brian. *Development Through Drama*. Atlantic Highlands, N.J.: Humanities Press, 1967.

IMAGERY AND IMAGINATION

Bagley, Michael T., and Karin Hess. *200 Ways of Using Imagery in the Classroom*. New York: Trillium Press, 1984.
De Mille, Richard. *Put Your Mother on the Ceiling*. New York: Viking, 1973.
Khatena, Joe. *Imagery and Creative Imagination*. Buffalo, N.Y.: Brearly, 1984.
Lazarus, Arnold. *In the Mind's Eye*. New York: Rawson, 1977.
Osborn, Alex F. *Applied Imagination*, 3d ed. New York: Scribner's, 1963.
Richardson, A. *Mental Imagery*. New York: Springer, 1969.
Samuels, Mike, and Nancy Samuels. *Seeing with the Mind's Eye*. New York: Random House, 1975.
Shorr, Joseph E., Gail S. Whittington, Pennee Robin, and Jack A. Connella. *Imagery*, Vol. 3. New York: Plenum, 1983.
Singer, Jerome L. *Imagery and Daydream Methods in Psychotherapy and Behavior Modification*. New York: Academic, 1974.
Singer, Jerome L. *The Child's World of Make-Believe*. New York: Academic, 1973.

THEATRE ARTS

Boleslavksy, Richard. *Acting: The First Six Lessons*. New York: Theatre Arts Books, 1949.
Chekhov, Michael. *To the Actor*. New York: Harper & Row, 1953.
Cole, Toby, and Helen Krich Chinoy. *Directors on Directing*. Indianapolis, Ind.: Bobbs-Merrill, 1963.
Corey, Irene. *The Mask of Reality*. New Orleans, La.: Anchorage Press, 1968.
Jones, Robert Edmond. *The Dramatic Imagination*. New York: Theatre Arts Books, 1941.
Machlin, Evangeline. *Speech for the Stage*, 2d ed. New York: Theatre Arts Books, 1980.
Parker, W. Oren, and Harvey K. Smith. *Stage Design and Stage Lighting*, 4th ed. New York: Holt, Rinehart and Winston, 1979.
Rosenberg, Helane S., and Christine Prendergast. *Theatre for Young People: A Sense of Occasion*. New York: Holt, Rinehart and Winston, 1983.
Smiley, Sam. *Playwrighting: The Structure of Action*. Englewood Cliffs, N.J.: Prentice-Hall, 1971.
Stanislavski, Constantin. *An Actor Prepares*. New York: Theatre Arts Books, 1936.

RELATED ARTS

Baker, Paul. *Integration of Abilities: Exercises for Creative Growth*. New Orleans, La.: Anchorage Press, 1977.
Dimondstein, Geraldine. *Exploring the Arts with Children*. New York: Macmillan, 1974.
Franck, Frederick. *The Zen of Seeing*. New York: Vintage, 1973.
Hendricks, Gay, and Thomas B. Roberts. *The Second Centering Book*. Englewood Cliffs, N.J.: Prentice-Hall, 1977.
Joyce, Mary. *First Steps in Teaching Creative Dance to Children*, 2d ed. Palo Alto, Calif.: Mayfield, 1973.
Masters, Robert, and Jean Houston. *Mind Games*. New York: Delta Books, 1972.
Nash, Grace C. *Child Development with Music, Language, and Movement*. New York: Alfred, 1974.
Newman, Frederick R. *Zounds!* New York: Random House, 1983.
Paynter, John, and Peter Aston. *Sounds and Silence*. Cambridge, England: Cambridge University Press, 1970.

CREATIVITY AND COGNITION

Copple, Carol, Irving E. Sigel, and Ruth Saunders. *Educating the Young Thinker: Classroom Strategies for Cognitive Growth*. Hillsdale, N.J.: Erlbaum, 1984.

Flavell, John H. "Metacognition and Cognitive Monitoring." *American Psychologist, 34,* 10, October 1979.

Jastrow, Robert. *The Enchanted Loom*. New York: Simon & Schuster, 1981.

Kagan, Jerome, ed. *Creativity and Learning*. Boston: Houghton Mifflin, 1967.

Koberg, Don, and Jim Bagnall. *The Universal Traveller*. Los Altos, Calif.: William Kaufmann, 1972.

Nickerson, Raymond S., David N. Perkins, and Edward E. Smith. *The Teaching of Thinking*. Hillsdale, N.J.: Erlbaum, 1985.

Parnes, Sidney. *Creative Behavior Guidebook*. New York: Scribner's, 1967.

Perkins, David N. *The Mind's Best Work*. Cambridge, Mass.: Harvard University Press, 1981.

Raudsepp, Eugene. *More Creative Growth Games*. New York: Putnam, 1980.

Von Oech, Roger. *A Whack on the Side of the Head*. New York: Warner Books, 1983.

Index